MANAGRA

DOCTOR WHO – THE MISSING ADVENTURES

Also available:

GOTH OPERA by Paul Cornell
EVOLUTION by John Peel
VENUSIAN LULLABY by Paul Leonard
THE CRYSTAL BUCEPHALUS by Craig Hinton
STATE OF CHANGE by Christopher Bulis
THE ROMANCE OF CRIME by Gareth Roberts
THE GHOSTS OF N-SPACE by Barry Letts
TIME OF YOUR LIFE by Steve Lyons
DANCING THE CODE by Paul Leonard
THE MENAGERIE by Martin Day
SYSTEM SHOCK by Justin Richards
THE SORCERER'S APPRENTICE by Christopher Bulis
INVASION OF THE CAT-PEOPLE by Gary Russell

MANAGRA

Stephen Marley

DOCTOR WHO

THE MISSING ADVENTURES

First published in Great Britain in 1995 by
Doctor Who Books
an imprint of Virgin Publishing Ltd
332 Ladbroke Grove
London W10 5AH

Copyright © Stephen Marley 1995

The right of Stephen Marley to be identified as the Author of
this Work has been asserted by him in accordance with the
Copyright, Designs and Patents Act 1988.

'Doctor Who' series copyright © British Broadcasting
Corporation 1995

ISBN 0 426 20453 0

Cover illustration by Paul Campbell

Typeset by Galleon Typesetting, Ipswich
Printed and bound in Great Britain by
Mackays of Chatham

*All characters in this publication are fictitious and any resemblance
to real persons, living or dead, is purely coincidental.*

This book is sold subject to the condition that it shall
not, by way of trade or otherwise, be lent, resold, hired
out or otherwise circulated without the publisher's prior
written consent in any form of binding or cover other
than that in which it is published and without a similar
condition including this condition being imposed on the
subsequent purchaser.

For Anita, for reasons known by few.
And for Tom Baker, for reasons known by *everybody*.

Acknowledgements

Many thanks to Peter Darvill-Evans, Rebecca Levene (the long-suffering) and Andy Bodle, noble souls all. Thanks also to Desmond and Sonja for – whatever, and Jim Newcombe for the videos and slim volume. To Paul Campbell, for his superb cover illustration, I owe a debt of gratitude (which I may or may not pay). And a nod to Andy Lane, for reasons which will be revealed in a month or so. Above all, my regards to all those readers who have (preferably) bought this book and (hopefully) got round to reading it.

Prologue

London: 29 June 1613

The reddest of flames licked the bluest of skies.

The Globe Theatre's first staging of Will Shakespeare's *Henry VIII* had turned out to be its last performance. Gone up in smoke, bracket and beam, stage and balconies.

The squat wooden tower of the Globe was a column of fire, disgorging a terrified multitude. Crammed in the gateway, the crowds that had flocked to witness Shakespeare's farewell play now jostled and trampled one another in a stampede to flee the blaze.

It had been a full house, the theatre packed to its two-thousand capacity.

' 'Tis a pity,' Francis murmured under his breath. 'But it had to be done.'

Francis stood on the Southwark bank, an easy pebble's toss from the bridge, and watched the inferno at a hefty stone's throw distance. He stepped to one side as a merchant rushed past, wreathed in flames, and dived into the Thames, disappearing in a splash and wisp of steam. Others, their garb a fiery flamboyance, soon dived in his wake.

London's towers tolled their bells, a carillon of alarm, the air percussive with fear.

Francis kept his eyes fixed on the mighty conflagration. Inside the burning theatre was his tinder-box, evidence, if any should find it, of his guilt in starting the fire. But the act of arson had been planned meticulously: no one had spotted him switch the flame from his tobacco pipe to the paper and straw he'd crumpled under the bench.

The tinder-box that created the fire would be consumed in the fire it created.

'I think that's dramatic irony,' he mumbled, frowning his uncertainty, then he caught sight of a bowed figure standing nearby, draped in the makeshift cloak of a scorched blanket.

Wincing in the mounting blast of heat and clouds of smoke, he strode up to the distraught man, took him gently by the arm. 'Will . . .'

Will Shakespeare looked all of his forty-nine years as he raised smoke-smudged features to Francis. Then the playwright shook his head, turning desolate eyes on the blazing theatre and terrified crowds. 'God,' he groaned. 'God . . .'

Francis shifted his hand from Will's elbow and gripped him tight by the shoulder. 'Remember your own lines from *Richard II*, Will?' He took a deep breath before declaiming:

> 'His rash fierce blaze of riot cannot last,
> For violent fires soon burn out themselves . . .'

Shakespeare, absorbed in the fiery catastrophe, wasn't listening. Blank-eyed, he continued to shake his head. He shuddered, and swerved a piercing glance at Francis, quoting from the first scene of *Henry VIII*:

> 'Heat not a furnace for your foe so hot
> That it do singe yourself.'

Then he stared back at the inferno, lost in grief.

Disturbed by the aptness of the quotation, Francis let fall his hand and left the dramatist to his distress. He'd taken barely ten paces when the chorus of screams intensified, underscored by low, bestial growls. He squinted into the billows of smoke and drifting cinders, and saw shambling shapes emerge.

A shadow, bulging from night into light

' 'S'blood!' he swore, backing away, as much bedevilled by the shadowy phantom in his head as frightened of the approaching silhouettes. Then the silhouettes hardened into clarity and the dark devil fled his mind at the prospect of a more immediate threat. The menace wore fur and padded on four legs and bellowed fit to burst.

Bears were on the loose, the pelts of some flickering with flames. The fiery bears were not in the best of moods. Either the beasts had broken out of the bear pit adjoining the theatre or the keeper had set them free. Accident or folly, burning bears were on the loose . . .

Moments after Francis took to his heels, he spotted a smoke-blinded woman running straight into the path of one of the enraged creatures. A blistering paw swiped the side of her head and spun the wretch clean off her heels, her neck a snapped stalk.

Running along the Southwark shore, he tried to blank out the horrors at his back, struggled to smother the upsurge of guilt. *He* had created this disaster. *He* was responsible for the suffering.

The author of all their woes.

'Author of all their woes,' he mumbled, staring into the dregs of his tenth cup of sour wine.

He lifted bleary eyes to rove the squalid interior of the Black Boar Tavern, one of the lowlier drinking dens in the stinking slum known as the Stews. The tavern had few customers this evening. Most of the regulars had joined the vast crowd gathered to watch the bonfire of the Globe light up the evening. The bears, it was reported, had been laid low by infantry musket-balls.

Heat not a furnace for your foe so hot —

All over London the bells were still tolling. For Francis, the peals had a funereal tone.

'I had to do it,' he whispered, returning his abstracted gaze to the wine cup. 'I had good reason. It had to be done. But no one will ever understand.'

Kelley and Bathory, they're to blame. If it wasn't for them . . .

A dark memory skimmed across his mind. A shadow, bulging from night to light. Hard to grasp . . .

A croaky tone dispersed the elusive memory. 'Good e'en to you, Francis. Fancy a bit of a tumble in a bed made for tumblin'?'

He glanced up and scowled at the swollen bulk of Alice, two score years and ten with a wart for every year. Her tongue wiggled suggestively.

'A doxy with the pox,' he sneered. 'I'd sooner stick my head in a piss-pot.'

She spat at him and hurled a stream of colourful insults as he shouted for another flask of wine.

The flask was duly delivered and Alice eventually withdrew to a corner, muttering to herself.

Francis downed three cupfuls inside a minute. 'Must be getting drunk,' he said. 'This slop doesn't taste like bilge-water any more.'

A pot-bellied behemoth of a tavern-keeper glared in his direction. 'King James himself has praised my wines!' he bellowed, shaking a meaty fist.

'That's what you always say,' Francis responded dully, gulping another draught. 'Besides, yon canny Scots king has no liking for strong drink — or is it tobacco?' He reeled in his chair. 'Well, something like that . . . wrote a book . . . Counterblast . . . or suchlike —'

Something had happened to his head. He felt as though there were a hole in it, and his liquefying brains were gushing out.

I had to do it. I had good reason.

Time dissolved into the stale wine. Past and future acquired a fluid quality. He swam in it.

He blinked twice, and between one blink and the next he composed an epic poem. He blinked again, and forgot every word of it.

For several aeons, he wandered in Arcadia. A rare delight it was — until he walked into a waterfall.

Spluttering, he swam up into a lamplit room that was vaguely familiar. He was soaked in some foul liquid. He stared up at the raftered ceiling for a long moment before he realized that he was lying on the floor. Faces loomed over him, guffawing.

He put a name to one of the laughing faces: Alice. She waved a metal bowl in front of his eyes. 'Sooner stick your head in a piss-pot, would you, Master Francis? Your wish has been granted, from my very own pot.'

Wiping the rank liquid from his face with the back of his sleeve, he heaved himself on to his elbows. 'Now I know where the tavern wine comes from. Just as well I've no intention of paying,' he heard himself say. His voice seemed to issue from inside his boots.

From a prone position he found himself suddenly yanked upright, feet dangling above the rush-strewn floor. He heard his doublet tear in the tavern-keeper's grip as the burly man shoved his bearded face up close. 'Not – paying?' the beard-fringed mouth snarled. A gust of foul breath hit Francis in the face. His nose wrinkled in revulsion.

'I'm the author of all our woes,' he croaked.

A meat-slab of a fist put paid to any further ramblings. He felt himself sailing through the air to land with a thump.

He was dimly aware of the next couple of punches and kicks, then the sweet waters of Lethe washed over him and he sank into blessed oblivion.

After several ages of the world, or a fleeting second, he opened an eye. Closed it again. Opened it once more.

Time and place were askew; it took some effort to slot them back into position.

At length, he managed to take in his surroundings. It was night. He was sprawled in a greasy alley in the Stews, his body battered, skin and clothes steeped in Alice's urine and his own blood. Inside his ruined physique, he could sense the fatal seepage from damaged organs.

He might as well give up the ghost. His ambitions had foundered. His plans had unravelled. He'd been betrayed.

'Betrayed,' he wheezed, then broke into a harsh spasm of coughing.

There was a rosy glow above the rooftops. The Globe Theatre was still providing London with a lusty bonfire. His handiwork. The last act of a desperate man, whose motives would be known and understood by nobody.

Roused by sudden rage, Francis forced himself to his feet – or rather, to one foot; the limp left leg was well and truly broken. Swaying to keep balance, he shook a fist at the frost of stars.

'You betrayed me! Edward Kelley, Elizabeth Bathory, you betrayed me! Damn you to the sulphurous pit of Hell!'

'*Hell* . . .' echoed an immense voice.

Francis's heart drummed in his shattered rib-cage.

Night congealed into what might have been a shape and walked towards him down the thin alley. A shadow bulging from night –

His befuddled wits couldn't cope with what he was seeing. A coagulated darkness, prowling between the leaning houses. The sight of it convinced him that either the world was insane for containing such a thing, or he was insane for imagining it.

'Who are you?' he wheezed.

'*Who are you?*' boomed the advancing spectre.

Losing his equilibrium, Francis toppled to the cobblestones. 'Christ protect me,' he moaned softly.

'*Christ protect me*,' the voice repeated.

The nonsense shape of night leaned over him, a cold, starry twinkle in its eye.

'I'm damned,' Francis sobbed.

'*I'm damned*,' came the vast echo.

It was close now, close as breath. Essence of dark filtered into Francis's shrinking pores. He looked the nightmare nonsense in its impossibility of a face.

He felt as though a cat had licked his heart.

'I know you,' he gasped as the darkness seeped into the red life in his veins. The invading dark worked a spiritual

alchemy. A transmutation. A merging of souls.
'*I know you.*'
'You're the Devil.'
'*You're the Devil,*' the voice mimicked.
Francis's mouth opened, then froze in a rictus. His body lay quiet and rigid as a corpse on the slab.
A long silence of deepest night was finally broken by a vast whisper.
'*WE ARE THE DEVIL.*'

Castle Ludwig: the Black Forest, Bavaria

Tomb night.
Skull moon.
The scenery and theatrical props were in place, the scene was set, the audience of two settled in their thronelike chairs, and the actors awaited the cue of a raised curtain.
A fanfare of trumpets.
The red velvet curtains parted, revealing a stage-set that resembled the interior of a spacious tomb, or the most austere of bedchambers. A skull-featured moon peered in through a wide crack in the upper wall. Centre-stage, on a bed of stone, lay a man in white robes, his head crowned with the papal tiara that proclaimed him Pope Supreme of the Catholic Church Apostolic.
Enter the Archangel Michael, stage left. The warrior angel, attired in silver armour, hoisted a long spear.
Enter Lord Byron, stage right, sabre in hand.
The drama had begun.
As the scene unfolded, one of the two spectators — a young sybarite dressed as a late eighteenth-century fop — turned to the man at his side. 'May I speak, Doctor?' While posing the question, he nervously stroked a pink poodle nestled in his lap.
'You will be silent, Prince Ludwig.' The speaker's voice was mellifluous, his smile broad, his face hard and white as marble.

Prince Ludwig held his tongue. The stroking of the poodle became brisk and insistent, an expression of frustration.

Finally, Ludwig moved his mouth close to the poodle's fluffy pink ear. 'Did you hear that, Wagner?' he whispered under his breath. 'The Doctor orders the Prince to keep silent. And after all we've done for him, placing Castle Ludwig at his disposal.' His delicate hand weaved in a circle, indicating the soaring, gloomy arches, the stained-glass windows, the ranks of gargoyles, the general neo-Gothic extravagance of the castle's Chimera Hall. 'A melancholically magnificent setting for a drama of fear.'

'I told you to be silent,' the Doctor said, the smile fixed on his rigid features.

Trembling, Ludwig inclined his head to the sinister Doctor, astonished that the man at his side could have heard so faint a whisper. 'Forgive me. It's just that I *am* a Prince of the House Glockenstein, and – and –' He tried not to stutter. 'Th-this is my castle. Much as I admire your drama of f-fear –'

The perpetual smile imprinted on his mouth, the Doctor rose to his feet, carefully adjusting the black folds of his full-length opera cloak. 'I will show you fear, and not in a handful of dust. And I will teach you to be silent.'

A quivering Ludwig hugged the poodle tight as his gaze followed the tall man's fluent movements. The Doctor placed long, manicured fingernails under his chin, and deftly peeled off his smiling face.

Aghast, Ludwig crushed the poodle to his breast as though to absorb its warmth and comfort. 'Uh – uh –'

The Doctor brandished his white face from an outstretched hand. On the front of his head was a blank, pink oval, framed by long, auburn hair. Smooth and featureless as an egg, the non-face paralysed Ludwig with a horror of – well, the faceless.

The white mask spoke from the man's hand, its smiling lips murmuring satin-soft words. 'I have shown you fear. Now I will teach you silence.' The arm stretched forwards, and pressed the mask to the prince's face. The white lips greeted his with a kiss. Sealed them with a kiss.

Ludwig's fingers flew to his mouth – and contacted only smooth skin. A flat expanse of smooth skin from nose to chin.

Where is my mouth? he tried to scream, but had no mouth for screaming.

With a graceful gesture, the Doctor replaced the mask over the pink blank of his face. 'Now, Prince Ludwig,' he said, resuming his seat. 'Let us watch the play – in silence.'

Bathed in the hot sweat of fear, the prince watched the drama, hardly daring to blink lest the Doctor blind his eyes with another kiss.

Onstage, the performance was gathering momentum. There was blood on Byron's sword, and blood on the Archangel Michael's spear.

Ludwig barely caught the Doctor's faint whisper: 'The play's the thing . . .'

Part One

Crimes at Midnight

Crimes at midnight would wail
If torn tongue could tell the tale
In this castle incarnadine
With rare juice, heart's wine.

Pearson's *The Blood, the Horror, and the Countess*

One

'The pope is dead.'
Cardinal Agostini flickered open his eyes at the panicked words, tilted his head on the pillow and, under lowered lids, studied the intruder who had presumed to invade his bedroom. The portly figure of Father Rosacrucci hovered beside the cardinal's bed, dithering hither and thither, rosary beads rattling.

'What was that about the pope?' growled Agostini, pulling back the monogrammed silk covers.

'His Holiness Pope Lucian has — has been taken to the bosom of Christ,' Rosacrucci spluttered. He leaned close, his plump face sheened in sweat that glistened in the muted torchlight. 'There is evidence of — foul play.'

The cardinal glowered at the priest. 'Have you been overdoing the flagellation again, Rosacrucci? If this is another of your visions —'

'It's true, your eminence. The Enclave is gathering in the papal night-chamber and the Camerlengo urgently desires your attendance.'

Agostini pursed his lips, then nodded. 'Tell him I'm on my way.'

Father Rosacrucci backed away across the spacious bedchamber, bowing until he reached the bronze double doors and slipped quietly through.

Observing the priest's departure, Agostini leaned back on his pillow and surveyed the fresco that adorned the ceiling. The painted expanse depicted the Sufferings of the Damned in a tangle of tormented limbs, howling heads, and demons rampant. The fresco had acquired an additional figure overnight: a fresh recruit to the company of the damned. The new lost soul in Hell bore the unmistakable features of Pope Lucian.

'So it's true,' the cardinal whispered. His gaze descended to the crossed-keys papal insignia above the door. '*Sic transit gloria mundi.*'

Expelling a short breath, he eased his tall, chunky frame out of the bed. His bedchamber was on the upper level of the Apostolic Palace, thirty paces down the corridor from the papal apartments. If he hurried, he'd be there before the rest of the Enclave. On the spot, ready to take action.

As Cardinal Agostini dressed, he kept his stare fixed upward on the Sufferings of the Damned. Pope Lucian glared down at him from his heights of woe.

Clad in red robes and a gold pectoral cross, Agostini finally lowered his gaze as he crossed the marble floor.

'So it begins,' he murmured. 'It begins.'

Miles Dashing stalked Bernini's colonnades bordering St Peter's Square, wondering whether he was supposed to be somewhere else. The rendezvous was in Vatican City, he was sure of that, but was it St Peter's Square or St Peter's Basilica? Blast it – if only he could remember . . .

Miles swept back the long, blond fringe from his youthful face with one hand as his other kept a tight grip on his épée. The twenty-year-old ex-Earl of Dashwood was in enemy territory, and every muscle of his tall, lithe figure was on the alert.

At any moment a prelate or military guard of the Exalted Vatican might step from the shadows and discover Miles for the interloper he was. Then there would be much sounding of alarms and much rousing of Vatican minions. A prudent man would make a run for it right now, rendezvous or no rendezvous.

Miles swished his blade and swirled his black opera cloak. Miles Dashing of Dashwood was not one to fail an appointment with a comrade, even if he was having problems finding him. And find him he would, or perish in the attempt.

'Now,' he whispered, 'Square or Basilica? Or was it the Apostolic Palace? I *know* it was at stroke of midnight.' His brow furrowed. 'Or was it at first stroke past midnight?'

Épée in hand, black cloak billowing in the rising breeze, Miles Dashing continued to stalk the colonnades of St Peter's Square.

Giovanni Giacomo Casanova lay in bed with his latest conquest, a comely wench of sixteen, and stared through the open windows of the balcony at the star-haunted night above Venice, resonant with the amorous songs of gondoliers.

Casanova turned to the sleeping girl at his side. What was her name? Maria ... something. He'd ask her when she awoke; he liked to keep a full account of his affairs.

He glanced at the sword by the bed, and his thin lips formed a wry twist. Tonight, if he had put duty before passion, that sword would be in his hand and he would be far from here, in the shadow of St Peter's. Casanova, despite his reputation, set great store in keeping his word, fulfilling an honourable duty. But Maria-something had been so exquisite, so beguilingly innocent, and passion had won out over duty.

He exhaled a slow breath and closed his eyes, head sinking back to the pillow. His comrade would have to make do without him.

'Forgive me, Byron,' he murmured regretfully.

'A sorrowful moment, eminence,' acknowledged the Camerlengo, Cardinal Maroc, as Agostini entered the papal bedchamber. Maroc, like Agostini, struggled to suppress his emotions at the grim spectacle laid out on the bed.

'A sorrowful moment for us all, eminence,' Agostini solemnly greeted, echoing Maroc's formality of address. He noted, with disapproval, that the dumpy figure of

Torquemada was standing at the side of the tall, austere Camerlengo. Agostini had hoped to be first on the scene.

His gaze moved to the papal bed. The pontiff, in full pontifical regalia, was sprawled face down on the sheets. Above his prone figure was an inverted statue of St Michael the Archangel, three metres long from upended feet to helmeted head. The spear gripped in the silver-plated St Michael's hand was lodged in Pope Lucian's back, pinning him to the mattress. A glance under the bed revealed that the spear had been driven clean through the mattress to bury its point in the tiled floor.

'Skewered,' Cardinal Maroc said. 'Like a lamb on a spit. It would take several strong men to hoist the statue above Pope Lucian and drive it down with such force.'

'Either that,' Torquemada said in his silky tone, 'or some deviltry has been at work. I smell the warted hand of Lucifer in this unholy deed.'

Agostini shook his head. 'Lucifer works most often through human hands. The Heretic Alarm must be sounded and the guard mobilized.'

Cardinal Maroc raised a Gothic eyebrow. 'Should we not wait for all members of the Enclave to arrive before taking action?'

'While we wait, the perpetrators escape. As Camerlengo, the papal chamberlain, you must take the role of acting pope, and must act accordingly.'

Maroc deliberated a moment, then inclined his head. 'The alarm will be sounded.'

Stroking his heavy jowl, Agostini studied Pope Lucian's body. 'There was a rumour,' he mused. 'I paid scant heed to it at the time . . .'

The Camerlengo's brows contracted. 'What rumour?'

'Well – it may be nothing, but there was a whisper in the corridors that His Holiness planned a secret meeting with Lord Byron this very night.'

'Byron!' Torquemada spat out the word like a dose of poison. 'The devil incarnate, cloven-hoofed. If that degenerate was here, then I have no doubt who committed this sacrilegious murder.'

'He would have needed assistance,' Agostini said, pointing at the massive metal statue. 'But still, we can proceed on the assumption that Byron was the ringleader. Any henchmen –'

'Why was His Holiness dressed in full regalia at this time of night?' Torquemada interrupted, his normally smooth brow creased in puzzlement.

Agostini lifted burly shoulders. 'More proof that he was meeting someone in his formal role as head of the Catholic Church Apostolic, perhaps?'

'Someone like Byron,' Torquemada grunted.

Agostini studied the skewered pontiff. 'There's no one like Byron.'

Mad, bad, and dangerous to know.

That's how that titled doxy Lady Caroline Lamb had described him. He was the first to admit that the lady had a point. George Gordon, Lord Byron had few illusions about himself.

His present predicament was indubitably mad, bad and dangerous, and he was in great part the author of it.

Prowling through the baroque labyrinth of the Apostolic Palace, blood on his bared sabre, Lord Byron – poet, satirist, politician, pugilist, swordsman, marksman, seducer, adventurer and general hell-raiser – was in peril of his life: the taste of danger had a distinct relish.

The hue and cry had just gone up, resounding from deserted halls and *galleria*. Ah, so they'd found the pope's body, and were after blood. One sight of Byron, and the Vatican prelates would know whose blood they sought. Already the Vatican guard might be on the scent.

Catching the pounding of booted feet up ahead, signalling the approach of the heavily armed Switzia Guardians, he ducked into a side-chapel and hid behind the wrought-iron grille of a rood-screen.

He peered through the grille as the military guard

stormed past, their barbed halberds glinting in the flicker of wall-mounted flambeaux. He counted seven halberds raised above seven gleaming helmets. At a pinch, and in different circumstances, he might have taken them on with a blade in hand and an apt quotation on his lips, but tonight was a night for stealth and flight.

The rumble of booted feet receded down the corridor.

He sat down in a pew and ran strong fingers through his red-brown hair as he considered his situation. His co-conspirators had let him down: Miles Dashing and Casanova had failed to appear for the rendezvous in St Peter's Basilica. The pox on the both of them for leaving him in the lurch, alone in the middle of a hostile Vatican City. With alarms screeching all over the Vatican, and the Apostolic Palace sealed off by now, he was in a spot as sticky as a dead man's gore.

The line of his mouth hardened. 'Well, the son of Mad Jack and grandson of Admiral Foul-weather Jack is no wee, sleekit, cow'rin tim'rous beastie to be caught in a trap.' A smile bent his lips as he glanced at the blood on his sword.

The shriek of the alarm stopped as abruptly as it started. That boded ill, implying that his whereabouts had already been located.

He scanned a row of incongruous gargoyles on one wall. The Gothic additions to the baroque chapel served more than a decorative purpose but, for the moment, the stone faces seemed nothing more than ornamentation. The gargoyles, however, could stir to life in the blink of an eye . . .

Jumping to his feet, he studied the shrine, whose paintings and statuary had a twitchy shadow-and-shine life of their own in the dance of candle- and torchlight. His attention centred on the altar, above which loomed a marble statue of St Anne.

The front of the altar was decorated with a rococo riot of imagery in bas-relief, purportedly telling the tale of the Virgin Mary's birth. The eyes of all the figures were hollow. Byron smiled as he recognized a cryptic pattern in the bas-relief.

Sheathing his sabre, he knelt down and pressed his fingertips in the hollows of the eyes in a sequence according to a basic Baconian code. He was rewarded with a click and a low humming sound as the altar rose from its base and ascended two metres, revealing the black square of a portal in the chapel's back wall.

A secret door to a secret passage. The Vatican was honeycombed with hidden tunnels, and a man with such sharp wits as Lord Byron needed no Ariadne's thread to weave his way through the maze.

He stepped towards the white marble frame of the portal.

And leaped back as the doorway filled with Switzia Guardians, halberds jabbing, teeth bared as they chorused: 'HERETIC!'

Unsheathing the sabre and whipping out a dagger, Byron stood his ground, bellowing words of defiance from his own *Childe Harolde's Pilgrimage*: 'War, war is still the cry, War even to the knife!'

Sharp steel sliced the air. Hot splashes of red decorated white marble.

Two

The fresco of *The Last Judgement* blazed electric blue.

A burst of electromagnetic frenzy illuminated the painted wall of the barrel-vaulted hall. Displaced air fled down the hall with a rush as supercharged ions unleashed a manic dance of crazed lightning. A flamboyant novelty was arriving with a flash and a bang.

The lightning fizzled out and the luminosity dimmed as a blue object intruded itself upon the candlelit expanse with a noise like an asthmatic tank engine afflicted by grating gears. At first more phantom than substance, the intruder phased from image to solidity. In seconds, a blue police box stood on the marble floor.

It stood there for some time, quiet and still, devoid of pyrotechnics, behaving as a proper police box should.

Its door began to open. 'No need to check the screens, Sarah,' a cheery male tone announced from inside. 'Sorry about the tricky touchdown, but *this* time I've landed us right on a Shalonarian beach.'

'That's what you said *last* time,' muttered a woman's voice, loaded with irony.

The door opened wide and a tall man stepped out, hands thrust in the pockets of a brown overcoat, a brown fedora planted on the coppery bramble of his hair. An inordinately long multi-coloured scarf swung down from his neck and scraped his shoes. From head to toe, he was the essential bohemian, and his toothy grin exuded bonhomie.

'Sun and sands,' he declared.

He pulled to an abrupt halt and confronted the dark,

vaulted spaces, the light and shadow of the frescoed hall.

His pale blue eyes bugged and his mouth fell open. 'Ah . . .'

A young woman, almost a foot shorter than her companion, emerged from the box. She was dressed in a black bikini, her heart-shaped face adorned with sunglasses, a towel in one hand, a bottle of sun-tan lotion in the other. Slowly, deliberately, she placed the towel and lotion bottle on the floor and pushed her shades to the top of her head, revealing hazel eyes and a peeved look.

He bent an apologetic smile in her direction. 'Ah . . .'

'This doesn't look like a sun-drenched shore of Shalonar,' she said dryly.

'Just a teeny bit off course,' he conceded. 'But what's a couple of centuries and a few light-years between friends, eh, Sarah? Sarah? . . .'

Sarah Jane Smith pursed her lips. 'Don't – don't tell me you've landed us in "a spot of bother" again. I still haven't recovered from the last one.'

'Yes, that was a bit of a rum do, of somewhat apocalyptic proportions, in which I played a not insignificant role, if I say so myself,' he said, taking several strides to a baroque altar fronting the near wall.

Sarah heaved an exasperated breath and tracked his steps.

'Doctor,' she said in a warning tone, 'if you start *exploring* again I'll –'

'Jelly baby?' offered the Doctor, cutting her off in mid-threat as he whisked a paper bag from a pocket while simultaneously pointing at the immense fresco. 'The end of the story,' he murmured, gaze roving the depiction above the candlelit altar. 'A graphic story. What does it tell you?'

Ignoring the proffered bag of sweets, Sarah's mouth formed a moue as she studied the fresco. She'd recognized the spacious chapel almost at first glance; she'd visited it on a tour back in 1971. But she was in no mood to play the Doctor's games, not with a bikini barely covering the necessary on her goose-pimpling skin she wasn't. 'Why don't you tell me a graphic tale,' she said, all wide-eyed innocence.

The Doctor, however, had lapsed into a thoughtful silence. His features, although partially shaded by the wide-brimmed hat, betrayed a hint of uneasiness as he scanned the painting. Despite accompanying the Time Lord through two of his incarnations, Sarah still found much of his character a giant question mark, but she'd learned to pick up on the little signals of content or anxiety. Something troubled him now, as he studied the images on the wall. 'Eschatology isn't what it used to be,' he mumbled to himself.

Curiosity aroused, she examined the fresco. It was familiar from a hundred popular reproductions: *The Last Judgement*, Michelangelo's towering nightmare in paint. Her stare was drawn to the stern, Grecian Christ hovering high above the altar. His athletic physique seemed to move in the light-and-shadow-play of the flickering altar candles. Christ brandished his right arm at the cascade of lost souls tumbling down to Charon the Ferryman who waited to ship them off to Hell. The damned were suitably horror-struck. But then, even the faces of the blessed appeared less than ecstatic as their souls were sucked into Heaven.

A macabre picture, but Sarah couldn't spot what was bothering the Doctor. She glanced over her shoulder at the murky chapel, sparsely patched with the illumination of flambeaux and the candles of side-altars. If the scene was intended to evoke reverence and awe, it didn't succeed. It was downright spooky: she could almost imagine a painted Renaissance spectre stepping off a wall.

'Astounding!'

The Doctor's loud exclamation made her heart do the hop-skip-and-jump. She darted a glance at his animated expression: a near-childlike excitement had got the better of him. You could always rely on the Doctor to be erratic.

He was engrossed in the portrait of St Benedict. 'Look,' he said, indicating Benedict's aged hand. 'The attention to detail is remarkable.'

She already knew what to look for; she was educated, she was an astute journalist: besides, she'd read the guide books. Michelangelo had painted his own features into the wrinkled flesh on the back of the saint's hand. A neat little touch, sure, but what was so amazing about it?

She gave an indifferent shrug. 'Just a portrait in wrinkles. Michelangelo's face.'

'Do you recognize Michelangelo?'

How the blazes was she supposed to identify the Renaissance artist in a maze of wrinkles? 'No,' she said in a flat tone. 'Sorry. Don't recognize him at all.'

He peered closer at the painted hand. 'Neither do I, Sarah. Neither do I. Most curious.'

Puzzled by his remark, she was about to pose a question when he spun on his heel and marched swiftly down the hall, his arms spreading expansively. His energetic tone boomed in the cavernous space as he hurled his personality in all directions. 'You know where we are, Sarah Jane? I'll give you a clue: there's no place like Rome.'

Cursing under her breath, she ran after him, the soles of her rope sandals slapping on the marble. By the time she drew alongside his gangling figure she'd traversed more than half the length of the floor.

'Of course I know,' she snorted. 'We're in the Vatican's Sistine Chapel. Judging by the wall-torches, sometime before the mid-nineteenth century. And, if you hadn't noticed, I'm strolling around the Vatican in a skimpy bikini.'

His pace didn't slacken as he headed for the far wall. 'Hmm... The TARDIS has materialized inside the Sistine Chapel – makes a change from the cargo hold of an alien spacecraft.' Momentarily, there was a distant glint in his stare. 'Inside the Sistine Chapel, within the Vatican.'

'Yes, so, this is the Sistine Chapel. What of it?'

He flashed one of his disarming grins. 'A rose is a rose is a rose – and if you believe that, you'll believe anything.'

'You call that an answer?'

'No, but at least it's a point of view.'

They'd reached the far wall to confront the first of the nine panels portraying the narrative of Genesis: the *Separation of Light and Darkness*. The Doctor's gaze moved up the wall, then travelled along the frescoes of the vaulted ceiling.

'What neurotic splendour!' he marvelled. 'Rather like Michelangelo himself, in fact. He didn't want to do all this, you know. Pope Julius II badgered him into it. But then, Michelangelo chose the subject – the Bible, from Creation to the Last Judgement, a graphic story from beginning to end.'

As he was speaking he walked to a side-altar, beckoning his companion to follow.

She stood her ground. 'Doctor, if this is turning into another of your investigations I'll nip into the TARDIS and slip into something more – uncomfortable.' She nodded in the direction of the time-travelling police box that contained a mini-universe. 'Let's face it, I'm not in suitable attire for a Vatican visitor.'

He pointed a finger at the ceiling, indicating the depiction of the *Creation of Eve*. 'You're more fully clad than Eve,' he said.

'Tell that to any passing cardinal.'

'This won't take more than a few seconds, Sarah, I promise.' He held out a hand. 'Please?'

She did her best to muffle a smile as she joined him by the altar. 'Oh, OK. You always know how to get round me. Too fond of you by half, that's my trouble.'

'Really? I'm *terribly* fond of you, Sarah, and I don't find it any trouble at all.' Beaming genially, he nodded at the lighted altar candles. 'Try putting one of the candles out.'

She raised a quizzical eyebrow, but stepped up to the altar and slammed a hand down on a candle. Her eyes widened as she witnessed the flame flickering *through* her hand. There wasn't the slightest sensation of heat. Light without warmth.

Sarah glanced questioningly at the Doctor. 'A holo-flame,' he informed, 'like the fires on the wall-torches. The programmed flicker is an absolute give-away.'

She withdrew her hand. 'Puts paid to my guess about the century. OK, you've had your little demonstration. Let's get back to the TARDIS and head for the sun-kissed beaches of –'

'The face.'

The Doctor's incisive tone and remote aspect silenced her. In an instant, all trace of the clown and prankster had vanished from his features. In the blue of his inward gaze was the light of an alien world, exposing his habitual tomfoolery for what it was, the froth on the surface of the ocean.

He looked a young forty going on eternity.

At times like these, mercifully rare, she felt as small as a mouse.

'What about the face?' she heard herself whisper.

His baritone thrilled right through her. 'The image on St Benedict's hand was a composite face. Faces within faces. I thought I recognized the pattern – from long ago.'

The moment of abstraction lengthened, then he shook his head and broke into a smile as he pulled out a yo-yo and put it into play. The froth was back on the ocean, obscuring the depths.

'A composite face?' she said.

'Oh, heed me no heed,' he grinned, performing a figure-of-eight with the yo-yo. 'A little trot down memory lane to a door I never opened, into the rose garden.'

Quicker than she could blink, the yo-yo was back

in his pocket. He raised his arms and circled on his heels, taking in the surroundings. 'Impressive. A near-perfect reconstruction. The artificial ageing is particularly noteworthy. However, the patterning of the marble floor is distinctly anachronistic, to say nothing of those gargoyles up there.'

She frowned. 'A reconstruction? This is the Vatican, isn't it?'

'It's *a* Vatican.'

She scratched her head. 'Just how many are there?'

'Oh, very few. In fact –' His hand flew to his mouth. 'Oh dear.'

'What's wrong?'

'We're on Earth.'

'Is that bad?'

'It is if I got the time co-ordinates right for Shalonar – AD 3278. Vatican City was remodelled in the 31st century by colonists from the Overcities, signalling the inception of the Europan era. If this is the Europa of 3278, or even a century either way . . .' He grabbed her arm. 'Quick, Sarah, back in the TARDIS. I'll be right behind you.'

She didn't need any more prompting to take to her heels as fast as her flip-flops would allow. Her sprinting strides devoured the distance to the vehicle, the Doctor's heavier steps thumping close at her back.

Something was about to go seriously wrong, she just knew it.

But only a few more paces to the open door of the police box. Inside, safety.

Almost there . . .

The police box dropped clean through the floor.

Sarah skidded to a halt at the rim of an empty black square where the TARDIS had stood an instant earlier.

She spun round to confront the Doctor's dismayed expression. 'What happened?' she demanded, heart thudding. 'Don't tell me you managed to land the TARDIS right on top of a trapdoor.'

'A drop-slab,' he responded. 'I thought the patterning

of the floor was peculiar – interlocking squares. Any one of them can function as a drop-slab. Should have realized that at first glance.'

A low rumble resounded from the square-framed pit as a slab of marble slammed up and slotted back into place, leaving the floor intact as before, minus the TARDIS. Sarah stared forlornly at the spot where the TARDIS wasn't.

'Somebody knows we're here,' she said bleakly.

'Yes.' The Doctor's tone was sepulchral. 'They must have known it from the moment we arrived.' For a moment, he wore a woebegone expression, then switched from the funereal to the happy-go-lucky. 'Oh well, that wily old girl of a TARDIS must have had one of its "tendencies", depositing us here for some jolly good reason. After all, the TARDIS is a sort of extension of my psyche. No doubt, deep in my unconscious, I *intended* to come to this space-time co-ordinate. And so – here we are . . .'

Sarah closed her eyes and counted to five before speaking. 'Do you actually believe that?'

'Not a word of it,' he said. 'But a fool who persists in his folly becomes wise, as a friend of mine once said on Brighton sands. Mind you, he thought he was talking to Moses at the time . . .' He straightened abruptly, snapping to attention. 'No time for chit-chat. Must get the TARDIS back. Bothersome thing is, you left the door wide open.'

'*I* left the door wide open?' she snorted, hands on hips.

He raised a hand in absolution. 'Don't blame yourself, Sarah. A mistake anyone could make.'

On the verge of delivering a barbed retort, she bit her lip. 'Are you trying to rile me so I forget to be scared?'

He appeared genuinely baffled. 'Am I? Oh well, if you say so.'

'Tell me, just what should I be scared of? Dropping through the floor like the TARDIS? Being attacked by a mob of demented monks? What do you know about –

what did you call it – Europa?'

'Its reputation,' he said darkly.

'Oh, come on. You can tell me more than that.'

He scratched his brambly hair, as if trying to tease memories from his head. 'Not much more. I've never visited Europa. All I know is a little something I picked up once from the TARDIS data banks. Europa is an area reconstructed on the site of the original Europe – East and West, and – er, this is slightly embarrassing . . .'

'Go on, be embarrassed.'

'Whatever you say. Well, how shall I put it – Europa is infested by ghosts, vampires, werewolves, ghouls and other grotesques spawned from old European folklore. I think we're in a spot of bother, Sarah Jane.'

She gave a slow shake of the head. 'I don't think I want to hear this . . .'

The Doctor breezed on regardless. 'And the whole kit and caboodle is ruled by the Inquisition under a renegade branch of the Catholic Church. The official papal seat is, I believe, situated in the Betelgeuse system during this era.' The Doctor's grin broadened into a crescent that was positively devilish. 'If you want an idea of what it's like travelling through Europa, imagine running scared in the Black Forest under a bad moon.'

'But you're talking about that old, black magic!' she protested. 'Has science just got ditched out the window?'

He twitched his shoulders. 'Someone once said that advanced science becomes indistinguishable from magic, or words to that effect. Besides, I'm only quoting the data banks, which are not immune to the occasional gremlin. Perhaps this era has developed highly sophisticated psionics and – oh, never mind.' He started to move away. 'Now, Sarah, let's introduce ourselves to the local ecclesiastic dignitaries before they introduce themselves to us.'

Breaking into a brisk stride, he made for a pair of imposing double doors. With a philosophical shrug, she tracked his long paces. At the doorway, he paused, and shot up a finger. 'Take me to your pontiff! How does that sound as an introduction?'

'Ho hum,' she responded. 'Although it has a resounding ring. The ringing tone of a ham actor. Lead on, Macduff.'

Pushing open the doors, he gave her a conspiratorial wink. 'That's the spirit, Sarah. I do so admire a plucky journalist.'

She scowled. 'I hate it when you call me that.' The scowl faded. 'Or are you deliberately riling me again?'

'Am I?' he said, his bugging eyes the soul of innocence.

'Hard to tell.'

A rumble from the floor startled the pair. Alternate drop-slabs had plunged out of sight, leaving the floor resembling a chess board with empty gaps for black squares.

'Time to run?' Sarah urged.

He raised a hand. 'I don't think so. Better wait and see what happens.'

Bare seconds passed before the slabs ascended back into place. On each slab stood a man garbed in livery reminiscent of the Swiss Guards, a score in all, bearing cruelly barbed halberds.

The nearest soldier, whose insignia marked him out from the rest, jabbed an accusatory finger at the time-travellers. 'Protestant heretics!' he roared. 'Captain Emerich of the Switzia Guardians places you under arrest for the murder of Pope Lucian!'

'You were right, Sarah,' the Doctor confided out the corner of his mouth. 'Time to run.'

Three

The sabre slashed as halberds jabbed in the chapel of St Anne.

Byron, blade streaking fast as thought, dispensed with poetic quotes and saved his breath for battle. Two Switzia Guardians had felt the edge of his keen steel and been split wide open, spilling their hot life on to cold marble. Five more to go.

The poet's sabre flashed across a throat. Four to go.

In a blur of thrust, counterthrust and parry, Byron bedazzled his adversaries, spinning their wits. The sabre ripped through one man's chest as the knife drove into another's heart.

'He's a fiend!' shrieked the foremost of the two surviving guards.

'One of the devil's own crew,' the Englishman snarled, booting the man in the stomach and stabbing between the ribs.

A final swing of the sword severed the remaining man's head from his shoulders. No enemies left standing: the way to the secret passage was clear.

He jumped over the heaped bodies, some still twitching, and cast a backward look at the chapel. His feet froze in mid-stride.

A granite gargoyle was turning its demonic head on a chapel wall. Its scaly neck craned towards him, stony eyes fixing the lord with a baleful glare.

Breaking free of the gargoyle's dire spell, he sprang into the portal's shadows.

'Now they know where I am,' he muttered under his breath. 'Hell's teeth.'

'St Anne's chapel,' Agostini announced as a picture formed on a stained-glass window, obliterating the coloured glass depiction of Christ's Harrowing of Hell. Framed by the window's Gothic arch, the scene of slaughter in the chapel was revealed in three-dimensional detail, transmitted by a Gargoyle Vigilant. The assembled members of the Enclave caught a glimpse of Byron before he disappeared into the secret passage.

'The ringleader,' Agostini pronounced, then switched his attention to another window which displayed the interlopers in the Sistine Chapel. 'And two of his accomplices. The accomplices are in our hands. Their leader may prove more elusive if he's gleaned knowledge of the hidden maze.'

'He'll not last long,' Cardinal Maroc stated confidently. 'Who can outwit us in our own labyrinth?'

Agostini's stare swept over the other six members of the Enclave, the innermost cabal of Vatican City, gathered in the circular Chapel of Witness beneath the Apostolic Palace. The faces of Inquisitor General Torquemada, Cardinals Maroc, Borgia, Richelieu, Altzinger and Francisco met his stare, unspeaking.

'The murderers of Pope Lucian must be brought swiftly to punishment,' he declared. 'Europa must be left in no doubt of the fate awaiting those who dare strike against the Church Apostolic.'

Torquemada, exuding his customary aura of oily saintliness, uplifted his hands to heaven. 'The apprehension of murderous heretics must be swift,' he said. 'But the punishment must be *slow*.'

Six heads nodded in accord.

He was all at sevens and sixes on this piggledy-higgledy night.

Miles Dashing sneaked out of St Peter's Basilica and

resumed lurking in the shadows of Bernini's colonnade, perplexed and undecided.

No sign of Byron anywhere. Miles was mortified by the prospect of letting down his poetical comrade – despite the fellow being a bit of a scallywag – but what to do? Either it was the wrong place or the wrong time or maybe the whole thing had been called off. Come to think of it, where was Casanova? Wasn't he supposed to be here too?

What to do? What to do?

'Alack, unhappy night,' he groaned, covering his exquisite features in a long-fingered hand.

Ashamed of his momentary lapse, Miles straightened his shoulders, flicked back his long blond hair, and determined to resolve his predicament. If neither Byron nor Casanova was here, it stood to reason that they were probably somewhere else. Well, yes, that was blindingly obvious, now he thought about it. So where else should he go? If not St Peter's Square in Vatican City . . .

'Yes!' He snapped his fingers. 'Casanova. There's a clue. And where does that saucy scoundrel live – Venice. St *Mark's* Square in Venice.'

Decision reached, Miles Dashing raced from the piazza, his long, athletic legs taking him to the brink of – nothing. Beyond the entrance to St Peter's Square, Vatican City ended in a rim which overlooked the Roman hills two kilometres below, the moonlit vista puffed with cumulus cloud. Tonight, the Vatican was Exalted, hovering high above the earth.

Miles sheathed his sword and leaped off the edge of Vatican City.

Sarah didn't need the Doctor to tell her it was time to run.

She'd already kicked off her sandals and was speeding down the corridor to the Borgia Apartments.

The Doctor delayed his flight, standing in the doorway to cover Sarah's escape. Captain Emerich led the charge, halberd lowered. 'Apostate necromancer!' the captain screeched, froth speckling his blubbery lips.

With the prestidigitation of a conjurer, the Doctor drew the yo-yo from his pocket and unleashed its spinning disc to impact at lightning velocity between the captain's eyes. The man's onrush continued for a second from its own momentum, then he toppled, pole-axed.

The yo-yo was whisked back into the Doctor's hand an instant after braining Captain Emerich, ready for a repeat performance.

The Switzia Guardians skidded to a stop, mouths agape.

'Ah-hah!' the Doctor chuckled wickedly, giving a convincing portrayal of a desperado. It was evident that these men were unaccustomed to defiance. 'Are you ready to surrender?' he demanded imperiously.

They were impressed. But not that impressed. The onslaught was resumed with redoubled intensity. 'Heretic! Pagan! Blasphemer!'

'Now you've asked for it!' the Doctor thundered, lashing out again with the yo-yo, downing two assailants in a fleet figure-of-eight. 'Beware the Flashing Lemniscate!' he boomed, whipping the yo-yo in another figure-of-eight, disposing of a couple more guards. 'Devastation to flesh and bone!'

Two more soldiers hit the floor, senseless.

The Switzia Guardians finally faltered, unable to make rhyme or reason of the bizarre weapon launched at them, then dropped their halberds and executed a swift about-turn, beating a panicked retreat.

The Doctor was already hot on Sarah's tracks the instant the guardians turned their backs. By the time the men had replenished their meagre stock of courage he'd be long gone.

'Ah,' he murmured. 'But gone where?'

Sarah raced from the grandiose Borgia Apartments on to the seemingly interminable Lapidary Gallery skirting the

Court of the Belvedere. The night sky was just visible above the far side of the grassy court.

She gave a breath of relief at the distinctive sound of the approaching paces.

'What took you so long?' she said as the Doctor rushed round the corner.

'Just keep running.'

'Where to?' she gasped, legs pumping as she pushed herself to the limit.

'Keep running down the corridor and I'll think of something.'

They'd covered hardly thirty paces when a figure in black darted from the right, a sabre glinting in his hand.

'Stand, or be chopped up fit for the butcher and baker!'

The Doctor grabbed Sarah's arm and slowed her to a halt. They confronted the stranger, who was dressed in a black velvet suit over a flared white shirt. Reddish-brown curls framed a saturnine face. An imperious air belied the man's medium height.

'George!' the Doctor exclaimed. 'It's a small universe. But what are you doing a millennium or so out of your time?' He threw a glance at Sarah. 'I told you I'd think of something. Meet George, an old friend.'

'Lord Byron to you,' the man scowled, although lowering his sword.

Sarah gazed, awestruck. *Byron*. Mad, bad and dangerous to know. The roistering poet whom no self-respecting career woman should look up to. But — she couldn't help it — her skin tingled as Byron's gaze roved her bikini-clad body. Besides, she was in a tight corner, and the mad, bad poet was a good man to have on your side in tight corners.

'Good to meet you,' she smiled, feeling thoroughly naked under his probing stare.

A wicked grin bent the lord's lips. 'Running near-nude through the Vatican. A shameless Diana of the chase. An honest slut. I approve.'

'Don't call me a slut, you male chauvinist pig!' she exploded, sensual thoughts dispersed with a word.

'A filly with spirit too,' observed Byron. 'If we find the time, I shall enjoy the taming. So shall you. On second thoughts . . . I couldn't be bothered.'

'George,' interposed the Doctor before Sarah could hurl a well-chosen insult. 'I'm the Doctor. We once sat by the Parthenon and I gave you a critique of a poem you hadn't yet written. I know I look different now, but surely you remember that little episode with the five oranges and the purple handkerchief and the misplaced nostrum?'

The lord's brow furrowed. 'I remember nothing of the kind. Your wits are obviously addled.'

The Doctor stroked his chin in meditation. 'Hmm . . . curious.'

'Doctor!' Sarah implored. 'We're up to our eyebrows in trouble. No time for reminiscences. We've got to –'

'Are you the assassins who sent Pope Lucian to his Maker?' Byron cut in.

The Doctor darted a glance down the passage. 'The Switzia Guardians seemed to think so.'

Byron snorted. 'They're also saying it was me. I've been hunted through every hall and gallery in the Apostolic Palace.' He stared deep into the Doctor's eyes, then gave a small, knowing nod. 'You're no assassin.'

Without warning, he sped past them in the direction of the Borgia Apartments, a flick of the hand indicating a farewell.

'No, not that way!' the Doctor warned.

'Adieu,' Byron called out as he ran speedily, despite a slight limp, to the near end of the corridor.

'Good riddance,' sniffed Sarah, but with less conviction than she felt at the loss of a potentially valuable ally.

'Shame about him running off like that,' the Doctor murmured. 'I find his amnesia about our meeting quite baffling. And why's he in this epoch? Pope Lucian . . .'

He thumped his head. 'Pope Lucian. Of course! Now it's coming back to me. It is the year AD 3278, or very close. That means we're bang in the middle of the High Dogmatic period.' A low sigh. 'We really are in a spot of bother, Sarah Jane.'

'This is news?' Despite her affection for the Doctor, he certainly took the biscuit for driving her clean up the wall. 'Let's get out of here. Fast!'

'Absolutely right,' he said, launching into a sprint down the gallery. 'Follow me.'

The precise instant she resumed running the walls came alive. Faces grew out of them. Stone faces. From floor to ceiling, the full length of the corridor, gargoyles sprouted from the masonry, stony tongues flicking from their gaping mouths.

The myriad gargoyles screamed the same refrain, a high-pitched, eardrum-drilling shriek, incessantly repeated: 'HERETICS . . .'

Sarah's pulse accelerated its tempo to panic stations. 'What in God's name's going on?' she gasped.

The Doctor glanced over his shoulder. 'Heretic Alarm, I suppose. Don't let those ugly mugs on the wall worry you. They're just a type of plasmic extrusion – I think. Anyway, I find the mixture of Gothic and Baroque elements decidedly unaesthetic.'

Sarah couldn't resist a smile. You had to give it to the Doctor for bare-faced insouciance in the middle of bedlam.

'Bare-faced cheek, more like it,' she said under her breath.

Ignoring the strident gargoyles, she focused her attention on the Doctor's back and told her legs to run, run and run. The metres flashed by, and she forgot about her thumping heart and strained limbs. Run like the devil with a bigger devil at your back.

Her gaze still focused on the Doctor, his overcoat swirling, ludicrous scarf flying, she gave an extra push to draw alongside.

It was then she noticed something untoward about him. Sarah couldn't identify the wrongness at first. Her mind shifted several notches out of kilter when she realized that she could see *through* him. In a few blinks of the eye, he was becoming transparent. A phantom.

'Doctor!'

His fading silhouette elongated, twisted out of shape. A thin cry of pain issued from the distorted spectre: '*Sarah* . . .'

The cry fled into the distance and the contorted residue of the Doctor vanished.

The corridor stretched ahead, empty and limitless. Her heart turned to lead and sank. 'No!' she railed. 'No!'

She fell to her knees and thumped the mosaic floor with her fist, biting back the tears. A corner of her mind registered that the gargoyles had fallen silent. She didn't care one way or the other. The Doctor was gone.

She had no idea how many minutes passed while she knelt on the floor. At length, she told herself not to give up, give out, give in. The Doctor wouldn't have wanted that. Keep going, mourn later.

When she raised reddened eyes on the way ahead, she could see no end to the corridor. She rose to her feet and peered into the distance. The Lapidary Gallery lost itself in some unguessable vanishing point. The gallery had put space on the rack and stretched it beyond the limits.

'Oh well, start moving.' Her voice was weak and small.

She started forward. And stayed put. She looked down at her feet planted on the marble, the soles stuck fast. What the hell? Sarah shook her head in bemusement. What was doing this to her, and why?

As she gazed around helplessly, she noticed that the light of the holo-torches was dimming. As the illumination lowered, a chant rose, mounting wave by wave.

It was Gregorian chant, the discordant voices souring the natural beauty of the harmony. The Latin phrases clanged like funeral bells in the air:

Dies irae, dies illa,
Solvet saeclum in favilla . . .

She mentally translated the familiar words: Day of wrath, day of mourning, Heaven and Earth in ashes burning . . .

'Who's the requiem for?' she muttered. 'Me?'

Her sense of balance suddenly went haywire.

The rapid forward motion was so abrupt that she reeled backwards, arms flailing. It took a few seconds for her senses to reorientate. When they did, she groaned aloud.

Her feet were still glued to the floor, but the floor was moving. The walls slid past at some ten miles an hour. Inexorably, the speed increased until the gargoyles streaked by, mere smears in the shadows. She was racing along at fifty miles an hour, minimum, and the velocity kept on increasing.

Sarah was on an express conveyor belt whisking her to an unknown destination at a rate of knots.

'What's happening?' she yelled. Then the acceleration escalated to a point where the breath was forced from her lungs.

At that point she saw the end of the corridor hurtle towards her. Rubbing water from her eyes, she made out a black door that blocked out the entire corridor.

The door enlarged in moments, glinting metallically. End of the line. A terminal full stop.

Sarah slammed into it at killing speed with a despairing scream: 'DOCTOR!'

Four

Clad in the hooded robes of Convocation Extraordinary, the dignitaries of the Enclave sat in the seven thrones of the Crypt of the Seven Sleepers. Each of the fabled Sleepers, dreaming or otherwise, was entombed behind an icon set in the granite walls.

In front of the Altar Ipsissimus, flanked by congregations of holo-candles and a small group of mechanical monks, rested the two-metre-high blue box taken from the two intruders in the Sistine Chapel. Although the object's door was open, no one had yet succeeded in entering the outlandish container.

Fidgeting on his throne, Torquemada folded his arms and glared. 'What is this infernal, heathenish machine? What sorcery obstructs us from walking through an open door? And what is the diabolic meaning of the legend on its crest: Police Public Call Box? And the rest of its words of witchcraft on the side: police telephone free for use of public –'

'The point, surely,' said Richelieu, 'is that the entrance is invisibly barred.'

Agostini, accepting a proffered glass of wine from a mechanical monk, ushered the cowled robot away before flicking a hand at the box's open door. 'Whatever force prevents access, we'll circumvent it.'

'It is the gate to Satan's domain,' Torquemada insisted.

Cardinal Rodrigo Borgia waved a lazy arm at the Spanish Inquisitor General. 'You're so naive, Tomas.' Ignoring the bristling Torquemada, he continued in a robust tone. 'It's merely a device, like an Angelus or viewing gargoyle or mechanical horse. Like all devices when mastered, it will serve a purpose.'

'I beg to differ,' Agostini said. 'There are forms o technology which undermine the dominance of th Catholic Church Apostolic and the Holy Inquisition This contraption here may be a product of just suc technological expertise.' He glanced across at Torque mada. 'The intruders must be interrogated as to th nature of this – this apparatus. I trust the man and hi shameless female companion are secure in Hell?'

The Inquisitor General bent a pious smile, small eye brimming with anticipation. 'Yes, indeed – interrogate – in Hell.' The words were honey on his tongue.

Maroc raised a hand. 'The candidature for the papac has not been decided. In my capacity as Camerlengo, must deal with this matter without delay. Rodrigo Borgi would seem the obvious choice –'

The Borgia cardinal nodded vigorously.

Agostini gave a firm shake of the head. 'Until th identity of the pope's assassins is irrefutably established, i would be unwise to institute a papal election. Many ou there in Europa would be only too willing to believe tha the murder was arranged – *in Vaticano*. There is, after all, long history of ambitious cardinals disposing of popes i order to ascend the Throne of Peter and wear th Fisherman's Ring.'

'Why are you looking at me?' Cardinal Borgi rumbled, glaring under his bushy eyebrows.

'I wasn't,' Agostini replied wearily. 'Until this matter i settled, a cloud hangs over the entire Vatican Curia. I short, Lord Byron and his two accomplices must b sentenced to an auto-da-fé. Justice must be seen to b done. The arts of the inquisitor will ensure a satisfactor outcome in that area, I have no doubt.'

'You may count on it, eminence,' Torquemada said.

'As regards this puzzling device,' said Agostini, indicat ing the police box. 'The dungeons of the Inquisition wil supply us with answers from Byron's co-conspirators.' H looked around for confirmation. 'Agreed?'

One by one, heads inclined.

'Excellent.' Agostini leaned back in the throne. 'Then, Torquemada, I suggest you introduce the two accused to the torments of Hell.'

'The Pit and the Pendulum,' chuckled Rodrigo Borgia.

'Oh no, eminence,' Torquemada purred. 'That would be too great a mercy.'

Sarah recalled a phrase from Milton: *darkness visible*.

The dark pressed in on her with all the force of a sentient presence, intimating the blackest of revelations. She wondered if she'd died and gone to Hell. There were no pits of lurid fire, no sulphurous smoke, no gibbering demons with pitchforks at the ready. This was a cold, light Hell. Hovering weightless in this nothingness, aware of neither up nor down, she recalled the metal door she'd seemed to slam into at fatal speed.

Had it been an illusion of the dying, or had her rapid forward acceleration altered into an abrupt *downward* tilt? For all she knew, she might have been plucked from the gallery and deposited in a psionically engineered Pit somewhere in the Vatican.

To keep terror at bay – and terror was damn near breathing down her throat – she cast her mind back to childhood. Think back to the happy days.

Behind her eyes, she resurrected the streets of South Croydon, the tiny playing field of her primary school where she frequently lost her ball over the blue railings. And there was Julie with her mass of freckles, always laughing. And Billy, forever giving her the wink, while she thumbed her nose at the tow-haired scamp. Coming home, satchel swinging in one hand, choc-ice in the other, socks collapsed round her ankles. Home to Mum and Dad.

Until that day when Mum and Dad weren't there. She'd wandered the too-empty house for an hour, then the phone rang. The caller was Aunt Lavinia, ringing

from Morton Harewood. There'd been a car acciden[t]
Mum and Dad hadn't suffered. It had all been very quic[k]
Quick and painless . . .

The darkness visible bored back into her. With a[n]
effort, she thrust it away. Recall a face, a voice . . .

Aunt Lavinia.

After the car accident came the sharp transition t[o]
Morton Harewood and the slow tempo of village lif[e.]
Aunt Lavinia had done her best to be father and moth[er]
to the orphan under her roof, but nobody's best woul[d]
have been enough. Sarah's parents had been the best [in]
the world. She still believed that.

When she moved back to South Croydon, it w[as]
chiefly the memory of Mum and Dad that prompted th[e]
return. She'd always ensured the grave was kept tidy . . [.]

The past images deliquesced like water-colours in th[e]
rain.

The darkness visible was back in full intensity, drivi[ng]
out each light-and-life recollection.

She wasn't a child any more, nor a teenager. And sh[e]
wasn't in the London suburbs. She was either dead a[nd]
damned, or alive and in a hell contrived by a pseud[o-]
Vatican.

The only fixed point left was the Doctor. When sh[e]
first met him in his third incarnation as a crease-feature[d,]
grey-haired man, apparently in late middle age, sh[e]
almost came to look on him as a father-figure.

Father-figure? She'd kidded herself back then. For a[ll]
that he was a Time Lord from the mysterious planet [of]
Gallifrey, he just didn't measure up. No one could stan[d]
in her Dad's shoes.

But with the Doctor's regeneration into a younger ma[n]
with hair like an exploding Brillo pad, the father-figu[re]
issue never arose. The Fourth Doctor was her idea of [a]
mad uncle, and she'd always wanted a mad uncle. Gifted b[y]
the experience of his seven-hundred-whatever years, h[e]
still looked like he'd come down with the last shower.

If he was dead . . .

No, she refused to accept that. Many times, when she thought him dead and done for, up he popped again like a jack-in-the-box. She even believed him capable of negotiating an escape clause from the Last Judgement.

She needed him now. Needed his tomfoolery, his clown's wisdom.

The darkness visible lapped over the fringes of her mind, threatening to swamp all the memories in the locked cupboards and cabinets – her parents, Aunt Lavinia, the Doctor, steeped in oblivion.

Terror, no longer at bay, leapt like a tiger, ravenous to devour her, piece by piece.

Of one thing Sarah was sure; living or dead, she was in Hell.

The Doctor hung in the middle of a black void, arms folded, feet crossed, body leaning against a metaphorical lamp-post.

He had tried shouting out for Sarah, but the muffling dark all but swallowed up his voice, and he caught no response from his companion. Oh well, if whoever put him here had decided to keep him alive, the chances were good that they'd done the same for Sarah. If they hadn't, they'd answer to him.

Whoever they were, they possessed considerable skill in the field of somatic transmatography. He had been phased from the Lapidary Gallery to – wherever he was – with ruthless efficiency. The transdimensional distortions, warping his physique during transit, were decidedly uncomfortable.

Where exactly was he? Limbo? No, that was a catch-all name, another way of admitting that you hadn't a clue where you were. It wasn't E-space – or N-space for that matter.

Lifting his battered hat, he scratched his head, trying to solve the puzzle.

'Hmm . . .' he mused.

* * *

Miles Dashing plummeted three metres from the brink of the Exalted Vatican City and landed in the seat of his Draco, the golden hover-scooter fashioned in the likeness of a stylized dragon, wings partially unfurled.

'Must check it's still hovering in the same spot I left it before I jump next time,' he muttered.

Releasing the camouflage device that disguised the craft as an Angelus, one of the Vatican's air vehicles, he sped north towards Venice. As the kilometres raced below, his native melancholy reasserted itself. Two hours to Venice at full Draco speed. About half that time to Florence, where his beloved dwelt – his divinity in female form.

'*Beatrice* . . .' he sighed soulfully. 'Beatrice Florentino.'

He had glimpsed her first as he stood on the Ponte Vecchio over the River Arno that wound through Florence's glorious cityscape. In that one look, he had become her worshipper, her idolater. For a time he worshipped his goddess from afar, then he made his reckless move, made mad by all-consuming adoration.

A rose gripped between his teeth, he swung in through her open window in the depths of the Florentine night –

– and discovered it was the wrong window. He landed on top of Beatrice's mother where she slept in bed. There followed a session of screams and gunshots and unseemly language, culminating in his expulsion from the villa with the tidings ringing in his ears that his divine Beatrice had fled her home on the very eve of his importunate entrance. He set off in quest of his Queen of Heaven, scouring the numerous Dominions of Europa.

He found her at last in the Demi-monde area west of the Wall in Franco-Berlin. She had grown very fat and exceedingly common in that brothel in the Demi-monde. No longer the radiant idol of his youth (well, of nine months earlier), she stubbornly refused to leave the house of ill-repute, speaking in the most foul-mouthed manner of 'good money' and 'liking 'em rough'. Oft-times he beseeched the fallen lady to turn from her sorry state and take up residence with him in a small but serviceable castle in one of Bohemia's Black Forests, but ever she spurned him with unladylike scorn until he desisted and rode away on his mechanical horse, wracked with sorrow and steeped in irredeemable gloom.

'A sad tale, but mine own,' he sighed mournfully to the wind. Then, slowly, the importance of his mission dawned on him. Enough of past regrets and *tristesse*, no matter how deeply lodged in his wounded heart. He had a duty to fulfil, and a gentleman always did his duty.

Miles Dashing's obligation now was to Byron — wherever he may be. The poetic lord was involved in some kind of deal with the pope that would advance the cause of the Dominoes and diminish the flourishing power of the Inquisition. A high, noble ambition.

'If only I could play my part,' Miles muttered, brow troubled with a frown. 'I hope Byron's in Venice. At least, there's a good chance that Casanova will be there.'

The torchlights of Florence came into sight on the horizon.

'Oh, my lost Beatrice,' Miles Dashing moaned soulfully.

'What the —'

Casanova flung back the sheets and blankets and rubbed his pounding head. His vision gradually focused on the tall, aristocratic figure standing by the bed. Taking in the heroic posture, the tragic aura, the flowing blond hair and outrageously good-looking features, he gave a low groan. 'Oh — it's *you*.'

Miles Dashing gave a curt bow. 'Miles Dashing of Dashwood, at your service.'

Casanova yawned, still partly in his dreams. 'I thought the name was Miles Dashwood.'

'I had to adopt a pseudonym, for political purposes.'

'You're hardly likely to pass incognito with a minor alteration like that, are you?' Casanova said, blinking sleep from his eyes.

Miles politely waved aside the sardonic observation. 'You may not be acquainted with my reasons for secrecy, but two years ago, the nobly born but vampiric Mindelmeres, owners of an estate neighbouring Dashwood House, attacked my family while I was elsewhere engaged in a duel over a lady's honour –'

Casanova was now fully awake, despite the throbbing in his skull from too much wine. 'Oh, wait, you've told me all this before, *several* times –'

Miles, however, was in full flood. 'Little was I to know, as I passed the gloomy fastnesses of the Mindelmere estates, what horrors that foul brood had visited upon the Dashwood family. Yet, a curious despondency and chill foreboding settled on my spirit as the lofty towers of Dashwood House loomed into view –'

'Yes, we're all familiar with your family tragedy and very sympathetic, but –'

'Hesitating a moment at the threshold of my family home, strangely hushed in the spectral gloom, I summoned my courage and entered, sword in hand –'

Casanova buried his head in his hands. 'Oh *God*,' he moaned.

'I was soon to discover that my sword would serve me naught, for my family had become – *vampires*. They advanced upon me, fangs bared, eager to bestow the bloody kiss of the undead. "Avaunt!" I cried at the ghastly sight, and reached for my stake-gun –'

'And staked the lot of them,' Casanova broke in, 'which led to the charge of kin-slayer being laid at your door, chiefly through the influence of the Mindelmeres, forcing you to escape execution by fleeing Regency Britannia, since when you've wandered through the Europan Dominions with a price on your head.'

Miles's graceful eyebrows arched in surprise. 'Oh, I see.

I've told you all this before.'

'And about bloody Be—' Casanova checked himself. 'And about Beatrice,' he concluded lamely.

Miles averted his elegant profile. 'Yes, but that was all long, long ago.'

Casanova sat up. 'Anyway, what did you want?'

Pulling himself together with a mighty effort, Miles squared his shoulders and flung back his head. 'Plans are afoot and the Dominoes are on the march. The ignoble alliance between the Inquisition and Cardinal Richelieu is about to be sabotaged. But I must locate Lord Byron for the first blow to be struck. Would you happen to know his whereabouts?'

The Venetian shrugged and sprawled crossways on the bed. 'I'd like to know Maria Fiore's whereabouts. I arranged a tryst with her last night. She didn't turn up.' He grunted. 'Sleeping alone is best left to when one is in one's coffin.'

'You slept alone,' Miles remarked in a tactful tone.

'It *has* been known,' Casanova retorted. 'Anyway, about Byron — he's not here. I should try Britannia if I were you.'

'Which one?'

'Either of the two main ones.'

Miles rubbed his finely chiselled chin. 'Hmm . . . You don't think he'd be in the Vatican then? I was under the impression that you also had a meeting with him in the Exalted City.'

'Are you joking? That's hardly likely, is it? No, if I were you, I'd try Regency Britannia first, or — wait a moment — I heard rumour of Byron taking up residence in the Villa Diodati again.'

Giving a resigned lift of the shoulders, Miles exhaled a short breath. 'The Villa Diodati would seem the most probable choice.' He swirled the opera cloak around him. 'Adieu.'

An instant later he leaped through the open window.

Casanova slumped back on the disordered pillows, and

mulled over Dashing's strange visit. Then he thumped his head, and winced at the pain it caused.

'Of course! Miles has got it wrong again. He found the wrong man. Oh well . . .' As he dozed off, his lips stirred in a dozy mumble: 'That's the trouble with Reprises.'

Five

Grunting and puffing in the leather traces, six nuns of the Sisters of the Heart of Superabundant Sanguinity pulled the Cart Venerable down the Via Benedictus to the arched entrance of Domain Purgatorial. Seated in the cart's red velvet chairs, Cardinals Agostini and Borgia and Inquisitor General Tomas de Torquemada discussed torture.

'It is a cleansing,' Torquemada insisted fervently. 'A heretic who recants under the Torture Extraordinary is redeemed in the Blood of the Lamb. No holier task exists than that of the inquisitor.'

'It keeps the laity in line and us in business,' said Rodrigo Borgia. 'What do you think, Agostini?'

Agostini shrugged. 'There is much to be said on both sides.' He stabbed a glance at the toiling sisters. 'Come on, you lazy women, put your backs into it. At this rate it'll take all night to reach the Pit of Perdition.'

'They lack strength,' Rodrigo admitted. 'But their comeliness more than compensates.' His mouth formed a wicked curve as he turned to his fellow Spaniard. 'Care to use the whip on them, Tomas?'

The Dominican inquisitor squirmed. 'All women should have the build of an ox, fit for child-rearing and menial work. Comeliness in women is Satan's snare. Females are stinking pits of iniquity —'

The Borgia Cardinal waved a dismissive hand. 'Sing a new psalm, Tomas. We've heard this one before. Call yourself a Spaniard —'

'I represent the true Hispania! The mortification and

the blood and the ritual —'

'We're all part of the Catholic Church Apostolic,' said Agostini. 'Members of the Mystical Body. If there is division among the members the body will fall, especially now that we lack a head.'

'Pope Lucian is even now lying in state,' Rodrigo said. 'The Enclave could vote in another pontiff by tomorrow night.'

'Not all of the Enclave will back you,' Torquemada growled. 'You're not getting my vote — I'll tell you that for nothing.'

'Not everyone is as free from the taint of greed as you, Tomas, and I have a generous purse.'

'Not in front of the nuns,' Agostini warned in a low voice. 'They pretend they're in some perpetual God-struck trance but they listen to everything. Besides, the sentencing and execution of the assassins are our immediate concern. Remember, Pope Lucian became an ardent reformist. We are renowned anti-reformists. Many of the laity and all of the heretics will accuse us of his murder.'

'Politics, politics,' snorted Torquemada.

'Politics is our business. Let's leave the religion to hermits and Cistercian monks.'

'*I* am a monk!' Torquemada shouted, the loose folds of his flesh aquiver.

'A *Dominican* monk. Doesn't count.'

Torquemada sank into his seat, simmering, as the Cart Venerable entered the vast chambers of Domain Purgatorial, dripping, stone walls echoing to the grim strains of Sepulchral Chant.

'Time to deliver the man and the girl from Hell,' said Agostini. A ghost of a smile brushed his lips. 'Before we send them to the Hell from which no traveller returns.'

The darkness visible began to retreat.

The gradual reappearance of light, grey though it was, blinded Sarah like a lance of brash sunlight after the utter blackness of limbo. Eyes shut tight, she sensed the restoration of gravity.

Abruptly, her perceptions became confused, telling her that she was simultaneously standing up and lying down. The impression of lying flat on her back quickly established itself. She could feel hard stone, chill on her bare back. Slowly, she opened her eyes. Hazy impressions coalesced into a rectangular view of a dark stone ceiling. Tilting her head, she looked to one side. It took several moments before the truth struck her, morgue-cold.

'God,' she gasped, heart drumming its dread, 'I'm in a stone coffin.'

'Hmm . . . A sarcophagus, based on a fifteenth-century Roman design of a distinctly inferior aesthetic standard,' the Doctor observed, studying the stony recess which imprisoned his long body. 'I was buried alive in one like this once. Thoroughly unpleasant experience.'

Although he could move his head, the rest of his anatomy failed to react, whereas his skin retained tactile response. Ah, he realized, selective nerve paralysis, restricting the limbs but preserving the powers of sight, hearing and speech, and response to stimuli. If he was any judge, the stimuli would be of the painful variety.

Hey-ho . . . *Dum spiro, spero.*

'Sarah!' he called out.

He grinned from ear to ear when he heard her answering voice.

'Doctor!' Sarah exclaimed, heart flooding with relief. 'Where are you? I – I'm in a coffin. No – I mean a sarcophagus.'

'So am I,' came the Doctor's strong baritone from somewhere nearby. 'I suspect we've been in them for some time.'

'I thought I was in Hell.'

'A perceptual construct, no more. Probably generated by a psychomorphic field inside the sarcophagi.'

'Is that guess wild or informed?'

Before the Doctor could reply, Sarah's sarcophagus tilted sharply forwards until she was left standing upright, although still imprisoned in the container by some magnetic coercion.

She was in a vaulted chamber of prodigious dimensions, dimly lit by torches that partially illuminated body-cages, iron maidens, racks, roasting-seats, and a score of elaborate torture devices that didn't belong in the history books: equivocal glimpses of diabolic machinery in the chiaroscuro.

At a few metres' distance, in his own stony niche, the Doctor was upright and smiling. 'Ah,' he said. 'A distinct improvement in the view. Cheer up, Sarah. Things are improving.'

'Domain Purgatorial is no place of cheer,' resounded a solemn tone.

A dumpy, middle-aged man in black robes walked into view, followed by two taller figures in the red attire of cardinals.

At sight of the man in the black habit of a Dominican, the Doctor's face split into a toothy grin. 'Well, Tomas de Torquemada, as I live and breathe!'

'Torquemada . . .' Sarah whispered under her breath, pulse thudding. The notorious founder of the Spanish Inquisition. Oh, hell.

Torquemada peered at the Doctor. 'Have we met before, heretic?'

'Yes indeed. Once in Toledo – a steely encounter, and a second time in Avila.' The Doctor's broad smile acquired a sharp, canine edge. 'You died on the second occasion.'

The Inquisitor General drew back, crossing himself. 'Do you seek to threaten me with sorcery, necromancer?' Quickly, he collected himself, his voice lowering to a sanctimonious purr. 'Soon, I promise you, you will confess each and every sin. You will howl to the Lord for deliverance.'

The taller and heftier of the two cardinals moved forward. 'First things first. Confess every detail of Pope Lucian's murder, particularly that fiend Byron's role, and I, Rodrigo Borgia, guarantee a merciful death by strangulation.'

'That's awfully decent of you, but I'm afraid I can't oblige. Didn't do it, you see? Nor did Byron. Quite out of character. By the way, you don't look anything like the historical Rodrigo Borgia. Adopt the name as a sign of respect for that rapacious old goat, eh?'

Borgia bunched his fist, then thought better of it, moving back to make way for the other cardinal, who bore himself with a more dignified posture.

'I am Cardinal Agostini,' he announced. 'Named after none. More to the point, what is your name, and the name of your trollop?'

The Doctor silenced Sarah's protest with an urgent look. 'I'm the Doctor.'

'Doctor what?'

'Just – the Doctor.'

'Doctor *of* what?'

'Oh, this and that, bits and bobs, odds and sods.'

Agostini turned away in contempt. 'Deal with him, Tomas.'

The cardinals left the Dominican to his work, moving towards a line of pews in the near distance. Torquemada, watching their withdrawal, called out: 'You will find the seats most comfortable, eminences.'

'Any chance of a brief demonstration of the Pendulum, Torquemada?' Borgia requested. 'Just for an amusing diversion.'

Torquemada scowled, disdaining a reply.

'I say, Tomas,' the Doctor called out. 'You haven't seen a blue police box around here anywhere, have you?'

The Inquisitor General narrowed his eyes. 'A blue box? As it happens, that fiendish contraption is one of the subjects I wish to discuss, at length. I think we'll dispense with the Ordinary Torture. We'll proceed with the Special Torture.' He flicked a grimy hand. 'Sprenger! Kramer! Let us begin. The torture will commence with suitable musical accompaniment.'

Two hooded Dominicans shuffled forwards at his bidding as the turgid strains of a dirge filled the chamber.

'Couldn't we have a choice of sacred chant?' the Doctor enquired. 'Gregorian, or even plainsong. Oh, and do you have any Hildegard von Bingen – sublime stuff, don't you think?'

'Sepulchral Chant is what you'll have,' the inquisitor snapped. 'The music of the dark night of the soul. By the time you've been cleansed by agony, you will appreciate its ecstasy of mortification.' He signalled to the two brethren. 'Take them to the Pit.'

The Doctor gave her a look. 'That sounds ominous, Sarah.'

'Sounds like a line from a Roger Corman film to me.'

'The pendulum swings both ways,' the Doctor stated sonorously.

The two silent monks, arms folded, kept their shadowed gaze fixed on the prisoners. She felt the hidden stare penetrate her flesh, bone, the very stone at her back.

'Thought-waves converted into para-acoustic rhythms, by the feel of it,' the Doctor was saying. 'An interesting form of mind/matter interfacing.'

'Doctor,' she groaned. 'Who *cares*?'

The sarcophagus suddenly fell backwards, jarring her spine. Then the stone coffin was sliding along the floor. Watching the vaulted roof pass overhead, she quailed at the prospect of where she was headed.

The Pit, Torquemada had said. Didn't sound too good.

'*Dum spiro, spero*, Sarah,' the Doctor boomed out.

'Where there's life, there's hope,' she acknowledged with a wince. 'Great time to be spouting Latin clichés.'

The scrape of stone on stone was replaced by silence, and the swift halt of the sarcophagus. Somehow, the Dominicans were controlling the whole operation without lifting an unwashed finger. Their telekinetic powers were formidable, and alarming.

Think positive.

She focused her mind on all her narrow escapes since stowing away on the Time Lord's TARDIS, all the light-years she'd travelled since then in the space-time vehicle. The memories sparked a spirit of defiance.

It was simply a matter of keeping that defiant spark lit. No small feat in the chambers of the Inquisition. Candle in the wind . . .

Red liquid suddenly seeped from the porous stone, splashing on her skin. That unique, coppery scent was unmistakable. She was no stranger to the smell of blood.

The seepage of blood from the stony pores mounted to a glutinous flood. Eyes shut, she fought the good fight against panic.

They're going to drown me in blood.

Coffin of blood. B-movie material. Cheap melodrama, sure, but it scared the bejesus out of her. Then she realized that she could no longer feel the touch of rough stone on her back. Peeking through half an eye, it seemed that the sarcophagus rim was closer.

The return of mobility surprised her with its suddenness. Motor functions restored, she thrashed her limbs, and discovered that she was floating. Now she was thankful she was still dressed only in a bikini, buoyant in the gore.

Blood's thicker than water.

Then she realized that the Doctor was clothed in shirt, trousers, waistcoat, jacket, overcoat, eighteen-foot-long scarf, and whatever mysterious underwear he might or might not be wearing. If blood was pouring on him he'd go under, weighted down.

'Doctor – can you hear me?' she yelled.

* * *

'Glug-glug-glug,' the Doctor said, his body rising on the surface of the extraordinarily dense fluid, too dense for your average haemoglobin. Must be a form of semi-liquefied haemogel, possibly Aldeberan in –

Sarah's shout disturbed his speculations.

'Make the gruel thick and slab: *Macbeth*, act four, scene one,' he declaimed in a stentorian tone. 'I was in that play with Will Shakespeare when it opened at the Globe Theatre. Played the part of the Doctor . . . quite a story behind that.'

'Never mind the story! Can you keep afloat?'

'Rather fine story, as a matter of fact. But yes, I'm afloat. The gore is thick and slab. Straightforward question of valency. Now – the Globe Theatre and Will Shakespeare. The whole adventure started in Venice long ago, when I had just the one heart –'

'Doctor! Think of something. We're in the soup again.'

He had risen to the top of the sarcophagus, buoyed up by the haemogel. A sidelong glance showed Sarah struggling to rise from her sarcophagus, a couple of metres from his own. He heaved himself to one side and peered over the edge. A huge black pit yawned below, some thirty metres in span, its depth unguessable.

'Er, Sarah, I'd stay where you are if I were you.'

She followed his glance, blanched, then lay back on the thick blood. 'I think I'll take your advice.'

He gave her a wink, then faced Torquemada. 'Tomas,' he called out. 'Don't you recall our last meeting in Avila? It was *awfully* eventful, what with the personification of Death making a dramatic appearance and that scythe whizzing about and everything.'

'We never met in Avila!' Torquemada snarled.

'And Toledo, seven years earlier? The auto-da-fé that didn't quite work out as you planned, the mini-Beelzebubs that threw you out of bed the following night –'

'The Devil is ever a liar!'

Brows knitted, the Doctor studied Torquemada intently. 'What about that time you locked yourself in the San Diego chapel, and prayed to be relieved of your doubts of the Inquisition? All too fleeting doubts, alas.'

Torquemada was aghast. 'How did you know? I was alone. Sorcery –'

'Interesting,' the Doctor observed. 'That one isn't in the history books. But those other events – for you, they never occurred. Yes, I think I'm catching on.'

Gathering his dignity, Torquemada drew back several paces. 'Falsehood will be scoured from your lips when the Special Torture begins. Which is now.'

'Oh, and what happens now?'

Torquemada's glee was poorly hidden under a devout guise. 'You expressed a dislike of Sepulchral Chant. Now the Pit of Perdition –'

'I was wondering what sort of Pit it was.'

'– will deliver Sepulchral Chant in its full glory. The superabundantly ensanguined sarcophagi you lie on will amplify the dread strains, plunging you into a pit of spiritual desolation.'

'Sounds nasty,' the Doctor said. He winked at Sarah. 'Chin up. I'm sure the chant's bark is worse than its bite.'

'Yeah, right . . .'

'The chant is merely an overture,' Torquemada said with relish. 'Other tortures will follow. If you refuse to confess, then you'll experience the final horror of the Pit. You'll be thrown into it, and plunge into that individual, unendurable nightmare that each mortal carries deep in his soul.'

Mouth agape, the Doctor stared down into the impenetrable blackness. 'A sort of Room 101. Gosh.'

'Begin the chant!' commanded Torquemada.

'Oh, hell,' muttered Sarah.

'*Hell*,' she repeated, as a doleful chorus emanated from below, resonating through the sarcophagus. Hell. The word was singularly appropriate.

The swelling dirge seemed to rise more from the pit of her stomach than the Pit of Perdition, each phrase a wave of depression ending not so much in a dying fall as a prolonged death-rattle. Liturgid.

She covered her ears, but the Sepulchral Chant wasn't to be muted by an inch or two of flesh and bone. It was lost soul music.

The mournful chant, a dismal ebb and surge, was a weight of misery that brought her spirits down. And down.

And down.

And

down.

Then, a clarion call in the distance, she heard a merry voice: 'Let's face the music – and dance!'

Peering through a haze of dejection, she saw the Doctor standing on the narrow rim of his sarcophagus, arms outspread, hat in hand, pure vaudeville.

'Come on, Sarah,' he urged. 'Kick your legs and wave your arms like an old hoofer, and sing an old-fashioned song!'

'What –' she mumbled.

'There may be troubles ahead . . .' he sang, then stopped, eyes big with disappointment. 'Come on, join in. One, two, three . . .'

'There may be troubles ahead,' she croaked, in unison with his rich baritone as he performed a jaunty dance number on the stone ledge.

'You're not taking this seriously!' Torquemada protested, brandishing a fist.

That did it. 'Sorry –' she spluttered. Grief was a giggle away. And the grief of the Sepulchral Chant was a bit of a giggle. Always look on the bright side of death. She threshed about like a maniac, singing of moonlight and love and romance.

'Stop the chant!' thundered Torquemada.

The Sepulchral Chant ended abruptly, and Sarah heard the echoes of her hysterical mirth in the ensuing silence.

Her knotted stomach muscles were in agony by the time she regained control.

Then she heard Agostini's authoritative command. 'Don't waste time, Tomas. Put them to the final test. Drop them into the Pit.'

Sarah glanced at the Doctor, hoping that his inventive mind had produced another trick. 'Now what? Thought up any scheme?'

His response chilled her. Sitting on the viscous blood, ashen-faced, skin glistening with perspiration, he slowly shook his head. 'No, Sarah. I'm afraid not. Sorry.'

His defeated posture and flat tone told her volumes. According to the Doctor, his telepathic ability was 'just this side of not terribly good', but frequently he'd appeared to pick up faint signals in the aether, sensitive to the unvoiced thought, the unplayed tune. He knew what was down in the Pit, and he knew he couldn't survive it.

'Goodbye, Doctor,' she whispered under her breath.

'The Pendulum!' shrieked Torquemada. 'Did you release it, Borgia? For an – an amusing diversion?'

Sarah whirled round to glimpse a streak of glittering metal high above and far behind Borgia's head. The Pendulum, end on, heading straight for her.

Cardinal Borgia spread his palms, all innocence. 'Nothing to do with me, Tomas. That device goes off on its own all the time.'

Sarah quailed as the thin slash of steel arced down. In a couple of seconds she formed a notion of the Pendulum's prodigious length, a crescent of steel as long as the Pit was wide.

And, no doubt, razor-sharp.

The onrush of the enormous scimitar drove her flat on her face before its keen edge whished overhead, fanning her back.

Looking up, she saw the Doctor still seated, his attention on the blade as it disappeared into the shadows. 'The Pendulum swings both ways,' he muttered.

After long moments the Pendulum emerged from the darkness.

Her heart thumped when she perceived that it was discernibly lower. It had missed her by a fair distance on the first swing. This time . . .

'How low is it?' The words were almost strangled in her contracting throat.

'Low enough,' he said, rising to his feet. 'Stand up, Sarah.'

'What?'

'Stand up – now!'

'Suicide,' she murmured, but got to her feet. Suicide. But maybe that was the point. Spare themselves from the Pit.

The blade whistled down. She tensed her hands, fingernails digging into the palms.

Then she saw a shape at the centre of the curved blade. An instant later the shape was discernible as a man, one arm gripping the Pendulum's chain.

The man was Lord Byron, and his free hand dangled a loop of rope. 'Grab hold!' he yelled.

The Doctor was already leaping for the rope as the Pendulum swished over the Pit. 'Quick, Sarah, jump!' he shouted.

Again she'd misjudged the blade's elevation. It was still a good two metres over her head, and the rope out of arm's reach . . .

Not for the first time, she was glad of the Doctor's ludicrously long scarf. She caught its trailing hem as it whisked past, established a firm double grip, and drew knees tight to chest as she skimmed over the rim of the Pit.

'*Unngh* . . .' the Doctor gasped as the scarf's noose throttled his neck.

She darted a look over her shoulder at the shrinking black pit. She could taste her relief. Saved from the Pit by the Pendulum.

'You know where you can jump!' she taunted the prelates.

Byron's sombre voice sobered her a little. 'In five seconds the blade ends its swing. Jump when I shout, or back on down you go.'

Point taken. It was a long, long drop to the flagstones. A scant two seconds after delivering his order, the poet yelled, 'Now!'

Trusting the Doctor's judgement, Sarah kept hold of the scarf as he let go. The Pendulum's swing had taken them into a narrow wall-niche, floored with a mooring mechanism.

She barely had time to take in her surroundings, rubbing her scraped knees, before she realized that she and the Doctor were alone. Byron hadn't jumped.

Or jumped too soon.

Six

Vast powers lurked in the peaks of Switzia, a shunned region, haunted by terrible Swiss gods.

Miles Dashing, clinging for dear life to his airborne but errant Draco, squinted into the snowy maelstrom bedevilling the Teufelstein range, and regretted his decision to seek out Lord Byron in the Villa Diodati by Lake Geneva. After all, the Concocters had created *three* Switzias in Europa in the time of the Great Concoction, some two centuries past, just as they had formed four Rhines, six Danubes, and dozens of Black Forests.

Three Switzias, but a Villa Diodati in only one of them.

The Switzia he'd decided upon was built on the original site of Switzerland after the fall of the Earth Empire. He had discounted the sinister stories of this lofty range of lonely pinnacles, enshrouded in perpetual snowstorms and blighted by vast, inchoate Presences. He had laughed them off as peasant tales in darkened inns. Now, he knew better.

In ancient days, the strange folk of the original Switzerland were made of living chocolate and wore short trousers and stood on mountain tops, emitting soul-chilling ululations.

At least, that was how the dark tale went.

Normally, Miles Dashing was inclined to the more reasonable account of the ancient Swiss as people made of clockwork. Now, in the teeth of a preternatural gale that blew him inexorably eastward towards Transylvania, he was not so sure.

Within sight of the tiny, Puritan Dominion of Geneva, the Draco, programmed to land when its sensors registered Byron's proximity, had started on a gradual descent, confirming the poet-lord's presence. Then a cloud had condensed into a dumpling face, and blown him clean over Lake Geneva at a speed that took his breath away.

Other cloud-faces had formed on his enforced flight east, each blowing him far off-course and further from Byron.

Then the Presences manifested themselves, invisible but for the roiling mist and snow that clothed them. The impression of sheer *massivity* they conveyed was near overwhelming. But he battled on, regardless.

Miles was, after all, no superstitious peasant. He was familiar with the theory behind the genesis of the Swiss gods, whether of cloud, snow or mist. The ancient Swiss, it was said, paid little heed to the Inner Dark, the wild, weird, romantic depths of the psyche. The imprisoned Inner Dark erupted after centuries of confinement, manifesting the hidden fears and dark dreams of the Swiss in the virtually tangible form of pseudo-matter. At least that was the theory put forward by the twenty-third-century Jung the Obscure in the Eiger Apocrypha.

If his Draco had been working properly, he would have been free of Switzia by now: he'd had several chances to make a break for it, when the puff-clouds had temporarily ceased puffing, but the crystal-seeded canopy above the peaks blocked the morning sunlight and depleted the already low energy of the air-scooter's solar cells.

So, perforce, he flew east, to the dread Dominion of Transylvania, where few mortals dared tread.

Vampirism was rife in many of Europa's Dominions, but in Transylvania it was compulsory.

The motives behind Transylvania's exclusive ruling were understandable. Vampires, like mortals, came in all shapes and sizes, good and bad. Throughout Europa, the undead were persecuted en masse. Many vampires lived happily on black puddings, but that didn't save them from the stake. A Nosferatu refuge was required, and Transylvania provided it. The trouble was, hordes of tourists descended on the Dominion's silent, wooded hills on unauthorized staking parties. Even the purely voyeuristic tourists upset the locals, gawking at the undead rising from their coffins at sunset. So a law was passed, and mortals were barred from the vampiric realm.

Miles wasn't expecting a warm welcome when he flew into Nosferatu territory. The penalty for such a violation was live burial.

But, as the Draco struggled over the last peak of the Teufelstein range, beyond which lay the border of the Transylvanian empire, it became clear that his ailing air-scooter was gliding down to the precincts of Castle Borgo, home of an Ipsissimus order of vampires. The Ipsissimus undead, aristocrats all, were the fiends of the Nosferatu breed. Legend traced their origins to two vampires from space, known as Lord Jake and Lady Madelaine, destroyed in the twenty-fourth century by Jonquil the Intrepid.

The Mindelmeres, who had infected his family with their unholy contagion, were of the Ipsissimus Order. Since that fateful night in Dashwood House, when he faced the bestial onslaught of his own kin, stake-gun pumping, blood splashing all over the place, he had sworn to rid the world of Ipsissimus vampires. He had set about the task with true Britannian determination.

And always, he sought an explanation to his expiring father's last, cryptic word, delivered in a gasp: *Managra*.

Was Managra the secret head of the Ipsissimus brood? Or was it a code, a verbal key to a realm of power? Or – whatever.

The Draco slid down an air current to the woodland skirting the base of the Alps – one of seven separate Alpine ranges – and coasted to a glade barely five kilometres from the soaring towers of Castle Borgo. He alighted the instant the vehicle thumped on to a grassy rise, and set about recovering his implements from the Draco's hidden compartments.

'Should have a servant for this sort of menial labour,' he grumbled.

Chore completed, he glanced back at the mountainous expanse: at least he'd left the Swiss gods behind. However, on the debit side, Transylvania was steeped in night, although the hour was close to noon. The populace had clearly decided to play safe and opt for holo-night, canopying the Dominion in a perpetual starry, moony sky, like Venice. Or perhaps, unlike Venice, they turned the holo-image off when true night fell.

Miles looked up at the full holo-moon and felt for the comfort of his stake-gun under the opera cloak. The stake-gun was intact, but he was low on ammunition. Eight stakes left. And even they might prove inadequate against a full-blown Ipsissimus. For such creatures, only the traditional full-length stake – with optional hammer – would suffice.

For a moment he debated whether to press onwards or head for the nearest pass into Switzia. His business with Byron was Domino business, high affairs of state and anti-state. But he had sworn an oath to the House of Dashwood, and that too was a bounden duty . . .

He flung back his head and squared his shoulders. Duty was duty. He couldn't depart this region without destroying *one* Ipsissimus. Besides, he needed a question answering.

Domino obligations could be resumed immediately the deed was done.

There should be a cemetery somewhere near the castle . . .

Vampire Disposal pack slung over one shoulder, Miles crouched in the moonshadow of a clump of yew trees and studied the mossy tombs that crowded the graveyard.

None of the Borgo's direct lineage would be interred here – they'd be laid to rest in the castle's crypt – but a lesser offshoot of the family, or some petty lordling, was likely to be found in the middle of the sarcophagi and effigies of fallen angels. Ipsissimus undead, if bereft of castle walls, invariably sited their places of rest at the centre of graveyards, surrounded by ranks of lesser vampires who served as lines of defence against intruders.

He pulled out a crucifix from a pocket of his black frock-coat, and pointed the silver cross at the leaning headstones and ivy-garlanded tombs. The crucifix began to emit a steady pulse of light, betraying the presence of vampires. Of itself, no surprise inside Transylvania. Arm held straight, he moved the crucifix in a slow sweep. The light-pulse increased in rapidity to a swift flicker, indicating the centre of death's little acre.

Just as he thought, at least one Ipsissimus in the midst of this unhallowed ground. The Crucifix Indicatrix pointed the way with its flashing beacon.

Heart drumming its blood-beat, breath bated, he emerged from the shadow of the yews and tiptoed through the outer ring of graves, wary of rousing the undead despite the relative safety of the daylight hour. Above the holo-night shroud of Transylvania's sky, it was noon, and the resting vampires were responsive to circadian rhythms.

Miles's progress through the cemetery was stealthy, but no icy voice challenged or chill hand outreached as the Crucifix Indicatrix guided his steps down the aisles of tombs.

Directed by the crucifix, he arrived at the doors of a mausoleum, its walls enwrapped in a special silence. He checked the Vampire Disposal pack. Each item intact, from garlic clove to the metre-long heart-of-oak stake.

Pocketing the manically flashing cross, he gave the doors a push. They opened with the long protest of a reverberating groan, drawing a pained wince from the vampire-hunter. He hoped the rest of the cemetery's occupants were deep in sleep, let alone the Ipsissimus within the mausoleum.

The arch-vampire he sought would have the keenest hearing. Now, speed of execution was all.

Gripping the stake in a high hand, he darted into the mausoleum, booted feet kicking up dust inside the domed interior.

His feet skidded to a stop.

In front of him an elaborate coffin reclined on a dais, barely discernible in the moonlight streaming through the open portal.

'*Who dares?*' rumbled a voice from the coffin, bone deep.

A chorus of howls ascended, near and far, answering the master's summons. No time to prise off the coffin lid.

Miles leaped on to the coffin, stake grasped in a double grip, hoisted the sharpened branch above his head, and, combining instinct and experience in judging the spot, drove the point clean through the lid.

Snap-cracking, Transylvanian elm gave way to English heart-of-oak, and the stake penetrated deep into the coffin, boring into flesh. A roar of agony soared with a fountain of blood.

'Bang on target,' Miles Dashing declared. 'I shall say a prayer for you to Our Lady of Manifold Misereres at some later, more suitable moment. But now, one question –'

The ferocity of the vampire's reaction, bashing feet and fists on the coffin lid, toppled Miles from his perch. By the time he'd regained his feet, the lid was blasted to smithereens by a combination of pounding arms and legs and a geyser of spiritual steam. Shattered planks and a foetid miasma hurtled to the roof.

Miles flung himself over the coffin, face to face with the expiring occupant.

Lord Byron, fangs foaming, features contorted, glared up at Miles.

Byron? Momentarily, Miles was taken aback, then wheels whirred at the back of his head, and something clicked.

Byron forced words through blood-speckled teeth. '*You – bastard . . .*' His hands reached to pull the stake free, then sprang back as though burned.

'I know it hurts, but I make no apologies for delivering your soul,' Miles said, then posed the question he'd put to every Ipsissimus on the point of expiry. 'Tell me – what is Managra?'

'*Bastard . . . cut your balls off . . .*'

'Crudity will avail you nothing. What – or who – is Managra?'

Blood erupted from Byron's mouth and hit the ceiling. His muscular, writhing figure subsided into a nerveless mass of bubbling flesh. The flesh dissolved into a broth of frothy red.

Miles stepped back from the spectacle. Yet again, his question had gone unanswered.

As for discovering Byron in a vampire's coffin . . .

A voice hissed at his back. '*We'll pluck out your heart, mortal, then stick in the heart of a cat.*'

Miles whirled round, swishing back his opera cloak and whisking out the stake-gun from its shoulder-holster. The weapon, resembling a stubby harpoon gun, rested steady in his grip as he aimed it at the creatures thronging at the tomb's threshold, their moonshadows spilling across the dusty floor. Eight mini-stakes lay in the gun's chamber, awaiting release by the gas compression system. Miles's finger tightened on the trigger. Eight stakes, and at least five times that number of enemies.

He confronted the foremost of the peasant-class undead, who still possessed both his eyes, although one orb dangled on its optic nerve and jiggled about whenever the creature moved his head.

'Go back home to your graves and nobody will get hurt,' Miles advised, giving the stake-gun a meaningful shake.

'*A cat will lick your heart . . .*' came the congregated hiss.

Framed by the flood of bright moonlight, the vampires

drew out their own stake-guns. Vampire-killing weapons in the hands of vampires . . .

An intuition of a deadly presence at his back made Miles glance over his shoulder.

A shadow was rearing out of the coffin, its outline that of Lord Byron.

'Dash it,' Miles muttered under his breath. The moonlight in the mausoleum had provided the Ipsissimus with a shadow, imbued with the puissance of the incarnate Nosferatu. Those of the Ipsissimus Order were gifted with detachable shadows, and staking was not sufficient if the body cast a moonshadow. The science of the phenomenon was bewildering – something to do with anti-light amplification in concert with lunar cold light modulations and photon-evading psychoform lattices. Miles hadn't a clue about it. Prosaic, unromantic stuff, quite out of tune with his Gothic life-style.

He knew what he needed to know: the detached shadow was as deadly as the original vampire, and a lot trickier to pin down.

As he watched, the shadow slid up the far wall, then sprang into the air, riding on a moonbeam.

Miles Dashing flicked his gaze between the oncoming Shadow Ipsissimus and the creatures at the portal.

A vampire Byron – and a throng of undead peasants with stake-guns.

This was all beginning to make sense.

Decayed skull in one hand, glass of red wine in the other, Lord Byron leaned back in his armchair and stared gloomily out of the window at the incessant rain that deluged the lawns of the Villa Diodati.

'For the rain it raineth every day,' he quoted glumly.

'You must be out of sorts if you've given up quoting your own verse,' said a woman's voice, light in pitch but strong in sarcasm.

'If not myself, then the Bard of Avon will more than

suffice for a swan-song,' he drawled. 'But if it's beef of Byron you want –'

'I don't.'

'– then how's this for a threnody?' His gaze rested on the surface of Lake Geneva, drab in the downpour, and recited in a slurred tone:

> 'He sinks into thy depths with bubbling groan,
> Without a grave, unknelled, uncoffined, and unknown.'

Byron raised his glass to the lake, then downed the contents in one gulp. 'Damn me if I know how you managed to drown yourself *twice*. Here's to you in your watery bed, Percy Shelley.' Turning the relic to and fro in his left hand, he studied the skull of the Black Monk, unearthed in the grounds of Newstead Abbey, his ancestral home. 'Do you miss Percy much, Mary?'

'Um – not particularly.'

He frowned. 'Damn it, woman. You and Percy were lovers!'

'We still are,' Mary Shelley replied.

'What? Oh –' He returned to his scrutiny of the skull. 'How's that cursed *Frankenstein* sequel coming along?'

'So-so. What's another word for "unhallowed"?'

He stood up and faced the young woman who sat on the far side of a desk, her arms folded as she concentrated on the auto-quill which, for the present, hovered above the page, awaiting her instructions.

'There are a multitude of synonyms for unhallowed,' he said. 'And you've done each and every one of them to death. Uh, why bother, wasn't *Frankenstein* enough? Must we now endure *The Return of Frankenstein*?'

'Benighted,' she said, her delicate face brightening under the fringe of brown curls. 'I haven't used that one for at least a dozen pages.' She addressed the auto-quill that dangled in mid-air. 'Quill-resume.' The nib touched the sheet as she recommenced dictation: '– his benighted soul now yearned for the succour, not of a Creator, but a

Creatrix, a Mother of Creation, as his weary feet trod the illimitable expanses of desolate ice and snow, devoid of —'

'Let it rest, Mary,' he groaned, cutting her short. The quill instantly ceased its furious scribbling. '*Frankenstein* made the point perfectly well. To labour the point is inelegant.'

With a snort, Mary Shelley shot up straight in her seat. 'The female point of view was ill-represented in my first work. The symbolism was Miltonic in the extreme, and as for the characterization of Elizabeth — a mere cypher.'

Byron turned on his heel and strode to the fireplace, flinging his empty glass on to the roaring logs. 'The *female* point of view . . .' he growled. Then, attuning his voice to recitation mode:

> 'There is a tide in the affairs of women,
> Which, taken at the flood, leads — God knows
>   where.'

Mary Shelley grimaced. 'A quote from *Childe Harolde's Pilgrimage* and another from *Don Juan* is twice more than enough. But then, men like to have twice as much say as women.'

'Tarrah!' he exclaimed. 'The Trumpet of the Rights of Women blows again! The daughter of Mary Wollstonecraft, defender of the female faith, shows her colours. I marvel there's so much red blood in such a blue stocking.'

'And I marvel how I put up with you. If it weren't for Percy . . . Where is he, by the way?'

Byron stared into the sockets of the Black Monk's skull. 'At the bottom of the lake,' he murmured, then collected himself. 'Oh, he mentioned something about tying a cat to a kite and flying it in a thunderstorm up in the mountains.'

She shook her head. 'The things he gets up to.'

'On the subject of flying, did you spot a Draco flitting overhead this morning? You didn't? Well, no matter. I hope it wasn't a Puritan spy from Geneva.' His heavy brow glowered. 'For all I love the Villa Diodati, it's too close to the Geneva Dominion for my ease of mind.'

'Puritans don't fly Dracoes,' she calmly pointed out.

'They might have stolen one.'

'Puritans don't steal. They just burn people in vast numbers.'

He gave a shrug. 'As they chiefly burn each other I thoroughly recommend the practice.' Expelling a sharp breath, he strode back to his armchair and slumped into the seat. 'I'm bored. Where's that half-sister of yours?'

'Claire's in her room, reading *The Castle of Otranto*,' she said wearily. 'What did you have in mind?'

His smile was a lascivious curve. 'The usual. The whip and the chain. And –' He kissed the skull on the mouth. '– raising the Devil.'

'What Claire lets you do to her is her business, but remember what happened last time you summoned Satan.'

'Yes,' Byron breathed softly. 'He came.'

'I'll tell him you're here.'

Giovanni Giacomo Casanova waved a languid hand at the servant. 'Tell him quickly, as a certain lady is waiting for me in a certain palazzo.' The bit about the lady was a lie, but one had to keep up appearances.

The servant scurried up the steps of the Villa Cadenza, leaving Casanova waiting in the hall, viewing a painting of the Grand Canal by Canaletto.

'*Bernardo* Canaletto,' Casanova sniffed scornfully. 'I have an *Antonio* Canaletto, nephew Bernardo's elder and better.'

He tensed at the bellow of an angry voice from an upstairs room. 'Tell him to go to Hell!'

Casanova's lips tightened. 'Tell me yourself.'

Taking the stairs two at a time, he brushed past the startled servant and burst into the master bedroom. Noticing the woman who snuggled up to the man under the bed-covers, Casanova's refined nostrils flared.

'Maria Fiore! So this is where I find you!'

Maria's hand flew to the gaping oval of her mouth. 'Oh – don't tell me it was you . . .'

Casanova turned his ire on to the woman's companion. 'What do you have to say for youself, Casanova?' demanded Casanova.

Casanova sat up in the bed, lifting a nonchalant eyebrow. 'I admit I took your place. After all, you've done the same to me on occasion.'

'How was I supposed to know?' Maria was grumbling. 'You look exactly the same. Damned Reprises!'

'I came to inform you that Miles Dashing entered my dwelling last night on Domino business under the misapprehension that I was you,' Casanova said coldly, trading glare for glare with his doppelganger in the bed. 'He was in search of Byron. I suggested the Villa Diodati. There, my duty has been performed. Now, Giovanni Giacomo Casanova, there remains the matter of honour concerning the lady. Shall we say rapiers at midnight in the crypt of the Palazzo Intaglio?'

Casanova waved a hand in resignation. 'If we must, we must.' He rubbed the vestiges of sleep from his eyes. 'I should have kept to the rendezvous with Byron,' he murmured. 'Come to think of it, I promised Prince Ludwig the service of my blade for the week or two following his showing of *Twelfth Night*. Two promises broken. Unpardonable lapses on my part.'

'Till midnight,' said Casanova, and swept out of the room.

Casanova watched his double's departure, and smiled ruefully. 'Well, at least Casanova will still be alive after this midnight duel.'

Seven

The Pendulum's swing was slow and steady, unerring in its aim. Unless a little weight was brought to bear on the matter. A man's weight was quite sufficient.

So delicately poised was the crescent of steel that a redistribution of poundage could steer the blade's course a fraction off-centre. As the Pendulum progressed, that fraction doubled each instant.

Lord Byron, riding the Pendulum, put all his weight to one side and kept his eyes on the wrathful figure of Torquemada on the far side of the Pit. A swordsman to the hilt, Byron was a fine judge of aim and distance.

'Blasphemer!' Torquemada screeched, brandishing a fist. 'Devil-worshipper!'

The Inquisitor General lowered his hand as the whistling crescent streaked over the Pit, realizing Byron's intention. The Pendulum was veering to one side — towards Torquemada. Adamant in his faith in his own Pendulum, Torquemada stood his ground, a metre away from the blade's standard course.

'A maximum variation of one half-metre off-centre!' Torquemada shouted confidently. 'I know my own Pendulum!'

'Are you sure about that?' called out Agostini.

The massive steel blade hurtled down.

And passed the Inquisitor General with a good half-metre to spare.

'Missed!' Torquemada scoffed.

'Next time, inquisitor!' Byron sped into the shadows of the further wall.

Torquemada folded his arms. 'I'll still be here.'

The Pendulum whished into the dark of the far chamber, reached the end of its swing, then swept back, its size belying its speed. Once more, the blade veered towards Torquemada.

The Inquisitor General stood erect, immovable in his certitude. The Pendulum arced down, parting the air with a thin, whistling sound. 'I know my own Pendulum!' he repeated as the keen edge sped at his head.

And passed by again with the same distance to spare.

'Missed again!' he sneered as Byron flew alongside, straddling the Pendulum.

Byron's booted foot lashed out and caught the inquisitor square in the midriff. The blade's momentum and the lord's vigorous kick lifted Torquemada clean off his sandalled feet and back through the air.

The monk sailed several metres, arms flailing.

And fell to where the ground wasn't.

Screaming, Torquemada dropped straight into the Pit.

Byron laughed as he steered the Pendulum back on course to slot into its mooring-niche. 'Adieu, you religious caterpillars!' he called down to the cardinals.

'Laugh away, blasphemer,' Agostini shouted back. 'You'll never escape the Vatican!'

'I'll give you a run for your money!' came the parting shot as the Pendulum disappeared into the dark.

'Whew!' Sarah exclaimed. 'Now that was something. I wonder if even you could have managed that, Doctor.'

'That was something I wouldn't want to have managed,' the Doctor responded, a touch of ambivalence in his blue gaze.

Squeezed one to each side of the niche, they watched the Pendulum swing back, and Byron alight with athletic grace on to the floor, leaving the mighty crescent to resume its progress.

'Before you ask,' Byron said, 'I saved you because you're the Inquisition's enemy, and I knew where they'd take you. Does that suffice?' The poet nodded to a tiny door at the end of the niche. 'Now let's go. Keep close behind me – the Vatican's a warren. The secret passages doubly so, and bristling with traps.' As he ducked into the doorway, he glanced at the Doctor. 'Can you use a sword?'

'For defensive purposes, yes. But don't expect me to start hacking into all and sundry.'

'Then you'll not live long,' Byron retorted, slipping into a narrow corridor.

'Oh, I've not done too badly on that score,' the Doctor replied, tracking the poet's steps as the corridor angled into a steep spiral stair.

'Aren't you going to ask me if I want a sword?' Sarah said, starting on the winding descent.

'You have neither the build nor the spirit of a fencer,' Byron said without looking back.

'Uh-huh,' she sniffed, then decided to needle him. 'That's because I'm a woman, right?'

He saw straight through the affectation. 'No. Because you're the kind of woman you are. You have neither the physique nor poise nor reach of arm nor killer instinct. I'd thank you not to strike bogus political attitudes with me, madam.'

Sarah's mouth tweaked in a begrudging smile at Byron's unabashed machismo, but the *language*... 'Political attitudes?' she queried. 'Was that expression used in Regency times?'

'We live in an eclectic world. Now for the time being I bid you keep your voice low. The Vatican is chock-a-block with listening devices.'

'You're the boss,' she whispered under her breath. 'For the time being.'

The spiral steps ended in a passage that led to an angled staircase. Halfway down the passage, she jumped at the abrupt shriek of alarm.

'HERETICS...'

Her shoulders relaxed. 'There goes the Heretic Alarm

again.' Her mind went back to the Lapidary Gallery. 'I hope this floor doesn't start whizzing along like it did back in that gallery. I thought they were going to splatter me all over that metal door.'

'*They* didn't do that,' said Byron. 'I did.'

'You –'

'I saw your friend being translated to the Domain Purgatorial, and activated the slide-floor at maximum speed.'

'But you ran to the other end of the gallery – I saw you.'

'I ran into a parallel hidden passage, with a faster slide-floor. I was about to open the door and rescue you when the Enclave translated you into the Vatican's Purgatory. Feminine curiosity satisfied?'

She bit her lip.

'Now hurry your feet,' he snapped. 'We've a long way to go.'

The stairs ended in a passageway flanked by apocalyptic bas-reliefs. Byron darted to a depiction of an angel breaking open the Seventh Seal, and jabbed his fingers into various crevices with bewildering speed. The panel slid up, but instead of entering the space beyond, he ran several paces down the corridor and, on the opposite wall, performed a similar routine with a bas-relief of Apollyon rising from the Pit. The slab ascended and Byron sprang into the revealed aperture. Sarah followed suit, with the Doctor on her heels. Unlike the Seventh Seal panel, the Apollyon slab slammed shut behind them.

'Standard misdirection,' she heard the Doctor mutter quietly at her back.

Sure enough, she recognized, it was standard, but the ruse would probably work for a while, luring any pursuers down a false trail.

Padding down the dim, narrow corridor, she shivered. 'I don't suppose there's any chance of grabbing some clothes?' she stage-whispered. 'I came dressed for the beach.'

She was mildly surprised when the poet gave the nod. 'Soon,' he spoke softly. 'Now, we're coming to an area of traps. Get ready for my signal. Then jump when I jump, and crawl when I crawl.'

'Trapdoors?' she said, keeping her tone as low as his. 'Spikes and darts shooting out of the walls – that sort of thing?'

'That sort of thing. Now save your breath and concentrate. I don't want you blundering into my back if I have to stop suddenly.'

She was about to retort that she didn't make a habit of blundering, but clamped her mouth tight and kept a close eye on Byron, alert for any signal.

For a time, Byron kept up a brisk pace, traversing passages, descending twisting stairs three steps at a time, then, as they emerged into a comparatively wide corridor, he lifted a hand.

'Watch the spot from where I leap,' he instructed. 'And start your leap from the moment I land. Then run like the devil.'

He broke into a run and, opposite a bizarre figure of a saint holding a holo-candle, launched into a three-metre-plus jump. The instant his feet touched ground she raced and sprang with all the energy in her adrenalin-hyped body. She had to be leaping over a trapdoor. No doubt of it. She landed on a floor that mercifully didn't give way under her feet, then set off in Byron's wake, flicking a glance over her shoulder at the Doctor as he soared in a mighty jump that almost skinned her heels.

'Show-off,' she whispered, then winked.

'Hurry!' Byron ordered, sprinting ahead to a distant archway. She put down her head and set about some determined running.

Within twenty breaths she was under the archway and on a landing, the Doctor loping easily at her back, matching her speed.

Byron had halted, hands planted on hips. She stopped beside him.

'I hope I passed the sprint qualification,' she said, sweet poison in her smile.

He gave her a disdainful look. 'What you lack in wit you compensate for in superficiality.'

'George,' the Doctor butted in. 'What would have happened if we'd stayed too long in the corridor?'

'The entire floor would have dropped beneath you, plunging you to certain death,' the poet replied, descending the steepest of stairways.

'Really? How does the mechanism work?'

'Who cares?' Sarah and Byron chorused, then exchanged glances. Byron's laugh echoed Sarah's.

'At least we agree on something,' she said, then dug the Doctor in the ribs. 'Only kidding.' She caught Byron's glance. 'Oh, we'd better keep going.'

The descent continued, punctuated at rare intervals by the poet's warning to avoid treading on this or that innocuous-looking step. Travelling through the Vatican's interior was like wending a way through the intestines of a rococo dragon. Like it or lump it, they needed the notorious lord.

Eventually, the succession of stairs ended in a series of chambers that arched in all directions, a regular maze.

'Now, for those clothes you wanted,' said Byron. 'There's a chamber three to the left with some cast-offs in chests.'

'Clothes,' she sighed. 'At last.' She slanted a look at the poet. 'From now on, you'll just have to dream about my body.'

He raised a haughty eyebrow. 'Don't flatter yourself.'

Agostini and Borgia lingered by the Pit of Perdition, gazing at its black O of a mouth.

'Well,' said Agostini. 'He's been down there too long, facing his worst fear. Too late for restoration. The terror will have killed him by now.'

'What was his worst fear?'

'No idea. He probably didn't know either, until now.'

'And what's *your* worst nightmare, Agostini?'

A ghost of a smile touched Agostini's lips. 'That's between me and my God and the Devil.'

'Eminences,' greeted Torquemada.

They spun round, alarmed at the familiar, oily voice, then relapsed into nervous laughter.

'Catches me every time,' chuckled Borgia.

Torquemada approached the cardinals with mincing steps. 'I hear my services are required as Inquisitor General.'

Borgia threw a look at the Pit. 'The Inquisitor General is dead. Long live the Inquisitor General.'

'But try and take more care than the previous holder of the office,' advised Agostini. 'We've only got a couple of Torquemadas left, and some stupid oaf has burned the lock of hair in a thurible. Our inquisitorial future went up with the incense.'

Profound unease troubled Torquemada's features. Borgia shot Agostini a warning glance.

Agostini bowed his head. He had mentioned what should not be mentioned. 'Apologies, brothers in Christ.'

Torquemada's inherent self-assurance got the better of his discomfort. 'Well, eminences, any news of that devil Byron and his lackeys?'

'Their apprehension is a matter of time,' Borgia said.

Torquemada scowled. 'Meaning, they've so far eluded Cardinal Agostini's security.'

Agostini scowled back. 'I think it's time for a Conclave Extraordinary, wouldn't you say, brethren? Otherwise, Cardinal Richelieu will make his move in our absence.'

'Good point,' Rodrigo Borgia acknowledged, then lifted his arm: 'Cart Venerable!'

In the distance, the Sisters of the Heart of Superabundant Sanguinity began to huff and puff, dragging the oversized, ornate cart towards the Pit area.

'The Ascension Towers would be far quicker,' the Inquisitor General said, with a twist of the lip.

'Undoubtedly.' Borgia threw a conspiratorial look at

Agostini. 'But they lack the *style*.'

The cardinals walked at an easy pace to meet the advancing cart. After they had covered some distance, Agostini gave a backward glance.

Torquemada stood near the rim of the Pit of Perdition, peering into its lethal plenum-vacuum.

Agostini's lips twitched in a smile. '*Plus ça change . . .*'

'An altarboy.' Sarah stood with arms folded, expressionless.

The Doctor gave her black cassock and white cotta an appraising look. 'I wouldn't know about such things, but I imagine you'd turn a few heads with that outfit.'

'I know a couple of nobles who'd pay you a tidy sum to dress up as an altarboy,' Byron said in a matter-of-fact tone.

She slammed the chest shut and marched purposefully out of the chamber. 'I won't be anyone's plaything – at any price.'

'I would,' the poet said casually, keeping pace with her. 'Money for old rope. I've done a lot worse in my time.'

'That I can believe.' Her gaze wandered around the labyrinth of chambers. 'Which way?'

He walked in front of her. 'If you take your proper place – behind me – you'll have no need to ask.'

She followed in silence, speculating on how much longer she could go on biting her lip before the bloody thing dropped off.

The arched chambers gradually evolved into a series of tunnels with fluted walls emitting low, monotonous organ music. Up ahead she suddenly heard a sequence of high-pitched, piping notes.

Byron raised a hand. 'These walls are semi-organic, liable to be roused by swift movement. We'll lie low until they settle down.'

Sarah, following the poet's example, sat down on the faintly vibrating floor.

The Doctor stood bolt upright, staring at the rounded

ceiling. He spoke in a low voice: 'I presume you were in the Vatican for a clandestine meeting with Pope Lucian?'

Byron glanced up. 'Indeed, Doctor, well surmised. Lucian proved to be a reforming Pontiff, and sent a message requesting a secret discussion with Domino representatives, the aim of which was to form a truce between the Vatican and the Dominoes, and destroy the power of the Inquisition. Myself and Casanova were chosen as the diplomats —'

'*The* Casanova?' Sarah queried.

'If by that you mean Giovanni Giacomo Casanova, yes.'

'Another character from history. Just how many of them are there?'

'They're known as Reprises,' he said wearily. 'Historical recreations. Are you *so* ignorant?'

'Let's leave the Reprises till later,' the Doctor advised. 'Do go on with your story, George.'

Byron expelled a short breath. 'Casanova and I were to go on the mission, with Miles Dashing as an extra sword in case of trouble.'

'Miles *Dashing*!' Sarah exclaimed. 'What a name! I don't recollect any mention of him in the roll of history.'

'That's because he wasn't an historical character. Like the majority of Europa's population, he isn't a Reprise. He was natural-born twenty years ago in Regency Britannia. Miles is, however, the finest swordsman in all of Europa — with the possible exception of the villainous Comte d'Etrange of Bordeaux, of course.'

'Of course,' shrugged Sarah, hands outspread, fingers splayed. 'Goes without saying.'

He subjected her to a stare worthy of Olivier's Heathcliff. 'What a supercilious wench it is. Now, may I continue? The three of us planned to rendezvous in St Peter's Basilica, then take a secret route to the papal apartments. Neither of my Domino comrades appeared, the Devil knows why.'

Sarah swayed her head from side to side. Reprises . . .

Dominoes . . . It was a major job keeping up with it all.

'I went alone to Pope Lucian's bedchamber,' Byron continued. 'I remember passing a tall, metal statue of St Michael on my way . . . Myself and Lucian had barely exchanged a dozen words when the Archangel Michael burst in, spear lofted. Although nimble as a stag, the angel's body – some three metres tall – was metallic in appearance. But he bled like a man when my sabre took him in the side. He gave me a blow that floored me, dazing my wits. I watched as the warrior angel flung the pope face down on the bed. Then the angel launched himself into the air and, head first, bore down on Lucian, spear extended. The spear plunged clean through body and bed. A moment later, the angel had metamorphosed back into a statue. I took that as my cue to depart.'

'Your meeting was not so secret, then,' the Doctor concluded. 'Someone laid a trap for you. Kill the pope – blame the Dominoes.'

'Evidently. But I'm not so easily trapped. And Lucian imparted one vital piece of news before St Michael's intrusion – the Dominoes have an ally in the Enclave, but he didn't have time to give me the name.'

The organ notes had subsided to a *basso profundo* rumble.

'Time to go,' the poet declared, jumping to his feet.

They set off down the fluted passageway, and were soon in another maze of ribbed tunnels, unpleasantly organic in appearance. Again, she was reminded of rococo intestines.

After a prolonged trudge, interspersed with periods of crawling on her stomach to avoid whatever devilish traps were hidden in the walls, she felt a warm breeze fanning her face.

'Almost there,' Byron announced. 'We've been lucky so far. Very lucky.'

'Where is *there*, exactly?' said the Doctor, peering ahead.

'You'll know it when you see it.'

'If you say so.'

The lord signalled them to crawl down a gentle slope to a circular hatch. 'Slow and careful,' he ordered, 'or you'll be in for a long scream.'

Reaching the hatch, he depressed a lever. The metal surface slid aside. Inching forwards, Sarah peeked over the rim. It took a couple of seconds for the view to sink in.

'That's a city down there,' she said. 'A long way down.'

'Two kilometres,' informed Byron, regarding her closely. 'Renaissance Rome, minus the Vatican. We are looking down from the Exalted Vatican. My compliments, madam. For a woman, you have an excellent head for heights.'

'Oh, Byron,' the Doctor groaned. 'Stop being so – byronic. You know, when we chatted in the Villa Diodati, you were a much more affable fellow. No need to live your own legend, you know.'

A small spasm plucked Byron's cheek. 'When were you at the Villa Diodati? I don't remember . . .'

The Doctor's mouth split into a huge grin. 'Oh – touched a raw nerve. So sorry. The episode wasn't in the history books.'

'Doctor,' Byron said softly, with an undertone of menace. 'Either you are irredeemably ignorant of Europan etiquette, or you are deliberately provoking me. Not wise.'

The Doctor's mouth formed an innocent oval. 'I wouldn't dream of doing such a thing. We're not quite *au fait* with Europan etiquette. We've just arrived in this world, you see.'

Byron frowned. 'From where?'

The Doctor waved a vague hand. 'Oh, elsewhere, elsewhen.'

For protracted seconds, the lord studied the Doctor. 'Very well,' he said at length. 'It would explain your companion's ignorance of Reprises. Against my better judgement, I'll accept your word. You're obviously not a Vatican spy, but you might still be an enemy of the Dominoes.'

'Dominoes?' Sarah mouthed to the Doctor, but he raised a silencing palm.

The Doctor peered through the hatch. 'Ah, the distinctive shimmer of a chameleon-field cloaking some form of aerial vehicle, shaped like a dragon, I believe.'

'You can see through a cloaking-field?' Byron said in surprise. 'Or are you simply guessing?'

The Doctor winked. 'I have good eyesight.'

Sarah looked good and hard. Couldn't see a blasted thing.

'Hmm . . .' Byron mused dubiously. 'Well, you'll find it a lot easier to jump when you can see what you're aiming for, won't you?' He stretched out an arm in invitation. 'After you, Doctor.'

Sarah pulled the Time Lord's sleeve. 'We don't have to go. We could just look for the TARDIS.'

He smiled wistfully. 'Would that I could. I miss the old girl. But she's locked up tight and well beyond my reach, I fear. Besides, I think she brought us here for a reason. We can't run away from this one.' He adopted a derring-do grin. 'Follow me, Sarah.'

With a spring, he vaulted into empty space.

A moment later, he was sitting on empty space, little more than a metre below. 'Just climb down and plant your feet directly behind me,' he called up.

Her mind told her one thing, her senses another. As far as she could see, there was nothing down there but air and a lot of gravity. But she kept up a brave front and sank through the hatch. She released a breath of relief when her legs contacted an invisible something. Settling into place, after an awkward adjustment of the cassock, she found her seat comfortable, similar to straddling a motor-bike.

'I landed in the middle of this aerial scooter,' the Doctor shouted up to Byron. 'I presumed you'd wish to take the front seat.'

'You really can see through a cloaking-field,' the poet

said admiringly, dropping in front of the Doctor. 'You could prove a useful ally.'

Sarah saw Byron's hand twist an unseen something or other, and was jerked back by a sudden acceleration.

'Hold on tight,' the Doctor called over his shoulder.

'I am. I am.'

The activation of the air-scooter had apparently cancelled the chameleon-field. She was no longer riding on air, but a stylized red-golden dragon, the half-unfurled wings providing a partial buffer against the wind.

The Exalted Vatican's baroque underbelly sped overhead until the hovering city's rim came into sight and they were flying with free blue sky above. Glancing back, she got the impression that the Vatican's underside seemed to stretch forever. This pseudo-Vatican City had to be ten, twenty times the size of the original.

The Doctor appeared unimpressed. 'Overblown,' he remarked, then tapped the lord on the shoulder. 'What do you call this nippy little scooter?'

'A Draco,' Byron shouted over the whooshing wind.

'Fast on the straight, quick on the turns, is she?'

Byron nodded. 'But she's built to hold two. We're overloaded. Pray to whatever gods you hold dear that the Angeli don't spot us too soon.'

'Angeli – Vatican fliers, no doubt. Are they shaped like angels?'

Byron looked into a rear-view mirror and emitted a groan. 'Look for yourself.'

The Doctor and Sarah turned in unison. Viewed at this distance, Vatican City was a stupendous, though disturbing spectacle. Gargantuan domes and colossal pillars, a deranged meld of the Baroque and Gothic, an architectural wonder and monstrosity. It was a nightmare of epic proportions.

And issuing from ports in its side were Angels of Wrath, pursuing the Draco head on, mouths agape. She reckoned that each mouth was large enough to swallow the Draco.

'They can't be made of grey stone,' she muttered.

'A convincing imitation,' the Doctor said. 'Probably feels like stone to the touch. Have you noticed the spear pressed to each flank? They're all St Michaels. The Warrior Archangel.'

'I'm a bit rusty on my angels,' she said through gritted teeth.

'We appear to be outdistancing them,' the Doctor shouted to Byron.

'We haven't outdistanced their firepower,' the lord said grimly. 'Take a look at the nearest Angelus.'

'I see what you mean. Looks like pseudo-sentient thermoplasmic soma-seekers to me.'

'If you mean cold fireballs that freeze their targets in mid-air, yes,' Byron grunted.

She twisted round, and then wished she hadn't.

From the yawning mouth of the foremost Angelus, a stream of blue-white spheres poured in abundance, resembling ball-lightning. They homed in on the Draco at an alarming speed.

Sarah leaned up close and spoke into the Doctor's ear. 'Do you think we're in a spot of bother now?'

He glanced round. 'Oh, not at all,' he reassured, his mouth set in a ghastly grin, stark eyes bulging from his sockets.

Eight

Shadow Ipsissimus to the rear, stake-gun-wielding vampires to the front, Miles Dashing was forced to think quickly. He came to a swift decision.

Shoot at everything and see what happens.

Swinging his stake-gun at the pouncing Shadow Ipsissimus, he pressed the trigger and let fly a mini-stake.

The stake sent the black phantom flying across the tomb, burying its point in the masonry and pinning the vampiric shadow to the wall. Blood spurted richly from the wound.

The Shadow Ipsissimus was new to the discarnate state, hadn't yet found its forte. It had reacted to the mini-stake as though still incarnate and vulnerable to physical weapons. But it would soon learn.

In the meantime, the vampiric commoners . . .

Miles vaulted over the coffin dais and dived for cover an instant before the undead peasants unleashed a volley of mini-stakes. The needle-sharp stakes whizzed over his head.

Bobbing up, he let loose three rounds in rapid succession. Three stakes struck three hearts.

He ducked under cover before the next salvo. The projectiles smashed harmlessly against the wall. As they impacted, he popped up again and pumped three more stakes into an equal number of hearts, then dropped before the answering fire drilled holes in him.

Taking a quick breather, he pulled out one of his crucifixes. There was scant chance of his adversaries so much as flinching at the sight of the cross — even peasant ampires lacked the necessary credulity to react to such a ackneyed talisman – but there was no harm in giving it a o.

Thinking faith, faith and more faith, furiously projecting devout thought patterns into the psycho-conductive metal, he flung the crucifix over the dais. It landed with a clink.

'Retreat before the symbol of Light!' he shouted, conviction ringing in his tone. He held his breath for protracted seconds.

The crucifix flew back in two pieces, neatly snapped in half.

'*Cat lick your heart . . .*' resounded a composite growl.

He had faith in the cross. They didn't.

'Oh well, it was worth a try.'

Now, with just one stake left in the gun's chamber, it was do or die. Face grimly set, he took out his concentrated garlic balls.

'For God and Saint George,' he declaimed.

Tossing a scatter of the concentrated garlic balls to clear his path, he leaped over the dais, rolled across the floor, and kicked the legs of the nearest peasant from under him. As the smelly commoner dropped, Miles back-shot him through the heart and grabbed his stake-gun.

Holding the twitching creature as a shield, Miles downed four more adversaries with the fresh weapon before the shielding vampire flopped. He let the body fall.

The portal was now free of enemies. But the cemetery must be teeming with Nosferatu.

Those peasants, however, had Byron as their Ipsissimus Lord. Thus a trace of Byron's élan should have permeated the dull clods. The stake-guns were evidence of that. Vampire duels or shoot-outs were rare, but when undertaken required pistols that shot stakes. Byron must have introduced the madcap custom to the locals – a dash of panache.

If so, those common folk out there might just have a

vague notion of gentlemanly honour.

'I challenge you to a duel!' he called out. 'Let your best man stand forth!'

'*Cat lick your heart . . .*' came the sibilant response.

Didn't sound promising. Miles had the greatest respect for the common people, living or undead, but perhaps it was too much to expect them to rise above their station and acquire a modicum of aristocratic style, with attendant *noblesse oblige*.

'*I accept your challenge,*' said a whoosh of a voice as the Shadow Ipsissimus whipped past and out of the portal.

Miles flinched back instinctively at the shadow's rush, then realized his luck was in. Byron's swashbuckling style hadn't been completely submerged by his vampiric condition. His active shade would possess the body of one of the commoners out there, and confront Miles face to face, stake-gun to stake-gun.

'*Leave the mortal to me . . .*' issued a vasty voice from the cemetery.

'You're a true gentleman, sir,' Miles Dashing acknowledged as he retrieved his concentrated garlic balls.

He straightened up at a strangled yelp and a glupping sound from out in the cemetery. Byron had incarnated himself in one of the peasants. Placing the stake-gun in its shoulder-holster, Miles stepped out into the graveyard.

The undead ranks had parted, leaving an aisle flanked by mouldy bodies. At the far end of the aisle, facing Miles at a distance of some fifteen paces, stood a tall, gaunt man in shabby dress. His lantern jaw moved as though pulled by strings. '*Let the duel begin.*' The voice reminded Miles of crunched gristle.

He glanced around. 'We are somewhat hemmed in by commoners here, who might fall foul of a stray stake. What about that open space near the weeping willow?'

Byron nodded the head he inhabited. '*It shall be so.*'

At each step to the designated spot Miles kept a wary eye on the peasants, who were staring at his jugular and smacking their lips. But none dared break the lord's command, and he reached the moist sward without mishap.

Byron halted in front of a ruined mausoleum at the far end of the sward, observing Miles who stood under the weeping willow. A mere ten paces separated them.

'First, we must choose our seconds,' Miles announced. 'Now, I'll have –'

'*As the intervening distance is so short,*' said Byron's gristly voice, '*I suggest the Borgo manner of duelling. We stand where we are, face to face, then draw on the third tolling of the bell.*' A bony finger indicated a squat commoner standing under a death-bell a couple of tombs away, rope in hand.

Miles frowned. 'Gentlemen stand back to back, walk ten or fifteen paces, then turn and –'

'*There is no option, Dashing of Dashwood.*'

'I little thought you would descend to such barbarous, foreign practices,' Miles reproached. 'But, if needs must, I agree – under protest.'

'*At the third stroke, Dashing of Dashwood.*' A cadaverous hand hovered over the holster of the gun-belt.

DOOOMMM . . . the death-bell resounded, echoing solemnly through the memento mori of the graveyard. Somewhere beyond the gathering mist, a chorus of wolves greeted the gloomy peal.

Miles tossed one side of the opera cloak over his left shoulder, eased back the frock-coat from the shoulder-holster.

DOOOMMM . . .

Byron's hand dangled over the stake-gun, fingers twitching in anticipation.

Breath clouding the frosty air, Miles inched his finger-tips to his holster.

DOOOMMM . . .

One instant Miles's stake-gun was in the holster. The next it was in his hand and firing.

A mini-stake was buried in Byron's chest before his gun was fully drawn. He reeled as two more stakes joined the first, making a mash of his heart.

He spun and toppled, still struggling to draw his weapon. The lord's confusion was Miles's opportunity to make a dash for it. The duelling area he'd chosen was between the Ipsissimus mausoleum and the cemetery wall. A quick sprint and he might just make it, while the commoners were still distracted by their master's defeat.

Drilling the few intervening vampires with well-aimed mini-stakes, he'd covered more than half the distance when a rush of noxious air suggested that the Ipsissimus had departed its host body. A backward glance confirmed the suspicion.

A shape of congealed night soared from the peasant's carcass and sped in Miles's tracks, soughing, '*Cat lick your heart . . .*' in the most coarse of tones.

The lord's brief sojourn in the rustic's anatomy had evidently obliterated the last vestige of Byron's nobility. The Shadow Ipsissimus was no more than an uncaged beast, ravenous for blood and life-essence.

Miles forced his legs to pump harder. The boundary wall, an effective barrier to the Nosferatu while actual daylight reigned above the black holo-sky, was just twenty metres distant.

He felt a frosty breath on the nape of his neck. Another instant and shadow pseudo-substance would seep into his flesh.

The wall was a jump away. He jumped for all he was worth, and sailed over the stone border, cloak flying.

Landing with a thump, he was up and running again, not slowing until he'd put a good ten metres between himself and the cemetery boundary. Skidding to a halt, he spun round, stake-gun levelled.

The Shadow Ipsissimus loomed above the wall, swaying like an underwater frond. Although radiating menace, the shadow was baulked by the barrier.

'*Come true nightfall . . .*' threatened the arch-vampire.

'Come nightfall, I'll be over the border and in Switzia,' Miles retorted. 'And that's a boundary you can never cross. Now answer me: who or what is Managra?'

'What's in a name, Slime . . .'

Miles straightened his back. 'Very well. If that's your attitude, I'll be on my way.'

With a swirl of the cloak he wheeled round and headed for a track that meandered through an elm wood. Yet again, his burning question remained unanswered.

Well, there was always next time.

As for the apparent coincidence of the Draco landing near the vampiric Byron, no coincidence at all. The airscooter's sensors, attuned to locate Byron, had done so. Although short on power, he now realized that the vehicle could have travelled a little further into Transylvania if it had wished. It wasn't the Draco's fault that it was the *wrong* Byron. Mistake any Draco could make.

Twenty minutes' vigorous walking brought him to his flier. Should be a few minutes' flying left in the old bird, sufficient to take him over the border.

A frown crossed his brow as he noted the dull energy panel. He wiggled the boost toggle, but to no effect. Starved of sunlight, the Draco's battery was flat. The effort of expending its energies homing in on Byron must have been too much for it.

And, he reflected, the sun would not be shining here to stir life in the dormant dragon.

He heaved a sigh. He'd have to leave his trusty old steed here for some time, until he could return and recharge the cells.

For now, he faced a long walk to the border – a six- or seven-hour trek, at least. And the hidden sun would be setting in five hours.

He thought of the Shadow Ipsissimus and its vampiric minions, down in the dell beyond the woods, not to mention the noble arch-vampires of the Castle Borgo.

He scanned the castle's crenellated walls and spindling turrets, rearing from a jagged crag, stark against the frost of stars.

'Do your worst,' he challenged, then spun on his heel and set out for the border.

Part Two

A Walk in the Black Forest

Let us take a walk in the Black Forest,
Just you and I.
In the deepest, darkest dell of the Black Forest,
Just you and I.
What's there to fear when we're all alone
In the deepest, darkest dell of the Black Forest –
Just you and I.

    Pearson's *Third Ghastly Tale of the Black Forest*

Nine

'I aspired to be the Official Antichrist before you.'

'Huh! I am officially recognized as the veritable Beast of the Apocalypse. My mother knew that I was when I was *thirteen*, when I seduced –'

'Gently, sirs, gently,' interposed the stooped, ageing Cardinal Richelieu, raising a conciliatory palm as he continued to stare through the portal of his personal Angelus. 'We'll soon be over the Francian Alps and still you squabble. You have some five minutes left before I must leave you at the place appointed. Five minutes for us to achieve an understanding, gentlemen.'

Aleister Crowley furiously scratched his shaven head and continued to glare at the foppishly attired Johann Faust. 'I,' he declared, 'am the Beast. *Ipso facto*, I am, apodictically, the Antichrist.'

Faust, magician of Wittenberg, bent an indolent smile at the tetchy Britannian. 'Your speech is as execrable as your prose. And try to get through a single minute without saying "apodictic" or some derivation thereof.'

Crowley hefted a brute of a fist. 'There's one way of settling this. I'd back an Englishman against a German any day in a straight fight.'

The willowy Faust waved away the stocky Britannian. 'Englishman, German . . . such antique language, rather like yourself, Crowley.'

'Master Therion to you.'

'Whatever. May I remind you that I'm under the personal protection of Mephistopheles, guaranteed for twenty-four years? Strike a blow at me, and watch your hand rot on the bone.'

'Let's try it and see,' snarled Crowley, swinging back an arm.

'Gentlemen!' reprimanded the cardinal. 'You know our situation. You are familiar with my plan. You are aware of the alternatives. We swim together or sink apart.'

Mastering his rage, Crowley sank back in the aircraft's seat. 'An alliance between Church and Anti-Church? That'll take some explaining to my disciples.'

'You think you've got problems?' snorted Faust, running ringed fingers through his long, lank hair. 'I've got to answer to Mephistopheles!'

Cardinal Richelieu steepled his fingers, the tips brushing his goatee beard. 'On that matter of the pact with Lucifer, arranged by the demon Mephistopheles, I have recently put my humble diplomatic skills to work. Behind the scenes, you understand. I think you will find your Tempter most accommodating should you enter into a pact with me.'

Faust gazed incredulously at the cardinal who was King Louis XIII's Chief Minister, and effective ruler of Francia. 'Are you implying that you've forged an alliance with Lucifer?'

'An – understanding.'

'You really do have good contacts,' Faust said admiringly. 'But how can you, a man of the cloth, make a pact with the Church's arch-enemy?'

'I have no enemies but the enemies of Francia.' The statement was delivered with such conviction that neither of the Antichrist aspirants doubted it.

'So, gentlemen,' the cardinal resumed. 'Let us start from common ground, then proceed speedily. Who is *your* greatest enemy?'

'Theophrastus Bombastus, alias Paracelsus,' growled Crowley. 'The oaf who thinks the post of Official Antichrist is his by diabolic right.'

'nemA to that,' said Faust. 'Do you know he intends to

change the Black Mass from Latin to the vernacular? It just wouldn't be the same without the Latin . . .'

'So,' Richelieu said. 'You have a common enemy. I have the means to oust that enemy from the contest for Official Antichrist. Then the two of you, *amicably*, can vie for the post. But remember that you have an additional enemy, far more threatening. An enemy common to us all.'

Crowley fixed his basilisk stare on the cardinal. 'The Dominoes.'

'Yes, the Dominoes. In particular, Byron, Casanova and Miles Dashing.'

Faust gave a slow nod. 'True enough, the Dominoes have trodden on the toes of the Anti-Church Lowerarchy once too often, especially that chivalric lunatic Miles Dashing.'

Crowley's lip curled. 'I hate Miles Dashing.'

'As for myself,' Cardinal Richelieu stated, 'I have good reason to see Dashing destroyed. He once aided the so-called Four Musketeers against me in a plot concerning the king's double and a mysterious item of lady's attire.'

'The Four Musketeers!' scoffed Crowley, his muscular frame shaking with mirth. 'They were created from a *film*, damn it. Fictional reconstructions. They're not even true Reprises, and they've been a quadruple thorn in your side for years. Casts a cloud over your vaunted skills, *n'est-ce pas*, Frenchman?'

'Francian,' corrected Richelieu. 'And may I remind you that Athos, Porthos, Aramis and d'Artagnan are themselves Dominoes, and receive the full support of that subversive confraternity? Gentlemen, both Church and Anti-Church share a common foe – the Dominoes, who upset the delicate balance between God and the Devil. We must join forces against that foe. Only I, of all the Enclave, understand the necessity. With myself as Pope Supreme of the Catholic Church Apostolic, not only will Paracelsus and his followers be exterminated, but the Dominoes will be crushed. And – you have my word –

the claims and integrity of the Anti-Church will be fully recognized, whichever of you is elected Official Antichrist. But, I *must* be made pope.'

'With a little help from your devil-worshipping friends?' remarked Faust.

'I have no friends. Only allies.'

Crowley and Faust traded glances, then nods. 'All right,' said Crowley. 'It's agreed.'

'Agreed,' echoed Faust. 'I've long ago given up the hope that the Anti-Church will overthrow the Catholic Church Apostolic. Tell me, cardinal. I've often wondered . . . how is it that the devils we've launched against the Vatican have constantly been overcome?'

A thin smile curved Cardinal Richelieu's mouth. 'It's as Casanova once remarked – the Vatican commands more devils.'

'Our play is done,' said the white, smiling face. 'One play is past. Lo! Another cometh!'

Prince Ludwig didn't answer. Couldn't answer. Where his mouth should be there was a smooth expanse of flesh from nose to chin. The Prince of the House Glockenstein hugged the pink poodle to his breast and regarded the Dramaturge with pale, frightened eyes.

The Dramaturge, his white mask face inscrutable, waved his assembled troupe of actors to the door. 'Our revels here are done, dead popes and dread poets all. Another stage awaits. Another masque, tragical and comical. And soon – soon – Thirteenth Night.'

Slowly, the troupe filed across the extravagant Chimera Hall to the arched exit. The masked dramatist observed them for a moment, then caught the eye of a tall, elegant woman in a crimson gown, dark golden hair framing her blanched, exquisite features. Her slow smile was a mortal sin.

'Milady Incarnadine,' the dramatist greeted with a bow of the head and a flourish of the hand. 'Your performance, as always, was a triumph.'

'I am what you made me, Doctor Sperano,' Incarnadine said, her voice a dark melody. With a sensual grace, she strolled on her way, giving a graceful wave. The shadow she cast behaved otherwise, arms gripped tight round its waist and head drooped in a posture of grief.

'Enchanted, madam,' he said softly, then switched his attention back to the prince.

'Ah, I cannot leave you so — speechless after our performance. Besides, how would you ever eat? You'd wither away to a shadow of yourself.'

A hand disappeared under the full-length opera cloak, and emerged with a long, curved knife in its grip. 'Would you like me to put a smile on your face?'

The prince shrank back at the knife's descent.

The blade's keen edge arced across Ludwig's face, slicing deep into the flesh. The prince spasmed in his chair, fingers digging into the armrests. The pink poodle jittered in his lap, emitting little yelps.

'There,' declared the Dramaturge, stepping back and appraising the curved, red rent. 'Ruby lips. And a permanent smile.'

Struggling to vocalize from the throat, Ludwig forced out guttural words. 'Doctor Sperano . . . Heal me — with a kiss . . .'

'Undo my own handiwork?' said Doctor Sperano's white, rigid lips. 'Rewrite a single line? What's done is done; sad, but true.' He pocketed the bloodied knife. 'But look, your little dog is alarmed. Here, let me take it awhile.'

The poodle was swept from Ludwig's lap to Doctor Sperano's embrace before the prince could lift a hand or voice a protest. Pale fingers stroked the soft, pink hair.

'So, wan prince, you have been graced with a performance from the Theatre of Transmogrification. Transformations most rare and curious. And you, yourself, have been transmogrified. A small part in the show, so to speak, but not a speaking part.'

He inclined his mask-face to the departing troupe. 'They did well, my little company of angel-devils. But –' The mellifluous voice lowered in tone. 'There was a small departure from the text, an improvisation, a fleeting character not included in the *dramatis personae*. I think he, like me, was a Doctor. I wonder who –'

The dramatist recovered from his abstraction, and bent his white smile over the anguished Prince Ludwig. 'When I'm gone – if you will, remember... But as *I* will, *forget*.'

Ludwig spread out his arms, silently beseeching Doctor Sperano to return his beloved pet.

'Oh, you want your little dog back? Most certainly. But first, let me give it a big, big hug. Make it part of the show.'

Sperano held the pink poodle close, and squeezed. And squeezed.

When he finally dropped the crushed, limp creature into Ludwig's lap, Sperano spoke soft words to the horrified prince: 'There, now it's red.'

Ten

'I wish I had my sonic screwdriver,' grumbled the Doctor, absently going through his numerous pockets. 'I'm sure I could get more speed out of this flying contraption if I did a little tinkering.'

Byron hunched over the controls, teeth bared in the wind. 'Touch my Draco and you're dead.'

Sarah darted another backward look at the pursuing Angeli and, racing in front of the Vatican aircraft, a trail of shimmering spheres. 'Those freezing ball-lightnings are right on our tail,' she yelled at Byron. 'Do you have a thermal decoy – anything like that?'

Byron disdained a response. The Doctor stepped into the breach. 'The thermoplasmic globes home on to DNA codes, Sarah. Ours, in this case.'

'Can you think of anything?'

'Er, no.' His face brightened. 'Can you?'

'No.'

His features relapsed into clown's sorrow, Pagliacci to the last smear of grease-paint. 'Oh . . . Would you like to hear an aria?'

'Not at this precise moment.'

'Ah . . .'

'We're not done yet,' Byron said. 'If we can keep clear for maybe a minute the freeze-spheres will lose energy and impetus. A minute, perhaps more, and the skies will be ours.'

'There you are, Sarah!' the Doctor smiled. 'It's one of those times when you hang on to your hat and hope for the best.'

'*Dum spiro, spero*,' she said, wearing the thinnest of smiles.

'Hmm . . . possibly. I was thinking more along the lines of *nil desperandum*.'

Amounts to the same damn thing, she thought, but took his contrariness in her stride. She was used to it. And two could play at that game, even with the imminent threat of death at their backs. 'What about "put on a happy face"?'

'Why, have you got one?' Then his banter faltered, and he stared into a distance she could only guess at. The froth on the ocean was gone, the depths partially visible. 'Faces,' he murmured. 'Faces within faces. A rose is not a rose is not a rose.'

Sarah opened her mouth, then closed it again. The Doctor was prone to mood-swings – maybe it was a Gallifreyan form of manic-depression – but he'd been a regular see-saw since the Sistine Chapel. Since viewing the wrinkle-face painted on St Dominic's hand. Later, if there was a later, she had a few questions to ask. As for now . . .

'Hell's blood,' Byron cursed. 'We're not going to outrun the freeze-spheres.'

She twisted round and observed the swift approach of the nearest globe.

The Doctor was also eyeing the spheres. 'You're absolutely right, George. A plan is urgently called for.' He glanced at Sarah. 'What's the first rule?'

'How should I know?' she shrugged. 'You keep making new ones up.'

'Never overlook the obvious!'

'Oh, *that* first rule,' she said casually, then did a double-take at the nonchalance of her tone. Was the Doctor's flip attitude infectious, and had she picked up a dose of it? 'I'm scared,' she said frankly. 'Think of something – please.'

'Think of something . . .' His brow frowned furiously, then cleared. 'No sooner said than done, Sarah. The spheres home in on DNA, yes? So let's give them some.'

He produced a needle and thimble like a conjurer. 'By the pricking of my thumbs and all that hugger-mugger . . .' Jabbing the needle into his flesh, he shook a few drops into the thimble. 'Now you, Sarah. Yes, that's it. Now – Byron . . .'

Byron's mouth angled in a dubious slant. 'If I guess your scheme aright, I'd say that it's too simple. They couldn't have overlooked such an elementary ploy.'

'Never overlook the obvious,' the Doctor repeated. 'But people do, with tiresome regularity.'

'Worth a try,' the poet conceded, letting fall a few droplets of blood into the thimble.

The Doctor swivelled round. 'Here goes!' He let go the thimble and watched it dip behind the Draco. 'Yes!'

The foremost globe dipped after the blood-trailing thimble. And froze in mid-air, metamorphosing into a giant snowball. Then it plummeted to earth.

Sarah punched the air in victory. 'You did it, Doctor!' *Well done, mad uncle . . .*

He gave a slight shrug. 'It was on the trail of our DNA. I gave it what it wanted. Twice more for luck?'

'You've got it,' she smiled, checking on the pursuers. The Angeli had given up the chase, and the closest spheres offered minimal danger.

'You're a capital fellow in a crisis, Doctor,' Byron complimented. 'From now on, consider me your friend. And a friend to the Dominoes.'

'That's very decent of you.'

'What *are* the Dominoes?' Sarah said.

'Let's ensure our escape,' the Doctor broke in. 'Then all will be revealed.' He tapped the poet on the shoulder. 'We're heading for the Villa Diodati, I presume?'

'Yes. How did you know?'

'Oh, a wild guess. Now – who wants me to give them the needle?'

The cardinal slipped into his chamber and carefully locked the door. A meticulous survey of the rooms revealed that the screening mechanisms were in perfect working order, obstructing any prospective eavesdropper.

Security ensured, he knelt before a large, silvered mirror and spread out his hands. His image showed scared eyes in the glass. He took a deep breath, hearing the rapid tempo of his pulse.

'Persona,' he summoned in hushed tones. 'Persona.'

For a long spell, there was no response.

The holo-candles suddenly flickered and dwindled, defying their programmed activity.

Briefly, the glass misted. When it cleared, he saw the reflection of a man standing behind him. He knew from experience that if he turned round he'd perceive no one in the room.

The man in the mirror stood as if waiting, a perpetual smile on the white, rigid face that reminded the priest of a marble mask.

'Master,' the cardinal acclaimed.

Gathering his full-length opera cloak about his tall figure, the man tilted his white, smiling face and spoke in a mellifluous tone. 'You called?'

'Eminence,' greeted Agostini, bending his lips in a smile. 'I feared you might miss the Conclave Extraordinary.'

'Eminence,' acknowledged Richelieu with a minuscule inclination of the head. 'I wouldn't miss it for the world.' With dignified steps, he descended from an Angelus emblazoned with the *fleur-de-lys*.

'King Louis is well, I trust?' Agostini radiated sincerity.

'Exceedingly,' replied Richelieu, walking alongside Agostini as they traversed a Vatican landing-port crowded with Angeli. 'He sends the best wishes of Francia.'

'Of *one* Francia,' the Italian stressed. 'Francia Bourbon. There were four others, at last count.'

'The true Francia is that which is built on the soil of ancient France.'

'Come now, more than half of that soil is populated by a score of Dominions — two miniature Britannias, three small Germanias, a single Esperantia. Why, there's even a nineteenth-century Francia on the old Alsace-Lorraine border.'

'Is there a point to this tedious catalogue?' Richelieu sighed as they neared the doorway to an Ascension Tower.

Agostini arched his eyebrows. 'Simply stating realities, eminence. No more.'

'As you say.'

'And in what state of grace did you find Francia Bourbon?'

'Improving,' said Richelieu. 'The Huguenots have fled to the Nederlandias and Britannia Gloriana, three Cyrano de Bergeracs are in prison, and the Four Musketeers are on the run.'

'I marvel that you gleaned so much in so brief a visit. Your Angelus seemed to return almost as soon as it left.'

'Economical use of time, Agostini. The Vatican could learn from it. Incidentally, I heard Byron and his accomplices slipped through your net. Flying free as birds.'

Agostini frowned. 'There is evidence that the one who calls himself the Doctor has a considerable command of sorcery.'

'As you're fond of repeating, Agostini – no comment.'

The two prelates entered the Ascension Tower gateway and stood on the small ring of flagstones that floored the interior of a granite tower which stretched eight hundred metres overhead. In unison, the cardinals pressed their palms together in an attitude of prayer.

The Ascension Tower's sensors, hidden between slim cracks in the granite blocks, registered the exact posture of the praying hands, recognized them as valid, and activated the ascension procedure. Reverse gravity mechanisms hummed into action, and lifted the cardinals off their feet. They levitated ten metres from the floor in as many seconds.

The two priests ascended the tower, hands upraised in

prayer. In their levitation they passed a dozen gateways, each affording access to one of Vatican City's many levels.

They ascended to the very top of the tower and, parting their hands in the prescribed manner, informed the tower to deposit them on the threshold of an elaborate archway. Stepping through the arch, they stood at the end of a long corridor whose floor gave every appearance of marble-bordered mosaic.

'Glide,' instructed Agostini.

The floor molecularly bonded the soles of their sandals to its surface, and rolled into action, speeding the pair down the passageway.

Gliding towards the Doors Beatific at the end of the corridor, Cardinal Richelieu turned to Agostini. 'Why the haste in calling a Conclave Extraordinary? We arranged a Convocation Extraordinary last night, and little came of that.'

'That,' said the Italian, 'is precisely why we require a Conclave Extraordinary.'

'Specious reasoning,' sniffed Richelieu.

'*Introibo*,' Agostini commanded the Doors Beatific. The tall bronze doors swung open and the cardinals slid to a halt, the floor releasing its molecular grip.

Bowing their heads, they entered the Shrine of Exaltation, crossing the voluminous hall with downcast gaze. Not until they were seated in a pew, between Francisco and Maroc, did they lift up their eyes.

Pope Lucian reposed on empty air three metres above the heads of the Enclave, arms crossed on his chest, the ravages of his murder disguised by vestments and the mortician's art.

The Enclave sat in silence as the sunlight gradually faded from the stained-glass windows. At the moment of sunset, the silver peal of a delicate bell resonated in the vaulted roof.

The seven Enclave members rose as one, arms uplifted. 'Exaltation,' they chorused.

The verbal signal slid open a panel in the roof and redirected the stasis-gravity that buoyed up the deceased pontiff. Pope Lucian rose heavenwards, grace of magneto-gravitational technology, ascending sedately to the open square in the ceiling.

The Exaltation increased in acceleration as the body neared the roof, prefiguring the imminent launch of the pope through the stratosphere and into star-dusted space.

With the departure of the pontiff, the panel slid shut. For a time, the seven remained silent. Then Cardinal Maroc stood up and addressed the brethren: 'Our silent farewells are completed. The time of mourning is over. Now is the time for action — immediate action. News has come to us that the one called the Doctor, far from being the fool he pretended, is a threat to the delicate balance of Europa, and to the very heart of the Vatican itself.'

Agostini stirred in his seat. 'Are you sure of this?'

'Certain. All forces must be mobilized to hunt him down.'

'Locating the Doctor will not be a straightforward matter if he's aided by the Dominoes,' Richelieu said.

'Indeed,' nodded Maroc. 'That is why I propose total war on the Dominoes. No more skirmishes and diplomatic dealing. Look where it's brought us — the pope murdered in his own chambers by Dominoes, or their agents. I advocate the complete extermination of the subversives. And top of the list — the Doctor.'

'An extermination policy will turn many of the Dominions against us,' Richelieu warned.

'Then we'll exterminate them too!' exploded Torquemada, springing from the pew.

Richelieu raised a calming hand. 'Before we rush into mass slaughter, I'd require the source of your information on the Doctor, and what kind of threat he represents.'

'Amen to that,' said Agostini.

Maroc smiled at Cardinal Richelieu. 'My source? If you'd care to meet him, he's just outside the door.'

'You can't bring an outsider into a Conclave

Extraordinary!' exclaimed Cardinal Altzinger, who up until now, true to form, had sat and observed in silence. 'It would be sacrilege.'

'Not this outsider,' Maroc said. '*Introibo!*' he called to the Doors Beatific.

The bronze doors swung wide, revealing a slender man in a white cassock and white skull-cap. He advanced with steady paces.

The Enclave members, all but Maroc, shrank back from the approaching figure as though it were an apparition.

'A ghost,' breathed Rodrigo Borgia.

Agostini stared at the familiar features. 'Pope Lucian,' he whispered.

Eleven

'I once met a man who wore a hat *inside* his head,' the Doctor said. 'Most odd.'

Sarah, hunched over the crackle and sparks of a wood fire, hugged her knees, then pulled back as the hem of the altarboy's cassock started to smoulder.

She resettled, her eyes roving the dense woods surrounding the small glade, black silhouettes against the stars. 'A Black Forest,' she muttered. 'I don't believe it. A Black Forest in northern Italy.'

'Italia,' corrected Byron, standing up from inspecting the Draco. 'And there is a superfluity of Black Forests in Europa.' He glanced down at the Draco. 'We won't risk it,' he decided. 'They'll be watching the sky. The old dragon will be a sitting duck. Once it's light, we'll go on foot until we can lay hands on a mechanical horse or three.'

The Doctor abruptly fell flat on his back, simultaneously pulling the fedora over his face. 'I wholeheartedly agree. Very wise.'

Sarah's gaze returned to the Italian Black Forest, a congregation of tall firs. In the deeps of those trees, the damp, dark silence of the forest. What was in there, the full cast-list of the brothers Grimm? A werewolf prowling through the thickets? A wicked witch with a cooking pot, beckoning to a wide-eyed Hansel and Gretel? The Big Bad Wolf grinning at Little Red Riding Hood?

Or maybe nothing more than your average big, hairy ruffian with a big, shiny axe.

The more she thought about it, the less she felt like a walk in the Black Forest.

The branches of several fir trees shivered, dispensing an unearthly chorus of sighs. '*Echo my echo . . .*' the trees whispered.

She shot to her feet. 'What the hell was that?'

'Tree ghosts,' Byron said casually. 'If you control your fear, they won't approach. So master your fear.'

'And if I don't?'

'I strongly suggest, madam, that you do.'

'They're doubtless arboreal psychic parasites, a form of necrodryad,' the Doctor said. 'The trees absorb moisture. Necrodryads absorb fear.'

Sarah suppressed a shudder. 'Anything else I should know about the Black Forest?'

'Perhaps a bit of a chat's in order,' the Doctor suggested. 'There's nothing better than a good chin-wag to keep the spooks at bay.'

'True enough,' she said, averting her eyes from the surrounding trees. 'And —' She glanced at the poet. '— I think it's time for a few explanations.'

Byron walked from the Draco and squatted down by the fire, warming his hands. Sarah laid a long, hard stare on him. 'It's time. Explanation time.'

'Absolutely,' the Doctor said. 'Time is what it is.'

The poet threw up his hands and sat down. 'Very well. What do you wish to know?'

'Everything,' the Doctor said, the hat muffling his voice. 'In that order.'

Byron chuckled heartily. 'I'll start with Reprises —'

'You mean clones, programmed with a facsimile memory lattice?' the Doctor said into his hat. 'Oh, I figured all that out back in the dungeons of the Inquisition. Tell me about the creation of Europa, its political checks and balances — that sort of thing.'

'Excuse me,' Sarah interrupted, waving a hand. 'I'm here. Can't you see me?'

'Difficult not to, altargirl,' Byron riposted.

'*I* want to learn about Reprises, if that's OK by all and sundry.'

'Fine by me,' the Doctor shrugged.

The lord mulled it over for a space, then lay back, folding his arms. 'Reprises it is. As the Doctor said, Reprises are clones encoded with virtual memories from a data bank. The historical data bank is known as the Chronopticon. It transfers a cognitive/perceptual matrix of an historical character's life into a newly formed clone of that same character.'

She began to see where this was leading. 'Now that definitely isn't Regency speech,' she observed quietly.

'Indeed. I'm not from the early nineteenth century. I was – created – in the middle of the thirty-third century, and implanted with memories, instincts, drives reconstructed from the Chronopticon's Byron archive. My first clear memory as a Reprise is dying of a fever at Missolonghi. His last memory was my first.'

The lord's face betrayed nothing as he stared up at the vivid stars. 'I was cloned from a single hair of George Gordon, Lord Byron. And other Byrons were cloned with me.' His mouth bent in a rueful smile. 'One was created from a toenail clipping. When he discovered that uninspiring fact, he was never quite the same man again.'

'Dispiriting news that, learning you were made out of a toenail,' the Doctor said into his hat.

Sarah felt a rush of sympathy for Byron – pseudo-Byron – whatever he was. She wondered how she'd take it if told that she had been cloned from a hair, and that all her memories, everything she thought of as herself, was an artificial creation, a scientific construct. A frightening prospect.

I'd feel desouled . . .

'Echo my echo . . .' the trees sighed.

She pulled herself up abruptly. The necrodryads had homed in on her faint sensation of dread. Better watch herself, or they'd be coming for her.

'I remember my mother when I was a child in Aberdeen,' Byron was saying, his tone subdued. 'I remember Newstead Abbey after my mad great-uncle died. I remember Harrow. Oxford. Swimming the Hellespont. I remember the Villa Diodati, where Mary Shelley started to write *Frankenstein: the Modern Prometheus*. I remember dying. But none of it happened to me. I wasn't there.'

His voice came from a remote, lonely place. 'We are all Frankenstein's monsters, we Reprises.'

He shook himself, regaining what she now understood was a façade of bravado. 'And to the Devil we go, ship and crew. There are just three of us Byrons left. We distinguished one from another by Lady Caroline's frustrated bleat: mad, bad, dangerous. Mad Byron moved to Transylvania. Bad Byron rarely leaves the Villa Diodati. And I, as you'll have gathered, am Dangerous Byron.'

'But you all turned out differently,' the Doctor said, abruptly sitting up and thrusting the hat back on his head. 'Month by month you diverged, changed by each diverse decision. You were created the same, but you made yourself into unique individuals.'

'Overstating the case, Doctor, but I thank you. True enough, there *are* differences. Mad Byron became obsessed with vampirism, Bad Byron with the Marquis de Sade tradition. And I . . .' The voice tailed off.

'You identified with Byron the humanist,' Sarah said. 'The man who stood up in the House of Lords and defended the Nottingham weavers against the millowners. The man who died trying to aid the Greeks in their struggle with the occupying Turks.'

Byron sat up and gave a bow. 'Your selectivity flatters me, madam. You have omitted the multitudinous scandals of my pre-existence, and you know nothing of my amorous exploits as a Reprise. Nevertheless, I thank you, and regret my earlier *hauteur* in our dealings.'

'Forget it,' she smiled. 'I'm not so blameless. I said some pretty trite things. Mouthing off. And I haven't even thanked you for saving our lives.'

'No thanks expected,' he drawled, the byronic Byron

once more. 'And I've chattered too much about myself. Many other historical figures were Reprised. My friend, Percy Shelley — a dozen of him — and Mary, his lover. There were clutches of Casanovas, Cyrano de Bergeracs, Torquemadas, a Cardinal Richelieu who killed off all his duplicates, Marquis de Sades, Goethes, Mozarts, Beethovens, Tchaikovskys, Metternichs, Leonardo da Vincis, Emily Brontës — the list is interminable. Reprises, in general, behave in accordance with their historical prototypes. Some became moving forces in the government of Dominions, others sided with the Vatican, and a great many formed a confraternity of adventurers, opposed to the Vatican and the more oppressive Dominions. This confraternity became known as the Dominoes, after its members' custom of wearing the *domino* cloak and eye-mask whenever they met in secret.'

'You know, I'm a bit in the dark about these Dominions,' Sarah interrupted, still trying not to dwell on those damn necrodryads in those damn night trees. 'What are they, nation states?'

'One topic at a time, or your head will start spinning,' he said. 'Apart from authentic Reprises, there were also a number of fictional recreations. The Four Musketeers were "reprised" from cells taken from four twentieth-century film actors who played the roles of Athos, Porthos —'

'Not the Richard Lester films?' Sarah butted in. 'Were the actors Oliver Reed, Frank Finlay, Richard Chamberlain and — Michael York?'

'Yes, I think they were. The actors' clones were encoded with personality-matrices extrapolated from the films.'

'God . . .' she exclaimed. 'Michael York is running around thirty-third century France as d'Artagnan! And as for Oliver Reed . . .'

Journalist though she was, words failed her.

* * *

He rode a mechanical horse to Liechtenstein, the steed's robotic legs making light work of the Transylvanian lanes.

Miles Dashing had appropriated the horse from the stables of a disreputable-looking mansion whose walls were splashed with blood and decorated with impaled trespassers. Any household who saw fit to behave in that sort of manner didn't deserve to keep a mechanical horse, which was in a shamefully neglected condition, creaking with rust.

The sleeping vampires within the mansion hadn't stirred as he quietly led the steed from the hushed precincts. That had been an hour ago, shortly before true sunset, and the Transylvanian border, at its long western arm that extended over ancient Austria, was mere minutes away. The walls of Liechtenstein's citadel of Vaduz were already in sight.

'Soon be there, Oberon,' he said to his freshly named horse. 'A dash of oil for you and a bite of food for myself in some suitable hostelry.'

The steed, covered in synthetic equinehide that partially disguised its metal joints, giving a rudimentary imitation of a jerky, organic horse, grated its neck-joints as it turned its head to Miles. It gave a convincing whinny, then put its head down and got on with the task of galloping.

Oberon, as its design revealed to Miles's expert eye, was manufactured in Britannia Edwardiana – most mechanical horses were, major export – and you couldn't beat Britannian workmanship. The mechanical beast's period of neglect on foreign soil hadn't impaired the steed's mechanisms one jot.

'Oh, well done, Oberon!' Miles congratulated, sighting the border some hundred strides down the lane. The Switzia border was marked with a continuous fence bedecked with preserved garlic plants. The plants were more of a warning than a defence against vampires, a warning that Nosferatu accustomed to Transylvania's necrotic atmosphere were likely to perish if they transgressed the boundaries of the living.

Miles threw a backward look as Oberon raced towards Switzia. And caught sight of a shadow, denser than the night, black on black, speeding on raven wings.

Byron's Ipsissimus Shadow, in hot pursuit.

'Too late, shade of Mad Byron!' Miles called out, waving a hand as the horse leaped the fence. 'Remain forever in your benighted domain.'

The Ipsissimus Shadow slid to a stop at the boundary.

'*Cat lick your heart*,' it seethed, its shape distorting with the rage of frustration.

Miles kept darting the occasional glance over his shoulder, just in case, but the shadow remained on his side of the fence, impotent.

Long before Miles approached the walls of Liechtenstein's citadel he had put the vampire to the back of his mind. Other priorities demanded attention. A bed for the night, and then the long ride to the Villa Diodati. As in most Dominions, there was a price on his head in this Switzian fiefdom, but he trusted his sword against any soldier of Vaduz.

'And I must acquire a servant,' he muttered to himself. His last servant had been crushed to death during the devastating appearance of the Dutch Mountain, that eerie, Dominion-rambling peak sprung from the metapsyche of the ancient Dutch.

Riding through the gateway, he hailed a passing commoner. 'Hey, fellow, is there a hostelry nearby, preferably run by a Britannian host?'

The scrawny yokel scratched his thin beard, then launched into a spate of German.

Miles gave a low groan. He'd forgotten to turn on his polyglot, the micro-translator embedded inside his ear. Polyglots, useful as the devices were in multilingual Europa, reduced the variety of languages to a thin, logicogrammatical gruel, and degraded everyday sounds to a monotonous buzz. He kept the blasted thing turned off as often as possible.

'What was that again?' he said, polyglot reactivated.

'There's a Britannian inn second lane on the right. Name of The Questing Beast,' gruffed the commoner.

Miles headed his steed in the direction indicated, tossing a coin to his informant. 'There's a florin for your pains, fellow.'

'What use is a bloody florin to me?' the man complained vehemently. 'This isn't bloody Florence!'

Miles gave a dismissive swish of the hand. 'Away with you, bumpkin.'

A colourful stream of abuse followed in his tracks, which he studiously ignored.

A short canter took him to The Questing Beast where he whistled up an ostler to oil the mechanical horse before striding into the parlour.

'Your pleasure is my pleasure, God bless ye, sir,' greeted the paunchy, thick-bearded inn-keeper, greasy hands rubbing the apron over his frilled shirt.

'Regency Britannian?' Miles guessed, turning off his polyglot.

'That I am, sir.'

'Cornwall man, by the edge of your speech and the cut of your jib,' Miles said, adopting a jocular air.

'That's a sharp eye and ear you've got there, sir. Penwallis is the name, from close by Nampara Cove, Master Ross Poldark's property.'

'I'm acquainted with your former master. A gallant gentleman. Now, before I take advantage of supper and bed, would there be any chance of acquiring a Britannian servant in the vicinity of your redoubtable hostelry?'

Penwallis threw up his hands. 'We've got Britannian servants galore for a blue-blood such as yourself, sir. There's half a dozen of them guzzling this very moment in the Toby Jug Room. By the time you've quaffed a draught of my finest ale, they'll be lined up for your inspection.'

Miles sat on a stool, accepted the proffered flagon of

ale, and took a deep draught, closing his eyes as the cool liquid trickled down his parched throat.

On opening his eyes, he witnessed six men shuffling into line in front of him. The inn-keeper was a man of his word.

Miles instantly waved away two applicants. Although lacking his height, they were too tall to accentuate his stature. Then he dismissed two more: their skin diseases looked infectious.

Studying the remaining pair, he addressed the taller and younger man. 'Have you any education, fellow?'

'None at all, sir. Pig-ignorant.'

Miles observed him shrewdly. 'I detect mendacity in your repudiation of scholarship.'

'No, sir! I'm not lying about my ignor—' The man winced, his mouth forming a wry twist. 'I walked straight into that one, didn't I?'

'Indeed you did. The vocabulary of my previous sentence would have been quite beyond an ignoramus. Your services are not required.'

Miles assessed the remaining candidate. He was short, fat, balding, and about fifty. In appearance, most suitable. But as for mentality . . .

'Do you have an imagination?'

The man scratched his flaking scalp. 'Dunno. Have to think about that one.'

'Who was your last master?'

'Haven't got one. Nobody would have me.'

Miles nodded his approval. 'Ignorance and desperation. An ideal combination in a manservant. You're hired. The wages are a penny a day, with a bonus for exceptionally hazardous enterprises. You also get to eat my left-overs. And, of course, I'll supply you with a mechanical pony.'

'A pony!' the man gasped. 'Can I – can I ride it?'

'That would be the general idea. So, fellow, what do you call yourself?'

'Crocker, if that's all right with you, sir.'

'Well, Crocker, you will address me as either sir or Master Dashing. Tonight you will sleep outside my door and then wake me an hour before dawn with a cup of Olde English tea. For the present, you may depart and resume drinking with others of your station.'

Crocker bobbed up and down in gratitude as he quitted the parlour.

Miles downed another draught of ale, and reflected on the journey ahead. First, locate Byron. After that, take on the might of the Catholic Church Apostolic, a daunting prospect for even the most foolhardy of Dominoes.

But, for tonight, a little rest. Peace before the storm.

The Shadow leaned over the Switzian border fence, gradually acclimatizing itself to the zoic air of mortal lands.

It had been a Transylvanian vampire for a mere few months, and was not yet dependent on that Dominion's necrotic atmosphere.

Centimetre by centimetre, the Shadow Ipsissimus eased over the fence, enduring the agony of transition for the sake of a single, fixed purpose.

Track down Miles Dashing.

At all costs.

Sarah leaned forward eagerly. 'About Michael York . . .'

'Sarah,' the Doctor broke in gently. 'I'd say a sketchy overview of this world would be rather handy, wouldn't you?'

'Sorry. It's just that I have this thing about Michael York . . .' She glanced at Byron, and was instantly ashamed of her lapse. Reprises, fictional or historical, might be an entertaining prospect viewed from the outside, but to *be* a Reprise, aware that all your pre-Reprisal memories were manufactured — it was monstrous.

She averted her gaze, eyes scanning the encircling forest, then wished she'd kept her stare aimed at the fire.

The injunction *not* to be scared had the opposite effect, unless you kept your mind on another topic, and that was no simple matter, what with fear-scenting necrodryads out there in the dark.

'*Echo my echo . . .*' issued the frailest of breaths from the trees.

Think of something else . . .

'Sorry,' she said again, attention fixed firmly on the crackling fire. 'You're right, we need an overview.'

'How about starting with Europa's foundation, George?' the Doctor invited.

'As you wish,' Byron nodded, settling down by the camp-fire. 'Europa was fashioned over two centuries ago from Earth's ruins by a cabal from the Overcities, a cabal later dubbed the Concocters. The Concocters were a mixture of genius and insanity, with both elements reflected in their Concoction: Europa. For various reasons, they restricted Europa's time period from the late fourteenth century to the early twentieth. Europe was remodelled on a grand scale: new Alps were raised, new copies of old lakes were formed, new imitations of old rivers. In Europa, there are several Lake Comos, Lake Genevas and Lough Neaghs, and numerous Rhines, Seines, Danubes. Black Forests here, there, everywhere. The aim was to accommodate each nation's sundry time periods somewhere in Europa. In all, there are five Britannias, reflecting different eras. The general idea was recolonization from the Overcities – choose your favourite historical period.'

'It's a bloody great Theme Park!' Sarah exclaimed.

Byron glanced at her uncertainly. 'But the Concocters didn't stop there . . .' he murmured.

'No indeed,' the Doctor said. 'They concocted a supernatural realm through psychotronic engineering. A realm based on old European folklore.'

'That's so. In Europa, vampires walk, right out of the storybooks. Werewolves prowl. Ghosts of considerable variety haunt hearth and home, wood and wild. Witches dance on the blasted heath. Demons from the *Malleus Maleficarum* and angels from the *Zohar* come visiting at all hours. Through science, the Concocters invented the supernatural.'

'Fascinating,' the Doctor said. 'Remarkable. It truly is. There's just one thing strikingly wrong about that account.'

'Oh – what?'

'The psychotronic and chronoptic expertise is far too advanced, light-and-dark-years ahead of thirty-first century Earth technology. The sole origin for a technology of that character and magnitude is, well, a planet I used to know.'

Sarah observed the Doctor's expression, secretive, a touch regretful. She knew that look. He was thinking of home.

'Gallifrey?' Sarah ventured.

His strange, penetrating leer was never more pronounced. 'Yes, Sarah. Gallifrey.'

The suddenness with which he fell back to the ground startled her. He slid his rumpled fedora over his eyes. His voice was distant: 'Faces within faces . . .'

'Doctor, a small observation,' she began delicately. 'Since the Sistine Chapel your moods have see-sawed, even by your standards. That Michelangelo fresco. The wrinkled face on St Benedict's hand. Did you recognize it?'

'It was a face in constant change.'

Constant change? Looked fixed enough to her. 'It must have been altering itself at a pretty slow rate.'

'Rather slower than the hour hand on a clock,' he said. 'Too gradual for you to spot in a brief observation.'

'So, what did the changing face remind you of?'

'Transmogrification.'

She couldn't tell if that was a reply or the Doctor's private musing. Behind his blue eyes, he was a universe away, where she couldn't hope to reach. Most of the time it was easy to forget that the Doctor was an alien, a

Gallifreyan, but at times like this it was hard to recall his apparent humanity, his downright *Britishness*.

'There's a Theatre of Transmogrification,' Byron said, gazing intently at the Doctor. '*Grand guignol*, dripping with gore, spectacular in presentation. The plays, however, are execrable.'

'About the Dominoes –' Sarah began.

'About the plays –' the Doctor said. Sarah cursed inwardly.

'– are the dramas established works, or freshly penned?' he continued.

'They're penned by the Dramaturge,' Byron replied. 'Playwright, producer, director rolled into one, under the name of Doctor Sperano.'

'*Dum spiro, Sperano*,' the Doctor declaimed, then winced. 'Gosh, what a ghastly pun. I'm sorry I said it now. This Doctor Sperano – doesn't go in for the classics then?'

'Shakespeare *et al.*? Not at all. In fact, the great Elizabethan and Jacobean dramas are rarely performed anywhere. The Vatican, and most Dominions, have prohibited their performance. To my unceasing disgust, the populace abjectly acquiesce to this suppression. Thomas Kyd, Christopher Marlowe, Will Shakespeare, Ben Jonson, John Webster – all proscribed.'

The Doctor slid a finger across his lower lip. 'Hmm . . . English dramatists of the Elizabethan and Jacobean periods were given the chop. For Shakespeare, the unkindest cut of all.' He sat up suddenly, hat planted firmly back on his head. '*All* dramatists of that era, you say.'

'That's what I said. I listed only the more famous, but lesser talents came under the axe.'

The Doctor mulled that one over, then seemed to shoot off at a tangent. 'So, what sort of plays does this Doctor Sperano write?'

Byron snorted. 'The titles should suffice. *Three Gentlemen of Venice on a Killing Spree – Edward II's Horrible*

End – Vampires: the Froth and the Frenzy – The Blood Countess of Transylvania – The Adventures of Macbeth's Head – and multitudes more such worthless works, five, maybe six hundred *in toto*. His next work, much trumpeted as a magnum opus, is *Thirteenth Night*.'

The Doctor's expression was enigmatic. 'I hear the ringing of bells. Memory's bells. Are you familiar with the deeds of the Blood Countess of Transylvania, George?'

'How would I not be familiar with one of the most notorious women in history? Countess Elizabeth Bathory, widow of Count Nadasay, and blood-relation to the kings of Poland and Transylvania. She slaughtered some three hundred women and bathed in their blood in the maniacal belief that the ritual had rejuvenating properties. After her trial and conviction in 1611, she was walled up alive in her castle.'

The Doctor nodded, uncharacteristically sombre. 'Yes, I remember. Elizabeth Bathory made an art-form of sadism. She engaged a German clock-smith to manufacture a mechanical device in the shape of a red-haired girl, wearing teeth extracted from the mouth of a servant-girl. She called the metal female Incarnadine. Incarnadine was designed to grip any girl pushed against it in a close embrace, activating spikes that sprang from the device's breasts. The blood was gathered in a channel and heated for the Countess's bath tub. There was a girl . . .' The sentence trailed into silence.

The silence lengthened, relieved only by the crackling of burning branches.

'I read about that device when I was researching an article a couple of years back,' Sarah said hesitantly, watching the Doctor's face for any tell-tale hints. It was easy to misinterpret his facial signs, but she sensed a buried phobia in his expression, an underlying magma of nightmare. 'One gruesome lady,' she prompted. 'Hammer made a film about her: *Countess Dracula*.'

'The film, although it has merit, hardly skimmed the surface,' the Doctor murmured absently, staring into the murk of the Black Forest. 'Castle Bathory and the Countess held more secrets than were revealed at the trial. She appeared middle-aged to her judges, but appearances, as they say, can be deceptive.'

'You were there, weren't you,' Sarah said. 'At the trial. In Castle Bathory. Was it that time you dropped me off in Skye for a couple of days?'

Byron was staring intently at the Doctor. 'The clockwork device in the shape of a female is part of the historical record. Its name is not. The name of Incarnadine was mentioned neither in the trial nor the tales surrounding it. You evidently possess some form of time-vehicle, Doctor. I've heard of such contraptions, but never seen proof of one.'

'You will,' the Doctor said, still lost in introspection. 'If I can retrieve it from Vatican City.'

'Doctor . . .' Sarah insisted. 'What happened to you in Castle Bathory?'

He lowered his gaze, haunted by the past. 'It's a long, monstrous story, and one best left untold.'

He slumped forwards, elbows propped on knees. She barely caught his hoarse whisper. 'Bathory . . . Kelley . . . Pearson . . . Faces within faces . . .'

Startled by his abnormally dark mood, she stretched round the fire and gripped his arm. 'Doctor – what's wrong?'

'*Echo my echo . . .*'

The rustling whisper of the fir trees prickled her skin, tingled her maze of nerves. Something bad was coming her way.

'I told you to control your fear!' Byron snapped, jumping to his feet.

'It's not my fear,' Sarah said, glancing at the Doctor. 'It's his.'

The Doctor rose to his feet. 'I'm sorry, Sarah. We have our nightmares on Gallifrey, you know. We have our nightmares.' He shook off his malaise. 'And now we have necrodryads to deal with.'

'ECHO MY ECHO...'

The susurration blew into her ears like a swarm of tiny leaves. She shook her head violently but the dark woodland spell drifted round and round in her skull.

Through cloudy vision, she saw the Doctor rummaging furiously through his pockets. 'I might just have it,' he muttered. 'You never know. Serendipity was always my strong suit.'

She barely caught his words. Her gaze was drawn to the black silhouettes of the fir trees. Second by second, the Black Forest trees lost their blackness. A silver radiance emanated from branch and bole.

The forest was lighting up.

A circle of silver luminescence formed around the glade.

The Doctor, fishing inside his overcoat for something or other, darted a look at the shining fir trees. 'Ah yes, the psionic law of correspondences. Trees of the variety *abies alba* – silver firs.'

Byron was busy booting the camp-fire in every direction. 'Doctor! Sarah!' he shouted. 'Make yourself useful. Kick the branches into a circle, then jump into the middle!'

'I'm otherwise engaged,' the Doctor said. 'But making a ring of fire will give the necrodryads pause – wood spirits aren't too fond of flames. Go to it, Sarah.'

She didn't feel like arguing. Hoisting her cassock, she hopped into a spot already cleared by Byron and laid into the branches, doing her best to kick them into a rough circle.

Busy about her work, she still couldn't fail to notice the mounting brilliance of the silver trees. Or the decorations on the boughs. Each fir was bedecked with myriads of baubles and bangles. '*ECHO MY ECHO!*' they jangled.

'Christmas trees!' she exclaimed. 'With *decorations*.'

'It's the eighth night after Christmas,' Byron grunted. 'The decorations don't come down until Twelfth Night.'

'Huh?' Weird. 'They sure as hell weren't there before.'

'That was before a psionic storm was stirred up,' he snapped. 'Now keep kicking those logs. They're coming . . .'

'Who? Oh – yes . . .'

The shiny bark was peeling off the firs, revealing yet another layer of bark beneath. 'An extra skin,' she breathed.

'A parasitic skin,' Byron said. 'Malevolent and versatile.'

The doffed strips of bark congealed into clumps. And the clumps morphed into palpitating stick men, standing one to each tree, surrounding the glade.

The camp-fire had been redistributed into the roughest of rings, with more gaps than burning tinder.

Byron glared at the figures of bark. 'The patchy fire ring won't keep them at bay for long. They'll already be probing the gaps. We've got to come up with something . . .' He shifted his glare to the Doctor, who had just jumped into the circle. 'Anything up your sleeve?'

The Doctor was still searching inside his overcoat with mounting frenzy. 'More a matter of pockets, George,' he said in a flustered tone. 'Don't normally carry it with me, but I could have sworn I had it. Where is the blasted thing?'

Sarah leaned towards Byron. 'Those necrodryads, when are they going to attack?'

'Any moment now.'

'They're just standing there,' she said, scanning the figures beneath the trees.

'They won't move from the host tree. They don't need to. But they can touch you, and when they do, they'll pump sap into your veins, and absorb you into themselves. You'll become one of them.'

'Pleasant thought,' she said, giving an involuntary shudder. 'But if they don't *move* . . .'

In unison, the necrodryads raised an arm, each arm pointing at the trio inside the circle of flame.

Then the arms stretched into slim branches, reaching

to the centre of the glade. A hundred elongating limbs approached with increasing rapidity. The supple limbs, tentacular in motion, extended twig fingers hooked into barbs.

One arm looped around the Draco, and whiplashed the vehicle clean over the tree tops. It spun out of sight, and landed somewhere with a crash that sent echoes flying into the forest.

'God!' Sarah whispered hoarsely. 'The strength of the things. And there goes any chance of escape.'

A limb sneaked through a gap in the ring, creaky hand clutching, thorns protruding from the fingers.

'How long do they take to pump you full of sap?' Sarah heard her voice shake like a – leaf.

'Seconds,' Byron replied, drawing his sabre. 'But I'll spare you that, madam. I'll cut off your head.'

The Doctor searched frantically inside his overcoat. 'Where is the blasted thing!'

A hundred thorny hands shot to their targets.

Byron swung his sabre at Sarah's neck.

Twelve

Rapiers flashed and clashed in the candlelight.

The two duellists sprang back and circled one another in the enormous crypt of the Palazzo Intaglio, its stepped walls thronged with thousands of candles in hundreds of candelabra.

Maria Fiore stood amongst a crowd of spectators, hand clutching her breast as she followed the midnight duel.

Casanova, dressed in a white silk shirt and black velvet breeches, weaved his rapier as he studied his opponent, who wore identical attire. 'A hit,' he said, eyeing the rip in his adversary's sleeve. 'A palpable hit.'

Casanova glanced down at the rent in his sleeve. 'An expensive shirt is ruined,' he said. 'But the skin bears not the slightest scratch.'

Casanova gave a gracious bow. 'I accept your word, although I suspect at least a pin-prick. Shall we retire for a glass of Madeira before resuming?'

'A kind offer, but I must decline. Five breaks for a tipple in as many minutes is quite sufficient. Let us allow another minute, and if I've not killed you by then I'll join you in a glass.'

'Agreed. *En garde*, sir.'

'*En garde!*'

Rapiers flickered.

'Would you take your hat off, please, miss?' piped up a short man behind Signora Sforza at the back of the spectators. 'Can't see a bloody thing.'

'Silence, runt,' she sniffed, fluffing up the feathers on her hat.

The Casanovas darted in and out, rapiers blurring as the two executed a nimble dance of death.

A nobleman nudged Maria Fiore, who was watching the contest in a mixture of concern and confusion. 'Well matched, aren't they, signora?'

She fluttered a haughty fan. 'Well, they would be, wouldn't they? And keep your hands to yourself.'

'Could you take your hat off, please!'

Signora Sforza stretched herself up to full height.

A swift lunge from one Casanova drew a gasp from the crowd. The thrust came within a centimetre of the other Casanova's jugular.

'I could do that,' said a podgy man, nodding at the two Casanovas. 'Got the speed and everything. You should see me practise on my own. Reflexes like lightning. Run rings around any Casanova, you just see if I don't.'

'Oh, shut up,' Maria snorted.

The Casanovas sprang simultaneously, swords extended. One Casanova withdrew, blood on the tip of his blade. The other peered at the hole in his chest, spurting rich red.

'Oh,' the wounded duellist said. 'Straight through the heart. My compliments on your accuracy, sir.' Then he fell flat on his face.

The victorious Casanova gave the vanquished Casanova a deep bow. 'You go to your Maker with impeccable manners, sir.'

'What happened?' piped up a voice from the back. 'Can't see a bloody thing.'

Casanova blew Maria Fiore a kiss, flung on his cape, and swept up the stairs, hand circling in farewell.

'Why won't you take your bloody hat off? What happened? Who won?'

The spectators exchanged glances. Good question. Who won?

Casanova emerged from the crypt of the Palazzo Intaglio and hurried through the thick mist to a branch of the Grand Canal.

Leaning over an arched bridge, he peered into the swirling vapour. No sign of a gondola.

'Damn you, Antonio,' he hissed. 'Where are you?'

'Under the bridge, sir,' a voice called up.

The prow of a gondola nosed out and slid over the waters, steered by a young gondolier.

'Hurry,' Casanova urged. 'When the Doge gets wind of my duelling I'll be a dead duck.'

'Better a dead duck than a live chicken, sir.'

'As no one is in a position to consult a dead duck, the point must remain debatable.'

Passwords exchanged, the gondolier gave a nod of recognition. 'Congratulations on winning the duel, sir.'

He heaved on the oar, and the gondola ascended from the canal, hovering on a level with the bridge parapet. Casanova leaped in and settled into a padded chair. 'Take me out of here, fast. How far can you glide before committing major anachronism crime?'

Antonio stroked his chin. 'Well, Austria Hapsburg has recently extended its boundaries. Can't take you more than twenty kilometres past Porto Maghera – and that's pushing it.'

'Then let's go!'

The glide-gondola coasted over the bridge and gathered speed as it cornered into the Grand Canal and flew at a constant ten metres' altitude above the waves.

'I feel a song coming on,' said Antonio.

'If it's *O Sole Mio*, you'll find my rapier stuck in your throat.'

'I've never sung an anachronistic song in my life!' the gondolier protested. 'What about an air from *La Serva Padrona*?'

'As you will. But don't expect a tip.'

'In that case I won't bother. Where are you headed?'

Casanova stretched back in the chair and closed his eyes. 'The Villa Diodati, by way of Castle Ludwig,' he murmured, half to himself.

* * *

'A chamber with a mushroom-shaped console,' said the pope. 'From your expertise in these matters, Maroc, would you say this was the contraption's main control room?'

'This, or that wood-panelled room just down the passage,' Maroc said, gazing around the white interior of the blue box, its defences recently circumvented. 'The rest of the rooms appear to be for living or storage space. As for the total size of the interior, I couldn't even guess. For all I know, the plasmic shell of the box might contain a private universe.' Breaking off his speculations, he adopted a dutiful air. 'Holiness, the rest of the Enclave is still somewhat shaken by what they regard as your miraculous return. I explained that a clone must have been killed in your place while you were confined by unknown abductors, but –'

'We'll deal with the matter in the Hall Excelsior,' Lucian said curtly. 'Call a meeting for one hour's time. As for now – this cornucopia in so small a container . . .'

The pope inspected the console, peering at the central column, then straightened and stared at the inner door, leading to an apparently limitless number of corridors, one allowing access to a lake-sized swimming pool. 'An exceptional example of Dimensions Extraordinary, would you think?'

Maroc prowled the control room, inspecting this, experimenting with that. 'Far beyond our world's understanding of Dimensions Extraordinary. I would suggest an alien origin. Why won't the controls respond?'

'Some form of lock is in operation, I presume. Have the Dimensions Extraordinary department work on it, eminence. Perhaps you would ask them to set about the task immediately? Oh, and ensure they seal it off while at work – I don't want the entire Vatican staff wandering in and out, and that includes the Enclave.'

Taking his cue to depart, Maroc bowed and walked to the outer door, whose rectangle framed the Crypt of the Seven Sleepers. 'Oh, a moment,' the pope called out. 'For now, let's keep the news of my survival within the

Vatican Curia. Let Europa believe I've been murdered. It will ensure greater security while the matter is being investigated. Have the Enclave swear an oath to preserve silence.'

'Yes, Holiness,' acknowledged Maroc, then made his exit.

Pope Lucian stood in the dormant chamber, still as a statue, trying to attune his mind to the psychic resonance at the core of this world in a box.

'A Pandora's box?' he wondered aloud. 'Well, good or bad, its secrets must be uncovered. Where there's a lock, there's a key.'

The door gave a faint creak and Miles Dashing instantly awoke and sprang out of bed, sword drawn.

Crocker crept into the bedroom, bobbing up and down in apology. 'Pardon me for intruding, sir. Some sort of supernatural shadow on its way up the stairs, sir.'

'What! The Ipsissimus...' Miles darted a glance around the room, taking in the small square of the window. 'Right, Crocker, take all my luggage and meet me at the nearest *schloss*.'

He kicked open the window and whistled for Oberon, frowning his anger at Crocker's whining complaint.

'What about me, sir? It's an 'orrible thing...'

'It's after me, not you, you fool. Get a mechanical pony and be about your business.'

'You haven't got me a pony yet!' Crocker yelled, approaching falsetto.

'There's money in the red leather bag.'

Crocker, instantly calm, broke into a broad grin. 'Money. Oh – that's all right then.'

A living shadow reared behind the grinning servant. '*Cat lick your heart...*' said a voice from the grave.

'Yikes!' squealed Crocker, ducking for cover.

Miles gave the Shadow Ipsissimus a flourish of the hand in farewell. 'Dawn's not far off, and I'm away ere break of day.'

He slipped through the window and dropped two storeys to land plumb on his horse's saddle, the impact cushioned by the inflatable crutch-pad in his trousers.

'Full gallop,' he instructed the steed.

Oberon sped off, almost dislodging the rider from his seat.

Within ten breaths the citadel gates came into view. Locked and bolted.

'I hate to do this,' Miles muttered, drawing his Hellfire pistol. 'But needs must.'

He pressed the trigger, and fired an explosive bullet. The missile zinged into the sturdy gates and blasted them to smithereens. Reeling in the shock-waves, Miles was carried by his steed out and under the archway.

'Hey!' shouted a voice from the ruined gateway. 'That'll cost you!'

Miles hardly made sense of the caution. His wits were on a spinning wheel.

Shaking his dazed head, he looked back along the road.

The Shadow Ipsissimus was right on his tracks. '*What's in a name, Slime . . .*' it soughed.

Wits restored, Miles shot a glance at the eastern horizon. Not a glimmer of pre-dawn. And the road ahead was long and the Shadow close behind.

'*Only commoners run . . .*' breezed the vast voice.

That did it.

'Halt!' Miles commanded.

Oberon slowed to a stop. Tugging the reins, Miles turned the horse, drawing his sword. The metal blade was no threat to the anti-light vampire, but Miles would at least perish sword in hand.

'No one,' said Miles, 'calls me a commoner. If I die, I die as Earl Dashwood of Dashwood, trusty blade in sturdy grip.'

The Shadow Ipsissimus wafted to a stop, hovering a few short paces from its target.

'*What's in a name, Slime . . .*'

'Call me by my name, or not at all!' Miles demanded. 'The Dashwoods don't suffer insolence gladly, you — shadow of a man. Come, do your worst!'

'*Your name*', said the shade, its outline acquiring the form of Byron, '*is a clue to the puzzle.*'

'Puzzle?'

'*I'm limited by my Nosferatu state. I must speak in riddles — and code.*'

Miles kept a firm grip on his épée. 'I'm not with you.'

'*Your name, Slime . . .*'

'My name is Miles, you hell-spawn.'

'*Yes. Miles. Think about it, Slime . . .*'

'How dare you —' he began, then thought about it. 'Miles — Slime . . . Oh, Slime's an anagram of Miles. But — to what?'

'*You asked me a question. I've answered it, as far as I'm permitted.*'

'What question? Answered what? What answer? Oh, enough of games. Come for me — I'll meet you with a blade in my hand and a taunt on my lips.'

'*I offer no threat. I wished to find you, before the Byron in me fades once more. I lost myself in Borgo cemetery, and sought your destruction. I've regained myself for a brief space. I've given you a clue, and I'll give you one more, there's a dark hidden in the name of Dashwood.*'

Miles lowered his sword a fraction. Perhaps a trace of the noble Byron did linger in the Ipsissimus. 'Er, could you speak a little more plainly? Not sure what you're getting at . . .'

'*Adieu, Miles Dashwood, I must return to Transylvania. A last thought — what is the name of the rose?*'

Miles shrugged. 'You tell me.'

'*The name of the rose — is Eros.*'

Miles thought for a moment. 'Name of the rose — Eros. Oh, it's another anagram . . .'

He looked up, but the shadow was lost in the night, trailing a faint, forlorn '*Adieu.*'

He gave a little wave. 'Adieu, Mad Byron.'

Reflecting on the vampire lord's cryptic words, and making neither head nor tail of them, Miles eventually gave a shrug. 'Sort it out some other time.'

He rode back slowly to the citadel, still teased by the enigmatic tidings.

Approaching the shattered gates, he encountered Crocker on a mechanical pony laden with Miles's luggage.

'Hello, sir! You're looking well. Enemy beaten, and all that? Hey, how about this pony — only cost three hundred marks. Oh, talking of cost —' He flicked a stubby thumb over his shoulder at the gateway. 'You'll have to pay a fortune for that, and the guard's on its way to collect.'

Miles straightened his back. 'A gentleman pays his debts.'

'Heard one of the guards say something in the region of twenty thousand marks, including the fine.'

Miles stroked his chin. 'Well,' he muttered. 'They're only foreigners, after all.' He swung the horse round. 'Come, Crocker, we've a long way to ride.'

'May I enquire where to, sir?'

'You may not.'

'Sorry, sir.'

Thirteen

'Got it!'

The Doctor yanked out a flute from an overcoat pocket.

Byron halted his sabre in mid-swing.

Sarah thought she was about to suffer a cardiac arrest.

The elongating arms of the necrodryads faltered, weaving around the circle of fire, twig-fingers flexing.

Maybe they sense the Doctor's confidence, she thought. It'll delay them – for the moment.

Byron stared at the flute, too long for any pocket, and shook his head. 'That's very strange, Doctor.'

'I should say so,' the Doctor replied, eyes big with surprise. 'I was looking for a recorder. Oh well, all the better.' He flashed a smile at his companions. 'Most appropriate, in fact. How's your Shakespeare, Sarah? *Henry VIII*, act three, scene one, lines three to five . . .'

'Haven't a clue,' she grunted, keeping a wary eye on those reaching limbs.

The Doctor's voice switched to recitation mode:

> 'Orpheus with his lute made trees,
> And the mountain tops that freeze,
> Bow themselves when he did sing.'

'Doctor,' she prompted. 'The stick-men with the long arms and thorny fingers and a bad attitude . . .'

Flute hovering near his lips, his gaze skimmed round the encircling figures. 'A flute for a lute, wood warbles to wood,' he said. 'The pipes of Pan would be ideal, but I'll give it a go.'

He placed the instrument to his mouth and blew [a] slow, wistful melody. At first, Sarah kept close watch on the tree ghosts, but the calm, ethereal refrain stole into her spirit. She felt the grass beneath her thin leather shoes. Felt the sap rising. Time slowed.

A nudge from Byron shook off the spell. 'They're motionless, like – wood.'

She scanned the necrodryads. The figures no longer gave an impression of sentience, but reminded her more of bizarre wood sculptures, one outreaching arm fifty times longer than the other.

'A musical charm,' Byron said.

The Doctor lowered the flute. 'A matter of vibrations, George. All matter operates at various levels of vibration. Music can alter the vibrational level. The necrodryads resonate at a higher pitch than the trees. I played music attuned to the slower life of the trees, and I slowed the necrodryads to that same pace. Then, of course, there's the consonance between the wood of the flute and the wood of the trees. Essentially, a transmission of arborification resonance.'

'In short, a musical charm.'

'Yes, that's right, a musical charm.'

'Time to go?' Sarah suggested.

'Too risky, stepping outside the fire circle,' the Doctor said. 'Might stir them up in an instant.'

'How long will your musical charm last?' Byron asked.

'Oh, a few minutes or so, then I'll have to play them to sleep again.'

'It'll be a long night for you, Doctor. Care to pass it in discussion? What about that planet you mentioned – Galumphrey, or whatever it's called.'

The Doctor was staring into the dark behind the ring of shining trees. '*Henry VIII*,' he said.

Byron nodded. 'If it's Shakespeare you want, I'll match you quote for quote. Now if you'd asked *me* about *Henry VIII*, act three, scene one, lines three to five, I'd have supplied chapter and verse, to mix a metaphor.'

The Doctor gave the poet an absent look. '*Henry VIII*, act one, scene one, lines a hundred and forty and a hundred and forty-one.'

Byron blew a sharp breath. 'Now I'll have to run through the whole scene in my head. Give me a while . . .'

'It's not a test,' the Doctor said. This time he recited in a low, quiet tone:

>'Heat not a furnace for your foe so hot
>That it do singe yourself.'

'Singularly apt lines,' Byron remarked, 'considering that the Globe Theatre burned down shortly after they were first delivered.'

'My very thoughts, George. Burned down on the first performance. Will Shakespeare was devastated. I wrote him a letter, saying he had more plays in him, but all he said in reply was that he valued our old friendship.'

Byron looked askance. 'You met Shakespeare?'

'Oh, I've met lots of people. Which brings me back to those proscribed Elizabethan and Jacobean dramatists, and Elizabeth Bathory . . .'

Sarah was troubled by the haunting that returned to the Doctor's face. It had been strong enough to awaken the necrodryads earlier. And if the memory was so terrible that it scared the *Doctor* . . .

'Dramatists. Dramatists. Why bring up that subject again?' Byron snapped.

'Connections, George, connections. Do you know the name of Edward Kelley, a man whose ears were cut off when young?'

'I've heard of him,' Sarah chimed in. 'He was assistant to John Dee, Elizabeth I's astrologer. And – wait – Dee, Kelley and their wives toured the Continent in the 1580s. They were welcomed by the king of Poland, Stephen *Bathory*. King Stephen Bathory, Elizabeth Bathory's blood-relative. So – no, doesn't add up, they weren't around when the Blood Countess started on her murders.

Dee returned to England in 1600 or thereabouts.'

'1589,' the Doctor amended. 'Dee came back. Kelley stayed, wandering Europe, earning a living as a scryer and alchemist. In September of 1610, he was in Prague. So was an obscure English dramatist. Together, they paid a visit to Elizabeth Bathory, to whom Kelley had already been introduced.' His voice sank to a near-inaudible pitch. 'I saw them there. I saw what happened during their stay. I saw the worse that followed after they left.'

The nightmare was back, behind his eyes.

'And you won't talk about that?' Sarah enquired softly.

A slow shake of the head. 'No. I won't talk about that.'

Byron tapped his foot impatiently. 'But you'll talk about connections, I presume? You seem to set great store on a play portraying Elizabeth Bathory. You mention Kelley, an acquaintance of the Countess, and an "obscure English dramatist" who encountered Kelley. Who was this playwright?'

The Doctor stared into the fire. 'Francis Pearson, of Stratford-on-Avon.'

Sarah and Byron exchanged glances, then shrugs. 'Never heard of him,' Sarah admitted, although pondering the Stratford-on-Avon reference.

'Nor I,' said Byron. 'So he *must* be obscure.'

'It might have been otherwise, if his manuscripts hadn't been destroyed in a fire,' the Doctor replied. 'Pearson blamed Shakespeare for the blaze, quite unjustifiably. He'd envied Shakespeare from childhood, and attempted to emulate his fellow-townsman's literary works. The results were a ghastly hash. Pearson's plays were probably the worst excuses for drama ever visited on an audience. For that alone, he would have gone down in history, despite his works never seeing the inside of a theatre. But a furious mob set fire to the wagons of Pearson's travelling troupe of players after an exceptionally dreadful performance in a Warwickshire village. His plays – all thirty of them – went up in smoke in March of 1610.'

'Six months before he met Kelley in Prague,' Sarah cut in. 'OK, I can pick up the connections, but where's all this leading? What's the point?'

'I've reached the point. *The Adventures of Macbeth's Head* was written by Pearson in 1603. *The Blood Countess of Transylvania* was composed in 1612. The Theatre of Transmogrification, purportedly staging newly devised dramas, is presenting plays written seventeen hundred years ago.'

'Lost plays, at that,' Byron mused. 'And from an English dramatist of the proscribed period. But then, perhaps the titles were mentioned in a manuscript kept in some locked chest for centuries, and Doctor Sperano came across them and took them for his own. Come to that, copies of the plays might have survived after all. Who's to say?'

'Sorry, Doctor,' Sarah said. 'I've got to agree. I'm sure there is a point, but I don't see it.'

He stared her straight in the eye. 'What's in a name?'

'That which we call a rose by any other name would smell as sweet,' she completed. '*Romeo and Juliet*, and never mind act, scene and line. What *is* in a name?'

A creak of wood in the night. A rustle of leaves.

'They're waking up again,' the Doctor said, putting the flute to his lips.

As he commenced the melody, Sarah studied his expression. 'That's all he's going to tell us for tonight,' she finally concluded.

Byron appeared dubious. 'How do you know?'

'Because I know him. Believe me, I know him.'

He gave a nod. 'A man's mistress knows the man.'

'What!'

'Yeah! I made out I was thick, and he fell for it!' Crocker chuckled, then took a swig of beer from a *stein* as he sat in the Commoners' Room of the *schloss*.

Guffaws greeted his narrative. A fair number of servants

were knocking back the *steins*, and they had similar stories of masters.

Crocker tapped his bulging pocket. 'Two hundred marks, easy as you please. Told him the pony cost three hundred. And he believed it!'

'No money-sense, these aristos,' said Quirrel, a fellow Britannian. 'Did you tell him you were from Britannia Victoriana? That's their favourite period for servants. I'm from Edwardiana – they're not quite so keen on hiring Edwardians.'

'Nah!' Crocker snorted. 'Told him I was Regency, like himself. Aristos can't tell the difference. We all sound the same to them.'

'Ain't that the truth. Where are you from, mate?'

'Britain. 1920s.'

'Uh-huh. Britannia Perfidia.'

'Less of the Perfidia, pal. And sod all this Britannia bollocks. I'm from Britain. Here – want another pint? I'm not short of the readies, thanks to his lordship.'

'I won't say no, squire. Where you headed? Grand Europan Tour?'

'No. Perilous quest job. My boss is one of those adventurers with a price on his head.'

'Whew, I wouldn't fancy that. Quiet life, me. What's his nibs's name, then?'

'Miles Dashing. Heard of him?'

Quirrel choked on his beer, froth flying. 'Miles-sodding-Dashing!' he finally spluttered. 'God Almighty, you're in for it. I say you're in for it.' While speaking, he made a secret commoner's sign with his fingers that told Crocker to keep his voice low.

'What's up?' Crocker's ruddy face split into a grin. 'He kill the pope or something?'

'No, just wiped out his entire family.'

'Eh?'

'Then joined the Dominoes and got pally with Dangerous Byron. The Vatican has a price on his head that would buy Buck House. Everybody knows that.'

'Nobody told me.'

'Where you been the last two years?'

'Alcoholic stupor.'

'Yeah, well,' shrugged Quirrel. 'That'd explain it. But you must have heard of the bloody Dashwoods.'

Crocker gulped and scratched his head. 'Yeah, course I have. Evil buggers, but what they got to do with the price of bread?'

'Dashing's a Dashwood, you silly sod. Last of the line. Well, he saw to that . . .'

Crocker crossed himself. 'Jeez. The Dashwoods. They were worse than the bloody Mindelmeres. But, hang on, I heard that the young lad – yeah, Miles his name was – turned out to be the white sheep of the family.'

'Well, in a manner of speaking,' Quirrel admitted. 'Bloody Sir Galahad. Saving posh ladies' honour right, left and centre. Wandering around writing poetry like a ponce. But then he went crazy and wiped out his family.'

Crocker peered into his *stein*. 'I know it's no excuse, but – I mean, your Dashwoods, they were a right bunch . . . mass murder, devil-worship, cannibalism. You name it, they did it. Perhaps it was all too much for the lad . . .'

'That's just it – he thought his family were *saints*. Bloody aristo family loyalty. Wouldn't hear a word said against them. Walked around Dashwood House with his eyes shut.'

'Then why did he kill 'em?'

Quirrel lowered his head. 'Aristo alert.'

'Fine master I've got,' Crocker declared loudly. 'One in a million. Too good for the likes of me. And his generosity fair breaks my heart, it does. A penny a day, you can't say fairer than that, can you?'

'We must depart, Crocker,' said a genteel voice at his back.

Crocker shot up and whirled round. 'Master! Didn't know you was there. Why, I was just saying –'

Miles swept out with a swirl of the cloak. 'Hurry

yourself, fellow. Fate beckons and duty calls, and we must keep to the low passes lest we rouse the Swiss gods.'

Crocker gave his drinking partner a wry grin. 'Been nice talking to you.'

Quirrel waved him close. 'I'll tell you the name of a good brothel, just between you and me,' he said cheerfully. As Crocker bent his ear, he whispered. 'Those two fellers in the corner, the short and thin, the tall and fat — they're Vatican agents. If you see 'em coming, run like hell. Your master's a marked man.'

'Thanks,' smiled Crocker. 'I'll try the place. Could do with a bit of rumpy-pumpy.'

He gave a wave and stomped out into the drab dawn light. Miles was already on his horse, gaze fixed on the road ahead. 'What took you so long?' he demanded.

'Beg pardon, sir, but we lowly folk was talking about brothels.'

'I hope that's all you spoke of. There were two Vatican agents sitting in the corner.' With that, the young lord rode off.

Crocker's mouth was still open when he climbed on his pony and followed.

'Thirteenth Night.'

Cardinal Richelieu raised a weary eyebrow. 'Another Venetian masque — must we?'

'The dignitaries of most Dominions will be there,' said Cardinal Maroc. '*Thirteenth Night* is, I'm led to believe, Doctor Sperano's masterwork. The play will crown Venice's Thirteenth Night festivals.'

'The Devil's revels,' growled Torquemada.

Agostini threw up his hands, glancing at Cardinals Richelieu, Borgia, Altzinger and Francisco. 'I'll go with the majority.'

'And,' said the pope, from the Throne Pontifical, 'I would suggest the majority choose to grace Thirteenth Night, both the Venetian carnival and Sperano's latest play. Venice is this year's setting for the Grand Inter-

Dominion Congress, with the largest number of delegates on record. We must send a commensurate number of delegates ourselves. The Vatican needs to show a new face to the Dominions.'

The seven prelates looked up as one at the figure in white on the high throne of gold and ivory, centre-piece of the sumptuous Hall Excelsior.

'Holiness,' Cardinal Richelieu said hesitantly. 'We are still coming to terms with your miraculous return, and –'

'Remember, Richelieu, officially I have not returned. As far as anyone outside the Enclave is concerned, I am dead. Break your vow of silence on that, and you'll answer to me.'

'I have no intention of breaking my vow,' said Richelieu. 'If, for professed reasons of security, you wish the proclamation of your death to stand for a time, I willingly comply.'

'As do I,' Agostini said. 'But, concerning your astounding return –'

Lucian gave a low groan. 'I never left. I would have thought that your able brain would have gleaned that by now. The man killed by Byron was a clone. A Reprise of sorts.'

'That has not been proven conclusively, Holiness,' Agostini pointed out. 'The body was Exalted before your appearance. A test could not be run on the remains.'

'And whose fault was that?' demanded Lucian, subjecting Maroc to a withering glance. 'I said to announce me *before*, not *for*, the Exaltation. And you saw fit to call me *afterwards*.'

Maroc hung his head. 'My profound regrets, Holiness.'

'Eminences,' Lucian sighed softly. 'I have passed through the Corridor Analytical, probed by every psychoform device known to the Vatican. Recognition of a Reprise would have been instantaneous. The Corridor Analytical confirmed me as natural-born, beyond all doubt. You contest this?'

'No,' said Richelieu. 'You are natural-born. Ergo,

your facsimile was a Reprise. The scandal of a Reprise as pope, in direct contravention of the Nicodemus principle of the Seventeenth Gospel, has been averted. I simply wonder, Holiness, who it was that locked you in the Chamber Impregnable and circumvented the alarms and Gargoyles Vigilant, and why anyone should wish to plant a Reprise in your place, and then kill him by Byron's hand.'

Torquemada was in like a shot. 'Byron himself?'

Richelieu shook his head. 'How? And for what reason? No, Inquisitor General. It was someone closer to home.'

'One of us?' Agostini said.

'Don't look at me,' Borgia rumbled, eyeing his brethren.

Agostini assumed a long-suffering expression. 'We weren't.'

'Enough of this!' the pope said sharply. 'We're going round in circles. Investigations take time, and other matters are pressing. We must appear at Thirteenth Night and present a message of reconciliation. That is all. Now leave and decide on the delegates for Thirteenth Night.'

The Enclave members stood, bowed, and made their exit.

As they passed through the Doors Chryselephantine, Richelieu angled his head to Maroc. 'My spies tell me that you suggested a major Vatican presence at Thirteenth Night. His Holiness was swayed by your arguments.'

The tall, angular Maroc sniffed his disdain. 'The day I concern myself with the views of a Reprise like yourself I'll join the Trappists.'

'At least, as a Reprise, I cannot be accused of scheming to ascend the Throne of Peter,' the Francian rejoined.

'It's significant that Pope Lucian made no such Thirteenth Night undertaking before today,' Agostini said, inflicting a benevolent smile on Maroc. 'One wonders, Maroc. One wonders.'

'I think it's an excellent proposal to trade ideas with the

Dominions,' Cardinal Francisco broke in, his youthful face agleam. 'After all, we're not living in the Middle Ages.'

'Some of us are,' hissed Torquemada. 'What *I* don't understand is why we were sworn to secrecy concerning the pope's survival. Why continue the pretence that he's dead?'

'I suspect His Holiness wishes to make a dramatic entrance on Thirteenth Night,' said Altzinger.

Agostini shook his head. 'Quite out of character.'

Richelieu gave Altzinger an encouraging nod. 'On the contrary, on the rare occasions when our Germanian brother speaks, it is always worth hearing. In the meantime, the report of Lucian's murder can be used to great advantage — in the destruction of the Dominoes, starting with Byron and Miles Dashing.'

'On that we agree,' said Maroc. 'But don't forget our foremost target — the Doctor. He is our chief enemy. Pope Lucian told us that himself.'

Richelieu gave a nod. 'Yes. But who told Pope Lucian?'

'Don't look at me,' Borgia muttered.

Fourteen

'Came the dawn.'

Byron looked up at Sarah's remark. 'Came the dawn — what?'

She shrugged, standing up in the dull light, and stirred an ember with her foot. 'Just — came the dawn.'

The Doctor sat cross-legged, the flute in his lap, and watched the layers of parasitic bark slide slowly back up the trees, restoring their extra coating. The silver firs were plain silver firs again, not lit-up Christmas trees. 'I wondered when they'd give up,' he said.

'Aren't they retreating from the daylight?' Sarah spoke in a low whisper, fearing to rouse the necrodryads.

Byron smiled indulgently. 'Now why should tree spirits fear sunlight? *Tree* spirits, of all things. Although I must admit you've come through this very well. You have admirable qualities.'

'Don't patronize me,' she snorted, adjusting the white cotta and brushing down the front of her cassock.

'All right. You're a spoiled, loud-mouthed, graceless brat.'

She lifted an eyebrow. 'Very funny. You enjoy bossing me around, don't you? God — it's times like this I appreciate Jeremy.'

'Who's Jeremy?'

'Oh, this guy I went with on holiday in Sicily a while back. He got on my nerves, but at least I could —' She broke off and resumed smoothing the cassock.

'At least you could be bossy with him, huh? There's a streak of the bully in you, Miss Smith.'

'Takes one to know one.'

The Doctor was back on his feet. 'Well, those parasites look nice and sleepy. Time to be off.' He replaced the flute inside his overcoat.

'I've often wondered whether you've got TARDIS pockets,' she said, summoning up a smile despite her weariness.

He gave a broad grin. 'Everyone has TARDIS pockets, Sarah. Haven't you noticed?' With that, he marched off, finger pointing into the forest. 'North is this way.'

'So is a rather dangerous tract of forest,' Byron called out, walking west. 'A few miles due west is a town where mechanical horses can be bought. I suggest you let me do the leading, Doctor.'

The Doctor spun on his heels and took Byron's lead. 'An excellent suggestion, George.'

They followed a narrow track through the fir forest, to the accompaniment of a chorus of birdsong.

The sudden burst of chirruping reminded Sarah of the absence of a dawn chorus. They should have been warbling for at least an hour. 'Why haven't the birds started singing until now?'

'The bad aura of the forest keeps them mute,' Byron said. 'Their song is a sign that the evil has sunk back into the soil. We won't have any more trouble today – not from the trees anyway.'

'Well, that's good news!' the Doctor breezed, striding along, arms swinging loosely. 'These mechanical horses – what do they look like?'

Byron shot him a wry look. 'They look very much like horses. What else would they look like?'

'Well, the trains of the American frontier were called iron horses, and they didn't run on four legs . . . Anyway, how fast can they travel?'

'About fifty miles an hour, full gallop. We might just cover five hundred miles by nightfall, if we manage to get a horse each.'

'Then –' The Doctor made a swift reckoning. 'We

should reach the Villa Diodati by dusk.'

Byron shook his head. 'You must be thinking of the old Europe. Europa's a very different cauldron of fish. If we travel by the direct route, we'll pass through fifteen Dominions, including a couple of Alps, and three Black Forests. Not to mention a Mediterranean.'

'*A* Mediterranean?' Sarah echoed. 'Oh, don't tell me — some miniature version of the original.'

'Yes and no. It's just north of Milan, and covers no more than five or six square miles of Dimensions Ordinary. But by Dimensions Extraordinary, it's the size of the original sea. When a wayfarer approaches its shores, he enters the Extraordinary, and sees the full expanse of the sea before him. It takes days to cross by ship.' He bent a smile at Sarah. 'I suppose you have difficulty with the concept . . .'

'Time and Relative Dimensions in Space,' she responded tartly. *Don't try it on with a TARDIS passenger, pal.* 'A transdimensional sea larger on the inside than the outside. An elementary concept.' *That'll teach you* . . .

Byron was unfazed. 'Time and Relative Dimensions in Space,' he recited. 'You mentioned TARDIS pockets to the Doctor. That would be an acronym of the term. Did you work out the principles of transdimensional physics yourself, or were you simply told? There was more in your speech of the parrot than the authentic natural philosopher.'

Sarah's retort was stopped by the Doctor's worried voice. 'I don't like the sound of this at all. This world is too advanced by half — by a million halves — psionics, psychotronics, chronoptics, and now transdimensional technology. I wonder who gave it to them?'

She studied his expression carefully. 'The Master?'

'There were others. The Meddling Monk *et al*. But the Master is the most likely culprit.' He wore a deep frown. 'You know, now and again, since I've arrived here, I've had the uncomfortable feeling that someone — familiar — is in this world.' He glanced at Byron. 'Tell me, where is this Chronopticon that scans history and programmes Reprises with artificial memory?'

Byron threw up his hands. 'Your guess is as good as mine. The Dominoes have been trying to locate it for years. We've all heard of its existence, and it stands to reason that such a device exists, but where it is and precisely what it is — a mystery.'

'Then where do Reprises come from?'

'They just appear, like actors on a stage.'

Sarah thought that over. It didn't add up.

'Actors on a stage,' the Doctor mused. 'Yes, everything points in the same direction, although it's hardly credible.'

'What is it you know?' demanded Byron. 'I have no patience with comrades who keep vital knowledge to themselves.'

The Doctor gave a shrug. 'All I can tell you is that someone immensely powerful is working behind the scenes. Perhaps it's the Master, I'm not sure.'

'This Master, is he an old enemy of yours?'

'An — adversary. He's his own worst enemy.'

'It's no good, Byron,' Sarah said, permitting herself a smug smile. 'He won't tell you anything until he's ready.'

Byron glared at the Doctor. 'When we reach the Villa Diodati, you tell me all you know. Agreed?'

'Hmm . . . I should have figured a little more out by then. Yes, agreed. Incidentally, how long would you estimate the journey to the villa, presuming we acquire the necessary transport?'

'We should arrive some time tomorrow afternoon. The route is circuitous.'

'And one last question. Where is the Theatre of Transmogrification performing at the moment?'

'No idea. Doctor Sperano's troupe was last in Franco-Berlin, a city divided by a wall separating Libertines and Puritans. He performed *The Dresden Dolls* in the licentious western half of the city — the Demi-monde. After that, who knows? Although he'll be presenting *Thirteenth*

Night in Venice on Thirteenth Night, if you're so eager to meet him.'

'Thirteenth Night will, I suspect, be far too late,' the Doctor said. 'Where did the Theatre of Transmogrification originate?'

'In Britannia Gloriana, a Dominion modelled on the England of Elizabeth I's reign, although its architecture and dress fashions are as much Jacobean as Elizabethan.'

'And are the dramatists of that era banned in Britannia Gloriana as well?'

'You ask a lot of questions, Doctor.'

'I need a lot of answers, George.'

The lord rolled his eyes in exasperation. 'Then yes. The dramatists are banned there as well. It's a capital offence to mention the name of Shakespeare. And – to answer yet another question I see in your eyes – none of the dramatists has been Reprised.'

'Thank you, George. And now I'll tell you something you already know. The Theatre of Transmogrification started out in a recreation of the Globe Theatre.'

'Yes,' Byron nodded. 'I look forward to hearing a full account of whatever's going on in your head.'

'You're not the only one,' Sarah said. 'But I'm more used to being kept in the dark. Doctor, does this all boil down to some sort of drama?'

The Doctor tapped the side of his nose. 'The play's the thing . . .'

'Milady Incarnadine,' the Dramaturge greeted with a bow. 'As ravishing as ever.'

The lady in question rose from her seat in the raftered, Jacobean room and walked across towards Doctor Sperano, her body-hugging crimson gown swishing over the floorboards. The shadow she cast in the candlelight had a life and shape all its own: its rounded contours folded in an attitude of defeat.

'Welcome back, milord,' said Incarnadine. Her crimson mouth smiled a slow smile, revealing sharp canines.

'My love is like a red, red rose,' he proclaimed, hand on heart.

'You honour me, milord. Was your visit successful?'

Incarnadine stretched out a pale hand. Sperano took it in a paler hand and gave it a kiss. 'Most satisfactory. I played my part well.'

'As always, lord.'

'Most kind, Incarnadine.'

'Here,' she offered. 'Let me take off your face.'

'Please do, I am rather uncomfortable with this persona, despite its droll appeal.'

Her long nails, crimson as her lips and gown, slid under Sperano's chin and peeled off the pliant mask. 'Oh,' she said. 'You're wearing your Droll Mask underneath.'

'It seemed appropriate, in the circumstances. Shall we repair to the Visage Attic? Here, lady, take my arm . . .'

They walked sedately up an angled staircase and entered a roomy, dusty attic crammed with wooden chests. 'So many masks,' he declared. 'So many roles to play.'

'You are a genius without peer,' Incarnadine declared, opening a chest and placing the mask with a pile of others. 'The creative force of the ages.' She tossed back her dark gold hair, blue eyes simmering. 'It angers me that your genius is unrecognized.'

'It will be, beloved, it will be. Very soon. Better to wait in the wings, unknown, biding the perfect cue, and then sweep onstage to thunderous acclaim. The right stage, the right audience, the right play and, of course, the right time. Timing is everything, in life as in drama.'

'Drama is life,' she intoned, reciting his credo.

He inclined his head in recognition of the doctrine, then lifted the lid of a heavy oak chest and fished out a mask. 'I must, alas, leave again soon,' he said, slipping on the new face.

He danced down the room, twirling. 'How do I look?'

'The part,' she responded, flinging out her arms.

'A small part,' he said modestly, spinning to a halt. 'A cameo, no more.'

'More than a cameo, Doctor.'

'Doctor . . .' he murmured. 'There are many doctors, as there are many masters. But there's a Doctor who has gate-crashed my drama — I can feel it. A not-so-little voice inside tells me so.'

'Then write him out of the play.'

He grinned. 'Oh, I will, I will. But I'll do him justice. His death scene will be macabre and protracted, a bravura performance.' Sperano gave a low chuckle. 'A performance with many repeats.'

They stood on the ceiling of the church of St Incarnata le Fanu and sang hymns to the Divine Diabolic.

The Anti-Church congregation, gazing upwards to the floor, saw not only inverted crosses, but inverted desecration altar, anti-saint statues, black candelabra, blood-scented pews — inverted everything: the entire church turned upside down, its steeple buried in the grounds of All UnHallows in Britannia Perfidia.

Dressed in black robes emblazoned with cabalistic sigils, Aleister Crowley and Johann Faust, for once, stood side by side on the roof painted with copulating angels, voices raised in the reversed chant.

Hymns finally concluded, Crowley and Faust sat down, a good arm's length apart.

'Infantile,' snorted Crowley. 'Inverted church, singing backwards, just what you'd expect of Faustians.'

'Your territory, my church, that was the agreement,' drawled Faust, picking his nose. 'So don't start complaining now. Anyway, singing and praying backwards was good enough for disciples of the Unspeakable One back in the sixteenth century. Never did me any harm. You and your Therionites don't know you're born.'

Crowley rubbed his forehead and groaned. 'Singing psalms the right way round can be a bloody pain. But doing them *backwards* is enough to give anyone a splitting headache. Just *remembering* the words back to front — gah!'

'Your crowd had it too easy,' muttered Faust. 'We had the original Inquisition after us, hammer and tongs. What did you have? A few British newspapers following your escapades and making a hero out of you at the same time they clucked their disapproval, that's what. In my day —'

'You're making my headache worse. By the look of my disciples, they feel the same.'

'Well, they made as big a hash of reversed praise as you did. I just can't see this Faustian-Therionite alliance working out, Crowley.'

'Master Therion to you,' Crowley insisted wearily. 'Think about bloody Paracelsus as Official Antichrist, and make it work. If we stick together until the elections, we will, apodictically, gain a few defectors.'

'Talking of defectors, what happened to Cagliostro?'

'Oh, he summoned up the demon Choronzon in a Carmelite monastery and can't get rid of him. But at least he won't be voting for bloody Paracelsus.'

'About the elections, I'm not too happy about holding them in Venice, not with the InterDominion Congress and the Vatican delegation running the show.'

'Why break with tradition? And no one will breach the Europan Pact, not even the Vatican. Besides, the Venetians, not the Vaticanos, are running the show, and they won't allow anyone to disrupt the Saturnalia of Thirteeth Night. Richelieu was adamant on that score.'

'Hope we can trust Richelieu,' Faust muttered. 'He's one of the slipperiest men in Europa. Do you think he'll keep his word?'

Crowley shrugged. 'He has nothing to lose by keeping it and everything by breaking it. As long as the Anti-Church stays out of Francia, he'll be content.' His voice lowered to a slight whisper. 'That's if you keep your part of the bargain, *Mephistopheles.*'

Faust tensed at the mention of his Domino code-name.

'You should watch what you're saying, Crowley. Even here.'

Crowley gave a leer. 'You worry too much, Faust. It's safe to talk here.'

'Not about the plan or my Domino identity, you loudmouth. If my fellow Dominoes had even a clue what I was up to —'

'Betrayal,' said Crowley, enjoying the other's discomfiture. 'Selling them out for the chance of ruling the Anti-Church.'

Faust shook his head in disgust. 'Some fellow-conspirator you are. Why not buy a megaphone and announce the news on Ranter's Corner?'

'Relax, it'll stay between the two of us.' Rising to his feet, Crowley pulled up the hood of his black robe, covering his shaven scalp. 'Now for a *real* Anti-Church mass, according to the Therion rite. A gnostic sex-magic ritual, as performed in my Abbey of Theleme.'

Faust made a face. 'The sex is fine by me, it's all that droning about Egyptian deities that sends me to sleep. Still, sex is sex, and I wouldn't say no . . .' His eyes roved the robed congregation. 'I'll have that one with the red hair.'

'That's my acolyte!' Crowley protested. 'Sister Lilith.'

'So what? I fancy her.'

'You can't have something just because you want it.'

'Do what thou wilt shall be the whole of the Law,' Faust quoted smugly, throwing Crowley's axiom back at him. 'Anyway,' he indicated a tall blonde with a regal air. 'You can have my own paramour — an authentic Reprise of Helen of Troy, the face that launched a thousand ships.'

'Helen of Troy!' snorted Crowley. 'Who do you think you're kidding? She's not even a Reprise. Her name's Gerda Gluck, and she's a prostitute you picked up in Prussia Hohenzollern. Gods, there are so many phonies about these days. Trust you to try and foist one on me.'

'All right, you can have Gerda *and* Heidi if I have Lilith. Deal?'

Crowley grimaced. 'I suppose so, but only if I can watch.'

'Goes without saying.' Faust extracted a sacrificial dagger from under the robe. 'Now, which of these ladies is the Living Altar?'

'The one with the jug-ears and the nose.'

'Right,' smirked Faust. 'Time to start carving.'

Fifteen

'Ride a crock horse to Banbury Cross,' Sarah muttered, thighs gripping the mechanical steed, arms encircling the Doctor who sat upright in the front of the saddle.

She had been wary of the disjointed parodies of horses at first glance, and experience had done nothing to reassure her of the robots' reliability.

The horse gave another jolt that almost unseated her. Every two hundred strides or so, the malfunctioning steed came near to bucking. The rutted track they were following through hilly terrain wasn't helping either. Sure, she was an experienced rider, but her robotic mount's erratic rhythm was putting her skills to the stiffest of tests.

She glanced at Byron who rode alongside. 'I thought you said these mechanical horses were smoother than the real thing?'

'Complaining again?' groaned Byron, fighting a wayward bounce of his own steed. 'What do you expect from a small village in the middle of nowhere? We were lucky to find two horses in some sort of working order. And they were cheap.'

'I wish I had my sonic screwdriver,' the Doctor said. 'With a little tinkering –'

'Doctor!' Sarah said. 'Will you stop rabbiting on about your sonic screwdriver. You haven't got it and that's all there is to it, OK?'

Byron frowned at the Doctor. 'Is she *always* complaining?'

'Not *always*.'

'Thanks, Doctor,' she said between gritted teeth. The periodic jolts had made her spine feel like squashed salami. She looked ahead at the staccato profile of the Tyrolean Alps – one of seven Tyrolean Alps, she reminded herself. 'Hey, Byron, how long before we take a rest? It's been hours and hours.'

'Two hours, and we'll soon be stopping. There's an oil-well up ahead.'

'Oh,' she said. 'Is that supposed to make sense?'

She lay on a grassy verge, her fingers massaging her back, and watched the horses trot to what appeared to be an old-fashioned water-well.

Byron had informed her otherwise. The small ring of stones enclosed a well of refined oil. Like the man said, an oil-well.

The mechanical horses stooped their necks into the well and started drinking.

'They should ride more smoothly once they've re-oiled their locomotive mechanisms,' the poet said, standing upright and stretching his arms. 'That should last them a couple of hours, at least. We'll have reached another wayside well by then.'

'What about us? That gulp of sour wine and bite of stale bread back in the village is all we've had since landing in this lunatic world.'

'That's all I've had in the last three days, so stop moaning, Miss Smith. And make an effort to comport yourself with a measure of dignity. Your manners are as common as your name.'

'Oh, she has her good points,' the Doctor broke in, leaning at a near-impossible angle against a cypress tree, gaze raised to the blue of the late morning sky. 'She'll surprise you yet, George. By the way, I think I might be able to iron out those little kinks in the horses' performance, even without my screwdriver. I've diagnosed the problem as a simple malfunction in the co-ordination master control. Give me five minutes and I'll have them galloping to the manner born, or I'm a Cyberman.'

Byron looked dubious, but flicked a hand in acceptance. 'I'll risk your tinkering if it means an end to Miss Smith's incessant whining.'

Sarah's fingernails sliced into her palm. She kept her tone even and moderate. 'I won't speak another word to you. Satisfied?'

Declining an answer, he followed the Doctor to the oil-supping horses, and kept a close eye on the repairs. Smothering her anger, she lay flat on her back and shut her eyes.

After a while, the anger evaporated. What did she expect of Lord Byron? A sensitive pro-feminist from her own era, willing to discuss gender roles? Wasn't going to happen. Let's face it, they were pretty rare in her own time, and some of those few turned her stomach with their relentless *understanding*. Having bounced about the breadth of the cosmos and the span of time she should know better. The civilizations of the universe were a bag of liquorice allsorts. Once you'd picked one, you had to like it or lump it.

Still went against the grain, though.

As for Europa, it was a bag of allsorts all to itself. A mish-mash of seven centuries. A plethora of mini-nations. Characters from history and fiction romping around the Dominions.

Back in that one-horse — well, two-horse — village, Byron had filled in a little more of the Europan background over wine and bread in the smallest inn she'd ever visited. She wasn't sure whether she was more confused after the account than before.

Europa was crazy. It shouldn't work, but somehow it did. The Dominions maintained something of historical integrity by blocking progress through inbuilt cultural limitations, legal and otherwise. Technological inventions were virtually taboo, except for a few invaluable contraptions such as mechanical horses. Anachronism was a crime, ranging from whistling a Regency ditty in Gloriana's

Britannia to buzzing Louis XIII's Palace of Versailles with a bi-plane.

Fine, each Dominion stayed roughly true to its own time period, but then there was the Vatican, hovering like an Overcity and bristling with psychotronic gadgets. A rule unto itself, above the anachronism laws that applied to everyone else. The original idea of the Concocters was to provide a focus of unity in the Vatican, roughly on the lines of the Christendom of feudal Europe. Bad idea. Over the decades, it aspired to become the seat of an empire, a Second Holy Roman Empire.

And the Dominoes arose as a protest against Vatican City, freebooters and swashbucklers forming an underground alliance against the spreading influence of the Catholic Church Apostolic. Dominoes cheerfully broke every rule going, inventing the anachronistic Dracoes, and flouting the Vatican at every turn, as well as any Dominion they took a dislike to. But even the Dominoes liked living in the past. Their Dracoes and psionic weapons were a necessary evil.

And then there was the supernatural realm, psychotronically generated and self-perpetuating. Trolls hurled rocks across the fjords of various Scandias. Elegant vampires rode glide-gondolas in the canals of Venice. The Little People haunted the hills of Eire. There were even Swiss gods, a baffling notion. Every dark legend of Europe was brought into existence. And why? Because the Europans *liked* it. Ghosts and ghoulies, succubi and incubi were – interesting. And Europans were all for an interesting life, whatever the cost.

Then there were the fictional Reprises, the weirdest clones of all. The Four Musketeers from the Richard Lester films, Ross Poldark and the entire cast of the TV series *Poldark*, Laurence Olivier's Heathcliff, who was apparently giving Emily Brontë a hell of a time in Regency Yorkshire, and there was . . .

Sarah opened her eyes with a low moan. This was all a bit too much. She'd need the Domino Encyclopaedia of

Europa and a spare week to get the hang of it all.

'Done to a turn!' the Doctor cried out cheerily, stepping back from repairing the horses.

Byron was still doubtful. 'We haven't tested them yet. When we've put another kilometre of road at our backs I'll give you my congratulations or a boot in the ribs.'

'What shall we call them?' the Doctor pondered, eyeing the steeds.

'Sturm and Drang,' came the derisive suggestion.

'Good,' the Doctor nodded. 'Yours is Sturm, mine's Drang.'

Sarah forced herself to her feet. Oh well, to horse, to horse.

'How about I sit in front for a while?' she said, foot already in the stirrup. 'I'm fed up with staring at your back.'

'Certainly, Sarah,' the Doctor smiled. 'At least the one in front gets a change of scenery.'

'With your height, you'll be looking clean over her head,' Byron said, mounting his horse.

'Good point,' the Doctor conceded. He glanced ahead at the Alps. 'About six hours' daylight left. We'll have to make camp in one of the mountain passes.'

'Worse than that,' Byron said, urging his steed forward. 'We'll be in another Black Forest.'

Sarah said nothing for the next minute as they rode along the track. She was too concerned with waiting for the next bump from the horse to dwell on the journey. But as a kilometre and more sped by with a steady rhythm and Byron shouted his congratulations to the Doctor on a repair job well done, she relaxed in her seat and allowed her thoughts to stray further ahead.

Another night in the Black Forest, and if she survived that, the Villa Diodati and Bad Byron. After that . . . Well, after that it looked like they would be taking on the power of the Exalted Vatican, and any Dominion that sided with it. Quite a prospect.

She stared at the mountainous expanse, summits

muffled in a cloudy micro-climate, and shivered, wishing she was back in the TARDIS, the closest thing she had to a home.

Then she thought of her real home, and instantly regretted the thought. Too strong a sense of loss, even now.

She had a mad uncle at her back, and that was some comfort.

But she wished her Dad was alive, and with her.

It would be good to be a small girl, just now and again, faced with so big a universe.

'Stop it,' she mumbled to herself. 'You're a grown woman in an altarboy's outfit with a bikini for underwear, riding on a mechanical horse with a Time Lord at your back and Byron at your side, taking on a futuristic Vatican in a Europe that lives in the past. There's high adventure or high farce for you. What would you prefer? A desk job and a bedsit in Ealing, travelling the Tube every day?'

The way she felt now, that's just what she'd prefer.

The cardinal bowed to the silvered mirror.

'The Doctor will soon be apprehended, Master. You have my word.'

The smiling white face in the mirror, rigid as a mask, gave a soft response. 'Apprehended by you, or me?'

Uncertain of the correct response, the cardinal hardly dared look the reflected apparition in its black eye-slits. 'By you – or me. If the Vatican seizes him first, he'll be delivered into your hands immediately.'

'I know, priest, I know. I suggest your spies concentrate on the Londia of Britannia Gloriana. The Globe Theatre, in particular.'

'Will he be there now, do you think, Master?'

'Not quite yet, I imagine, but very soon. He cannot help but investigate the Globe, if he's the man I think he is. Have your men ready to take him. By the way, you played your part well in the Hall Excelsior. I'm most pleased. On Thirteenth Night, you will be nominated Pope Supreme.'

'Much thanks, Master.'

'None required. I'm sure you'll do the part justice. Now go and play your part in the Conclave Ordinary, and ferret out the traitor who is supporting the Dominoes.'

'I have my suspicions, Master . . .'

'I want evidence, not suspicions. Go to the Conclave, and watch your fellow-cardinals for signs of treachery.'

'Yes, Master.'

The chalk-faced figure in the black opera cloak faded from the mirror. The cardinal rose to his feet, crossing himself.

He took a few unsteady steps to a chair and slumped into it, sucking in deep breaths and mopping his brow.

A semblance of composure regained, he studied the round mirror, made of rare crystal, and framed with antique wood. On its frame were carved, in Cyrillic script, three names: John Dee; Edward Kelley; Elizabeth Bathory.

The seventeenth-century scrying mirror, fashioned by Dee and appropriated by Kelley, had once been consecrated to Elizabeth Bathory, Blood Countess of Transylvania, but was now the possession of the man in the mirror, Persona.

Persona, who offered the cardinal the Throne of Peter.

He stood up, ready to face the rest of the Enclave, and lifted his glance to the ceiling, hands clasped in prayer.

Richelieu assumed his seat in the Crypt of the Seven Sleepers, and observed that one of the seven thrones ranged around the Altar Ipsissimus was empty.

'Where's Cardinal Francisco?' he asked.

'Late, as are you,' Agostini said, walking to the mysterious blue box beside the altar.

The crypt door burst open and the youthful Francisco bustled in, face flushed red. 'Apologies, brethren, I was delayed by a –'

'Well now you're here,' snapped Agostini. 'Assume your seat, please.'

Abashed, Francisco crept to his throne in front of the luminous icon of the Seventh Sleeper.

'Now that we're *all* here,' Agostini began, 'it behoves me to confirm that the box is a plasmic shell containing Dimensions Extraordinary, and that only Cardinal Maroc and a special team of psychotronic investigators are permitted inside its door.'

'How were its defences breached?' said Altzinger.

'By a select member of the department of Dimensions Extraordinary, as His Holiness has informed Cardinal Maroc and myself. The identity of the expert and the means employed must remain secret for purposes of security.'

Richelieu raised an eyebrow. 'Secret from the Enclave? Has Vatican security gone so far as to exclude its elect? Cardinal Maroc, even considering his rank of Camerlengo, seems to have acquired additional status overnight. I fail to see why he should be the only one of us to enter the device.'

Maroc glared daggers at Richelieu.

'Pope Lucian has chosen Maroc after careful thought, I can testify to that,' Agostini said severely. 'And may I remind you that I am included in the ban, an exclusion which I accept with grace.'

Richelieu inclined his head. 'Then so, eminence, do I. I am the servant of the pope as I am of the king of Francia.'

Maroc gave a grunt. 'But the pope's servant before that of Louis XIII, I presume, eminence?'

Richelieu's lips tightened. 'That, eminence, is a question undeserving of an answer.'

'Indeed,' Agostini interposed. 'To the business in hand. Pope Lucian will be remaining in his chambers for the next few days, to minimize the chances of any report of his survival leaking out. The vow of silence for the Enclave remains, until Thirteenth Night. As for now, the pope has agreed with Maroc on the matter of the Doctor. The interior of what has proved to be his space-time craft shows all the signs of alien manufacture, far in advance of our understanding of Dimensions Extraordinary. We can merely guess at what powers he has at his command. All forces will be mobilized to track him down. Any views on the most efficacious means to this end will be welcome.'

'The Villa Diodati,' Altzinger suggested. 'Byron might seek sanctuary there, and if the Doctor's with the Britannian lord . . .'

Agostini gave a slight shrug. 'A possibility. But only a possibility. The villa is at present under minimal surveillance.'

'Bad Byron is well ensconced in the Villa Diodati,' Richelieu broke in. 'He and Dangerous Byron were never friends, and often enemies. Besides, the villa is too obvious a hiding-place, and Dangerous Byron rarely resorts to double-bluff. I'd be inclined to believe his destination is Venice, with sabotage of the InterDominion Congress in mind. However, I'm still concerned over the murder of the false Pope Lucian and exactly who it was that abducted the pope . . .'

'That affair is closed for the time being,' Agostini said firmly. 'By order of His Holiness, as you well know. Keep to the issue in hand.'

Richelieu lifted his narrow shoulders in a Gallic shrug. 'You have my opinion on the Doctor's destination. Venice.'

'Or Transylvania,' said Maroc. 'Two of my agents have spotted Miles Dashing a few kilometres inside the Switzian border. Succeeding events also showed that he had spotted them. He rode west for a while, then doubled back in an adroit manoeuvre. The agents pretended that they had fallen for the ruse, and tracked him east with maximum secrecy. While I speak, he is within a few minutes' ride of the Nosferatu Domain. Miles Dashing is a frequent comrade of Byron, and Transylvania is a region more hostile than any other to Vatican City. Byron and the Doctor may well be heading for a pre-arranged meeting with Dashing in Transylvania.'

Agostini gave a nod. 'Your agents did well, and your

reasoning has merit. As Dashing pretended to ride west, that suggests he wished us to believe his destination was the Villa Diodati. Yes, the villa would present a diversion from the actual rendezvous, and that rendezvous could well be in Transylvania. I propose a maximum sweep of western Transylvania by a large contingent of the Switzia Guardians, replete with sacred talismans and accompanied by a squad of veteran exorcists. Who says Amen?'

'Amen,' six voices chorused in agreement.

'What about Regency Britannia, or perhaps Britannia Gloriana?' Francisco said, glancing around as though the idea would be met with derision. 'Byron's home is in the first Dominion, and he has many friends in the second.'

Agostini frowned, then indicated his approval. 'Both Britannias would offer him numerous hiding-places.'

'I propose three regiments of the Switzia Guardians for Regency Britannia,' said Borgia. 'And two for Gloriana's realm. A considerable number of spies will be required for both Dominions — five hundred, would you say?'

There was a general murmur of assent.

'Very well,' Agostini said. 'Now, to another matter . . .'

Agostini stared Borgia straight in the eye. 'We have a traitor in the Enclave. And I think I know his identity.'

'Don't look at me,' Borgia snorted.

This time, everyone did.

Sixteen

'I don't know – riding west, then riding back east, fair turns me head it does, your lordship.'

'"Sir" will suffice, Crocker,' said Miles Dashing, peering out of the cave mouth overlooking Liechtenstein's citadel. 'And keep the horse and pony back in the shadows.'

'Yes, sir, sorry, sir. Are those Vatican agents still on our tail?'

'I hope so. Do you know what a red herring is, Crocker?'

'Couldn't afford fancy fish, not a man of my lowly rank, sir.'

Miles groaned. 'A red herring's a false trail, poltroon. By now, the Vatican agents will have reported that we're heading for Transylvania. Time to eliminate them before they discover otherwise.' He pulled a dagger from under his frock-coat, and pressed the elaborate hilt to his forehead, eyes shut tight.

'What are you up to now, sir?'

'Concentrating. Hold your tongue, Crocker.'

'Sorry, sir.'

Miles's eyes sprang open at the same moment his hands flew apart, releasing the long-bladed dagger.

Instead of dropping, the dagger hovered, then rotated slowly until it faced the cave mouth. Then, slowly at first, it glided out of the cave, gathering speed as it veered east.

'Hey, that's a good trick!' exclaimed Crocker.

'That, my good man, was a smart dagger. A Domino weapon, perfected by Leonardo da Vinci. I projected an image of our trackers into the psycho-conductive hilt. On receiving the imprint, and the reasons for killing, the smart dagger homed in on its targets. It will be back in a short while.'

Crocker's eyes narrowed. 'How does it work, exactly?'

Miles gave a toss of his blond hair. 'How should I know? I'm a romantic adventurer, not a mechanic. I simply visualize the target, and the dagger picks up the image and flies to it. Something to do with engrams and DNA. Don't trouble me with idle questions, fellow.'

'Sorry, sir. Er – does it think then, this smart dagger? That wasn't no idle question, sir. Just trying to be a bit less ignorant.'

'Well, yes, it does think after a fashion, but chiefly on the ethical level. If it should decide that its mission is morally unjustifiable, it will desist and return. A necessary precaution, lest I make a moral misjudgement in the choice of victim. Taking a life is no light matter, Crocker.'

'That it ain't, sir. One of yer categorical imperatives.'

Miles frowned. 'Where did you hear of the Kantian categorical imperative?'

Crocker's narrow eyes narrowed further. 'Oh, this posh gent taught me to say it whenever killing was mentioned, so I wouldn't sound thick.'

Miles subjected the servant to a protracted stare. 'I'm beginning to wonder about you, Crocker.'

'Sorry, sir.'

'I hate Miles Dashing,' muttered Gratz, scanning the pass to Liechtenstein. 'Can't wait to see him hauled in. Hope the boss picked up the message all right. A lot of supernatural interference in the aether at the moment. Must be the time of year.'

'They got the message all right,' assured Gildern, riding at his side. 'Maroc will have a fleet of Angeli here in no time, you'll see. That bastard Britannian will get what's coming to him. *I* hate Miles Dashing too.'

'Everybody hates Miles Dashing,' grunted Gratz.

'The women don't. They all love him. All of them, crazy about him.'

'That's why I hate him so much.'

'Me too. Nobody should be that good-looking. Not natural.'

Gratz curled his lip. 'Work of the devil, if you ask me . . .' Something flashed in the noon sky. 'Hey — what's that?'

Gildern squinted into the bright sunlight. 'Looks metallic. Coming fast. God! I hope it's not a smart dag–' Speechless, he peered down at the blade stuck in his chest. With a wry twist of the lips he tumbled off the horse.

Gratz wheeled his steed round and galloped full pelt, darting terrified glances over his shoulder.

The smart dagger withdrew from Gildern's chest and sped after Gratz. It drove into his back, the force of the impact throwing him over the horse's head to land with a thump on the gritted road.

He felt the blade withdraw, leaving a punctured heart.

The world slipped away with the gush of his blood.

'I hate Miles Dashing,' he mumbled.

The dagger flew back into Miles's hand, its blade bloodied. 'Mission accomplished, Crocker. Now give this a good clean.'

'Be able to see your face in it, sir.' The servant took out a snotty handkerchief.

'Use the chamois leather, Crocker, and burn that obscene article in your hand.' He stood up. 'And be quick about it. We must resume our journey east with all speed. I only pray that Dangerous Byron can be found in the Villa Diodati. Bad Byron has, I hear, taken a distinct turn for the worse, from engaging rogue to utter cad.'

Crocker gave a wink as he wiped the blade. 'Bit of a bad 'un, eh? Heard of his goings-on. Whips and women's bottoms and suchlike.'

Miles grabbed the servant by the collar. 'I'll thank you not to speak so lewdly of ladies' private parts. Any more of that talk and I'll box your ears.'

'Quite right too, boss.' Crocker resumed polishing the knife with a will. 'A good trouncing's the only kind of language us uppity commoners understand.'

While Crocker was busy about his task, Miles brought out his horse and whispered into its ear. 'Oberon – the Villa Diodati, by the fastest route.'

The device's translation centres and location finders were evidently in trim shape. Oberon whinnied within a couple of seconds, nodding his head.

'Excellent, now let us away. Crocker – hurry yourself. A mere five hours of daylight remain.'

Crocker hurried himself, and master and servant were soon riding down the hill. Once back on the road, the mechanical beasts set off with a will.

After five minutes at a determined gallop, Crocker shouted out to his master. 'I hear there's promotion in this job, sir. That true?'

'Only under the usual conditions. Acts of extreme heroism or consistently interesting behaviour will permit a commoner to enter the lower ranks of the aristocracy. Derring-do, panache, élan – that's what marks the aristocrat from the plebeian. Only heroes and bohemians, not to be confused with Bohemians –'

'Eh?'

'– may hope to aspire above their born station. Equality of opportunity is thereby guaranteed in most Europan Dominions. A system most fair and just.'

'Yeah, but there's not much room at the top, is there, pardon me for speaking my mind. The big nobs hang on to their positions.'

'Not true. Each year an assembly of aristocrats gather and demote any of their peers who have exhibited boring behaviour as a standard practice, or who have been craven when faced with the blade or bullet. About a tenth of the nobility are demoted every year, and an equal number of deserving commoners promoted to their titles. Thus an elite of interesting people is maintained.'

'What about Dominoes – they easier to join?'

'Ha!' Miles laughed grimly. 'Easier to become the Earl of Effingham than to ride with the Dominoes. A Domino is a man or woman of dauntless spirit and noble mien, skilled in war and ardent in love, careless of danger and quick to defend the right.'

'Sod that then,' Crocker muttered under his breath. Then, in a loud but respectful tone: 'Um, about your family, sir. A bit of a tragedy, so I heard.'

'A tragedy indeed,' Miles said sombrely. 'The dastardly Sir Giles of Uppington impugned a lady's honour. I had my duelling glove about my person, and struck him across the face. Challenge accepted, we met in Gadding Meadow, pistols cocked. Once I'd shot the scoundrel, I repaired instantly to Dashwood Hall, home of my noble and kindly kin. Little did I know what fate held in store –'

Crocker kept a straight face as he listened to the interminable account. He'd heard the tale before, but not in such detail, and not from his master's voice. The young lad certainly had his facts about the Dashwoods upside down and inside out. He gave family loyalty a bad name. Talk about blind allegiance.

'– and then,' concluded Miles, 'my father, with his expiring breath, gasped the single word "Managra", his tremulous finger pointing at the window that afforded a distant view of Mindelmere Mansion. With that, he gave up the ghost in a fountain of gore.'

'And very sad too, sir. Er, read a lot of books when you were young, did you, sir? Go on a lot of walks?'

'What? Ah – yes, it so happens I did. I read Malory's *Morte d'Arthur*, Wordsworth, Shelley. High, inspiring works. And I spent many days – even weeks – rambling the rugged, romantic moors of Devon, flower in one hand, book of poetry in the other. Oft-times, I would compose an ode of mine own, dedicated to an ideal love.'

'Didn't see much of your family then, sir?'

'Sadly, no. From an early age I was sent to live with a succession of friends and distant relations. I was always packed off on my own. Apparently my four brothers were temperamentally unsuited to removal from the ancestral home. My parents insisted that the holidays — rather a lot of them — would further my education. Later, as I grew into a youth, they were equally insistent that I leave home and acquire lodgings of my own in Londia or Bristol or Exeter or Truro or — anywhere. They especially recommended the far north of Scotland. The recommendation was for my own sake, of course, but I refused to leave the family home. My parents pretended despondency when I assured them I'd never leave their side.'

'I'll just bet they did, sir. Weeping and gnashing of teeth.'

'In my last year at Dashwood Hall, my parents and brothers urged me to go on long walks — the longer the better, they said — for the sake of my spiritual growth. Indeed, the rare periods I stayed in Dashwood Hall were plagued by near-fatal accidents. Chandeliers fell from the ceiling whenever I walked under them. Broadswords and axes would drop from walls when I sat beneath. Stray bullets from my brothers' guns would graze me during the hunt. A cannon once discharged itself a mere second after I peered down the barrel at my father's invitation. It was as though a curse was on me. None of my family were similarly afflicted. To this day, I suspect the baleful influence of the Mindelmeres.'

'Oh yeah, the Mindelmeres,' said Crocker, shrugging his shoulders and rolling his eyes. 'I mean, who else could it be?'

Miles's eyes flashed with anger. 'The newspapers thought otherwise, especially those of Britannia Perfidia. They claimed that the Dashwoods were *allies* of the Mindelmeres, that on the very night preceding the attack, my family visited Mindelmere Mansion to witness a performance of *The Blood Countess of Transylvania*, presented by Doctor

Sperano's Theatre of Transmogrification.' Anger changed to troubled reflection. 'True, they did visit the mansion that night, but in the hope of arranging a peace pact, not to watch Sperano's dreadful spectacle.'

Crocker rubbed his chin. Doctor Sperano. Now there was a thought.

His master started muttering. 'Miles – Slime – name of the rose – Eros.'

'What was that, sir?'

'Nothing you'd understand, fellow. A cryptic puzzle.'

'Oh, you're right there, and no mistake. Don't know what cryptic means. Don't even know what puzzle means. Not too bright.' He was silent for a time, then asked: 'Ever had much to do with masks, sir?'

The Rite of Passage hurtled through the Passing Strange.

A black coach-and-horses dashed madly through the vortex of the Passing Strange, followed by a trail of carriages, wagons and carts, each pulled by a mechanical horse or donkey.

The leading coach, blazing a trail through the inchoate swirl of colours and non-colours, bore two names on its side: *Rite of Passage* and *Sperano*. The same title was emblazoned on every vehicle in its retinue. The Rite of Passage was a cavalcade, bearing its theatrical troupe through the sly interstices in space and time. It was the Theatre of Transmogrification on its way to church.

A pale face with crimson lips and dark gold hair stared out of one of the leading coach's windows, observing the flamboyant bedlam of the Passing Strange.

''Tis well named by the Master – Passing Strange indeed,' said Incarnadine, turning from the spectacle and strolling across the living room of the Jacobean house contained inside the coach, the large confined within the small. As she walked, arms swinging at her side, her shadow, fuzzy in the candlelight, crouched as though beaten, the epitome of wretchedness.

She sat by an oak table and uncorked a bottle of vintage

blood, pressed from twentieth-century Spanish Carmelite nuns rapt in the throes of mystical ecstasy. Pouring the liquid into a delicate blood-glass, she lifted the goblet and inhaled the mystic bouquet.

'Heavenly,' she murmured. Her shadow squirmed in anguish.

Then she raised the blood-glass high in a toast. 'To you, Doctor Sperano, Master Dramatist. You created me in her image. A whore exalted to a countess.'

Her blue eyes shifted to take in a portrait on the oak-panelled walls. The woman in the portrait might well have been Incarnadine's twin.

'May I play your part worthily, Countess Elizabeth.'

Sip by sip, Incarnadine drained the glass. With a contented sigh, she leaned back in the chair.

'Spectre!' she called out.

A gaunt apparition wafted into the room, a butler in stocking and hose, crowned with a powdered periwig. Through gaps in his diaphanous body, parts of the wall could be seen.

'Ma'am,' he said with a formal bow.

'We shall shortly be arriving in church. Pass the word on that the troupe must ready themselves for a major production of *The Adventures of Macbeth's Head* soon after our churchly performance. The Master has a fondness for it. It will serve well as a forerunner of *Thirteenth Night*.'

'Yes, ma'am. May I enquire when the Master will return?'

'In a few hours.' Incarnadine smiled the reddest of smiles. 'He has to pick up someone on the way.'

Seventeen

'Don't look at me.'

'But, for once, we are,' said Agostini, glaring at Cardinal Borgia. 'I accuse you of treachery to the Catholic Church Apostolic, of connivance with the Dominoes in the attempted assassination of Pope Lucian.'

Borgia roared like a bull, almost launching his powerful frame from the throne. 'How dare you? I'm no traitor. Why should I wish to assassinate the pontiff?'

Maroc took two paces and stood beside Agostini. 'It begins with the old Jesuit question: Who profits? As the most likely candidate to succeed Pope Lucian, you had most cause to speed up the succession. That is your motive. As to the proof –' He nodded to Agostini.

'Why you substituted a clone for the pope, then had him killed in so spectacular a fashion, we can only guess at. The Domain Purgatorial will wring the truth from you on that. What is certain is that you, probably with the assistance of Byron, the Doctor and the woman, locked Pope Lucian in the Chamber Impregnable oubliette, meaning to dispose of him later. He was extremely lucky that a guard discovered him on a random inspection.'

'That is insane!' Borgia bellowed, fist thumping an armrest. 'Where's your proof?'

'His Holiness was not quite unconscious when thrown into the oubliette. He saw you, Rodrigo Borgia. He heard you give the orders. Pope Lucian condemns you out of his own mouth.'

'Then why isn't he here to condemn me?'

'Such attendance is not required, by ecclesiastical law,'

said Maroc, his smile a thin slash. 'I was always wary of you, eminence, ever since you took the name of Rodrigo Borgia, a man who became pope through murder and maintained his power by murder.'

'This is outrageous!' exploded Borgia. 'I demand a curial trial as befits my position.'

'A trial would cause scandal,' Agostini said, stepping back and touching the Altar Ipsissimus. 'Vatican City cannot afford a scandal.' He pressed a stud on the altar. 'Better you go straight to the Domain Purgatorial and await the Inquisition.'

Metal bands sprang from armrests and pinioned Borgia to his throne. 'You stinking bastards!' he yelled, struggling against the bonds. Then the throne shot straight through the floor, leaving a square of emptiness. The rumble of a large throne sliding down tunnels reverberated from the gap, mixed with a receding cry: 'Rot in Hell . . .!'

Three members of the Enclave stared at Agostini and Maroc, amazement on their faces.

Richelieu wore a careful smile, the quintessence of diplomacy. 'Cardinals Agostini and Maroc are evidently privy to the pope's confidence. There must be an excellent reason why he informed the two of them and excluded the rest of us. One can only wonder why His Holiness waited so long before denouncing Cardinal Borgia.'

Agostini's smile was the match of Richelieu's. 'His Holiness hoped that Borgia, realizing his plot had failed, would attempt to contact his co-conspirators. We gave him a little time to do so, but could risk no more. That is all, eminences. The Conclave is at an end. We'll meet at a more opportune moment to elect a new member to the Enclave.'

Agostini and Maroc stood by the altar and watched as the rest of the members filed out of the crypt.

Francisco, last in the file, darted across to Agostini and gripped his hand. 'Much thanks for the suggestion, eminence.'

Agostini waved him away with good humour. 'Think nothing of it. Only too happy to assist a promising career.'

Flashing a smile, Francisco made his exit.

Maroc turned to his companion. 'What suggestion was that, eminence?'

Agostini lifted his shoulders. 'Francisco is grateful for small favours. Being young, he's ambitious. A suggestion of mine that he join the Confraternity of Biblical Interpolation gained him praise from the pope this morning. You know how keen Lucian is on Biblical Interpolation.'

Maroc crossed himself. 'Aren't we all, eminence. Aren't we all.'

'Time to leave,' Agostini announced, heading for the door. 'The search for Byron and the Doctor must be organized.'

Maroc followed in his tracks. 'As Camerlengo, I'll assume responsibility for the main search in Transylvania.'

'And I, if I may, will supervise the hunt in the two named Britannias.'

'Agreed. Young Francisco is voicing his opinions, at last. His idea that we look for the Doctor in Britannias Regency and Gloriana was sound, although far from inspired. I didn't know that Byron had a large number of friends in Gloriana, did you?'

Creases formed on Agostini's wide brow. 'I did not. I wonder how Francisco knew.'

Maroc summoned up what passed for a smile. 'Inspiration from above, perhaps?'

The Camerlengo barely caught Agostini's low murmur. 'Or below.'

'For a Black Forest, it doesn't look too bad.'

The forest they had camped in for the evening had a gentle, wistful appearance, an air of romantic *tristesse*.

Sarah sat by the camp-fire at the bottom of a hollow overarched by trees, and contentedly chewed mushrooms, savouring the taste. Food, at last. She swallowed the last morsel with regret.

'I'd give anything for dessert,' she mumbled, eyelids lowering.

'Jelly baby?' the Doctor offered, holding out a paper bag. Free hand dipping into a pocket, he pulled out another bag. 'Or liquorice allsorts?'

Sarah grimaced. 'I'd forgotten all about them! You had those all the time, and didn't offer me a single one.'

The Doctor made his Pagliacci face. 'I thought you didn't like them. You said they were unhealthy. Bad for your figure.'

'Did I? Well, let me be fat, I don't care.' She grabbed a bunch of jelly babies in one hand and liquorice allsorts in the other.

Byron strolled over and peered into one of the bags. 'Jellies in the shape of babies? What's this, Doctor, a magical form of infantile cannibalism?' He took one of the jellies and chewed.

After a few chews he winced and spat out bits of jelly. 'Gah! Tastes like a chemistry experiment.' He straightened up and headed for the slope. 'While you're stuffing that muck in your mouths I'll scour the area for danger. I'll be back before last light. Both of you, stay where you are.'

'Yes, boss,' Sarah muttered, polishing off the last of the sweets. She glanced at the Doctor, who was back in a prone position, hat covering his face. 'Tell me,' she said, 'did you ever eat jelly babies and allsorts in your previous incarnation? I don't recall you doing anything like that.'

'Oh, my lesser self didn't do lots of things I do,' he replied. 'He – I mean I, or *is* it he – was inclined to the self-important. All he – I – did was wave a sword about from time to time.'

She chuckled, rising to her feet. She was still chuckling as she headed for the nearest slope.

'Where are you going?' the Doctor called out.

She cast a mind-your-own-business look over her shoulder. 'Nature calls.'

'It does indeed,' he said, staring at the trees above the hollow. 'But for whom?'

'Making mysteries again?' she asked, starting on the upward climb.

He lay back, hat over his face once more. 'Curiouser and curiouser, Celia,' he intoned.

'In a world of his own again,' she muttered. She left him to it, climbing out of the hollow and wending a path through the firs, their colours muted in the afterglow of sunset.

She glanced around. Now where was a good place to take a pee? She didn't want the prowling Byron catching sight of her in a compromising position.

Ah, the ideal spot — a clump of hawthorn bushes, good and thick. She pushed through the foliage, whose delicate scent reminded her of hawthorn in full bloom of white and pink blossoms.

So peaceful here, she thought dreamily. Hard to imagine this is a Black Forest. She remembered that the hawthorn was called the mayflower tree in England.

She stopped in front of a bush rich in white and pink blossoms, and wondered why she wasn't surprised. The air was drowsy with glamour. She reached out a hand and touched a white bud.

A mask on a stick appeared from behind the bush. The mask was the green and brown of nature, mouth set in a smile. From somewhere, she heard the strains of an antique flute.

The mask was withdrawn, then a man stepped out, dressed in motley, the green and brown mask held before his face, the mask-stick gripped in the whitest of hands.

Am I dreaming? she questioned. She didn't know. And didn't care.

'Who are you?' she breathed softly.

The answering voice was mellow as honey. 'I'm the king of the forest.'

'Who are you?' she found herself repeating, hungry to hear that voice again.

'I'm the spirit of the trees.'

The green-brown mask was instantly replaced by another, as if by magic. A golden mask of the sun beamed at her, encircled by solar flares. His costume had changed to a sparkling cloak.

'I'm the light of your life.'

The mask changed again. Now he held up a death-mask in front of his face. The features brought her father to mind, although the dead set of them made her want to cry. He was dressed in a tweed suit that had seen better days.

'I'm your father,' he said.

The death mask lowered, revealing her father's smiling face, just as she remembered it.

'I'm your father, Sarah,' he said softly.

'You can't be,' she whispered. 'He died.'

'The world's full of magic, Sarah,' he said. 'I told you that. Have you forgotten, now you've grown up? Have you forgotten everything, even that rhyme I taught you when you were very small . . .'

A fox mask appeared from nowhere and covered his features as he started to recite:

> 'Mister Fox
> Lost his socks
> And found them in a chocolate box.'

'I'm under a spell,' she said drowsily. But a little voice inside told her it was all true, every bit of it.

The fox mask was supplanted by a larger, hairier visage.

'Now I'm the Big, Bad Wolf from the Black Forest,' he growled.

Sarah cringed, trying to roll into a ball, a prickly hedgehog.

'Only playing,' laughed the Wolf. 'Playing the Big,

Bad Wolf. Remember how I used to do that? It's fun to be scared.'

She stuck a thumb in her mouth and gave a small nod. Yes, it was fun to be scared – just a *little* bit.

'Want to play another game?'

She nodded eagerly.

The Wolf disappeared and a full-cheeked, jolly man took his place. She giggled at his big stomach and old-fashioned clothes and top hat perched at a jaunty angle.

'Who are you now, who are you now?' she asked gleefully, jumping up and down.

'Why miss, bless your heart, I'm the Jolly Coachman.' He stepped to one side and indicated a black carriage with plumed horses in the shafts.

The Jolly Coachman doffed his top hat as he swept her a bow. 'Room for one more inside, miss.'

'Can I go for a ride, really?' she gasped in delight.

'A ride as long as you like, young miss. Over the hills and far away.'

She ran to the carriage doors. The Jolly Coachman opened a door and lifted her inside. 'Where are we going?' she said, settling into the padded seat.

He jumped up into the driving-seat and shook the reins. 'Over the hills –' he laughed merrily. The horses leapt from the ground and galloped through the air, drawing the carriage into the sky. '– and far away.'

Byron descended into the hollow, and threw the Doctor a glance. 'No sign of trouble, although I'm still uneasy . . .' He looked around. 'No sign of Miss Smith either. Where's she got to?'

The Doctor sat up abruptly from his prone position. 'Nature called,' he said with a frown. 'She answered.' He sprang to his feet. 'Something's wrong – I thought I sensed a presence in the forest. We've got to find her. Come, George, we must hurry.' He broke into a run, bounding up the slope, and cupped hands around his mouth. 'Sarah!' he called out. 'Sarah!'

Byron sprinted in his wake. 'How long has she been gone?'

'Five minutes.'

'That's not long.'

'Long enough.' His gaze roved the twilight forest. 'Sarah!' He raced down the aisle of firs, shouting at full volume.

Byron darted off in a different direction. 'Sarah! Where are you, woman? Sarah!'

When night fell in earnest, they were still calling out her name.

Part Three

A Bolt from the Black

It came like a bolt from the black
And pierced my heart as Cupid's dart.
Never to be drawn, never to give back:
My wound, my remedy, my death, my art.

Pearson's *The Man Who Sold His Ears to the Devil*

Eighteen

'Cardinal Borgia is dead.'

Agostini's hand froze over the chessboard, black bishop clutched tight in his contracting grip. The piece snapped and dropped in two beside a white rook.

He glared at the nervous messenger, then stared across the board at the dumbstruck Maroc.

'What brought about his death?' Agostini demanded of the messenger. 'The Inquisition—'

'The Inquisition had no part in it, eminence. He was crushed in the transit tunnels before reaching Domain Purgatorial. Such accidents have been known.'

Maroc had regained his poise. 'Perhaps it's the judgement of the Almighty.'

Agostini expelled a breath. 'Perhaps. But he's taken his secrets to the Almighty with him. Now we'll learn nothing.' He waved the messenger away, and leaned back in his chair, brooding. 'For Borgia's co-conspirators, a timely accident. Too timely. It must have been arranged.'

'But that could only have been done by a member of the Enclave!' exclaimed Maroc. 'No one else was aware of his transition to Domain Purgatorial.'

'That's so. It seems there were two traitors at the Vatican's heart. I said as much to you, but you wouldn't hear of it. I supplied the names of both suspects. The pope confirmed the guilt of one. Now — well, you know whom to watch.'

Maroc shook his head in confusion. 'Two traitors in the Enclave . . .'

'But only one left to find. And he'll have a contact on

the outside. When he makes that contact, we've g[ot] him.'

'Shouldn't we consult the pope?'

'He's in retreat. We must decide for ourselves.'

Maroc lowered his gaze to the chessboard, with [a] broken black bishop. 'Your move, eminence,' he invite[d] his tone loaded with significance.

Agostini held his head and groaned. 'I just knew yo[u] were going to say that.'

Cardinal Francisco couldn't keep his eyes off the mirror.

An hour ago, after returning in shock to his cham[-] ber, he had knelt down before a statue of St Sebastia[n] and prayed that the Inquisition would purify Rodrig[o] Borgia's soul. On hearing the news of Borgia's death i[n] the transit tunnels, his prayer was more urgent: may Go[d] claim Rodrigo before the Devil takes his own.

The guards, he was told, found it difficult to distinguis[h] between crushed cardinal and crushed throne.

The thought of Borgia's hideous end had put a stop t[o] Francisco's prayers. Such accidents were rare. And th[is] was a convenient accident for anyone who wished th[e] cardinal silenced.

What might he have said that was so damning?

It was with thoughts of damnation that Francisc[o] glanced in the mirror and saw the Devil.

The glimpse of horns and hooves had been fleeting, [a] flicker of diablerie in the glass, but it set his pulse pound[-] ing and rosary beads rattling.

Face the Devil with faith, that's what he'd been taught[.]

Now he paced his chamber, eyes constantly straying t[o] the mirror, daring the Father of Lies to reappear.

The glass reflected nothing but the room and his ow[n] frightened face. His steps slowed, and finally halted i[n] front of the mirror. He folded his arms, and levelled [a] steady stare. Nothing to be afraid of. Reflected at his bac[k] was St Sebastian the martyr, body pierced with arrow[s.] The martyr was the patron saint of his town of birth, an[d] his comfort and inspiration.

That was all he saw in the glass. Himself and St Sebastian.

Then he saw neither. Just the Devil, glaring out of the wooden frame. The Goat of Mendes, sitting cross-legged, with splayed horns and cloven hoof, covered in a grey pelt.

Francisco held up a crucifix in a trembling hand. 'Leave this place, Satanas! I conjure you by —'

The mirror exploded into the room in a blizzard of crystal daggers that swept him off his feet.

The storm of glass blew him through the air to crash-land at the foot of St Sebastian, his body a score of red fountains.

He whispered his life away: 'The Devil has my eyes.'

Wherever they walked, glass crunched underfoot.

Captain Emerich gazed around in stupefaction, taking in the devastation of Cardinal Francisco's chamber. He raised a hand to his bandaged head, memento of his encounter with the Doctor. 'What could have done this?'

Agostini indicated the mirror-stand, devoid of glass. 'There was the weapon, but not the one who wielded it.'

He knelt beside Francisco's corpse, bristling with shards. 'One in each eye. The executioner was an expert.' He stood up. 'Evidently the killer smashed the mirror and used the pieces as knives.'

Emerich shook his head. 'He'd have needed thick gloves. And why bother attracting attention with all that noise? An ordinary dagger would have been quick and silent.'

'Sir!' One of the Switzia Guardians dropped a shiny sliver, blood on his fingers. 'Satan's in the glass!'

A guard at his side stared into another fragment. His face blanched. 'He's in this piece too, sir . . .'

Agostini knelt down and peered into a shard. At first, nothing. Then a change of angle conjured an image: a tiny Goat of Mendes.

Emerich's shout of 'He's in this one as well!' told the

cardinal that the captain witnessed a similar sight.

Agostini picked up another sliver, tilting it in the light. Another miniature Goat of Mendes. The guards followed his example and, one by one, found their own Devils in the glass.

The Goat of Mendes was reflected in every shard. Thousands of Satans scattered on the floor.

'Holograms,' Agostini remarked. One term was as good as another.

The cardinal leaned over Francisco and studied the glass daggers in his eyes. Viewed from the right perspective, the Devil glared back.

Agostini gave a slow nod. 'They say a murdered man's eyes bear the imprint of his killer. Perhaps a mirror serves as well.'

Aleister Crowley slid back the panel and stepped into Cardinal Richelieu's sumptuous apartments. The nun at his back closed the wood panel, leaving him in an apparently empty chamber.

'Sister Mathaswentha can be trusted, if that's what you're wondering,' said Richelieu's voice from the other side of a high-backed chair.

Richelieu rose and beckoned his visitor to a couch. Taking a seat, Crowley gave the cardinal a wicked leer. 'I wasn't wondering about my guide's trustworthiness, just what she was like in bed.'

'I wouldn't know. And I wish you would stop playing the Beast of the Apocalypse, if only for a minute.' Richelieu steepled his fingers. 'Two of the Enclave have died in the last hour. Borgia and Francisco are no longer with us.'

Crowley scratched his bald scalp. 'That's fast work.' His brow contracted. 'That just leaves Agostini, Maroc and Altzinger. Torquemada is excluded from the Throne of Peter on the same grounds as yourself.'

'Yes, we're both Reprises, but Torquemada is doubly excluded on account of the dislike he engenders.'

'So the plan's on course — except that Sister Mathaswentha told me the pope's still alive.'

Cardinal Richelieu inclined his head. 'So it would seem.'

'That puts paid to your hopes of wearing the papal tiara, doesn't it?'

'Leave that to me. And keep Pope Lucian's continuing existence to yourself. For the present, the Throne of Peter is not vacant, and three mortal-born Enclave cardinals stand between myself and the succession even if it were not. The plan must proceed. Otherwise, I will be deprived of the triple tiara, Paracelsus will become Official Antichrist, and the Dominoes will not be destroyed. Will Faust do his part? Time is running out — tonight will be Tenth Night.'

Crowley shrugged. 'Who knows with Faust? But he has the goad of Paracelsus as Official Antichrist to spur him.'

'As have you, as have you. For myself, I have no other motivation than the good of France — of Francia.'

'Slipping into your pre-existence speech patterns again, Richelieu? Somehow, I get the feeling you serve only yourself. But that's fine by me, so long as you call off the attacks on the Anti-Church once you're enthroned. Come to that, what are you going to do about Pope Lucian? When I heard of his survival I thought maybe the whole plan was off. What will you do about the pope — sneak poison into his chalice?'

'No, I will not. I repeat, leave Lucian to me.'

'Then who's next on the death-list? Maroc?'

Richelieu shook his head. 'I think not.'

Crowley glanced around the room. 'I hope to Satan there are no miniature Gargoyles Vigilant hidden in the walls. Are you sure my presence is a secret? Someone might have seen me arrive.'

'When it comes to secrecy and security, I have no peer. The Angelus that delivered you was invisible and impervious to the most sophisticated of Vatican City sensors, and the passages to my rooms secret beyond belief. Your stay here will be unmarked, known only to my most trusted spies.'

'So when do we start?'

'Tomorrow night. Eleventh Night.'

'Then we'd better make preparations.'

Cardinal Richelieu stroked his gold pectoral cross. 'Yes. Events are rushing to a finale. Do your part, and the finale will be a triumph.'

Crowley gave a smile. 'You know, I can easily imagine you as Pope of the Catholic Church Apostolic.'

'So can I, Crowley. So can I.'

'Kneel before me,' commanded Byron.

'Yes, lord,' whispered Claire Clairmont, her voice tiny in the spacious chambers of the Villa Diodati's crypt. Shivering in her torn shift, she knelt on the greasy flagstones.

'Who am I, woman?'

'Bad Byron, lord of –'

'*The* Byron!' he bellowed, giving her a kick that sent her sprawling. 'There is only one Lord Byron. Now – who am I?'

Claire crawled back to his feet. 'You are Lord Byron of Newstead, master of the dark arts, prince of debauchery.'

Byron planted his boot on her head. 'I wish you were Mary Shelley. Mary Shelley under my heel.'

'May I speak, lord?'

'Speak.'

'I've tried to entice my half-sister into our rites, but she will not comply.'

'She can be forced to. Satan welcomes the unwilling sacrifice.'

He raised the skull of the Black Monk to his lips and kissed its eroded mouth. 'Darkest of monks, let us summon Lord Lucifer. Let him bestow a blessing most diabolic on our carnal revels.' Byron closed his eyes. 'Come, Lucifer. Come . . .'

A rapping resounded from the upper part of the villa, echoing down the stone stairwells. A rapping at the outer door.

A hand flew to Claire's mouth. 'He doesn't usually knock.'

'That's not Satan, you stupid trollop,' he snapped, giving her another kick. He sprinted for the spiral staircase, traced its winding path into the upper cellar, and kept up a brisk pace as he ascended the stairway into a wide hall lined with suits of armour, swords, axes and grotesque masks.

Percy Shelley was in the act of opening the front door.

'Stand back, Percy! I'll be the one to greet trespassers with a knife in the guts.'

Shelley, a thin, yellow-haired young man with twitchy face and nervous stance, shuffled to one side. He held a smouldering kite, from which dangled a frazzled cat.

'Sorry, Albé,' he murmured, taking another step back from the door. 'I thought you were occupied with necromantic businesss downstairs.'

'I was.' Byron slid out a knife. 'But I can't leave you to handle intruders, can I? You'd probably offer them hospitality and insist they take your bed for the night.'

He flung open the door to a rainy day, knife ready for the kill.

The figure in the doorway was dressed in a black eye-mask and an opera cloak, emblazoned with the letters DO, the insignia of a Domino.

The stranger doffed his wide-brimmed, plumed hat and gave a bow. 'Johann Faust of Wittenberg, 1480 to 1540,' he announced. 'I promised I'd drop in.'

The cardinal knelt before the scrying mirror, and bowed as Persona appeared in the crystal, his white face wearing its permanent smile.

'Well, priest, what news?'

'Borgia and Francisco are dead, master.'

'That is good. Two down, four to go. And the search

for the Doctor?' asked the rigid mouth.

'The main force has been diverted to Transylvania. A large contingent will be combing two Britannias – under careful guidance. They will be guided to Gloriana's Globe Theatre, as you requested. The suggestion to take part of the hunt to the Britannias came from Francisco.'

'Excellent,' Persona congratulated. 'Tracks well covered. You will make a splendid pope, come Thirteenth Night.'

'Come Thirteenth Night, master.'

'And need I remind you to deliver the Doctor alive into my hands? No, I need not, I'm sure. You know what will happen to you if you fail me in that.'

Persona's image faded from the glass.

The cardinal stood upright, hands clasped in prayer, and gazed at the ceiling. He gazed at the ceiling for a long time.

Sarah thought she remembered flying in a carriage over the hills and far away as a little girl. Soaring to a fleet of gypsy caravans in the sky.

The Jolly Coachman . . .

The recollection flickered and died. It was hard to hold on to any memory, keep any thought still long enough to look at it.

There was a lady with ruby lips leaning over her. She wore a gown of the deepest red. 'Can you remember your name, little girl?'

Of course she could remember her name! It was –

'Shara,' said the woman in red. 'Your name's Shara, isn't it?'

She nodded. 'That's right. I'm Shara.'

'And I –' The lady gestured at her gown. '– am Incarnadine. Do you know what the name Incarnadine means, Shara?'

'I'm – not sure . . .'

'It means "to turn red as blood". Would you like me to turn you red, Shara?'

A man in a black cloak and smiling white face came

and stood at her side. 'Not yet, Incarnadine. Not yet.' He reached down his hand. 'Here, Shara, stand up and look at yourself.'

Holding her by the elbow, he lifted her as though she were a doll, and plumped her on her feet in front of a rectangular mirror.

'Look at yourself,' he invited. 'And tell me what you think.'

She looked as bidden and, for a moment, the dire glamour lost its grip.

She was *Sarah*. Sarah Jane Smith. But she didn't look quite herself in the glass. It reflected flushed features and dithery eyes, teeth bared in a grimace. She was dressed in a shabby orange gown, bordered with white lace that was torn at the neck. A theatrical costume the worse for wear and tear.

Then her name and everything it meant began to slip and slide. She reached for the name Sarah. It slipped through her fingers and was gone.

She fished for a name. One was dropped in her lap.

'Shara . . .' said a mellifluous voice. 'Tell me how you look.'

Shara. Yes, that's my name. How forgetful I am!

She looked – dazzling. An exquisite Lady in Tangerine.

'How do you look?'

'A woman of many parts, milord.'

Nineteen

'The Villa Diodati.'

The Doctor, astride the saddle of Drang, nodded at Byron's words, staring grimly across Lake Geneva.

The outlines of the Villa Diodati were difficult to distinguish in the heavy downpour and fading light, made worse by gathering stormclouds. The villa was a villa in name only. It was a Gothic fantasy, merging Jacobean mansion and late medieval castle. Soaring ramparts, arched windows that steepled to a point, spindling turrets. Around this architectural grotesquerie there circled a wall surmounted by demonic statues, the whole macabre extravaganza wrapped in a visible gloom.

The Doctor gave a toss of the head, displacing the rain that spilled over the brim of his hat. 'That monstrosity bears not the slightest resemblance to the Villa Diodati of history.'

'Bad Byron's creation,' Byron said. 'He replaced a room with an entire wing, built a wing on top of the new wing, dug out a vault, dug a vault below a vault. Within two years, barely a trace of the original villa remained.'

'And where's the Villa Chapuis, the Shelleys' residence? Demolished by Bad Byron?'

'Yes. He never liked it. So, Doctor, shall we wend round the lake and meet my alter ego?'

The Doctor glanced at the surrounding Alpine peaks. 'Won't this area be under surveillance by the Vatican?'

'There are Vatican watchers, but Domino watchers watch the watchers.' He flashed a smile. 'The polyglot in my ear does more than translate. It sends and receives.

The Vatican is concentrating its forces on Transylvania – thanks to a piece of inspired bungling by Miles Dashing.' The smile faded. 'Besides, Lord Byron has set up a Miasma around the villa's precincts. A shield of disguise.'

'I'm aware of that – I spotted it miles off. Presumably, the Vatican is also aware of it.'

Byron gave a shrug. 'If there were increased Vatican surveillance, the Dominoes would have informed me. There *has* been a slight increase, but nothing of note. Why the concern? I'd have thought you had a lot more on your mind.'

'I have. That's why I need to discount Vatican City for the time being. I want all my wits saved for Doctor Sperano – and Sarah.'

'Yes – Sarah.' Byron lowered his gaze. 'I never took to the woman, but I was responsible for her welfare. And I wouldn't see any woman in mortal danger. Her disappearance was so strange . . .' He shot the Doctor a sharp glance. 'Once inside the villa, I want answers. Answers in abundance.'

'I'll tell you all I know.'

'Truly? That should be interesting.'

'Oh, by the way,' the Doctor said. 'I presume you know we're being followed. Followed with great expertise.'

Byron gave a faint smile. 'If it's who I think it is, we'll soon be meeting our trackers face to face. Come, Doctor, before the light fails entirely. It's still a good quarter-hour to the villa.'

Together, they rode along the banks, gradually veering towards the Villa Diodati.

'Miles – Slime – Rose – Eros,' recited Miles Dashing, recalling Vampire Byron's parting words. 'Anagrams. What of it? Still can't see what he was getting at. And what did he mean by saying that there's a dark in the name of Dashwood?'

Miles flicked back the drenched locks of his hair and

peered through the teeming rain at the Villa Diodati. 'Perhaps Bad Byron can fill in the spaces left by Mad Byron.'

'Er – those two gentlemen we've been tracking, sir – going at quite a gallop now,' Crocker said, squinting at a couple of dots in the distance. 'Shouldn't we hurry up our steeds a bit?'

'Silence, oaf, I'm thinking.'

'Sorry, sir.'

'Anyway,' muttered Miles, 'it's perfectly obvious they're heading for the Villa Diodati. The route to the Geneva Dominion, with its perfidious democracy and puritanism, lies in the other direction. And as they're riding straight to Bad Byron's residence, we can safely discount them as Vatican agents. Now – a dark in the name of Dashwood ... You can take six letters from Dashwood and form the word "shadow", leaving "do" – a verb signifying the performance and completion of an action or, more to the point, the code for the Dominoes. But still – what of it?'

'About Doctor Sperano and his Theatre of Transmogrification, sir. If you think about masks ...'

'Will you stop jabbering about Doctor Sperano! I have no interest in either him or his plays. They are, by the judgement of every person of aesthetic sensibility, tasteless, talentless, and derivative to the ultimate degree.'

'Saw one once back in the Old Vic,' Crocker mused. 'At the start of the first scene, Edward II walks on saying: "Oh, I do hope I don't get a red-hot poker shoved up my arse tonight." *Edward II's Horrible End*, the play was called.'

'Crocker – do you mind?'

'Sorry, sir.'

'Just because you threw yourself in front of that werewolf last night it does not mean you can give yourself airs. You did, after all, delay him only a moment while I was loading my Hellfire pistol with silver bullets.

And there were nine other man-beasts to deal with.'

'Yes, sir. But there was that time when we were lured into those endless caverns by a nest of them whatchamacallits . . .'

'*Nachzehrers* and *Neuntöters*,' Miles said. 'Unusual to find those two groups of vampires in the same nest. *Neuntöters* are plague-bearers, and *Nachzehrers* normally give them a wide berth. Tricky moment, that, when we were trapped in the Cavern of Oppression at the centre of the labyrinth.'

'You're not kidding! There were dozens of the blighters. Clever move that, sir, turning the – the Nuntrotters against the Knackersearers. But I did brain two of 'em with a rock. Chance of an adventure bonus on top of my salary, sir?'

'I'll consider it. What galls me is that we've lost an entire day, thanks to those minor scrapes. Who knows what disasters have befallen in matters of state in the interim? Richelieu's wicked plots might now be hatched, and darkness set to fall on Europa.'

'Sounds grim, sir.'

A flash of lightning lit up Miles's elegant profile. A roll of thunder underscored his sombre reply. 'Your commoner's mind could not conceive the horrors which the Inquisition might unleash on the world. You have no idea, Crocker, what perils I faced when I once duelled with the Comte d'Étrange on the rim of the Pit of Perdition.'

'What pit's that, sir?'

'Never mind. Those strangers approach the Villa Diodati. Caution now gives way to swiftness. At a full gallop, Crocker!'

Miles Dashing streaked off to the accompaniment of blaze of lightning and detonation of thunder.

Crocker was soon left far behind, struggling to prompt his pony from a slow canter to a gallop. The pony decreased in speed to a laggardly trot, Crocker's short legs thumping its sides in exasperation.

'Teach me to buy an old banger of a pony for a hundred marks,' he grumbled.

Byron hammered on the massive door with his fist. 'Lord Byron, sixth baron here!' he bellowed. 'Let me in, Albé!'

The Doctor shook the rain from his hat. 'Albé – the nickname Percy Shelley used with the historical Byron. Is that what we call Bad Byron to distinguish him from you?'

'It is. If you call him Bad Byron to his face, he'll part your head from its neck.'

The Doctor glanced at the graveyard at their backs, boiling with white mist. 'Are there dead bodies in there, or is it purely for show?'

'With Albé, who can tell? The cemetery is a recent addition. It wasn't here when last I called.'

The door swung open, and Albé Byron stood framed in the doorway, a black greatcoat draping his brawny physique.

Byron swept a mock-bow to Albé. 'George Gordon, Lord Byron, 1788 to 1824.'

Albé smiled and gave a nod. 'Likewise.' The smile vanished. 'Who's the fellow with a scarf as long as a bridal train?'

'I'm the Doctor,' came the instant response, with a flash of a grin and an outstretched hand.

Albé Byron ignored the proffered handshake. 'What do you want, George?'

Byron spread his hands. 'What do you think? A roof over our heads. A full table. And time to talk.'

Albé hesitated, a spasm plucking a cheek muscle. 'There shouldn't be two of us in the same place.'

The Doctor gave an understanding nod. 'Clone syndrome. The symptoms are loss of a sense of identity, double-illusion, et cetera. Best cure is to develop a personality based on purely individual experiences, combined with exercises of a –'

'Oh, come in, damn you!' Albé snarled, whirling round.

'But keep well away from me,' he shouted, striding down the hall.

A thin, ethereal man with yellow hair and a nervous smile ushered the visitors in.

'It's good to see you again, George,' the young man greeted. He glanced at the Doctor. 'I'm Percy. Er – Percy Shelley, 1792 to 1822.'

The Doctor met his glance with a keen stare. 'I've met the original. Pleasant fellow, if a trifle overwrought. And a greater poet than even you, George.'

Byron flicked a hand. 'I know it.'

'Your *Prometheus Unbound* was a magnificent work,' the Doctor complimented.

Percy blushed and mumbled something.

A petite woman entered the hall. Petite in size, imposing in all else, from her Domino costume to the intensity of her gaze. 'Good evening, Doctor. I'm Mary Shelley, by inclination if not yet by words mumbled in a marriage ceremony. Percy, would you please deposit that kite and lightning-fried cat out of sight and mind? Come, Doctor, I've been awaiting your arrival with impatience.'

The three men exchanged quizzical glances, then shrugs.

She conducted them into a room large enough to hold a concert with full orchestra. The chandeliers alone would have covered the roof of an average home. Bas-reliefs of classical antiquity covered the walls, their themes alternately violent and erotic.

In one of many armchairs reclined a willowy, long-nosed man with lank hair. He raised an indolent hand.

'Johann Faust,' she introduced. 'Domino code-name Mephistopheles, appropriately.'

Faust grinned. 'Christians have their saint's names, I my demon name. My demon is a deal more effective than their saints.'

The Doctor raised his hat. 'Your reputation precedes you, Faust, even if the historical facts were squalid in the extreme – thief, confidence trickster, blackmailer . . .'

Faust tensed, anger sparking in his gaze. A moment later, his expression lightened. 'All true, and more besides, including the tale that I sold my soul to the Devil, from which pact I gained not the slightest benefit. In my Reprise life, however, Mephistopheles has been most accommodating.'

The Doctor sat in an armchair opposite Mary Shelley while the others assumed their seats. 'Tell me,' he asked her, 'how did you know I was coming? The Domino grapevine?'

'Message from the Vatican,' she replied.

'From whom in the Vatican?'

'That must remain secret.'

Byron studied her closely. 'Surely you can tell me – in private?'

A shake of the head. 'Under no conditions.'

The Doctor, observing the interplay of characters, gave Mary a shrewd look. 'I think I've just met the leader of the Dominoes.'

'Dominoes don't have leaders,' Mary said. 'But I advise.'

'She's the nearest we have to a leader.' Byron's respect for Mary Shelley was evident in his admiring glance. 'I wasn't so impressed with Mary in pre-existence, but as a Reprise she excels.'

Faust leaned forward. 'Mary. This Vatican informant, he must be a member of the Enclave. Let me take a guess – Agostini.'

She spread her palms. 'Guess as much as you like.'

'Mary,' the Doctor broke in. 'Before we launch into matters of state and rebellion and suchlike, may I touch on a personal subject? A companion of mine, Sarah Jane Smith, disappeared in a Black Forest last night. Has there been any news?'

She shook her head. 'How did she disappear?'

'She walked into the forest on a call of nature, and didn't come back. By the time we started searching, it was too dark to see very much. The next morning, we found her tracks, along with those of another, most likely a man. We followed them to a small glade, where her and the man's footprints ended, beside the deep imprint of wheels and horses' hooves.'

Faust waved an airy hand. 'Your lady companion had an assignation and departed in a carriage or some such vehicle. Hardly the first time in history. May we move on to weightier concerns now?'

Byron shot Faust a barbed look. 'The wheel-prints showed the vehicle had travelled no more than five metres, likewise the horses. The carriage, if that's what it was, could only have travelled through the air.'

'And Sarah wouldn't have wandered off with a passing stranger,' the Doctor said. 'Believe me.'

Mary lifted her shoulders. 'I do believe you, but I'm afraid I can be of no assistance.'

'Now that's out the way,' Faust snorted. 'Perhaps we —' A loud knock made him start in his seat. 'That damned front door with its decibel boosters. Trust Albé to build in boosters that shake every room in the villa.'

'I'll get it,' said Percy, springing from his chair. 'If Albé opens the door the visitor's life won't be worth a cat in a thunderstorm.'

'Not one of your cats, anyway,' Mary scowled, watching him leave. 'He's almost as bad as the Demented Shelley that drowned himself in the lake last month. Albé took the loss badly. He's been getting worse by the day.'

'And concerning yourself, Mary,' Byron said. 'How is the sequel to *Frankenstein: the Modern Prometheus* coming along?'

'In fits and starts, but at least this time I can sympathize fully with the Creature.' She glanced round at her fellow-Reprises, her tone sinking to a wistful murmur.

'We are all Frankenstein's monsters,' she said.

The gazes of her companions lowered in the lull that followed.

'Speaking of Frankenstein,' Byron remarked, in an obvious attempt to lift the mood. 'Did you know, Doctor, that Victor Frankenstein has been Reprised from a gentleman of that title who once lived on the Rhine? He was encoded with a composite "Frankenstein" personality, drawn from the book and several films. At times he skulks in the grounds of the villa, calling down the wrath of Heaven on Mary for not accepting him as her creation. Once he broke into her bedroom and insisted that she recognize him as her son. How's that for dramatic irony, Doctor?'

Before he could answer, a tall young man swept into the room, black cloak billowing, hand on sword hilt. 'Miles Dashing of Dashwood,' he announced, with a curt bow. 'Delighted to be under the same roof as your esteemed self, madam.'

Byron had jumped from his seat and grabbed the newcomer by the shoulders. 'Miles, you lunatic!' he laughed. 'Where have you been?'

Miles broke into a smile. 'Ah – you're Dangerous Byron. Well met, sir!'

Byron arched an eyebrow. 'At *last*. What happened to you – and Casanova, come to that. I waited in St Peter's Basilica the best part of an hour.'

'Oh – I thought it was St Peter's Square. I didn't look into the basilica until much later. Shot off to St Mark's Square in Venice after that. Had a word with Casanova, but he wasn't aware of any rendezvous. On later reflection, it occurred to me that I visited the wrong Casanova . . . May I sit down? Thank you. So, how did your meeting with Pope Lucian go?'

'Pope Lucian went, skewered by a St Michael statue directed by persons unknown. I was blamed for the killing, as was the Doctor here. No, don't stand up, Miles, let's leave the introductions till later, shall we? Where have you been, what have you been doing?'

'Not a great deal. I staked Mad Byron in Transylvania, but his vampiric shadow pursued me.'

'Are you referring to a detachable shadow?' the Doctor interrupted.

'Er, yes, sir, I am. A shadow of Hell imbued with the puissance of the Ipsissimus Nosferatu.'

The Doctor shook his head. 'Way off beam. A shadow is a positive-negative, so to speak. It's the surrounding photon-frame that defines a shadow. The vampiric psyche is photon-evading by nature. Photon-evasion guides the vampiric psyche to the shadow. Anti-light is then created, capable of independent action within a field of cold light, especially moonlight. A plenum-vacuum, you might say. A shadow vampire is full of the presence of its absence, to paraphrase Jean-Paul Sartre.'

Miles gave the Doctor a long, cool stare. 'Are you making all this up?'

'The Doctor, as I've discovered, is a knowledgeable man,' Byron said. 'His erudition on a vast range of topics has earned my increasing respect.'

'Then I bow to your opinion, Lord Byron. Doctor – despite your medical title, I presume you are of noble birth?'

'Well, I'm a lord of sorts, but I –'

'I thought so. You have an air of bohemian nobility about you. Tell me, does your erudition extend to unusual names, codes, that sort of thing?'

'Managra again,' smiled Byron, winking at Mary.

'Yes, Managra,' Miles continued. 'Does the name Managra mean anything to you?'

The Doctor sat up in his chair. 'Indeed it does, Miles. The name's an anagram.'

'*Another* anagram,' the young lord groaned.

'Managra,' said the Doctor, 'is an anagram of anagram.'

'My God!' exclaimed Miles. 'I never thought of that.'

'We did,' Byron said, glancing at Mary.

'Then why didn't you tell me?'

'You'd only have puzzled over it the more. Face it, Miles. Your family were a bunch of monsters, and you the exception to the rule. Your father played a final mean trick on you, giving you a clue to nothing, that led nowhere.'

Miles's hand flashed to his sword hilt, then hesitated. 'If any but you insulted the honour of the Dashwoods, swords would be drawn and blood spilt. Have a care, Byron.'

'Miles has a point about the name,' the Doctor said. 'An anagram gave me the first clue as to the puppeteer who pulls the strings in Europa. What do any of you know about Doctor Sperano?'

The young lord, his anger subsiding, gave the Doctor a sharp glance. 'The said Doctor performed one of his dreadful plays in a neighbouring mansion the night before my family was — infected.'

'It's all in a name,' the Doctor murmured, settling back, eyes closing. 'Sperano is an anagram of persona. And the word persona, as you're doubtless aware, was originally taken from the masks worn by actors in classical Greek drama. The persona was the role, the false face. A theatre of masks. The Theatre of Transmogrification?'

He had everyone's full attention. Miles was utterly absorbed: 'Go on, Doctor.'

'Well, there's one anagram for you. And here's one more, of much greater significance . . . Sperano is an anagram of Pearson, and Francis Pearson was an English dramatist who disappeared in London on the twenty-ninth of June, 1613. Gentlemen — lady — it's my belief that Doctor Sperano is Francis Pearson, transported from the seventeenth century to this period. And, I suspect, he has united with an entity mentioned in an old tale from my home world. The name Managra is a jumbled non-name that leads you in a circle. The old tale I referred to also gives this entity an anagram of anagram as a name. A non-name. A non-entity, if you will.'

'And this — entity infected my family?' Miles said in a hoarse breath.

'That may have been Sperano himself. It's impossible as yet to gauge the degree of interdependency of Sperano and Managra.'

Byron regarded Miles with more than a touch of remorse. 'We should have taken your Managra more seriously, Miles, although we had no means of knowing better.' He turned to the Doctor. 'It was when I mentioned the banning of Elizabethan and Jacobean plays, combined with the name of Doctor Sperano, that you first realized the dramatist's identity, wasn't it?'

'And the titles of Sperano's plays – a number of them including Pearson's lost dramas. However, I gleaned my first inkling from the back of St Benedict's hand –'

He glanced up as the door slammed open and Albé Byron stormed in, dragging a near-naked woman by the hair. 'More guests in my home?' he growled. 'Ugh – it's you, Master Dashing. Saved any wenches from a fate they deserved recently?'

'Unhand that woman, sir!' demanded Miles, leaping to his feet.

Albé sent her spinning across the carpet. 'You want her, you have her.'

'Take this, my lady Claire Clairmont, for your shift is scanty and torn,' offered Miles, whisking off his cloak and dropping it over Claire's shoulders.

Albé threw himself into a chair next to Faust and glowered at his guests. 'What are you looking at?' he snapped.

'A man made from a toenail, if I'm not mistaken,' Byron said coolly, idly studying the ends of his fingers.

Suddenly, the room was crammed with silence.

Albé went white with rage.

'Now you've done it,' Mary breathed softly.

Albé rose menacingly from the chair. 'George Gordon, Lord Byron,' he said, slowly and deliberately. 'I challenge you to a séance.'

Byron returned the glare. 'Challenge accepted.'

The Doctor took in Byron's casual manner. 'Challenge expected. That was no provocation out of the blue.'

Miles nodded agreement. 'It seems Dangerous Byron wishes to be the only Byron in Europa.'

'*I* will soon be the only Byron in Europa,' Albé said in a tone of utter conviction.

The Doctor glanced at a round table near a window, its shimmer betraying the presence of psycho-conductive wood. 'A séance,' he muttered. 'I think I'll join in.'

Casanova fumed in the glide-gondola.

'This must be the longest gondola ride in history, Antonio.'

The gondolier threw up a hand. 'How was I supposed to know that a Mediterranean had slipped north of Porto Maghera? Dimensions Extraordinary are playing havoc with my navigation. Why can't these transdimensional Mediterraneans stay where they're put?'

'Reality shifts are becoming more frequent,' Casanova conceded. 'As though theatrical scene-shifters are at work behind the, er, scenes.' He peered down through the clumps of cloud. 'Can't see a thing. Are we over Bavaria Glockenstein yet?'

'Close enough.' Antonio pursed his lips. 'It's strange how the gondola was forced to take you the whole way to your intended destination. A suspicious man might be inclined to believe you had interfered with the steering mechanism.'

'No more than an example of synchronicity,' drawled Casanova. 'My life abounds in it. Console yourself that you serve a man on a noble mission. I promised to visit Prince Ludwig after viewing that superlative performance of *Twelfth Night* he permitted in Castle Ludwig. He was somewhat concerned about the repercussions of staging the play, and wished my keen rapier at hand if retribution should fall. Belated though my arrival, it will be welcome. Now drop me off in Glockenstein, Antonio, there's a good fellow, and do *try* not to hit any more pockets of Dimensions Extraordinary. They quite upset my constitution.'

Snorting angrily, Antonio steered the gondola on a steep descent.

'This trip will cost you a fortune,' Antonio muttered sullenly.

'A fortune I don't have, alas.'

'Now where have I heard that before?'

'Persona,' the cardinal summoned.

The round mirror shimmered. A figure in black with white, smiling face appeared.

'Well, cardinal. Trouble, so soon? I have little time now for our chats.'

'One last time, Persona, and then all's done.'

'Then speak, and to the point.'

'Should I supervise the surveillance of the Globe Theatre in person, or would that draw unwanted attention? Representatives of the Vatican are not welcome in Britannia Gloriana. But if I'm not there to supervise, the Doctor might slip through our fingers.'

'I already know the Doctor's whereabouts.'

'You do?'

'I do. Don't interrupt. I must be ready for him. The scope of his powers needs to be assessed. By the time he reaches the Globe, I'll have all the knowledge I require. In answer to your question, I consider a personal visit to Gloriana unwise in the extreme. Stay where you are, and send your most reliable agent to survey the mission. Your presence is required in the Vatican.'

The cardinal bowed. 'Yes, master.'

'Adieu,' said Persona. 'Until Thirteenth Night.'

'Until Thirteenth Night.'

The eerie figure faded from the ancient scrying mirror. Expelling a breath, the cardinal rose to his feet.

Then, as so often, he gazed up at the ceiling. If outdoors, or in a chapel, his gaze would have been lifted to Heaven. Here, in his private chambers, it was raised to Hell.

A fresco of the Sufferings of the Damned covered the ceiling. From the multitudes of lost souls, the face of Pope Lucian stared down, as woeful as its first appearance on the night of the pope's death.

'*Sic transit gloria mundi*,' Agostini intoned.

Agostini's mouth bent in a smile. The pope's demise, manifested in paint through a dash of Persona's mimetic magic, had corroborated the news brought by Rosacrucci. He had waited an hour for that news, feigning sleep.

When the pope's murder was confirmed by the apparition in paint, he had inwardly rejoiced.

Lucian's murder completed the first act of Persona's plan.

Agostini's rise to the Throne of Peter had begun.

Twenty

The carriages and wagons of the Rite of Passage swept down from the phantasmagoria of the Passing Strange and into the realm of the Ordinary.

The Rite of Passage retinue followed the leading two carriages into a spacious hall. The Theatre of Transmogrification was in town. Or rather, the theatre was in church. A church that flew upside down above the clouds.

The vehicles glided to a halt on the roof of St Incarnata le Fanu, the inverted church of Johann Faust. The Faustians and Therionites were lined up at the far end of the roof, sinking to their knees as a door of the lead carriage swung open.

Doctor Sperano, Master Dramaturge, descended arm in arm with Milady Incarnadine. 'Greetings, gentles all,' he declaimed with a flourish of the hand. 'Our humble players, shadows of substance that they are, are here for your diversion.'

Sperano's white, smiling face scanned the Church of the Fallen and alighted on the man who remained upright. 'Ah, Benvenuto Cellini, sculptor, metalsmith, writer of spicy memoirs, a true Renaissance man. Permit us to approach.'

'You're welcome,' said Cellini. 'A private performance from the Theatre of Transmogrification, and at no cost, is not to be sneezed at. Besides — anything for a laugh.'

Sperano approached the confident young man. 'You stand in the place of Faust and Crowley, Master Cellini? I had heard they chose you as a — representative. They are, I know, elsewhere engaged.'

Cellini gave a sneer. 'I stand in place of no man. The Faustians and Therionites have a new leader, myself.'

'Oh, let us not be disingenuous, kind sir. Great artist though you were in pre-existence, you were a mere voyeur of the necromantic arts, not even a dabbler. The necromancer in Rome's Colosseum gave you more than you bargained for.'

'Impertinent bastard,' snapped Cellini, bunching a fist. 'You were invited here as entertainers, no more. You need a lesson in manners, Sperano.'

A laugh trickled from Doctor Sperano's inflexible lips as he plucked out a quill from under his cloak. 'No, you need a lesson in obedience.' He jabbed the quill into a vein, and sucked up red blood for ink.

Too swift for the eye to follow, he scribbled blood-red words on the air. Exercise completed, in less than two seconds, he stood back, leaving a sentence hovering in the air, dripping red drops on to the roof-floor: '*I obey you in all things, Doctor Sperano, said Benvenuto Cellini in the upside-down church, meaning every word he said.*'

Cellini, eyes glazed, recited the written words. 'I obey you in all things, Doctor Sperano.' He stood meekly, awaiting instruction.

Sperano grabbed the shimmering words out of the air, popped them in his mouth, and gulped them down. 'I have never been afraid to eat my own words. Now order your followers to sit and watch. I have produced an amusing little one-act play for this occasion, entitled: *A Stab and a Scream in the Dark on a Gothic Night by a Big Lake: a Drama with a Point*. I'm not sure about the title, but it will suffice for a one-off performance. Please take your seat on the – roof.'

As the audience settled, Sperano resumed writing on the air. 'Now let me see,' he muttered. 'A large Gothic room, with a round table centre-stage. Lightning flashing through an arched window – no – make that three arched windows. A roll of thunder –'

With each scrawl of the quill, the scene described took

shape between the audience and the Rite of Passage vehicles. Walls rose with three arched windows. Lightning flickered. Thunder rolled.

He scribbled the cast list, then, quill poised, summoned the actors name by name, concluding with '– and Shara, stage-name Intangerine.'

The cast took their places on the psychotronic set. Sperano gave Shara an encouraging nod. 'You'll be a credit to the Theatre of Transmogrification on your first appearance, won't you, Shara Intangerine?'

Shara returned the nod, fingering the white lace collar of her orange Regency gown, then lifting the dagger in her grasp. 'I'll give it a stab.'

Casanova stormed into the Chimera Hall of Castle Ludwig, rapier at the ready.

What ailed the servants of the House Glockenstein? Not a one in sight. Empty hall after empty hall. Had the entire household fled, or been slaughtered for performing a Shakespearean drama? Such a performance did, indeed, carry the death penalty in all the Bavarias.

He skidded to a halt. The Prince was visible in the murky hall, slumped in a chair, hugging a small red bundle.

'Prince Ludwig!' he cried out. 'What fate has befallen the House of Glockenstein?'

Prince Ludwig raised a feeble arm, and beckoned.

A score of long strides took Casanova to Ludwig's side. Ludwig raised his face.

'Hell's teeth!' Casanova exclaimed.

The prince's mouth was – not a mouth. It was a mere rent, a loose flap, curved into a travesty of a smile.

At first he thought the lips had been cut off, then he perceived that the slash was too thin.

'Facial transmogrification,' he hissed. 'Who did this, prince? The Vatican?'

Ludwig shook his head and lifted the red bundle. 'He killed Wagner,' intoned a guttural, monotone voice that might have issued from a grave. The tone was in keeping with Ludwig's waxen appearance. 'He killed Wagner.'

'Well, there are plenty of Wagners to go around . . .' Then Casanova realized what the red bundle was. 'Oh, he killed your dog. Most – tragic.'

The monotone voice went on, dead as a cracked bell. 'He told me to forget. But I remembered him killing Wagner. The killing wasn't in his script. Remembered the dog.'

'But your face – the deserted castle . . . Never mind. Who killed Wagner?'

'Told me to forget, I think. But after he said Wagner was red. After that – remember, a little. Shouldn't have killed little Wagner. Told me to forget . . .'

Casanova stroked his chin. 'An example of Dr Mesmer's art, unless I'm mistaken. What has been imposed by mesmerism can be relieved by mesmerism, with a few improvements of my own, dispensing with the flim-flam of magnetic fluid. Fear not, Prince Ludwig, I shall banish this dark enchantment.'

Lighting the candles of a nearby candelabrum, he took out a crystal suspended from a slender chain, and waved it to and fro before Ludwig's crazed eyes.

'Watch how the crystal catches the light. Keep watching the crystal. And listen to my voice. Hear only my voice . . .'

'Gather round the table, and hold hands,' Albé commanded in a voice like the crack of doom.

Faust fidgeted, staying well clear of the round table. 'I think I'll sit this one out – on the other side of the room.'

'The legendary Faust shrinks from a séance?' Byron said scornfully. 'You've changed your tune. We need at least seven pairs of arms to encircle the table, and Claire is hardly up to the experience.'

'Definitely not,' the Doctor agreed, glancing at the woman sprawled on a couch. 'The lady requires rest. Besides, her mental turmoil would set up interference patterns in the composite telepathic lattice. With a psycho-conductive table of this high energy, the resultant psionic backlash –'

'Thank you, Doctor,' Mary smiled. 'Suffice it to say that Claire's instability will be amplified and transmitted to others in the circle. You verge on the pedantic.'

He looked stunned. 'Gosh, do you really think so?'

A knock boomed at the outer door, resounding through the villa.

'Gods!' bellowed Albé. 'Has the Villa Diodati become a hostelry!'

'That will be my servant,' Miles said. 'Perhaps he may be permitted to sit in the hallway. Do you have someone of low degree to let him in?'

'Voice-command will do,' Albé snorted. 'Outer door!' he shouted. 'Open!' He waited a moment. 'Visitor! Enter and remain in hallway!' He heaved a sigh. 'Now let us begin.'

'After Miles's servant joins the circle,' Byron said. 'This is, after all, a séance duel. A circle of seven leaves an unequal number of non-duellists between the protagonists. Séance duellists should face each other from opposite sides of the table, with an even count of non-combatants between.'

Albé nodded. 'That will make for a fair duel. Servant! Enter second door on the right!'

Miles drew himself to full height, dwarfing all but the Doctor. 'Do you mind, sir? Crocker is *my* servant.'

Albé flicked a hand. 'You tell him to take part, then. Just let's get on with it.'

When Crocker sneaked his head through the door, Miles signalled him forward. 'You have the honour to take part in a séance duel between Bad – er, Albé Byron and Dangerous Byron. You will be delighted to hear that you'll be linking hands with the noble and famous for the duration of a contest which will unleash supernatural forces in violent conflict. The combat will conclude when one of the duellists dies of terror.'

A gulp travelled down Crocker's throat. 'Too good for the likes of me, sir. Sure you don't want me to polish your boots instead? They could do with a bit of a shine . . .'

The Doctor strode up to Crocker and looped an arm around his shoulders. 'You come and sit next to me, Crocker. I'll make sure you come to no harm.'

Crocker looked up, cheered by the Doctor's assurance. 'Why, thank you, sir. You're a real gent.'

'Now can we begin?' Albé exhaled sharply, taking a seat. Speeding across the floor, the Doctor plumped himself down beside the owner of the Villa Diodati, who threw him a wary glance.

The others settled into place, Mary sitting between Crocker and Byron, and Faust, Miles and Percy sitting in an arc from Byron to Albé.

Faust twisted uneasily. 'I don't see why I should have to do this.'

Byron gripped Faust's hand. 'You'll do it. Now everyone link hands.'

Albé planted the skull of the Black Monk at the centre of the table and joined hands with the Doctor and Percy. The remainder followed suit.

Albé glared across the table at Byron. '*En garde.*'

Byron glared back. '*En garde.*'

'Can you see him, prince?' Casanova kept the crystal swinging to and fro although his arm felt as though it were about to drop off. 'He is killing your dog. Can you see his face?'

Ludwig's drowsy eyes tracked the crystal's arc. 'Squeezing . . . squeezing . . . pink to red.'

Casanova glanced at the patches of pink dye on the crushed poodle, and put two colours together and made a scene. 'Yes, that's right. He's squeezing Wagner. Crushing him to death. Look at the man's face.'

'No face.'

'Look at his face.'

'No face.'

'Is the face hidden?'

'Mask.'

Casanova sensed he was getting somewhere, at last. It had taken a good half hour to lull Prince Ludwig into a trance. And for the last ten minutes all the prince had produced was 'no face'.

'Look under the mask. Don't be afraid. Look under the mask.'

'Under . . . No face.'

'Look. I command you to look.'

He could tell that Ludwig was looking, peering into the past.

'No face.'

Casanova bit back his frustration. 'Very well. Look at the mask.'

'White smile.'

'Good . . . good . . . Keep looking.'

'White marble. Smiling.'

'Good. Now – who is wearing the mask?'

Ludwig forced his slit of a smile to move. 'No – spear.'

No spear? What did Ludwig mean? No Shakespeare?

'Again. Who is wearing the mask?'

'Rape – son.' Ludwig's brow was streaming with hot sweat. His legs spasmed.

Diagnosing an impending fit, Casanova spoke softly. 'The man in the mask has gone. You're lying in your bed now, warm and safe. You're starting to dream of a pleasant valley on a summer's day. There's a brook nearby. You're at peace. At peace . . .'

A look of serenity stole into Ludwig's features. He expelled a long breath as his eyes closed.

Casanova lifted the dog from Ludwig's lap and placed it on the floor. In a short while, he would bury the animal. Before that, he would carry the prince to his bed and leave him to rest.

But first of all, to decode the man's speech . . .

A mask. No face. No face because covered by a mask? Most likely.

No spear. Rape son. It took only a few seconds for him to realize that the phrases were anagrams of each other. Damn it, if he just had pen and paper.

He knelt down, pulling out his dagger, and scratched the seven letters on the flagstones, then sat and ran through all possible combinations in his head.

First, assume the seven letters add up to a single word: the permutations were lesser in number. Lips pressed tight, he frowned in concentration as he mentally shuffled the letters.

One word leaped out, suggested by the mask: persona. His shoulders sank. If that's what the anagram signified, the clue led in a circle: mask − persona − mask . . .

Minutes slipped by while he produced permutation after permutation.

He thumped the floor. He was getting nowhere. The anagram didn't mean −

Sperano.

The name came from nowhere. Doctor Sperano of the Theatre of Transmogrification, sometimes known as the man of masks.

'Doctor Sperano,' Casanova hissed between his clenched teeth. 'Could it be that you punished the prince's showing of *Twelfth Night* because of your forthcoming *Thirteenth Night*? Who are you, Sperano? More than a dramatist, or I'm no more than a librarian.'

The Theatre of Transmogrification would be in Venice for Thirteenth Night, but he had no wish to wait that long for vengeance. Sperano's travelling theatre made a habit of turning up unannounced. Had he mentioned his next venue to the prince?

He roused Ludwig from his dream of a summer valley, adopting Sperano's smooth tone.

'Prince Ludwig, I am Doctor Sperano. Do you hear? I am Doctor Sperano.'

The prince's eyelids flickered. 'Yes, Doctor.'

'I told you to forget. Now I order you to remember. Remember my visit.'

The eyes filled with dread. 'Yes – I remember.'

'Describe it – in detail.'

Through slurred speech, and frequent lulls, Ludwig told the tale of Sperano's visit, and the play staged in the Chimera Hall. The play's title was typical Sperano: *Lord George and St Michael and how the Subtle Dragon Killed the Pope*.

As the account progressed, Casanova grimly noted the coincidence of time and place between Byron's meeting with Pope Lucian (damn me for not being there!) and the enactment of the pope's murder. In the play, the pope was killed by St Michael, skewered on a spear, with an actor playing Sperano lurking behind a pillar, costumed as a serpent Satan, the hidden controller of events.

Casanova stroked his lower lip. 'Art mirrors life, but can life mirror art?'

Had Sperano's play caused the pope's murder? He listened attentively as Ludwig reached the end of his narrative.

'Then you left,' wheezed Ludwig. 'And you shouted out to Incarnadine: "Next stop, the church" –'

Casanova groaned inwardly. The church. There were over two hundred thousand churches in Europa.

'– and then, Verona,' Ludwig whispered. With that, he lapsed into silence.

Casanova rose triumphantly.

'Verona.'

'Sod this for a lark.'

'Did you just mutter something?' Mary Shelley asked, brows knitted.

'Me, miss?' Crocker said, eyes wide as he could make them. 'Just a wordless mumble, miss. A bit o' froth from the stream of consciousness.'

A suspicious glance from Miles silenced him. Oops. Better watch his tongue, or he'd be out of a job. Act thick, that's the ticket.

'What's this 'ere séance duelling when it's at home then, squire?' he asked the Doctor.

'We are *en garde*!' Albé barked, glaring his rage at Crocker.

'Oh, our friend here is entitled to know what he's letting himself in for,' the Doctor said jovially, tipping Crocker the wink.

'He's only a damned servant!' Albé roared.

'In the ideal world, there will be neither servant nor master,' Percy broke in. 'All men will be equal, and the Promethean fire of knowledge will be brought to all men.'

'And they'll scorch themselves with it,' Mary said. 'I'm not so blithe about progress as you, Percy. I never was. You never fully grasped the hidden message of *Frankenstein: the Modern Prometheus* back in the days of our pre-existence, did you?'

Albé banged the table, agitating its psychotronic shimmer. 'Enough! This babble of democracy and progress wearied me the first time round! Must I endure it again? Doctor, I give you twenty seconds to explain the duel to the dolt. After that, I'll slit the throat of the first jabberer, understood?'

The Doctor bent a smile to Crocker. 'Well, the two Byrons are the opponents, and their minds are the weapons. We provide a path for those minds to attack one another. Imagine a psychic bullet being fired by Albé. It will arc through us and hit Byron, while Byron's psychic bullet swerves through Faust, Miles and Percy to strike Albé. The psycho-conductive table magnifies the power of the bullets. The first ten rounds go clockwise, the next widdershins, then clockwise and so on. If you keep your thoughts on even keel – visualizing a brick wall helps – you'll suffer only minor discomfort.' He swung round to Albé. 'Twenty seconds precisely.'

Miles, who had been studying his fob-watch, snapped it shut. 'On the dot.'

'Now, link hands again,' Albé growled.

A burst of sheet lightning made a black silhouette of the Villa Diodati's lord. '*En garde*, Byron.'

A crack of thunder.

'*En garde*, Albé.'

Crocker gulped.

A brick wall, the Doc said. He shut his eyes and summoned the image of a brick wall.

A wall of bricks materialized behind his eyes, tall, solid, safe.

Then a dirty great fist punched a hole in it and bashed him right on the hooter.

Miles sat erect, eyes open, and allowed a galvanic current of Byron's sheer hatred of Albé to pass through his body-spirit. He saw Albé wince as the charge struck home. A simultaneous gasp was drawn from Byron.

Albé's hatred was stronger than Byron's. First hit to Albé. But it was early days. The spirits hadn't manifested yet, not to mention the Pandora's box of demons in the two men's psyches.

Crocker was moaning, in obvious distress. 'Right in the bleeding mush,' he groaned.

'Crocker!' he called out sharply. 'Don't let the side down. Pull yourself together, fellow. Think of something boring, like – Swiss history –'

'It isn't all cuckoo-clocks, you know,' the Doctor remarked.

Ignoring the interruption, Miles went on: 'If you make such a to-do in the first rounds, Crocker, how do you think you'll fare when we reach the stage of unnameable horrors?'

'Sorry, sir,' Crocker gasped, then reeled as the next bolt of malevolent mind energy swept through. 'Oh *God* –'

Miles spotted a transference of psychic energy from the Doctor to Crocker: those little blue flickers around the intertwined fingers said it all.

Crocker instantly relaxed in his chair. Miles gave an appreciative nod to the Doctor. A selective mind-block, transferred by touch alone. Impressive.

'Quite good fun this, innit?' Crocker grinned.

The round of ten was soon completed, and the psychic current was reversed.

Miles observed the heightening radiance of the table. The spirits were on their way.

He felt a jolt from Percy. The young poet was staring in horror at Mary. 'She's a witch!' he screamed. 'She's got eyes in her breasts! Eyes for nipples!'

'That's enough, Percy,' Miles said firmly. 'The lady is fully clothed and, I'm sure, perfectly formed.'

'Breasts . . . Eyes . . .'

'Percy! You're making an exhibition of yourself, and there are foreigners present.'

Percy, for whatever reason, mastered his fit.

The ten widdershins rounds completed, the circuit reversed clockwise. Both Byrons were showing the strain, shuddering in their chairs. The table's shimmer had intensified to a lunar glare.

'Metapsychic manifestations on their way,' the Doctor announced as a sorcerous swirl whirlpooled above the table.

A witch flew overhead with eyes in her breasts.

'I hold you personally responsible for that,' Miles muttered to Percy.

The young poet burst into laughter. 'You're priceless, Miles! Priceless!'

Bereft of Percy's phobic reaction, the witch cackled out of sight. A stream of apparitions followed, chiefly gibbering idiots from the subliminal undersurface of the Byrons' minds. The circle of Jabberwocky set up a miniature whirlwind. The table started to levitate, and the chairs with it.

The witless spooks went on circling for a while, then grumbled into non-existence.

The room was now irradiated with a moony glow. Miles prepared for trouble. They were phasing into the stage of the reification of the deep unconscious, death to all but the hardiest of duellists, and hazardous to all participants.

'Augusta...' the Byrons chorused the name of their dead half-sister, faces wrenched with the pain of longing.

'*George*...' soughed a desolate voice. A pale spectre of a beautiful woman rose from the region of the monk's skull. She swayed like a deep-sea plant, then dissolved with a forlorn 'Adieu'.

Miles threw a glance at Faust, whose features were clenched in concentration. A trickle of blood oozed from where Faust had bitten into his lip. What on earth was the Germanian up to? Everyone acquainted with the occult knew better than to tense up during a séance. Gritting the teeth, fighting to keep everything in was just asking for trouble. Whatever was in you, you had to let it flow forth.

'Relax, Faust,' he urged. 'Or you'll explode.'

'Mind – your own – bloody – business – you – Britannian – bastard,' croaked Faust, eyes tight shut.

'Commoner,' Miles retorted. Then he glanced down. The table and chairs had levitated a metre from the floor. Some distance away, Claire was threshing on the couch, froth bubbling in her mouth.

He switched his attention back to the duelling circle.

The Black Monk's skull, at the centre of the table, had begun to radiate a darkness, paradoxically brighter than the surrounding luminosity.

Byron's eyes sprang open and fixed on the skull. 'The black halo,' he whispered, then winced as a bolt of Albé's malignancy struck him.

Miles experienced no answering bolt aimed at Albé. Byron was fading. Nightmares jostled in his stark gaze. He shuddered at another charge from Albé.

Then Byron's eyes swivelled round and looked inside his head, forced to view his worst fear. He was undergoing transmogrification. The duel was almost over.

Mary let loose a cry of alarm. Like Miles, she wanted to aid the lord, but the rules of séance duelling were strict. No psychic assistance from non-combatant participants.

The table started to spin as it levitated several more metres, coming level with a chandelier. Miles, like his companions, held on like grim death. Faust was groaning with the strain of blocking out the psychic hullabaloo.

The skull's black halo had bulged to the table's rim.

Byron unleashed a cry of anguish. 'The worms are eating her!'

The black-shining skull creaked open its jaw-bones. 'And then *you'll* eat –'

'That's enough of the Mad Hatter's Tea Party!' thundered the Doctor, banging the wood with his fist. He broke contact with Crocker and grabbed the skull, swinging it round to confront Albé, his fingers working the relic's jaws like a ventriloquist's dummy. He cast his voice into the jerking mouth, producing a high-pitched squeal: 'See how you like your own back, sunshine!'

Albé stared into the sockets, and arced back in his chair, screaming.

Byron's eyes swivelled round from the impossible to the normal, although he was out for the count.

'You have broken the rules, Doctor,' Miles declared. Then he glanced at the black shine of the skull, and his psychic sense came fully awake. Albé had broken the rules from the start. He had hit Byron with two charges using the Black Monk as the second path, a path amplified by his affinity with the skull.

The Doctor had given Albé a taste of his own medicine. Miles gave the two combatants a swift inspection. Both Byrons were comatose.

They should have been dead.

'How is it they're both breathing?' Miles asked the Doctor.

'Because I chose to stop them killing one another. The séance can be turned to better use. Information.' There was no hint of the genial in the Doctor's tone.

From a seemingly happy-go-lucky fellow he was transformed into a man of authority, of what Miles regarded as natural nobility.

The Doctor replaced the skull in the centre of the table, which was gradually lowering to the floor. 'Everyone, link hands again. Concentrate on the skull. And summon up an image of Mad Byron.'

Miles smiled his approval. The correspondence between the Black Monk's relic and Byron – *any* Byron – was strong. Calling Mad Byron to the table might provide invaluable answers.

Crocker stirred uneasily. 'Not that bleeding shadow from the grave,' he muttered. The effects of the Doctor's mind-block were wearing off.

'If you know him as an anti-light lattice, then summon him as such. Now, all of you, focus your minds, and let the words of another great poet weave their spell. Imagination is a plasmamorphic field *par excellence*. Imagination is the key, not hocus-pocus.' His resonant tone filled the room, commanding attention, reeling them in, entrancing:

'Before me floats an image, man or shade,
Shade more than man, more image than a shade –'

A dark ascended from the black lustre of the skull, a shadow from a shell, and shaped itself into a silhouette of Byron.

'– For Hades' bobbin bound in mummy-cloth
May unwind the winding path –'

The shadow gave a dry, scraping breath. '*Unriddle a riddle –*'

'– A mouth that has no moisture and no breath
Breathless mouths may summon –'

'*Managra –*'

'I hail the superhuman;
I call it death-in-life and life-in-death.'

The Doctor, summoning completed, cast a cold eye on the spectre. 'Who is Managra?'

'*Jumbled. A mask. A mirror —*'

'Is he Francis Pearson, or is he within Pearson?'

'*Inside. Jumbled Pearson. Persona —*'

Miles shook with conflicting emotions. Managra was part of Pearson-Sperano. The true author of his woes was Doctor Sperano, not the Mindelmeres. 'Father . . .' he whispered hoarsely.

'We're losing him,' the Doctor snapped. 'Concentrate. Mad Byron is essentially a psionic creation, part of the shadow-play. He can sense the hand that casts the shadows. *Concentrate.*'

The shadow's outline quivered, an inconstant shade, then elongated into a different figure.

'*Miles —*' hissed a voice from the past.

'Father?'

'*Keep clear of Sperano, Miles. His secret name is Persona, his god Managra. Keep clear, and stay alive —*'

'A fortuitous intrusion,' the Doctor said. 'Ask him more of Persona and Managra, Miles.'

Miles had his own questions. 'Were the Mindelmeres allies of Persona, Father? Did they attack you at his bidding?'

'*The Dashwoods and the Mindelmeres were allies. Persona was our master. He works in secret, behind the scenes. And behind Persona — Managra. Stay clear of him, Miles. Stay alive —*'

Miles darted a look at a dumbstruck Crocker. 'So much for the rumours that my family hated me.' He switched back his attention to the tall shadow. 'Why did Persona have you — infected?'

'*We stole his quill, to write our own life-plays. The Mindelmeres retrieved the quill. Then Persona wrote a new play, in which we were given the blood-kiss by vampires. What he writes, happens. He hates you, Miles, for escaping his justice. Stay away from him. He can write you to death. Stay alive.*'

'Mimesis,' the Doctor murmured.

'Father,' Miles sighed, a tear trickling down his cheek. 'I always knew you loved me.'

'*Loved you? I hated you, you honourable, pious, self-righteous little bastard!*'

'But —'

'*I want you to stay alive because I don't want you over here with the rest of us, you sonnet-quoting prig! A hundred times the family tried to get shot of you when we were alive. And now we're dead the last thing we want is you coming over to join us. Stay alive, you chivalric bastard! Do you hear? Stay away from us!*'

Miles was speechless.

'Ask your father where Persona is now,' the Doctor urged. 'It's vital you ask!'

Composing himself, Miles framed the words. 'Father, where is Persona?'

The table and chairs returned to the floor with a combined thunk.

'*I told you to stay away from him, you little bastard!*'

'I — I need to know where he is to stay away from — wherever he is.'

A long, pained sigh from the netherworld. '*Very well, although he's hard to perceive. He journeys through the Passing Strange. From — from Castle Ludwig. His destination — a church? No — I must look —*'

Mary Shelley streaked across the table. Hand-contact broken, the séance circle lost the spectre. The shade of Miles's father swished out of sight.

'Mary!' Percy exclaimed in shock.

Miles had also glimpsed a glint of metal in her hand.

Face contorted into a parody of itself, Mary plunged a dagger in the Doctor's chest, burying the blade up to the hilt.

The Doctor yelled in pain, tumbling from his chair and crashing to the floor. Blood geysered. The Doctor gave a last convulsion, then lapsed into stillness, inert. The black radiance faded from the skull. The room lit up with sheet lightning and vibrated to a boom of thunder.

Blood trickling from her right hand, Mary Shelley stood immobile, her expression blank.

Miles, Crocker and Percy rushed to the Doctor's side. Miles gave the body a swift examination, then sat back on his heels and shook his head.

'The blade went straight through the heart. The Doctor's dead.'

Albé and Byron, rousing from deep sleep, blinked as they took in the scene of slaughter.

'What happened?' mumbled Albé.

Percy gave him a distraught look. 'The duel was cancelled. Then – Mary killed the Doctor.'

Mary Shelley was still lost in oblivion, gazing at nothing.

Albé, indifferent to the Doctor's murder, glowered at Byron. 'The duel was cancelled. I hereby resume it. Sabres?'

Byron nodded, his gaze straying to the sprawled body.

By the time Miles draped the Doctor in an old bedsheet brought by Percy, the clash of steel on steel resounded in the hallway.

Mary Shelley swayed on her feet, lifted her right hand, and stared at the bloodied fingers.

Shara held a blood-dripping dagger. The drops fell on the figure of the Doctor at her feet. She took a bow to a burst of applause that echoed in the inverted church of St Incarnata le Fanu. As she swept off her Mary Shelley mask, the psychotronic Domino guise vanished, revealing her torn orange gown.

Doctor Sperano joined in the applause. 'Your first performance was a tour-de-force, Milady Intangerine.' He glanced down at the actor who had taken the role of the Doctor. A mortal wound gaped in the motionless chest. 'Now,' said Sperano. 'Now we will know for sure.

Take him to my carriage.'

Incarnadine, eyebrow raised, studied the actor. 'If he's dead?'

'Then he's dead. And so is the real Doctor. We're not short of male actors in our troupe at the moment. Anyway, he has a perfectly good understudy.'

Incarnadine smiled her crimson smile. 'We get through so many actors with these one-off performances.'

'You should have seen the Theatre of Transmogrification a century ago,' Sperano reminisced fondly. 'We used to wipe out half the cast in a night, and garner fresh talent for the next performance.'

The Dramaturge swept a final bow to the audience, and followed the corpse-bearers to the leading carriage with the names *Rite of Passage* and *Sperano* emblazoned on its panels.

'Come, Shara,' he beckoned. 'The penultimate play, then – the big night.'

Shara, trudging at his heels, stared at the Doctor's corpse, lines creasing her brow. 'Doctor . . .' she mumbled. 'Doctor . . .'

Sperano grabbed her by the shoulders. '*Shara*, look at me. Look at my face. Who am I?'

She looked, and broke into a smile. 'You're – my Dad.'

'That's right, Shara. I'm your father, and you know what the Bible says? Honour thy father. Now follow, as you're bidden.'

Shara nodded meekly, tracking her father's steps past the Jolly Coachman's carriage to the small-outside, big-inside Rite of Passage coach. 'Honour thy father,' she murmured.

Then, a tiny voice, right at the back of her skull, completed the line: '– *and* thy mother.'

For a moment, she forgot her name, almost found another. 'Mum?' she whispered, seeking out a special face from the crowd, and catching no sight of it.

Then the moment was over. She was Shara once more – and Daddy was calling.

Twenty-One

Grunting, sweating and swearing, Byron and Albé cut and thrust, sabres flashing in the holo-torchlight as they advanced up the curved stairway.

Albé leaped on to the landing, and dashed into an open door.

'Running?' Byron sneered. 'I'd expect that of a turncoat.'

'I'm no turncoat!' A length of rope snaked from the door and lashed round a beam. Autoknot rope, beloved of Dominoes, self-tying and unknotting in response to vocal commands. 'I'm a Domino to the teeth, or I'm nothing!'

One hand gripped round the rope, Albé swung out of the doorway boots first. Byron dived to one side, evading a slash of the blade. He sprinted through the open door, seeking autoknot rope for himself. 'You converted your polyglot to transmission on a Vatican frequency, you bastard!' Byron yelled. 'You broadcast our conversation after you threw Claire to the floor!' He spotted a length of likely rope, swept it up, and rushed back on to the landing.

'I'm no traitor!' Albé bellowed swinging back to the landing, blade poised. 'Transmitting via polyglot – insane!'

'I can do it.' Byron lashed the rope at a chandelier. 'Quick-knot and sharp left swing,' he instructed the strands. He dodged Albé's sabre, then was launched off his feet as the rope looped round the chandelier chain and whipped him off his feet. He sailed over the bannisters, shouting, 'I had my polyglot tuned to pick up any signal on the Vatican wavelengths. A signal came from you, sending, not receiving. What price treachery, Albé, a life free of Vatican interference in the Villa Diodati?'

'If you picked up a signal, it wasn't from me, you dolt!'

The two men, voice-commanding the ropes to frontal assault, hurtled at each other, twenty metres above the marble-floored hallway.

Sabres sliced the air.

One sliced clean through a neck.

A head bounced down the marble floor.

A shroud sat up and Claire Clairmont screamed.

The shroud lay down again and Claire went on screaming.

'The dead rise!' Percy shrieked, throwing his hands before his face as forked lightning crazed the night sky. 'They rise to march, silent, sere armies . . .'

Unresponsive, Mary Shelley was slumped in a chair, head in hands, unable to believe what she'd done. 'What happened to me? What made me do it . . .'

Miles, hiding his dismay at his father's apparition, took command of the situation. 'Stay back, all of you. This may be an example of a discarnate *afreet* entering a corpse — I never liked the look of that Arabian jar over there with its broken Seal of Solomon. And will *somebody* go and see what the two Byrons are up to?' He knelt down and pulled back the bedsheet from the Doctor's corpse. Faust joined him, his grey eyes fixed intently on the body.

Miles tossed back his hair. 'So you've finally recovered your courage, Faust.'

Faust curled a lip. 'Go stick your head in a dung-bucket, Britannian.'

'Spoken like a Germanian.' Miles carefully extracted the dagger. A jet of red drenched his hand.

Faust frowned. 'Heart still pumping? Impossible.'

Miles felt for a pulse. 'My God, his veins are still

beating. Wait . . .' He pressed his ear to the chest. 'I can hear a heart – but it's in the wrong place. So . . .'

Leaning forward, Faust inspected the wound. 'That's a stabbed heart in there – in the right place. The Doctor has two hearts.'

Miles shook his head in mystification. 'Have you heard of the like? Perhaps the Doctor is not the human he seems.'

'An alien, maybe?'

'Alien or not, we must tend him as we can,' said Miles, stanching the wound.

Mary had rushed to his side. 'For whatever reason, I stabbed him. At least give me a chance to heal what I wounded.' She extracted a vial from under the Domino cloak. 'Anachronistic potion from the Overcities. It mends the most damaged organ in less than an hour.'

The door swung open and a man strode in, his sabre streaked red. When he entered the candlelight, they saw, by his clothes, that he was Byron.

'Albé is no more, I take it?' said Miles, leaving Mary to her work and approaching the lord.

Byron tossed the sabre on the floor. 'Albé will have difficulty carrying on with his life without the benefit of a head.'

Mary glanced up in consternation. 'Oh no, you'll bring the house down round our ears.'

'You've lost me, madam.'

'Albé installed a House of Usher mechanism, triggered by the fatal spilling of Byronic blood. By shedding Albé's blood you've – brought the house down.'

Faust held his head and moaned. 'Typical of Bad Byron – we can call him that now, can't we?'

Byron inclined his head a fraction. 'If you insist.'

'Excuse me,' Miles broke in. 'Leaving aside the anachronism of utilizing an Edgar Allen Poe theme, exactly what does a House of Usher mechanism entail?'

'Just as in the Poe story,' Percy said. 'The house decays and sinks into a mere.'

'But the villa isn't in a mere.'

'It soon will be.'

A ground thunder threw several of the company off their feet. A chunk of masonry smashed the table.

'See?'

Byron instantly assumed command. 'Mary, how many Dracoes does the villa contain?'

'A score or more. They're on this floor. Last chamber on the right of the hallway.'

'Good. The Doctor —' He glanced fleetingly at the prone figure. 'The Doctor has provided us with invaluable intelligence. As matters stand, an all-out attack must be launched on the Vatican before Thirteenth Night. It's what the Doctor would have wanted.'

Faust eyed Byron warily. 'Are you sure?'

'Certain. He also wished to investigate the Globe in Gloriana's Londia, and track down Doctor Sperano. Mary, Miles, would you go with the Doctor? And Faust, come with me and muster your Anti-Church friends for an assault on the exalted city.'

'Isn't that for Mary to decide?' said Percy. 'She makes most decisions.'

'No,' she said. 'Byron has the edge where military strategy is concerned. Now — someone help me get the Doctor to a Draco before the roof falls in on us!'

Percy made a dash for the door. 'I'll just flit off to the mountains and fly my cat, if that's all right with the rest of you. Campaigns aren't my strong point.'

'Goes without saying,' Mary muttered as she lifted the Doctor with the aid of Miles, Crocker and Byron.

The last straggler had barely quitted the room before the ceiling came down and met the floor. The impact threw them face down on the marble of the hallway. Crocker found himself staring eye to bloodshot eye with a severed head. ''Scuse me, your lordship,' he muttered.

'Hurry!' Byron snapped. 'Let's get on those Dracoes and fly out of here before we're squashed flat!'

The Doctor groaned and stirred. His eyelids flickered open. His sluggish gaze wandered, then settled on Albé's head. The Doctor's lips moved. Miles leaned close and strained to listen.

'No,' the Doctor whispered. 'Wrong man.' The eyelids fluttered shut and the head lolled.

'Move yourselves!' Byron barked, then swayed as a crack ran down the length of the hallway.

They needed no prompting. In less than ten seconds they were inside the Draco chamber. Percy had already activated its slide-window, the stained glass gliding into the side-wall of a Gothic arch.

'I'll take Claire,' Percy volunteered.

'Won't be the first time,' Byron grunted.

'I'll carry the Doctor,' Mary said. 'The rest of you – fly your own Dracoes.'

Crocker looked around, flustered. 'I can't fly a Draco!'

Miles pushed him on to a dragon-scooter. 'She wasn't talking to you, you're a servant. No – not there – sit behind me.' He glanced across at Mary, twirling a hand at the archway. 'After you, madam.'

Rolling her eyes, she flew her Draco through the arch. 'Keep close behind, Miles.' She waved a hand. 'The rest of you – adieu.'

Crocker shut his eyes the moment his vehicle took off, hanging on for all he was worth. His stomach lurched at the rapid upward acceleration. When he looked again, he wished he hadn't.

The Villa Diodati's topmost tower was already below him. The sheer drop spun his head with vertigo. The ground was for men, and the air was for birds. 'It ain't natural.' His voice was a harsh croak.

Miles glanced down at the tilting towers and crumbling battlements, sinking into a mere that had oozed from nowhere, exuding a spiritual miasma. 'Unnatural indeed, Crocker. The *grand guignol* of the House of Usher mechanism is an affront to the true romantic.'

'I meant – never mind, sir.'

Miles twisted in his seat. 'There go Byron and Faust's steeds, due south.'

'And there goes her ladyship, due north,' Crocker said, in an effort to be helpful. 'And his lordship Shelley and her ladyship Clairmont west by north.'

'I'm not blind, Crocker.'

'Sorry, sir.'

'And before long, there'll be others flying this way, alerted by the downfall of the Villa Diodati. Vatican fliers. Keep a lookout.'

Crocker looked back at the Villa Diodati. Its turrets were sinking into the mere with a giant glug.

'I'll keep a lookout, sir,' he said, closing his eyes and keeping them tight shut.

A man in a brown overcoat and fedora, neck encircled by a long scarf, stirred on the floor.

'Ah,' smiled Sperano. 'I thought so. Thierry, still in rôle, has returned from the dead.'

Incarnadine knelt beside the actor, touched the slight trickle which was all that remained of the wound from Shara's dagger, and licked a trace of blood. 'He tastes healthy, milord.'

Sperano backed away from the recuperating actor and sat in a chair, his gaze moving to a mullioned window and the riot of somethings and nothings that was the Passing Strange. 'Now I know. A man with one heart would have died. A man with two hearts would survive.'

He glanced at Milady Intangerine, standing meekly in a corner. 'You kept the knowledge to yourself, you *bad* girl.'

She sucked a thumb. 'Sorry, Daddy.'

'Not really your fault,' he breathed to himself. 'He would have prepared you in some way, built in defences, barriers.'

Thierry raised himself up on his elbows, and broke into a toothy grin. 'Good evening, I'm the Doctor.'

'Of course you are, of course you are.' Inside Sperano's

blue gaze, a distance. 'Now I know who you are, Doct[
A lord from a planet over the hills and far away.'

Incarnadine stole across the panelled room. 'A
Intangerine, master?'

'Of no use to us. On Twelfth Night she will give h
next performance as the fourth weird sister in *The Adve
tures of Macbeth's Head*. It will be her last.'

Incarnadine's smile was a lethal crescent. 'Oh yes,
well recall the fate of the fourth weird sister. We're s
looking for the pieces of the last player of the role.'

'Yes, she gave it her all.'

'And the Doctor, what of him? Shall we head for t
Globe Theatre, or straight for Verona?'

'I will consider the correct dramatic response. No
leave me with our own poor player of the Doctor, a
take Intangerine with you.'

'Come Shara,' summoned Incarnadine. 'Let's go a
pluck chords from moonbeams.'

Shara skipped to Incarnadine's side and, hand in han
they made their exit.

'Approach me on your knees, Doctor,' Sperano said.

The actor obeyed, shuffling to within touching di
tance of the Dramaturge. Sperano placed his fingerna
under the chin of his white, smiling mask, and peeled
off.

'Look at me.'

The Doctor, mouth bent in a pleasant smile looked
the blank, pink egg of a non-face.

Then Sperano pulled off the nothing face.

'Now – look at Persona. And Managra.'

Twenty-Two

The Doctor reeled in the Draco's saddle, muttering in half-sleep. 'Cagliostro was born Guiseppe Balsamo in Palermo in 1743, yes – hmm . . .'

'Doctor!' Mary shouted above the wind. 'Don't sway too much. Those autogrips aren't always reliable.'

'Of course, Cagliostro was a bit of a charlatan,' he rambled on. 'But what occult adept wasn't in the eighteenth century? Called himself the Grand Copt, the giver of power –'

'Doctor!'

'According to Cagliostro, the Grand Copt's disciples undergo twelve rebirths, from which they rise like a phoenix from the ashes. Twelve regenerations. Always meant to look him up and ask him where he got that idea. He met Casanova, you know –'

'*Doctor!*'

He sprang fully awake. 'Crisis passed. Saved myself from that little test.'

She glanced over her shoulder. 'Saved yourself from what?'

'Oh, just – saving face.' He twisted round. 'Is that the worthy Miles Dashing and estimable Crocker on our tail?'

'It is.'

'We appear to be travelling north.'

'Right again. That's a new Francia down there – Francia Art Deco. Just ninety kilometres more and we'll be over the Channel. Are you fully recovered?'

'No, but I'll get by. Incidentally, any particular reason

why you stabbed me in the heart?'

She looked at him, looked away, looked at him again.
'I don't know what to say. It was —'

'Like having your will drained and being used as a puppet?'

'Yes,' she said quietly. 'Precisely like that. Is that alien insight?'

'Alien. Never really cared for that term. Too many unfortunate connotations. Besides, I've spent more time on Earth than any person I know. I'm practically one of the natives.'

'That's known as dodging the question, Doctor, but I'll let it pass. I suppose I'd better tell you what happened after I — after you were stabbed. Byron killed Albé in a duel with sabres.'

'I know.' His tone was sombre. 'The original Byron wouldn't have taken a life so readily.'

'I suspect he had a hidden purpose. Or are you implying an unworthy motive?'

'I reserve judgement. Where have Byron and company gone?'

'Percy and Claire went to fly cats —'

'Dreadful! I adore cats.'

'I also. Byron and Faust went to gather a Domino army to attack the Vatican. According to Byron, that would have met with your approval.'

He digested the news. 'He presumed a great deal. Well, it so happens an assault on that bogus Vatican City would provide an effective diversion from the real mission. Stop the Vatican treading on our toes.'

'A diversion from the real mission! I hardly rate Doctor Sperano as a greater threat than the Exalted Vatican.'

'Oh no, Mary, you're very wrong. The Vatican is merely part of the props. Persona is the showmaster. And Managra could change the face of the world forever.'

'You make yourself obscure, Doctor.'

'I frequently do. Comes of thinking in scores of tangents simultaneously. But it should all come much clearer after we visit the Globe — and a nearby slum, known as the Stews. If Byron's to be believed, Gloriana's Stews was built on the site of the original.'

'You wish to go slumming?'

'Something happened in the Stews, many centuries ago. The past, as so often, might provide the key to the future.'

She peered ahead. 'Dawn's on its way. And the Channel's in sight. We'll have to ditch the Dracoes and proceed on foot once we reach Britannia Gloriana. Too risky to stay aloft.'

'From now on, Mary, everything is risky. And everything must be risked.'

'The game goes well.'

Crowley, in the middle of donning vestments, surplice half-way over his head, gave a low mutter. 'That's good.'

Cardinal Richelieu sank back into his armchair and reflected on the news recently communicated from the Villa Diodati.

Byron was mustering an assault on the Vatican. A timely move on the Britannian lord's part, and patiently awaited by Richelieu. Such vital information should be passed on to the Enclave. The cardinal hadn't the slightest intention of doing anything so foolish, not until the opportune moment. To move sooner would play right into Agostini's hands, the papal tiara given to the Italian on a silver platter.

Agostini had arranged Borgia's murder. To Richelieu, it was so obvious. And Agostini had played a part in Francisco's death — with outside help.

The identity of that outside help had preoccupied the cardinal of late. Agostini was pulling the strings in the Vatican, but it was increasingly apparent that an outsider was pulling Agostini's strings. It had irked the archschemer that the outsider's identity still eluded him.

Now he had a name, grace of the words transmitted via

polyglot from his agent at the séance. Or rather, he had several names: Pearson, Sperano, Persona, Managra, each an anagram, the last a beast of its own colour.

The name of Sperano loomed largest. The grotesque but seemingly inconsequential dramatist had never figured in the cardinal's schemes, not even a pawn in his game between the white of the Catholic Church Apostolic and the black of the Anti-Church and the Dominoes. Now he had put Sperano in the centre of the board, with instant promotion to knight, and the likelihood of further advancement.

Or perhaps Sperano should be an adventurous pawn, one step from the queen's crown?

Whatever the next move, the interests of France — of Francia Bourbon — came first. For all Crowley's disdain of foreigners, he served himself first and last, ever willing to betray the Protestant Britannias if it suited his needs. Richelieu trusted selfish men: you always knew where you were with them.

'Ready,' said Crowley.

'So am I.' He gave the satanist a brief scrutiny. 'You'll pass as a priest. Time to pay a call on Pope Lucian.'

Two wheeled thronelets, bearing Maroc and Agostini, rumbled down the Via Sanctus, each thronelet pushed by two nuns of the Sisters of the Heart of Superabundant Sanguinity.

'The pope's spiritual retreat is giving rise to rumour,' Maroc said, casting a sidelong glance at Agostini. 'The briefest of appearances would suffice to scotch the rumours before they spread throughout the Vatican.'

Agostini lifted his shoulders. 'His Holiness will appear on Thirteenth Night. A short time to wait.'

Maroc threw up his hands. 'If he had at least publicly confirmed the orders he gave us *before* entering retreat, there would be less ill-feeling. Why did he not condemn Borgia in front of other witnesses, instead of just the two of us?'

Agostini raised a silencing hand. 'Pope Lucian's wishes must be obeyed, whether we like them or not. Shall we move to more pressing matters? When are you leaving to supervise the search for the Doctor? Transylvania is a large Dominion to cover, eminence.'

'Come to that, when are you setting out on the Britannias search?'

'With Richelieu up to whatever he's up to, one of us must stay to keep an eye on him. As Transylvania is the more likely refuge of the Doctor, it stands to reason that I remain and keep watch on him. The task is beyond Altzinger's scope, and as for Torquemada — out of the question.'

Lips pressed tight, Maroc shook his head. 'While I'm in Transylvania, that leaves only four members of the Enclave in the Vatican. And two of them Reprises.'

'We'll make do with four. Why are you concerned about the equivalent number of natural-born and Reprises?'

'I'm not sure. It just worries me. What if the Reprises force through an alteration in the Nicodemus principle, thus permitting a Reprise to accede as pope?'

Agostini stroked his chin. 'I hadn't given the matter much thought.' He twisted round in his thronelet and glared at the nuns. 'Push harder. Put your backs into it. I'm late for mass.' He turned to Maroc. 'I wouldn't worry about the Reprises. The pope is alive and well, and the political climate no more unstable than usual. Even Richelieu wouldn't risk flaunting his ambitions at this juncture. After all, he's more dedicated to maintaining his hold on Francia than aspiring to the papal throne. He never tires of asserting that his only enemies are the enemies of Francia.'

Maroc gave a nod. 'There's some truth in that. I sometimes suspect his god is more the spirit of Francia Bourbon than the Father Almighty. For Richelieu, the Devil's a Britannian.'

'Then let Richelieu worry about his own Devil. Will

you be departing for Transylvania directly after mass, eminence?'

'Directly after. I leave the security of Vatican City in your capable hands, Agostini.'

Agostini smiled. 'I will hold it in a tight grip.'

Pope Lucian's chair was empty in his study.

The nineteen chambers of the papal apartments were vacant.

Crowley, dressed as a priest of the Malachian Order, ranged through room after room, feeling the absence. When a man has left a room an hour before, there's an afterscent, an afterglow. Not in these apartments. No warmth, only vacancy.

Crowley sat down in the pope's desk chair. 'Situation vacant.'

He entertained papal ambitions, for a minute or so, then made his way back to a secret panel in the second bedchamber.

Cardinal Richelieu had guessed right. The pope hadn't sequestered himself in his apartments.

Pope Lucian had been dead for days.

Sperano wandered alone through the Visage Attic, opening and closing oak chests, humming a tuneless air.

He stopped at a chest with wrought-iron hinges, broke into a chuckle, and lifted the lid. He delved amongst the contents and extracted a mask of Pope Lucian.

'*Sic transit gloria mundi*,' he recited, and donned the mask. His entire body transmogrified as the mask slipped into place. The false face became mobile flesh.

'Milord?' Incarnadine had whispered into the attic, Intangerine trailing at her heels. 'I have small Latin and less Greek.'

'Thus passes away the glory of the world,' he translated. 'In short, all is perishable.'

'Not you, milord. You go on, from transformation to transformation.'

'Call me "Holiness",' he said, stretching out the Fisherman's Ring on his finger. 'After all, I am in role.'

Pope Lucian from skullcapped head to sandalled feet, Sperano paraded with patrician grace. 'Ten thousand masks, ten thousand personae. My pontifical disguise was perfect, my performance faultless. The Enclave believed their own eyes and ears when the pope returned from the dead.'

Incarnadine gave a curtsey. 'Pontiff, merchant, king, beggar – you are always master. And when Agostini is made pope –'

'I will be his God,' Sperano broke in. 'But Agostini is of small account, although he counts himself great. Come Thirteenth Night, there will be only one master, recognized by all.' He pulled off the mask, and his form and dress transformed from Pope Lucian in pontifical regalia to a tall Jacobean gentleman, face covered in a stiff white mask.

'Milady Intangerine,' he said. 'No, let's not be formal. Shara, are you ready for your role as fourth weird sister? The play is tomorrow night – time presses.'

Shara dropped a curtsey. 'I hope I will do you justice, my lord.'

'Justice will be done,' he said, swishing a hand. 'Leave us now.'

Holding up her tattered gown, she scurried from the attic. 'Well,' sighed Sperano, watching her departure. 'I have a feeling you will glean immense satisfaction from playing a revenant Lady Macbeth in tomorrow's performance. Turning Intangerine a rich red will be much to your taste. After the delights of the prolonged torture scene, that is.'

Incarnadine burst into laughter, which froze as her face slipped, hanging lop-sided.

'Sorry,' she said, adjusting her face. 'The mask slipped. Must get it seen to.'

He eyed her shadow, jumpy in the trembling candlelight. 'And your shadow is up to its tricks again, I see.' Incarnadine's shadow, different in shape from the lady that cast it, was in an attitude of weeping, shoulders heaving, hands rubbing eyes.

'Oh, there she goes again,' scowled Incarnadine. 'Whine, whine, whine.'

'After Thirteenth Night, your shadow will be your own,' he stated with ringing conviction. 'And everything else in this world will be mine. The world my theatre, its people my players.' A spasm shook his frame. 'Go now. I must be alone.'

She quickly made her exit. Sperano, still shaking, shuffled to a mirror. His fingers touched the white, smiling mask. 'The face of Doctor Sperano,' he exhaled softly.

He peeled off the mask and, with interior vision, viewed the pink oval, smooth as eggshell. 'Persona,' he announced to the glass.

He peeled off the Persona mask, and looked at what lay beneath. His tone was heavy with reverence: 'Managra.'

His arms spread out and a vast, inhuman whisper resonated in the Visage Attic. It came like a bolt from the black.

'WE ARE THE DEVIL.'

Part Four

Persona Non Grata

Persona non grata in realms high and low,
I pull the heart-strings of puppet friend and foe.
Come twelve and one, the play will show
I am the author of all your woe.

Pearson's *Thirteenth Night*

Twenty-Three

'Eleventh night,' the Doctor said, stepping from a barge on the Thames into the torchlight fringing Southwark Bridge. 'We're running desperately short of time, Mary. Aerial surveillance or not, we'll have to fly to north Italia once this is done.' He gave a dour glance at the rotting heads at the bridge's entrance, relics of the pre-Christmas heretic hunts. A short distance from the bank loomed the squat, wooden tower of the Globe Theatre.

'There's ground surveillance, too,' Mary said in a low tone. 'Switzia Guardians in disguise, led by Captain Emerich. Someone in the Vatican has ordered close observation of the Globe. That someone seems to be ahead of the game.'

'Or a pawn in some other's game,' the Doctor responded. 'Miles, Crocker – ready?'

Miles flung back his opera cloak. 'My sword is at hand. Though family loyalty has failed me, and my true love in a house of fallen women, and dread darkness crouched to pounce, I'll still fight the good fight.'

'Feelin' quite adventurous myself,' grinned Crocker. 'Do or die, eh?'

Miles gave an approving nod. 'That's the spirit, Crocker. The ennobling company you are privileged to share is having an improving effect.'

Mary put a hand to her right ear. 'Hush. A message coming through.' After several seconds, she lowered the hand, brow lined in thought. 'The Switzia Guardians are keeping their distance from the theatre. It's as if they're inviting us to walk right in.'

The Doctor surveyed the theatre. 'So we'll oblige them, although I've a feeling a number of unmarked guards may be much closer.'

Miles shot Mary a quizzical glance. 'I knew Byron had a communications polyglot, but I had no idea you possessed such a device.'

'Well, she is the Domino leader, ain't she, sir?' said Crocker. 'Stands to reason she'd have some fancy thinga-majig in her ear.'

'Er — yes. You've got a point there. You're quite intelligent, for a servant.'

'Thank you, sir.'

'That was a reproach, not a compliment.'

'Shall we get moving?' the Doctor suggested. 'Despite the dark we'll soon attract attention if we stand around chatting. We hardly melt into the Gloriana scene, do we?' Head lowered, he loped towards the Globe.

'I wouldn't worry too much about the Glorianans, your lordship,' Crocker muttered, his stubby legs pumping to keep pace with the Doctor's strides. 'The present Gloriana — Elizabeth XII, gor' bless 'er — has called off heretic hunts for the Christmas period until after Twelfth Night. Besides, they don't make a habit of burning tourists — bad for business.'

'So I've been told, but we're breaking into the Globe, and there are Vatican soldiers and spies all round us, so a touch of caution wouldn't come amiss. By the way, just call me the Doctor — agreed?'

'Agreed, the Doctor.'

As the four neared the theatre's locked gates, the Doctor whispered quietly to Mary. 'The Globe was reconstructed in the late twentieth century, mostly through the sterling efforts of an American actor, Sam Wanamaker. Charming fellow. But the reconstruction proved to be a stone's throw from the original. I hope this Globe was built on the foundations of the Shakespearean theatre, not the twentieth-century replica.'

Mary gave a shrug. 'Is that so important?'

'Psychic resonance,' Miles said. 'Isn't that right, Doctor?'

'If you want to put it that way. I'd say that any site records the events associated with it. A temporal echo. When a replica of an earlier building is raised on that site, the echo effect is amplified. The same goes for the Stews, I hope.'

Mary expelled a sharp breath. 'What does it matter about the Stews?'

'Because that's where Francis Pearson disappeared.'

She glanced at him in surprise. 'You were there?'

He gave a curt nod. 'In the vicinity. I saw the Globe go up in flames. And I saw Pearson running from the scene. I'd been shadowing him for months. So had a power first summoned in Castle Bathory by the Countess and Edward Kelley. Or rather, by the legacy of that power. It followed Pearson across a dozen countries, and finally, it found him.'

Crocker observed the Doctor with a shrewd gaze. 'This power in the castle, did you defeat it?'

The Doctor's reply was barely audible. 'At great cost.'

'And this same power eventually tracked down Pearson, right?'

'No. Not the same power. Managra is a legacy — a by-product. The original being was far more terrible. Don't ask me about it, the memory is bad enough.'

Mary was studying his expression closely. 'So, although Managra is a mere by-product of the entity called down in Castle Bathory, it is still a fearsome force.'

'Strong enough to warp the Earth, to the last syllable of recorded time.'

'And what are our chances of defeating it?'

'Slim. One can but try.'

Mary gave a broad smile. 'I like you, Doctor. And I'd like to get to know you better, if we survive. I'm tired of Percy as a lover.'

His answering smile was enigmatic. 'I'm flattered by the compliment. But believe me, Mary, we're worlds apart.'

They had drawn to a halt in front of the gates. A swift

scan showed only a few late-night strollers in pseudo-Jacobean garb, interested only in their private affairs.

Mary drew a sword hilt from under her cloak. No blade extended from the hilt. 'Monomolecular épée,' she explained. 'It can probe through wood and not leave a mark, but it can cleave that same wood as though it were paper. Or –' Taking a double grip on the hilt, she thrust the invisible blade into the gate and cut two parallel upward paths. '– it can slice a cross-bar.'

Within a few breaths, they heard the thump of a fallen section of timber. The lock was picked by Crocker with a speed that raised Miles's eyebrow.

'Keep behind me,' the Doctor advised, moving stealthily inside. 'I give Captain Emerich three minutes, at most, before his men flood the theatre, and that's not much time to raise the dead.'

Captain Emerich rubbed his bandaged forehead at first sight of the Doctor. 'Watch out, lads,' he said. 'That Doctor has some strange weapons at his command.'

'So I heard,' muttered Sergeant Angio, crouched with thirty other men in Jacobean guise inside the bear-pit adjoining the Globe. 'And look who's with him – that whore Mary Shelley and Miles-bloody-Dashing.'

'I hate Miles Dashing,' a soldier snarled. 'When do we go, captain?'

'Give it two minutes to make sure they're well inside the building. Chances are one or more of them will be up in the galleries. No chance of slipping through the gate.'

Angio glanced around the pit, his gaze settling on a barred entrance. 'The sooner we get out of here the better. I keep thinking about those bears.'

'They're sleeping in the pens and there's a barred gate between us and them, all right? If you had any sense you'd be worrying about the Doctor and Miles Dashing. Dashing's killed hundreds of men. *Hundreds*. And the Doctor's got a lot of secrets up his sleeve. Keep your mind on the job.'

Emerich consulted his chronometer. 'One minute to go. Get your extendable swords ready, lads.'

From close by, a bear growled.

The Doctor strode across the stage of the Globe, arms outspread as he declaimed:

> 'O for a Muse of fire, that would ascend
> The brightest heaven of invention,
> A kingdom for a stage, princes to act,
> And monarchs to behold the swelling scene!'

Mary, sitting in the audience pit, gave an ironic clap.

Miles, standing guard by the gate, smiled as he realized the Doctor's intention. 'Poetic evocation of psychic resonance, although I would have thought *Henry VIII* more apt than *Henry V*, given the tragical history in which we're involved.'

Crocker was viewing the stage, pit and galleries with a wary eye. 'You mean he's warming up the ghosts?'

'Pay attention to the theatre, Crocker. Report any anomalies instantly. And don't tell me you've no notion what an anomaly is – I've got your measure, Crocker.'

'Yes, sir.'

The Doctor's voice swelled in volume, resounding in the timbered interior.

> '– But pardon, gentles all,
> The flat unraised spirits that hath dar'd
> On this unworthy scaffold to bring forth
> So great an object. Can this cockpit hold
> The vasty fields of France? Or may we cram
> Within this wooden O –'

His arms extended as if to embrace the circular interior.

> '– the very casques
> That did affright the air at Agincourt?'

Miles's preternatural sense prickled. Soon now, soon . . .

Crocker stiffened. 'Anomaly in a gallery, sir. No – two

anomalies. No – five . . . a dozen.'

Miles shifted his awareness into psychic mode, and the past came to life.

Merry spectres were manifesting in the balconies. They appeared to be eating nuts and throwing the shells at each other. Figures materialized in the pit, making their fellow-Elizabethans up above the epitome of decorum by comparison. One ruffian was exposing his parts private to a buxom matron. What was worse, the matron was giggling and making lewd gestures.

'Hey!' cried Crocker. 'Where did that bloody bear come from?'

Miles glanced at the phantom bear on the far side of the pit. 'From the past. Doubtless it was a side-show in its time: *Henry V* doesn't have any bears. Incidentally, mark the size of the theatre.'

Crocker stared, his eyes widening. 'It's expanding. Must be twice its proper size.'

Mary was sprinting through the riotous apparitions in the pit. 'Dimensions Extraordinary!' she yelled. 'The architect must have built it in as an option. Can you imagine the skill that would take?'

As far as Miles was aware, the architect was anonymous. Doctor Sperano, perhaps?

The far wall was receding at a rapid rate. Crocker's eyes bulged at the phenomenon. 'The Globe must have flattened half the neighbourhood by now.'

'The external shell retains the same dimensions,' Mary explained. 'It's enlarging on the inside.'

'How much bigger can it get?' shrilled Crocker.

Miles stroked his chin. 'A kingdom for a stage . . .'

The Doctor had halted his recitation, and was beckoning them furiously on to the stage. 'Come on! Hurry, before the distance is too great! Everything's working out perfectly.'

'Could have fooled me,' Crocker grumbled, but ran for all he was worth at a glance from Miles.

In the sprint for the stage, Miles slowed his paces and

kept to the rearguard, darting occasional backward glances. At the fifth glance, a batch of apparent Jacobeans swarmed through the gate. The extendable swords in their hands gave them away. Switzia Guardians.

The guards faltered an instant on witnessing the flowering of Dimensions Extraordinary, then the leader's voice urged them on: 'There they are! Follow them!'

Miles leapt on to the stage and whirled round, épée at full stretch.

'Centre-stage!' the Doctor called out. 'Group close together.'

With swift backward strides, Miles covered the swelling stage until he stood side by side with his companions. The Switzia Guardians streamed across the stage, blades flickering in and out of the hilts.

Crocker gulped. 'Cor, those in-out swords look bloody deadly.'

Miles assumed the *en garde* stance. 'They are. Extendable blades can jut out as far as a metre, or retract to a short dagger, according to the pressure on the hilt. They give the wielder a grossly unfair advantage over a standard sword.'

Mary had drawn her own épée. 'And that includes a monomolecular blade. If you've a plan, Doctor, use it now, or we're butcher's meat.'

The Doctor flashed a smile. 'It's all a matter of imagination.'

Crocker groaned, and viewed the boisterous Elizabethan ghosts crowding pit and galleries. 'I imagine we'll soon be spooks ourselves.'

The Doctor launched into a spirited speech, arms outflung:

> 'And let us, ciphers to this great accompt,
> On your imaginary forces work.
> Suppose within the girdle of these walls
> Are now confin'd two mighty monarchies,
> Whose high upreared and abutting fronts
> The perilous narrow ocean parts asunder.'

The stage vanished.

They were standing in a soggy plain. On one side, a long line of archers, unleashing a hail of arrows. On the other, hundreds of charging armoured knights on warhorses. The four companions, and the stunned Switzia Guardians, were right in the middle.

'Safe!' grinned the Doctor. The grin withered. 'Of course, it's a dangerous sort of safe.'

'It's bloody Agincourt!'

'A dramatic recreation, Crocker,' the Doctor corrected. 'However, the armies are flesh and blood and the weapons are real and battle is well and truly joined.'

Crocker threw up his hands. 'Talk about out of the frying pan –'

'And into the fire. Yes, but I know a way out of the fire – I think.' The Doctor jabbed a finger straight at the French cavalry. 'This way, if I'm not mistaken.' He raced towards the charging knights. 'Come on, don't dawdle.'

Mary and Crocker exchanged resigned shrugs and sped after the Doctor. Miles, assuming the rearguard, peered ahead as he ran, attuning his sight to the psychic. Yes, he could just distinguish spectral giants on the horizon. The Elizabethan audience, watching the battle of Agincourt.

An arrow thunked into the ground a pace in front of him. He whirled round at the English lines, shouting: 'I'm on your side, you damned fools!'

The Switzia Guardians were sprinting towards King Harry's troops, the less alarming of the two sides. That didn't stop five of them dropping with arrow-heads protruding from their backs. He saw Captain Emerich hesitate, glancing over his shoulder at Miles.

Miles left the guards to their fate, fixing his attention to the front. The charging cavalry was less than two hundred metres away, a daunting spectacle to the stoutest of hearts. The lowered lances bore down on the runners to a thunder of hooves. The nearest chargers were mere strides from the Doctor.

Increasing his speed, Miles drew level with his servant.

'Crocker! You're running with your eyes shut!'

A falsetto shriek. 'Do you sodding well blame me, you stupid bastard!'

'Language, Crocker, and the respect due my position. But given the severity of our plight, I'll overlook the remark.'

'Bollocks!' Crocker screamed, racing through a rip in the air and on to the boards of the Globe stage. He kept on running for a dozen paces, then slowed to a stop and sank to his knees, stroking the planks as though the wood were holy.

'All right?' the Doctor asked, putting an arm around the man's heaving shoulders.

Crocker glanced up at the audience of ghosts, watching an Agincourt now invisible to the living. 'After being stuck in the middle of that bloody battle, this place looks downright *normal*.'

'Whew!' Mary wiped perspiration from her forehead. 'I could swear that hoof touched my stomach before we slipped out of the scene. Look – there's the mud . . .'

Crocker rose and confronted Miles with downcast gaze. 'Er, sorry about the sodding and bastard and bollocks and all that, sir. Didn't mean it. Won't do it again, sir.'

Miles placed a gentle hand on the servant's shoulder. 'It's not your fault you're a commoner. As I said on that field of martial valour, I overlook your improper behaviour *in extremis*.' He gave Crocker a comradely punch on the shoulder as though they were equals. 'All forgotten. Of course, there'll be no adventure bonus on your salary.'

Miles gave a forgiving nod and walked over to the Doctor and Mary. The stage he crossed had swollen at least five times its normal size. At his back, Crocker muttered something suspiciously like bollocks.

The Doctor was staring at something near the back of the stage. Exactly what that something was, God and the Doctor only knew.

'Ah,' the Doctor smiled. 'Here he comes.'

A terrorized Captain Emerich burst out of a split in the

air that healed instantly behind him. Eyes starting out of the sockets, he gazed about, dumbfounded. 'Uh – uh – uh . . .'

The Doctor whisked the hilt of the extendable sword from his hand, retracted it to knife length and dropped it in a pocket. 'Calm down, there's a good fellow. How's that crack on the head coming along?'

'Give him back his sword so I can kill him!' Miles demanded. 'Have you no sense of honour?'

'He has good sense,' Mary put in, drawing her épée. 'The captain talks, or parts company with his anatomy, piece by piece. The reason you can't see the blade is that it's monomolecular. You know what that means, don't you, captain?'

'I'll talk!'

Mary grabbed him by the throat. 'Who sent you here?'

'Cardinal – Cardinal Richelieu.'

'Let's try it my way,' the Doctor interposed. He planted his hands each side of Emerich's head, closed his eyes, and started chanting a string of phrases that sounded like babble to Miles's ears. Chant concluded, the Doctor opened his eyes and bared his teeth in a devilish grin. 'There – your cortex has been acoustically programmed with a Truth and Consequences code. If you lie, your brain will instruct your autonomic nervous system to stop your heart. As a fail-safe mechanism, your brain will self-destruct in a major haemorrhage if you should later report that you located us here or repeat any word spoken. Now – who sent you? And –' The voice sank to a chilling tone. '– be very careful what you say.'

'Car-Cardinal Agostini.'

'Who killed the pope?'

'You did . . .' Beads of sweat popped on his brow. 'I mean, that's what I was told. I mean, the pope isn't dead, that's what I heard. Something about a clone dying in his place.'

The Doctor stroked his lip. 'Really? Was it verified that the dead man was a clone?'

'No. His body was sent into space before Pope Lucian came back.'

'How convenient. And where is Pope Lucian now?'

'Nobody's seen him, except maybe Maroc and Agostini. The pope has locked himself in the papal apartments. You know – spiritual retreat.'

The Doctor reflected a moment. 'Did Pope Lucian give any orders concerning myself and Byron?'

'Yes, he said you must be hunted down, with the rest of the Dominoes, but you in particular. He said you were some sort of special menace.'

'Did he indeed? How very interesting. And what's the state of play in the Enclave? Any notable events?'

Emerich was desperate to please. 'Yes, yes. Maroc and Agostini accused Borgia of conspiring with the Dominoes, and he died on the way to Domain Purgatorial. Then Francisco was killed by broken glass.'

The Doctor's brow contracted. Miles detected a glint of fear in the blue stare. 'Broken glass. Was it a mirror, a mirror whose shards displayed metaholograms?'

An eager nod. 'They showed pictures of the Devil, every last sliver.'

The Doctor seemed far away. Eyes full of distance, he stepped back from the captain. 'Ask what you will,' he said in a subdued tone. 'But keep it short. Others may be on their way.'

Mary planted fists on her hips. 'Why should Agostini believe we were coming here?'

'Don't know, don't know. I swear –'

'Is this the only area the guards are searching?'

'Oh no, not all. The largest number are scouring western Transylvania. That's where Miles Dashing, er – you, sir – was last seen heading. As you and Byron are close comrades, it seemed logical –'

Mary chuckled as she glanced at Miles. 'You're Parsifal to the tips of your toes, stumbling your way to the Grail. Whatever you do, it works to your favour – and ours.' She turned to the captain. 'One last question. Has the Vatican located Dangerous Byron, or any of his comrades?'

'No. Not since I last heard. Can't find him anywhere.'

She gave a nod. 'Good. Anything you want to ask, Miles?'

'Uh — one thing. You wouldn't happen to be acquainted with Casanova's whereabouts, by any chance?'

'Which Casanova?'

'The — the one that wins most duels.'

'Even so — hard to say. But it might be the one who's just been reported in Verona. Hey, is he a Domino? Never would have guessed...'

The Doctor spun round. 'Remember what I said about reporting our conversation. Instant brain haemorrhage.'

'Won't say a word. I swear. I'm not a man who breaks his word.' Emerich froze. His body managed to shake and rigidify at the same time. 'Oh God — oh God — I've just told a lie. Always breaking my word to rebels. My heart —' He doubled up clutching his chest. 'It's going to stop.' He glared up at the Doctor. 'If I'm going to die, you're not running off scot free.' He plucked a small whistle from a pocket and blew a piercing note before anyone could move. 'That'll bring them — fast,' he growled, then staggered across the stage, hand on heart, like a ham actor.

The Doctor made a wry face. 'That's the trouble with that particular bluff. We'd better get a move on. Besides —' His circling arm indicated the theatre. '— this makeshift TARDIS won't get us anywhere in its present state, although it served well enough as the Chronopticon.'

Mary's mouth fell open. 'This theatre is the Chronopticon? How did you reason that out?'

'Byron told me that Reprises simply appear, like actors on a stage. Pearson burned down the original Globe out of envy and resentment, at least that's what I believe. It would be in character for him to use a replica of that same building to create his own reality. In this case, living characters — Reprises.'

Mary Shelley's expression paled.

The Doctor's voice softened. 'This is where you were created, Mary. In a play. Perhaps Byron and Shelley were on the same cast list.' He glanced around. 'The theatre's psychotronics are staggering by Earth standards – you saw Agincourt. This was created to view history, and something, probably Managra itself, fashioned the artificial personalities to programme clones.'

She made a brave attempt at a smile. 'I'm Doctor Sperano's Monster.'

'You are yourself, Mary, with your own life in the thirty-third-century. You're not Sperano's property any more than Miles is his father's property.'

Miles gave Mary an encouraging nod. 'I had some difficulty adjusting to my own father's true character, but it's harder for you, madam, I know.' He turned to the Doctor. 'There remains a lot to be explained. Several gaps exist –'

'And many hostile guards are on their way. We must make haste,' the Doctor said, flicking a look at Captain Emerich who was storming towards the ever-receding gate.

'You bastards!' the captain shouted back. 'You almost stopped my heart because I *thought* it would stop. Wait till the rest of my men get here!'

The Doctor raised his eyebrows. 'As I said, we must make haste. Another speech to our ghostly audience is urgently required.' He stepped forwards and faced the Elizabethan crowd.

'Is he *serious*?' wheezed Crocker as Miles and Mary traded mystified glances.

The Doctor's sombre voice soared to the galleries:

'I come no more to make you laugh; things now
That bear a weighty and serious brow –'

'The prologue to *Henry VIII*,' whispered Mary. 'I've suddenly had a premonition.'

'– Sad, high, and working, full of state and woe,
Such noble scenes as draw the eye to flow,
We now present. Those that can pity here
May, if they think it well, let fall a tear . . .'

Miles saw the audience dissolve and resolve before his eyes. Faces changed. The colourful costume of the Elizabethan era gave way to the darker garb of the Jacobean. Now there were two spectral dancing bears on chains.

The Doctor looked over his shoulder. 'I've spotted Pearson. Now to re-enact an old calamity.' He swung back to the audience and his powerful baritone resounded in the theatre's hollow tower, open to the stars:

'Heat not a furnace for your foe so hot
That it do singe yourself. We may outrun
By violent swiftness that which we run at,
And lose by over-running.'

Miles caught sight of a flicker of red on the far side of the pit. He heard distant screams, echoing down the years. And he saw a tall man at the forefront of the crowd, his calm manner markedly different from the panicked mob.

Francis Pearson.

The Doctor was already sprinting in pursuit. 'This way! Quick!'

Miles didn't wait to play rearguard this time. He tracked the Doctor as fast as his legs would pump, traversing the now enormous stage. A good hundred paces took him skidding to the edge. The stage had risen in proportion to the overall expansion, and the drop would have broken his legs – if he was lucky. The Doctor was shinning down a heavy curtain. Miles followed suit, clutching handfuls of coarse cloth in the descent.

He hit ground and was up and running, still unable to gain on the gangling figure ahead. He ran through the gossamer phantoms of Jacobean England, screeching like tiny birds in a chimney. He ran through flames that didn't scorch a hair. Ghost fire.

Emerich and a pack of guards appeared in the gateway and charged into the theatre. Confronted by the spectacle of ghosts fleeing a spectral conflagration, they milled about in confusion, losing direction as they lost their wits.

'It's only illusion!' Emerich roared. 'Attack those four solid-looking ones!'

Deep-throated growls rumbled in the building. 'Bears!' screeched one of the guards. 'Bears on the loose!'

'Illusions!' shouted Emerich, grabbing a sword from the nearest man. 'I'll show you the real enemy.' He lunged at the Doctor, extending the blade to a full metre. The Doctor whipped out Emerich's confiscated sword and parried the stroke, then, with a flick worthy of Miles himself, swept the sword from Emerich's hand.

Drawing level with the captain, Miles cursed at the man's weaponless state. Honour forbade him to plunge his épée into Emerich's vitals, so he made do with a kick to the stomach, flooring the oaf. The other guards were rushing about like headless chickens.

He glanced over his shoulder. Mary wasn't far behind, and Crocker was outdoing himself, struggling close on the lady's tracks. In the distance, he saw two phantom, fiery bears running amok.

'Bears! Bears!' the guards were howling. Credulous clods.

He gave a final sprint, leaving the men to their fate, and was through the gate and out in the open, normal dimensions restored.

And he confronted a pack of maddened bears on the prowl. At first he thought his eyes had tricked him: the bears appeared quite substantial, nothing like ghosts at all. Then he realized they weren't ghosts. They were the flesh and blood beasts, broken free of their pens, crazed by the phantasmagoria in the Globe. Animals were sensitive to *outré* phenomena.

The Doctor ducked and dodged the bears' swiping paws, and Miles, deeply concerned over the welfare of animals, did likewise, taking care not to scratch the beasts with his sword.

Mary and Crocker burst out of the gate. Captain Emerich was hot on their heels. The lady's eyes widened at sight of the enraged beasts, then she waved urgently to Crocker. 'On my back, quick!'

He obeyed as quick as the command. Within moments, Mary was carrying her burden piggy-back, hopping and side-stepping expertly to avoid a surfeit of tooth and claw.

'Now there's real breeding for you,' Miles murmured in admiration.

He resumed his zigzag progress until he reached clear ground by the Thames. Mary soon joined him, dumping Crocker unceremoniously. Close by, there raged a pack of phantom bears, wreathed in fire. And all around them, the spectral citizenry of ancient London watched the ghost fire that burnt not a single plank of the reconstructed Globe. A few intrepid thirty-third-century Glorianans had mingled with the supernatural throng to witness the unearthly blaze light up the night.

'Help!' screamed Captain Emerich. 'Help!'

He was racing downriver, a ferocious bear in close pursuit. He kept on running, and the bear kept on pursuing.

'Come on!' Miles spun round at the Doctor's summons, and distinguished his tall figure disappearing into the murk beyond Southwark Bridge.

'You heard the man,' Miles said, setting off in the Doctor's tracks. 'Come on.'

This time the Doctor didn't force such a gruelling pace. Miles soon drew alongside, throwing a backward glance to ensure they hadn't lost Mary and the servant. 'Doctor, I presume you're tracking Pearson, but I don't see any sign of him.'

'His time rate seems to have accelerated far beyond

ours. We'll be lucky to reach the right spot in the Stews before Pearson gets there and Managra comes.'

Miles whipped out his épée. 'If Managra appears, we can defeat the monster here and now.'

The Doctor shook his head. 'This isn't St George and the Dragon. Besides, the scene will be a recording of sorts. A replay of a night in 1613. You can't change the past, except in the rarest of circumstances, and this isn't one of them.'

Mary and Crocker had caught up. Crocker was puffing and grunting as though ready to expire.

The Doctor pulled to a halt. 'This is the Stews, sure enough,' he said, eyeing the tangle of narrow streets, swimming in liquid muck. 'But its layout is rather different from the original. Hard to get my bearings. I think I'll give intuitional direction-finding a stab.' He pulled out a curious disc and let it fall to a stop, suspended from a length of string.

Miles peered at the disc. 'Is that a divinational device?'

'It's a yo-yo. Now, if you'd be so kind, I must concentrate.' He shut his eyes.

The yo-yo hung motionless for a score of seconds, then started to swing. The swing became pronounced. 'The pendulum swings that way,' the Doctor said, pointing down a crooked street.

The words were hardly out of his mouth before he was off at full pelt. 'Follow the Doctor!' Miles said, dashing in pursuit. Crocker gave a soulful groan.

After several twists and turns through the squalid maze, the Doctor darted down an alley, shouting a loud 'Yes!' Miles forced his legs to greater effort, but still lost ground. The Doctor's athleticism was astounding.

Swerving into the alley, he squinted to catch sight of the Doctor in the dense gloom. A vague but familiar figure was some thirty paces ahead, its identity confirmed by the outline of a hat and a swirling scarf.

Then he noticed something wrong with the night. It had taken a bewildering shape, oozing part of itself down into the alley. The Doctor had stopped in his tracks in front of the hobbling figure of a man.

The non-shape of night prowled between the leaning houses, approaching the Doctor.

Swaying on one foot, the Doctor's shadowy companion shook a fist at a sky that glowed with the ghost fire of the Globe. His voice had the distant resonance of a phantom, far away in years.

'You betrayed me! Edward Kelley . . . Elizabeth Bathory . . . You betrayed me! Damn you to the sulphurous pit of Hell!'

'*Hell . . .*' echoed a voice, large as night. For the first time, Miles was afraid of the night.

He attempted to push forward down the thin alley, but the barrier of congealed dread was like wading chest-high in treacle.

'Pearson,' the Doctor said, stretching out a hand that went clean through the phantom Pearson. 'Can you hear me? Pearson!'

'Who are you?' wheezed the phantom dramatist, facing the living dark and oblivious to the Doctor.

'*Who are you?*' boomed the advancing nonsense of night.

Pearson toppled to the cobble-stones. 'Christ protect me,' he moaned.

'*Christ protect me.*'

The Doctor fell to his knees. 'Managra,' he breathed hoarsely.

Miles's struggle through coagulated dread became slower. 'Doctor!' he gasped. 'Doctor!'

The nonsense shape of dark leaned over Pearson.

'I'm damned,' came a sob.

'*I'm damned.*'

'I know you.'

'*I know you.*'

'You're the Devil.'

'*You're the Devil.*'

Pearson lapsed into the stillness of a corpse. The Doctor

crawled to the prone phantom.

'*WE ARE THE DEVIL.*'

It came like a bolt from the black and struck Miles in the heart. A vast whisper vibrated to the marrow of his bones.

He saw the Doctor flung violently to a wall, then blackness flooded his brain.

He was nothing. Nowhere.

Awareness came back by painful inches. He saw a blur that gradually became Mary's face. He heard a voice, repeating a word that he recognized as his name.

'Miles . . .'

He eased himself into a sitting position. 'The night tried to kill me,' he mumbled. He searched for a dire memory, but the essence of it escaped him. 'Something about the Devil.'

'I know who he is,' said a weary voice, the tone flat. Miles peered to where the Doctor was slumped against a wall, like a puppet with severed strings. 'I know exactly what he is. The face behind the mask. Faces within faces. I underestimated it. Even in a replay, the effect was devastating.'

Miles struggled to his feet. 'What is he – this thing?'

The Doctor looked as though his flesh had absorbed death. 'A composite. Managra and Pearson. A symbiotic entity. Let's call it Persona. There was a face in the Sistine Chapel, a face on the back of St Benedict's hand. Persona has left his mark at the heart of the Vatican. I saw the face before on the walls of Castle Bathory. And, long before that, on my home world. The cult that formed the changing face on my world celebrated a ritual once a year. They called it Thirteenth Night. And they practised a monstrous form of theatre, known simply as Mimesis, long since banned by the Council.'

Partially recovered, Miles walked to the Doctor, his legs unsteady. 'Thirteenth Night was invented for Venice by the Concocters.'

'And one of the Concocters was Persona, transported

by Managra from the seventeenth century to the thirty-first. It's the only explanation that makes sense. The knowledge of transpatial dimensions in the formation of Europa, the Chronopticon — Gallifreyan knowledge. Persona masterminded the Concoction, under whatever pseudonym. The banning of his contemporary dramatists is a typical example of his petty enmity.'

'Are you saying that Managra is a fellow alien of yours?'

'Far from it. An old legend refers to a Mimic, an entity that copies what it sees, repeats what it hears. It had no mind of its own, no integral intelligence. It wandered aimlessly into my world, and absorbed its secrets. A lord named Rassilon expelled the creature, with abundant assistance, and after a titanic struggle. Since then, it drifted through the vortex, lacking the capacity to put its stolen knowledge to use, unless, one day, it chanced upon a thinking host.'

'And that host was Pearson.'

'Yes, he sought immortality from Elizabeth Bathory, who had made a pact with a far more terrible being.'

'*More* terrible?' Mary echoed. 'What was this being?'

He shook his head. 'That's one secret I'll keep. But suffice it to say that Managra was attracted to the being, and —'

'Copied it,' completed Miles. 'Managra is a faint reflection of this — being.'

'Yes. Pearson presumed to make a similar pact to Countess Bathory, with Edward Kelley's help. He presumed too much. Elizabeth Bathory was more to the being's taste and the playwright was cast aside. Pearson thought he'd been betrayed. But Managra was drawn to a kindred spirit in Pearson, the dramatist being almost as derivative as itself. It tracked him across the world.' He waved a feeble hand at the alley. 'And ran him to ground down here, after he burned down the Globe to silence Shakespeare forever.'

'Now there's an act of purest spite,' Miles said.

'Pearson was a spiteful man. A man of infinite hate, inclined to blame others for his own shortcomings. He wanted to destroy Shakespeare, so he assumed Shakespeare wanted to destroy him.'

'And now he's out to destroy us all,' Mary said.

'Transmogrify. Mould us into shapes he can play with. Over two centuries he's set the stage – Europa. The actors are in place – Europa's populations. And, come Thirteenth Night, Persona's play begins, with each of us forced to play their part.'

'We must set forth for Venice immediately!' Miles exclaimed. 'We can pick up Casanova on the way, if he *is* in Verona. His occult skills might prove invaluable.'

'By all means, go to Venice, but I must restore my energy, hatch a plan. I'll see you there, on Thirteenth Night.'

Miles hesitated. 'Are you sure about this?'

'I'm sure.'

'I'm staying with you, Doctor,' Mary stated in a manner brooking no contradiction.

The Doctor summoned up a weary smile. 'Who am I to argue with the author of *Frankenstein*?'

Miles gave a bow. 'Till Thirteenth Night.'

The Doctor raised his hat. 'Till Thirteenth Night.'

Twenty-Four

The Angelus swooped over Transylvania's Castle Borgo and veered to a landing in the middle of a cemetery, crushing a dozen tombs.

Cardinal Maroc frowned through the windscreen at the mausoleums and leaning headstones. 'Are you sure that Mad Byron has made his lair here?'

'Just a rumour, eminence,' said Captain Miracci, looking over the chief pilot's shoulder. 'But well worth checking. Byron, the Doctor and Miles Dashing wouldn't want to be *too* far inside Transylvania. You can walk from the Castle Borgo area to the Switzian border in five hours or so. Anyway, it makes sense that Dangerous Byron would join forces with Mad Byron.'

The cardinal rubbed his bony chin. 'Does it?'

'Oh yes, your eminence. Let the rest of the fleet chase around the Nosferatu Dominion while you're in on the kill, so to speak.'

'No killing, mind,' Maroc warned. 'We need them alive.'

Captain Miracci glanced back at the Switzia Guardians seated in the Angelus, all one hundred and fifty of them, armed with heavy-duty stake-rifles, and a batch of grim-looking exorcists at the back. 'When they see us, eminence, they'll surrender on the spot.' He jabbed a button, opening the slide-door. 'Right, men!' he barked. 'Head for that fancy central mausoleum with the bronze doors. Go! Go! Go!'

The captain jumped up, stake-rifle in hand. 'Want to be in on the metaphorical kill, eminence?'

Maroc preserved a dignified mask, hiding his elation at the prospect of claiming credit for the apprehension of Pope Lucian's assassins. 'It would only be proper if I share the hazards of our men.' As fast as his spindly legs could take him, he followed close behind the captain.

Once out in the graveyard, canopied by holo-night and a false moon, Maroc's nerves started to jangle. 'Transylvanians feed off each other, don't they?' he murmured, half to himself, half to Miracci.

'They have to, most of the time – but they much prefer visitors' blood.'

A gulp travelled down Maroc's scrawny throat. This was Twelfth Night – not an auspicious time to be abroad in a Transylvanian graveyard. At the far side of the cemetery, he glimpsed a couple of mouldering figures firing at each other. 'What in heaven are those two up to?'

'Stake-gun duelling, eminence. There's not much for vampires to do. The boredom drives them crazy. Stake-gun shoot-outs pass the time. Liven the undead up a little. Or maybe it's a Twelfth Night revel.'

The troops had surrounded the central mausoleum, rifles levelled. 'Right!' the captain bellowed. 'Attack corps! Inside!'

'I'll wait outside,' Maroc said, slowing to a halt as the guards stormed the tomb. 'I'll only get in the way.'

Staying well within the defensive circle of guards posted outside, he watched as the captain joined his men on the assault.

The soldiers outside the mausoleum barely had time to take a few pot-shots at wandering vampires when the assault team trotted back out.

Captain Miracci showed his face at the portal and beckoned the cardinal inside. 'Tomb secured, eminence. They're not here, I'm afraid, but there are some interesting signs that *someone* was here. Could you give us your expert opinion?'

Maroc heaved a sigh that was a mixture of relief and

disappointment. 'Certainly, captain, although it is a pity our prey have eluded us.'

He walked into the mausoleum's murky interior, eyes squinting to make out the shape of a dais in the centre of the floor. The captain stayed by the door. 'Take a closer look, eminence. Don't worry, I've got ten men posted around the walls.'

Maroc glanced around at the reassuring sight of ten Switzia Guardians. They wore broad smiles.

He approached the dais, noting the shattered remains of a coffin on the stone platform. Tentatively, he touched a fragment of wood.

'That's right, eminence, stand up close. Now – turn round.'

Maroc spun on his heel. Captain Miracci was pointing his stake-rifle, aimed at the cardinal's chest. 'Accidents happen on vampire hunts,' he grinned, reflecting the smiles of his men.

His finger squeezed the trigger.

A mini-stake flew from the rifle and pierced Maroc's heart, throwing him backward over the ruined coffin. Sprawled over the dais, he croaked out a bewildered 'Why?'

'Orders from the next pope.'

'Hair-shirt?' offered Richelieu.

Torquemada, sitting uncomfortably on a luxurious armchair in the cardinal's apartments, eyed the prickly item with a dubious air. 'I have a perfectly good hair-shirt of my own.'

'But this is sin-activated, Inquisitor General. The latest from the Office of Mortification. Tiny barbs extrude from inside the cloth, the penetration into the flesh attuned to the severity of the sin.'

'It will help mortify me to a state of purity,' Torquemada reflected. 'Gift accepted.' The small eyes narrowed. 'But not as a bribe.'

Richelieu assumed a shocked expression. 'Who do you

think I am, Borgia or – Agostini? The gift was freely given, from one priest of the old school to another. We Reprises do, after all, remember the good old days of the original Inquisition.'

Torquemada bowed his head. 'This is true.' The head rose, and the wary gaze was back. 'But you didn't invite me here to offer a gift.'

Richelieu leaned back in his chair, adopting a look of utter frankness. 'It's always refreshing to talk to you, Tomas. You are invariably direct – so unlike the Italians. So often I'm forced to –' He paused to emit a sigh. '– scheme and plot and dissemble in the cause of Christ. But with you I can be honest. You see into the hearts of men – there's no hood-winking you.'

'You'd better not try.'

'Indeed. We differ on so many matters, Tomas. But I've always believed that we agree on the fundamentals, which are the extension of the power of the Catholic Church Apostolic – and the salvation of souls.'

'The salvation of souls is paramount,' Torquemada said fervently.

'Quite so, but there is no salvation outside the Church, so I, perforce, must dabble and muddy my hands in political dealings to maintain that Church.'

Torquemada scowled. 'Politics is not my concern.'

Richelieu raised his palms. 'But that's understood, Inquisitor General. Your concern is souls.' He leaned forward, and stared Torquemada straight in the eye. 'Tomas, do you believe Reprises have souls?'

The Inquisitor General nearly bolted from his seat. 'Of course we have souls!' he spluttered. 'The doctrine is enshrined in –'

'I know where it's enshrined. But, if we have souls, why are we barred from the Throne of Peter? Why shouldn't a Reprise be pope?'

'The Nicodemus principle . . .' muttered Torquemada.

'A principle established a mere sixty years ago by an exclusively natural-born Convocation Extraordinary. But think, Tomas, you and I have souls that span centuries, or are you inclined to the Chronopticanimist heresy that the Reprise soul is created at the moment the mysterious Chronopticon refashions the Reprise?'

'I'm no heretic!'

'Perish the thought. You are the scourge of heretics. But don't you see, the Nicodemus principle, forbidding the papacy to such as we, *implies* that we are on a lower spiritual level than the natural-born. Whereas —' He spread his arms. '— in truth, we priests of the — old school could teach these thirty-third-century prelates a thing or two about *real* faith.'

'We certainly could,' snorted Torquemada, a speculative depth in his eyes.

'Do you know what I think in my heart of hearts, Inquisitor General? May I — confess this to you?'

'Confession is my profession.'

'Well, I'm convinced that you or I would make a better pope than the devious Agostini. Besides, why should the Italians rule the roost? Why not an Hispanian or a Francian?'

Torquemada was mulling it over. 'There's Maroc. He's a Francian. When the new members of the Enclave are in place, they may well vote for him.'

Richelieu assumed a surprised face, and let a dramatic pause extend. 'Oh — of course. I wondered why you hadn't referred to the tragic news. I simply assumed —'

'What tragic news?'

'Why, report came in some twenty minutes ago that Maroc was killed by a stake-gun. An accident — they say.'

Torquemada shook his head, the soul of suspicion. '*Another* accident —'

Richelieu clasped his hands in an attitude of prayer. Now was the time to strike. 'Inquisitor General, I must place myself at your mercy, like a lamb. If you have schemed with Agostini, I'm a dead man.'

An enraged Torquemada thumped an armrest. 'How dare you accuse me of scheming!'

'A dead man,' Richelieu continued, without batting an eyelid, 'because it's my conviction that Agostini murdered Borgia before your servants in Domain Purgatorial could – save his soul. I also believe he killed Francisco, with the aid of a demon that calls itself Persona, that he arranged Maroc's "accident", and –' A grand pause. '– that he conspired in the murder of Pope Lucian, also in league with the demon Persona. It's the old Jesuit question: who profits? Who profits from all these deaths?' He allowed the silence to hang in the air.

'Agostini,' Torquemada hissed softly. 'Agostini becomes Pontiff of the Catholic Church Apostolic. But – the pope isn't dead.'

'But he is, Tomas, he is. Killed on Eighth Night, just as we first thought. Killed by the demon that later impersonated him: Persona. This is Devil's work, Tomas. Haven't you suspected the Devil's hand busy behind the scenes?'

'I have – suspected –'

'This is what these natural-born priests have brought us to, with their new-fangled Nicodemus principle. Would you or I have invited the Devil into the Vatican if one of us wore the papal tiara?'

'We would *not*,' asserted the Hispanian, on fire with righteous rage. The fire subsided to a simmer. 'But we must have proof –'

'If I supply the proof that Agostini has been trafficking with the Evil One, will you consider a suggestion of mine, aimed at averting a recurrence of similar monstrous deeds?'

Torquemada gave a brief nod.

'Then,' said Richelieu, 'I suggest that, if Agostini's guilt is proven, you and I vote to remove the Nicodemus principle before the Enclave is restored to its full complement of seven – no doubt with a heavy majority of natural-borns. If Agostini is ejected from the Enclave for diabolic dealing, it's our two votes to Altzinger's one. Then, my brother in Christ, it's you or I as pope.

Altzinger will have the casting vote on that, and, guided by the Holy Spirit, I'm confident he'll make the right choice.'

Torquemada took hold of the hair-shirt, stroked its rough fibre. 'Your suggestion has merit,' he said at length. 'But there must be proof. Can you supply it tonight?'

Richelieu shook his head. 'I'm not sure. I'll do my best.'

Torquemada rose to his feet. 'Then summon me when the proof is found.' He left the room with short, hurried steps, hands clutching the hair-shirt.

With the departure of the Inquisitor General, the cardinal released a long breath. So far, so good. But now came the real test. Catching Agostini in the act. And much of that depended on luck as careful plotting.

If Agostini wasn't overthrown by early tomorrow night, it would mean the end of all Richelieu's ambitions, not to mention the extermination of Europa.

Thirteenth Night was the last chance, for the cardinal, the Vatican, the world.

He would need the luck of the Devil.

'Doctor?'

He didn't look up from his rapping of knuckles on wood.

'Doctor!' Mary Shelley hadn't lost patience yet, but she was nearing the edge.

The Doctor glanced up from his kneeling position on the Globe Theatre's stage. 'You shouldn't still be here, you know. I'm quite recovered and rather busy. And you should be on the way to Verona by now.'

He resumed knocking on the boards, listening intently to the sounds. 'It's all a matter of setting up an acoustic amplification effect in a self-generating field, establishing a hypersonic transdimensional displacement relation, to put it simply,' he muttered. 'I can handle it perfectly well, once I find the correct sequence of sounds. But there's not the slightest point to any of it if you're not where you should be before Thirteenth Night.'

'I understand the plan – I think,' she sighed. 'But I don't want to leave you here alone. The Glorianan palace guard is sure to come.'

He flashed a grin. 'They may come, but that doesn't mean I'll let them in.'

'At least let me send for a dozen Dominoes to protect you while you – tinker with this theatre,' she pleaded.

He glanced up at the sky. 'It's well past noon. Even with your Draco, you'll be hard pushed to make Verona by tonight. Mary, *please*, go now, or we haven't a hope.'

She threw up her hands. 'You win.' She strode off the stage, its dimensions restored to normal since the previous night, the phantom audience and ghost fire vanished. 'See you in Venice, Doctor – I hope.'

He didn't appear to hear, engrossed in his experimental tapping of the planks, but she caught a faint murmur as his lips stirred: 'Sarah . . .'

Twenty-Five

Casanova took his seat in the Theatre Fortissimo, primed to kill.

Twelfth Night was a major affair in Verona, and the full complement of the city's gentlefolk had turned out to witness Doctor Sperano's *The Adventures of Macbeth's Head*, announced, as was Sperano's custom, a mere hour before the performance. The Theatre of Transmogrification always arrived in town on a surprise visit, and departed more quickly. It was part of its appeal.

Just what *was* the general appeal of Sperano's witless dramas? Casanova, a connoisseur of the arts, deplored the Theatre of Transmogrification and all its works on an intellectual level, but once part of the audience he was held spellbound, as though in thrall. Not until now did he consider the possibility of theatrical sorcery.

His mind went back to the Castle Ludwig, and he stroked the jacket that contained the smartest of smart daggers, as adept in philosophy as it was deadly in execution.

Before the performance was over, he'd have added a dramatic flourish of his own. Vengeance for Prince Ludwig.

'Casanova!'

He almost jumped out of his seat at the abrupt intrusion, swerving to confront the man who'd plumped himself down in the adjoining seat. A slow smile curved his lips. 'Well, Miles Dashing, a fortuitous meeting.'

Miles shook his head. 'Not fortuitous. I flew in an hour ago, seeking you out, then I heard about –' He gesticulated at the red curtains. '– the Theatre of Transmogrification.'

The grimness of the Britannian's tone, and the loathing with which he mentioned the travelling theatre, intrigued Casanova. 'I thought you immune to Doctor Sperano's dubious dramatic delights.'

Miles leaned close and spoke in a whisper. 'Our meeting was not fortuitous, but Sperano's arrival here is. I intend to kill him.'

'Coincidences abound. So do I.'

Casanova launched into an account of Castle Ludwig. Before he could finish, the chandeliers dimmed and the curtains swished open.

'Permit me to strike the first blow with my exceptionally smart dagger,' Casanova said. 'After that, you're welcome to strike as many blows as you wish.'

'He may not be as easy to kill as you think.'

'Oh . . . How so?'

'Shh!' hushed a woman seated behind. 'The play's started.'

Casanova inclined his head. 'My apologies, madam. I'm sure tonight's performance will prove singularly eventful.'

Where was her Mum? She kept seeing her Dad, but never her Mum. And her Dad was so strange. He kept changing.

Sometimes, Shara thought he wasn't her Dad at all. Then she was afraid for thinking bad thoughts.

She stood in the wings, dressed as a witch. Not a proper witch, with a pointy hat and broomstick, but an old crone with a wart on her nose and smelly clothes.

Shara grinned as Incarnadine patted her on the head. She liked Incarnadine, especially the lady's funny shadow that had a different shape from the lady and was always behaving as if it had a life of its own. Most of the time the shadow looked like it was crying. Incarnadine told her that she should laugh at that, so she did. Incarnadine knew everything.

'Soon be your turn on stage, dear,' said Incarnadine. 'Do us proud.'

'I will. I will. That's a lovely big knife you've got there, milady.'

'It is, isn't it?' smiled Incarnadine, strolling back to the *Rite of Passage* carriage. 'You'll be surprised the tricks I play with it, once I'm on stage.'

With the lady gone, Shara awaited her cue and tried not to bite her nails. She was so nervous. If only her Mum was here.

Where was her Mum? She thought she remembered her Mum and Dad always together. Although she wasn't too keen when Mum called her 'little' Sarah in front of her friends.

Sarah.

Shar—

Shara.

Shara shook her head, all befuddled. There was a funny name kept popping into her head, and then she forgot it.

What *was* that name?

A big hand descended on her shoulder. She looked up and saw her father. Father was always smiling. 'Shara,' he said. 'Your cue's coming up.'

She bit her thumb. 'What if I forget my lines?'

'In my plays, nobody forgets their lines because they don't have to memorize them in the first place. The words and actions just happen, don't they?'

'Yes, they do, Daddy. And it's always such a big surprise when you don't know what's coming next.'

'Oh yes, Shara. You're in for a big surprise.'

'What an ugly old crone,' muttered a man in front of Casanova and Miles. 'Can't be make-up. Ninety if she's a day.'

'How crass,' remarked Casanova, loud enough for the man to hear as the fourth weird sister hobbled onstage.

Miles leaned towards Casanova. 'How can you be sure that Sperano will appear?'

'He plays Macbeth's head. He *always* plays Macbeth's head. Speak of the devil –'

A head was carried on a spike by Macduff. Various soldiers hailed Malcolm as king of Scotland, watched by the lurking weird sister.

Then the soldiers departed, leaving the crone alone with the head. She released a spate of mumbo-jumbo, anointing the head with a slimy potion. Then the head sprang off its spike and rolled along the ground.

Casanova pulled out his smart dagger, pressed its hilt to his forehead. 'Kill Sperano,' he said somewhere below a breath. 'Here's his image – a head of Macbeth.'

'Your time is not yet done!' cackled the crone, eyeing the rolling head. 'Many adventures still await, containing various episodes enthralling in nature.'

'Foul hag!' cried the head, bouncing up and down on a coiled spring that had sprouted from the neck. 'Desist from your blandishments for I have no hands to cover my much-offended ears. Place me in a box. A box, I say. A box! A box!'

'A pox on your box. Flap your ears now, and fly to England's court, there to talk with the dreaded but effective necromancer.'

'Foul hag! My wife is dead, and I'm pashed quite. A box! A box!'

'Your wife? Heh-heh-heh. Why here she is – I've just dug her up and nourished her on rook's blood. Lo! She approaches.'

Lady Macbeth sauntered on stage, hand on hip.

Casanova, glaring at the head, lifted the dagger.

And Miles's stare was drawn to Lady Macbeth's shadow, so at variance with the strutting strumpet in red. True love recognizes its beloved, even in shadows. He knew that shadow shape, its unique mannerisms.

He sprang to his feet. 'Beatrice!' he cried out with longing.

Casanova's dagger was already speeding on its way to Macbeth's head. Half-way through its flight, the smart dagger faltered, then hung in the air.

'Is this a dagger I see before me?' laughed the head, still bouncing on its spring. 'I am the man of many faces and none! What image shall your dagger strike? A false image? Your fate is sealed, Casanova! But – what's this?'

The audience was clapping furiously, believing the confrontation was part of the show.

Miles raced down an aisle, épée in hand, and sprang on the stage. 'Beatrice!'

'Miles Dashing!' sneered the head. 'I reserved a special punishment for you. You exterminated your own family because I had done them the honour of making them vampires. Turning your beloved Beatrice into Incarnadine is the first, and most exquisite of torments. Watch your beloved butcher a young woman, Miles. Incarnadine, kill Intangerine as her true self, as Sarah.'

Incarnadine ripped the crone mask off Sarah's face, and hoisted a carving knife. Sarah blinked, waking up to the world and herself.

'Two can play at unmasking!' Miles shouted, leaping at Incarnadine. 'Beloved,' he said, and ripped off her face.

Incarnadine's entire appearance altered on the spot. Her unmasked features were rounded and gentle, with big, scared eyes. She had lost height and acquired a curvy figure.

'Miles,' she said in a soft voice. 'Miles . . .'

'What's unmasked can be masked again,' the head jeered, bouncing towards the reunited couple.

It was at that point Sarah jumped forward and kicked the head into the orchestra pit. 'You're not my Dad!' she screamed.

The applause increased in volume.

Casanova had reached the stage. 'Miles, take your ideal beloved and let's get out of here!'

'I'm coming too,' Sarah insisted.

'Then, lady, I suggest you run with fleet feet,' said Casanova, sprinting down the aisle. Miles, Beatrice and Sarah were right on his heels.

'Run where you will,' raged the head bouncing on a drum, still caught in role. 'Come Thirteenth Night, you'll run to me!'

Mary Shelley raced through the streets of Verona to the Theatre Fortissimo. The Theatre of Transmogrification was in town, according to a dozen passers-by, and Miles Dashing was sure to be at the performance, sword in hand. The Doctor had been right to urge her to leave his side. She had left her camouflaged Draco a mere five minutes ago, and the performance was well underway.

She skidded round a corner into the Piazza Fortissimo, and was sprinting across its expanse to the theatre when she glimpsed the black swirl of an opera-cloak, individual as a signature, disappearing down a side-alley.

Miles Dashing.

She chased the black swirl through alley, lane and road, pushing past hawkers and crashing through vendor's stalls, yelling 'Miles! Miles!'

There were others with the Britannian lord; his servant, Casanova and two young women she didn't recognize. 'Miles!'

Eventually, he glanced round, slowed his pace momentarily, then beckoned her to follow without shouting her head off.

A short run took them into a secluded piazza, with a sputtering fountain, where she finally caught up. 'Miles! We've got to get out of here!'

'You're telling me,' grunted one of the young women, clad in a tangerine gown.

'Whatever we were runnin' from,' gasped Crocker, lying winded on the ground. 'It wasn't bleeding worth it.'

Miles made hurried introductions. Mary raised an eyebrow at Beatrice's name, and another at Sarah's.

She studied the young woman. 'The Doctor's friend?'

'You know the Doctor?' Sarah exclaimed. 'How is he? Is he all right?'

'Discussion later, I think, ladies,' said Miles, leaping to the top of the half-hearted fountain and sitting on mid-air.

'Nice camouflage,' Mary complimented. 'Do you have only the one Draco?'

'Only the one, sufficient to carry three, and no more. Your arrival was opportune, milady. I presume your trusty steed is nearby?'

'Just a couple of minutes' walk. I'll take Sarah with me. She's needed for an assault on the Vatican. Care to join the attack, Miles, Casanova? I know you were headed for Venice, Miles, but if events go our way both destinations will converge.'

He cast a look of adoration at Beatrice. She returned it with equal ardour. 'I cannot take my beloved into danger. But if I can leave her somewhere safe, I'll follow you, milady.'

'Do you know,' said the demure Beatrice, drooping her long lashes, 'Miles thought I'd deliberately left home to join a – a house of ill-repute, but there was no choice involved. The power of Doctor Sperano forced me. He was in my mind, making me – do things.'

'Foul fiend!' cried Miles, gripping his sword-hilt.

'Very well,' Mary said, stopping the lord before he was in full flood. 'You take Beatrice and follow me. Casanova?'

The Italian shrugged. 'My attempt at revenge failed. My smart dagger is probably still hanging in mid-air back in the theatre. I may as well vent my frustration on the Exalted Vatican.'

Sarah made a face. 'Isn't anyone asking me what I want?'

Mary turned on her with a haughty expression. 'No.'

'Oh.' She shrugged. 'So long as I know where I am.'

Mary broke into a run, signalling Sarah to keep pace. 'I'll fly ten kilometres due south, then uncloak,' she shouted to Miles. 'Make sure you don't miss me.'

'When did I ever, milady?'

'More than once,' she murmured to herself, ducking under an arch. She threw a glance at Sarah. 'The Doctor has a plan which I must help carry out. The chances of success were virtually impossible. With you to assist, the chances may be reduced to *almost* virtually impossible.'

'That has a familiar ring,' Sarah remarked.

Twenty-Six

Four Sisters of the Heart of Superabundant Sanguinit[y] pulled the Cart Venerable out of St Peter's Basilic[a] having deposited Cardinal Agostini on the steps of th[e] altar.

Passing through the Doors Adamantine, they steere[d] the cart into a side-chapel, and slumped to take [a] breather.

Sister Assumpta glared at the Doors Adamantine, lis[-]tening to the drone of Agostini's voice. 'If he tells me t[o] put my back into it once more, I'll swing for him, I will.[']

Sister Lucrezia, face flushed, cheeks puffing, gave [a] nod. 'Day in, day out, push, pull, push, pull. Jesus, Mar[y] and Joseph . . .'

Sister Hildegard just sat and muttered. 'Pig-pig-pig[-]pig-pig . . .'

Sister Assumpta looked around. 'Well, we've ha[d] enough, haven't we, girls?'

Muffled murmurs of assent.

'It's not as if we *volunteered*,' Sister Assumpta grumbled[.] 'We're *contemplatives*, for heaven's sake. We should b[e] back in our old convent, with the Sisters of the Deafenin[g] Silence.' She gave a sharp glance at Sister Laetitia, wh[o] stood silent, leaning against a wall. 'It's up to you, Siste[r] Laetitia. I hope you're not going to let us down. It'[s] Thirteenth Night come sunset – our last chance.'

Sister Laetitia gave a small shake of the head. 'I won'[t] let you down. I'll do the bloody bastard in, and hand yo[u] his guts on a steaming plate.'

* * *

Sarah, legs pressed tight to the invisible flanks of the Draco, clung to Mary Shelley as Italia sped far below, and tied not to dwell on the giant-sized trouble less than an hour ahead.

She threw a glance over her shoulder. A couple of hundred Dominoes were apparently riding on thin air. The Dracoes' flight-camouflage was holding up well.

Sarah drew a deep breath. Her brain was still absorbing the information that Mary had conveyed in dribs and drabs over the past night and day.

While she'd been in the thrall of the Theatre of Transmogrification, the Doctor had been busy, as usual. He had come up with a lot of answers, which he'd passed on to Mary Shelley.

The Chronopticon had turned out to be the Globe Theatre, of all things. At least, the theatre was a major aspect of the Chronopticon: an entity called Managra had something to do with it. The Globe – less of a mouthful than the Chronopticon – was a very rudimentary TARDIS, but a powerful history scanner. A theatre, what better edifice to resurrect the past?

She looked at the sun. Low on the horizon. Not much time left, and if she and Mary failed the Doctor, the world was in for a long nightmare. Her thoughts strayed, then gravitated back to Mary's account of the Doctor's deductions. Sperano, under another name, had been the driving force behind the Concocters, soon after he arrived in the thirty-first century from the seventeenth. He, or rather, the Managra within him, had taken advantage of the fledgling psionic theatre, developing it into an art form eight-years ahead of its time. The Theatre of Transmogrification was born in the Overcities, and through it Sperano had spread his area of control, leading to the Concoction of Europa, a giant stage for the performance of his dramas. As for Reprises, the cloning itself was simple. The tricky part was accomplished by Managra, using stolen Gallifreyan knowledge. The Globe absorbed Managra's memory store, then transmitted the personality

285

lattice by enacting the death scene of an historical figure with accumulated life memories lodged in the original unconscious.

Europa, Reprises, the Vatican itself – all Sperano creations, but he had stayed in the background, behind the scenes. For almost two centuries, he had bided his time for the right dramatic moment to make an appearance. The grand entrance. Overnight fame.

It was up to the Doctor and Mary Shelley's cohorts to ensure that fame was short-lived. OK, he could have his fifteen minutes of fame, but not one minute more.

She hadn't forgotten how Sperano – Persona – whatever, had played her father to the hilt. That hurt. That was cruel. The dramatist had violated her and, deep inside, there would always be the scar. She pushed that thought away.

There were still so many questions . . .

'Mary – why do you sometimes talk in period, then use twentieth-century speech patterns? Byron was the same.'

Mary didn't turn as she replied. 'It's an eclectic world.'

'That's what Byron said. And why aren't clones cloned from other clones? Byrons from Byrons, and so on?'

'There was a ban laid on that during the Concoction. Anything *else* you want to know?'

'Sure is. How come Sper– Persona managed to track me down in the Black Forest, but then leaves the Doctor well alone?'

'The Doctor suspects that Persona can locate people easily in Black Forests, something to do with the consonance of the trees and the wood of the Globe. He obviously left the Doctor alone because he hadn't yet taken his measure.'

'And what about –'

'What about nothing. In about fifty minutes we'll reach the Exalted Vatican. There are two hundred of us and three thousand Switzia Guardians still in the Vatican. If all the guards scouring Transylvania and the Britannia are recalled, there will be six thousand of them.'

Sarah grimaced. 'Three thousand sounds pretty daunting to me.'

'Exactly, now let's concentrate on the general plan, and our own little plan, all right?'

'All right. Sorry.'

'You're forgiven.'

Sarah was silent for a while, then her journalistic instincts sprang to the fore. 'You said something last night about a secret ally in the Enclave. Have you only just found out –'

'Sarah!'

'Sorry.'

'Are you ready, Crowley?'

Crowley gave a nod to Richelieu. 'It's all set. In three hours' time, you'll have what you want.'

'Three hours! That's two hours too long.'

Crowley shrugged. 'Best I could do. You know the problems.'

The cardinal expelled a sigh. 'Yes, I know the problems. Do your best to speed him up. They're on their way.'

'And *you* make sure my escape's in place, or all bets are off. Remember – I'll be checking.'

'Of course you'll be checking. Look through the fourth window, and your mind will be at ease.'

'Oh, I'll be looking, Richelieu, be sure of that,' growled Crowley, moving to the door of the cardinal's apartments. 'It's a high price I'm paying to become Official Antichrist.'

'A price worth paying. Faust will howl with rage.'

The door closed, and Richelieu placed a finger to his ear, tuning the polyglot to transmission.

'Faust?'

'I wondered where you'd got to,' snapped a sharp voice in the cardinal's ear. 'We've been flying for hours.'

'Give me the situation.'

'There are just over two hundred of us, with Mary Shelley leading, and Byron and Miles Dashing close behind. We're thirty minutes from the Vatican. I'm right at the back of the Draco fleet. You'll be able to pick them out of the air with ease, but make damned sure you don't hit *me*.'

'I'll take infinite pains over you, be assured. The post of Official Antichrist is as good as yours.'

'Has Crowley made you pope yet?'

'As good as. As good as.'

'Have you killed off Crowley?'

'Very soon, I promise. Contact me when you're within five minutes of arrival.'

Richelieu turned off the polyglot and leaned back in his chair. Then he pressed an armrest button for the Sentinel Office.

'Eminence?' said a voice from a panel in the backrest.

'My spies report intruders in Vatican City. Turn all sensors to interior scan.'

'But there's rumour of a Domino attack, eminence.'

'A rumour without foundation. For the time being, concentrate all sensors on internal surveillance. I will clear the order with Cardinal Agostini.'

'Yes, eminence.'

Richelieu settled back and heaved a slow breath.

His murmur was somewhere below a breath. 'Now it's up to you, Agostini. I'm counting on you.'

The Exalted Vatican emerged from behind a luminous cloud. The myriad domes on domes, pillars rearing above pillars, radiated a fearsome glare in the evening sky.

Miles Dashing drew his épée and aimed its point straight at Vatican City. 'For God and St George!' he proclaimed.

'Bloody suicide, if you ask me,' groaned Crocker, from the rear of the Draco. 'Two hundred against thousands? Stark, staring mad!'

'You'll be entitled to a hefty adventure bonus,'

encouraged Miles. 'I wouldn't be surprised if two bright new shillings dropped into your purse once this exploit is over.'

'Words fail me, sir.'

Miles peered ahead. Mary's craft had dipped below the Vatican's underbelly, with Byron a few metres behind. Still there was no alarm from the hovering city. Either the Sentinel Office had gone to sleep, or, more likely, the network had been sabotaged. The helping hand within.

He glanced to the west and the afterglow of sunset. Back in Venice, in the Theatre of Sighs, the curtains would be opening on Persona's *Thirteenth Night*. Time was running out, from what he'd gathered of Mary and Sarah's plan. If they weren't in the Crypt of the Seven Sleepers within two hours, Persona's dire drama would swamp Europa.

Mary's Draco swooped up into an Angelus duct in the underside of the city, with Byron on her tail. Miles was soon zooming up the twisting duct.

They had entered the citadel. Now there remained the task of defeating an enemy that outnumbered them fifteen to one, with the full panoply of inbuilt defences at ecclesiastical command.

'Bloody suicide,' moaned Crocker.

Twenty-Seven

The Rite of Passage stormed from the Passing Strange into the vaulted crypt of the Theatre of Sighs.

The lead carriage juddered to a halt and Doctor Sperano jumped out, still seething from his setback of the previous night. Incarnadine had been stolen from him. Well, Twelfth Night had never been auspicious for him, not even centuries ago when he was plain and simple Francis Pearson.

Tonight would make up for all other nights.

Tonight he would doff the mask of Doctor Sperano and become Persona, for all the world to see.

A lady in crimson stepped down from the carriage, Incarnadine to the teeth.

He gave her a curt bow. 'You fit your new role well, Celia. At first sight I wouldn't spot the difference. The virtual spitting image of the Blood Countess.'

She dropped a curtsey and smiled a slow, crimson smile. 'Have I got the walk right, milord?'

'Of course you have,' he snapped. 'I wrote it into you, didn't I?'

'Pardons, milord.'

Ignoring her apology, he stormed up the spiral stairs into the wings of the theatre. He peered round the side curtain and studied the audience.

It was a packed house, chock-a-block with the masters of Europa.

'I am the author of all your woes,' he breathed softly. 'And the stage is set.'

* * *

The Doctor paced up and down the Globe Theatre's stage in mounting exasperation. 'I've tried everything!' he complained, flinging up his arms. 'Every acoustic sequence in the book, and a couple more besides, and nothing works!'

Fists were thumping on the outer gate, but he ignored them; the dislocational field he had cobbled together would keep intruders at bay.

But what was the use of that if he couldn't get this blasted theatre to work?

They were all depending on him – Mary, the Dominoes, the unsuspecting people of Europa – and the price of failure was higher than any of them could imagine.

Persona's *Thirteenth Night* would have entered its first act by now, and there was nothing, *nothing* he could do about it. Persona's Globe kept its secret from him.

'Blast it!' he shouted, kicking a wooden pillar. 'Why won't you do anything?'

Then the theatre did do something, perhaps roused by the kick directed at its timbers. It tried to kill him.

The colossal Theatre of Sighs in Venice was renowned throughout Europa. And this was Thirteenth Night, the Venetian carnival of wildest revelry. To cap it all, Doctor Sperano's Theatre of Transmogrification was presenting his latest opus, *Thirteenth Night*. For sheer decadence, Sperano had no equal. His plays were so awful they were all the rage with the cognoscenti. Besides, his dramas had an inexplicable, mesmeric quality.

The Theatre of Sighs was packed to capacity, the front rows lined with dignitaries from the InterDominion Congress. The promised delegation from Vatican City was significantly absent, but few remarks were made. This was a Thirteenth Night *par excellence*, an occasion on the grand scale.

The lights dimmed. A roll of drums and a fanfare of trumpets.

The curtains opened.

Doctor Sperano stood on the giant stage, in his white, smiling mask and black opera cloak. The set was blank: white walls, unrelieved by door or windows, a floor bereft of a stick of furniture.

The Dramaturge raised his arms and declaimed in stentorian tones:

> 'Persona non grata in realms high and low,
> I pull the heart-strings of puppet friend and foe.
> Come twelve and one, the play will show
> I am the author of all your woe —'

As he recited, he jabbed a quill into his wrist and scribbled red words on the air: *Europa for a stage, its population for players.*

An impossibility blossomed around Sperano, the totality of Europa, squeezed into a proscenium arch. Clouded peaks, patchwork plains, teeming cities, contending armies. The panorama was not merely true to life . . .

'It's alive!' marvelled a commoner in the back stalls, gawking at the world that enwrapped Sperano. 'Bloomin' thing's bustin' out all over!'

'Shh!' hushed a dozen indignant lips.

A spectral butler walked on stage. He raised his hand and coughed politely. 'Excuse me, you who should be regarded as the greatest Dramatist of all time, as you know, but did you know it's Thirteenth Night?'

Sperano paraded up and down, eyes fixed on the middle distance. 'Yes, I was aware that this is Thirteenth Night, Buntering, you who are my butler. I am a master Dramatist, living in this passing strange house, as you know. For many years now lots of bumpkins and poltroons have said I'm not a great Dramatist, as you know.'

'What's a poltroon?' asked the commoner in the back stalls.

'Shh!'

'This is superlative avant-garde drama of the highest and most exquisite decadence, you Britannian oaf,' chided a lady with a lorgnette.

'It's crap.' The commoner tilted his cloth cap and folded his arms. 'Our dog could do better than that.'

Sperano stared at the Britannian in the back row. 'If I weren't the greatest Dramatist in history, Buntering, do you think I could make a man sitting at the back of the theatre explode?'

'Indubitably not, sir.'

Sperano pointed a finger, saying, 'The great Dramatist pointed a finger, and the cloth-capped commoner in the back row exploded.'

'Bollocks!' the man jeered, then exploded.

General applause.

'Oh, I see,' said the lady with the lorgnette. 'The fellow was part of the performance. I feel so *gauche*.'

Those sitting in the vicinity of the blood-splattered seat, their clothes soaked in anatomical gunge, weren't so sure.

'Looked pretty realistic to me . . .'

'This gown cost me a bloody *fortune* . . .'

'Excuse me, master Dramatist,' said Buntering, pointing at the psychotronic panorama of Europa, 'but is that Europa?'

'Yes, Buntering,' boomed Sperano. 'That is Europa, where I live and write things. Plays are mostly that which I write. I have written good plays like *To the Devil, a Doorknob*, and other good plays like that, as you know.'

'So, just as a matter of interest, if I may presume to make so bold, sir, what is the play you are happening to be working on now?' For some reason or other, Buntering executed a *pas-de-deux* with Sperano as he was speaking.

'You may well ask, Buntering,' bellowed Sperano, still tripping the light fantastic. 'And, forsooth, I will answer.' He performed a pirouette, then his spinning came to an abrupt halt. He lofted a finger. 'The moment approaches, Buntering! Bring the box!'

Buntering reeled back. 'Not – the box . . .'

'Yes, Buntering, the box! The box!' Sperano windmilled his arms. 'Hell may grump in disgruntlement infernal and Heaven raise a paradisiacal eyebrow, but the box will be opened. Fetch the box, I say! The box!'

Buntering reeled back again, hand on chest. 'Not – the box . . .'

'Yes, Buntering, the box! Though Hell gnash its teeth in breath halitosis and Heaven turn its cherubic posterior to our face and intent, the box will be opened . . .'

And so it went on, scene after scene of act one, Sperano demanding the box, Buntering aghast at the demand, punctuated by lines of naked chorus girls and the occasional swarm of monsters with axes who chopped each other's heads off, then put them on again.

The audience grew restless. This wasn't what they were expecting: where was the gore most gruesome of *grand guignol*?

A girl paraded across the stage wearing nothing but boots, a bowler hat, and a bow-tie.

'Get 'em off!' a commoner cried half-heartedly from the back stalls. 'Show us what you're made of, you saucy tart!' A number of his companions gave him puzzled looks.

'A box, I say! A box!' thundered Sperano.

Half the audience had buried their heads in their hands.

'Oh *God* . . .' bewailed a Venetian drama critic, eyes rolling. 'It isn't even incomprehensible rubbish.'

The first act dragged on for an hour. The curtains closed to a dead silence.

Seconds later the curtains reopened to a general groan.

The living scenery of Europa remained, the sole redeeming feature of the appalling production.

Sperano entered, stage left, holding a small cardboard box. 'The box!' he proclaimed triumphantly.

A chorus of ironic cheers.

Incarnadine sashayed onstage, to a burst of wolf-whistles from the commoners. She turned to the audience. 'Shall we open the box?' Her voice was a mortal sin, her semi-exposed legs doubly so.

More shouts from the back rows:

'Yeah, open the bloody box, for Christ's sake!'

'Show us what you're made of!'

'Are you *sure* you want to open the box?' she teased.

The commoners started up a chant. 'Open the box – show us what you're made of – open the box – show us what you're made of . . .'

'You might not like what's inside.'

'Open the box – show us what you're made of – open the box – show us what you're made of . . .'

Incarnadine placed the box in mid-air and stepped back as Sperano strode forward. 'I'll open the box,' he declared in a stentorian tone.

His voice lowered to the loudest stage-whisper in history. 'Then I'll show you what *I'm* made of.'

The effect on the audience was instantaneous. Suddenly, the farce was over.

Sperano stroked the lid of the box. 'I will show you fear,' he said, voice soft as cobweb. 'And not in a handful of dust.'

He lifted the lid. 'Eros is a rose is a sore,' he chanted.

With an elaborate gesture, he drew out the first item.

That's when the screaming began.

Twenty-Eight

Richelieu pressed his armchair communications button. 'Sentinel – switch immediately from total internal surveillance to external. A fleet of Dracos have been spotted fifty kilometres due south.'

'Too late, eminence. Internal sensors have identified two hundred and nine Domino intruders. Cardinal Agostini has ordered that maximum internal surveillance be maintained and the Dominoes destroyed.'

'Your orders are changed. External surveillance only.'

'I cannot comply, eminence. Cardinal Agostini is Chief of Security.'

Richelieu cursed silently. 'Very well, Sentinel. You must obey the chain of command.' He jabbed the button, terminating the exchange. He placed a finger to the polyglot, and tuned it to Faust's wavelength. 'Faust. Security has located you, so listen to what I say or you'll die with your companions. I can't show my hand now and declare you a Vatican agent. Persuade your leaders to take the secondary path to Domain Purgatorial. It's the least guarded route.'

The Dracoes ditched in the winding, tubular passages, Mary Shelley and Byron led the Dominoes through the labyrinthine belly of Vatican City. Sarah, Miles, Casanova and Crocker followed close behind the leaders.

'Rococo intestines,' Sarah whispered in distaste, eyeing the coiling passages, ribbed and fluted with extravagant extrusions. 'It's even worse than I remember.'

Mary smiled over her shoulder. 'Tasteless architecture

and interior decorating is the least of our difficulties.' Her smile faded as she watched Faust's hasty approach.

'This way is too heavily guarded,' Faust said. 'The secondary route to Domain Purgatorial would be our best bet.'

She arched an eyebrow. 'Is that so? What do you think, Byron?'

He pursed his lips. 'The man has a point, although his knowledge of the Vatican's layout is a surprise to me.' He considered a moment. 'All right, the Domain Purgatorial route, although it's bristling with traps.' A babble from the back of the ranks drew a frown from the lord. 'Will someone tell those Cyrano de Bergeracs to stop arguing? Bloody Gallic temperament.'

'I'll do it,' Faust volunteered with a grin.

Byron watched the Germanian's departure, then glanced at Mary. 'Just as you said. He'll guide us right for all the wrong reasons. But a reckoning must be made soon.'

Sarah gazed from Byron to Mary in puzzlement. 'What?'

Mary shook her head, indicating silence, while Byron went ahead and veered into a leftward passage.

To Sarah, the route seemed twice as long and winding as the one she escaped down five days ago. It went on and on.

Gradually, the passages ascended, depositing them in a series of vaulted chambers. 'I recognize this place,' she said. 'This is where I put on those altarboy clothes.'

Miles looked askance. 'Altarboy clothes?'

'It's not so strange, sir,' grinned Crocker. 'I knew this girl once —'

'I'm sure you did, but I'd —'

A lump was growing out the wall above Crocker's head. A lump that was forming into a face.

Miles's Hellfire pistol was in his hand and firing, blasting the emergent Gargoyle Vigilant to smithereens. 'Shame about the noise,' he said, holstering the pistol, 'but I had no option.'

'Quick reactions,' Byron complimented.

Passing through the vaulted chambers, they wound up a spiral staircase. Half-way up the stairs a scream burst out from below. Other screams came in swift succession.

Miles sniffed the air. 'Poisonous Incense!' he shouted. 'Up the stairs! Hurry!'

They needed no bidding, sprinting up the steps as an aromatic cloud wafted in their wake. Sarah blessed her decision to tear the tangerine gown at the knee; full-length, she'd never have made it.

A race up a series of stairs took them clear of the deadly incense. They waited while Miles retraced his steps a short distance. He returned, shaking his head. 'The incense took almost everyone. Just eleven left.'

Mary shot Sarah a sharp glance. 'We may already have run out of time to save the Doctor. And if we lose the Doctor, we lose everything.' She turned to Byron. 'How long to the Crypt of the Seven Sleepers?'

'About an hour, by the routes we're forced to take.'

Mary thumped her forehead. 'We haven't a chance. I shouldn't have trusted our so-called ally.'

'What ally is that?' Faust enquired, still shaking with fright from the incense.

Byron gave a thin smile. 'Cardinal Richelieu. You'll meet him soon enough, if you live.' He gave a nod to the ascending slope of a corridor. 'Domain Purgatorial is just ahead. From there, we work our way upward.'

Mary shrugged. 'Might as well, there's no way back.'

'I thought Richelieu was your enemy,' Sarah whispered.

'So did I until last night,' Byron answered in a low tone. 'Mary told me who our friends and enemies are.'

Several minutes' progress took them to an arched door. Byron pushed it open and stepped through, saying, 'Domain Purgatorial.'

'But the door wasn't even locked!' protested Faust. 'This must be a trap.'

Byron grabbed him by the scruff of the collar. 'Let's talk about traps, shall we, turncoat?'

Before Faust could respond, a swarm of Switzia Guardians raced across the Domain Purgatorial, the sharpest of barbed halberds in their hands. The door slammed behind the Domino vanguard, cutting them off from their few surviving comrades.

Mary gave a moan of despair. 'Richelieu betrayed us.'

Sister Laetitia grunted with exertion in the leather traces as she hauled Cardinal Agostini in the Chair Exalted down the Passage Furtive to the papal apartments.

'Quicker, trull,' Agostini ordered, enjoying the sense of power over the nun. He would soon be enjoying power over the entire Catholic Church Apostolic. Perhaps Sister Laetitia sensed his impending accession to the Throne of Peter. She had volunteered to carry him outside of hauling hours.

He activated the slide-panel that afforded access to the papal chambers, and viewed his surroundings with serenity. He would be at home here.

'Take me to the Chamber Sumptuous,' he commanded. 'Then go and lurk somewhere out of my sight.'

Sister Laetitia took him to the place appointed, bowed, and glided away. Agostini expelled a sigh of satisfaction as he sat in the Chamber Sumptuous. His schemes had come to fruition. The report would soon be put about that the pope had fled in fear for his life. The Throne of Peter would be announced vacant in days.

Agostini, with Persona's help, had accomplished his ambition. Pope Lucian was dead. Borgia was dead. Francisco was dead. Maroc had met with an accident, as arranged, in Transylvania. Altzinger was devoid of ambition. And the other surviving Enclave members were Reprises, banned from the papacy. As for the Doctor and the Dominoes, Persona would make short shrift of them. The small party of Dominoes that had the temerity to assault the Vatican had already been dealt with.

No one would ever know that 'the pope who returned' was Persona in one of his limitless guises. Agostini was in the clear. Agostini was safe.

Sister Laetitia stood at the fourth of the numbered papal apartment windows. She touched her ear. 'Ready,' she whispered. The nun extracted a pair of spectacles with blood-red lenses and peered through the reinforced glass of the fourth window, concentrating on a spot just below the outside ledge.

A smile curved her lips. The faint shimmer of a cloaked Angelus was visible through the thermographic spectacles. An Angelus, with the dim outline of an open hatch. A quick examination of the window revealed that it had been modified to a slide-window with the operation of a simple release mechanism.

The escape route was in place. Cardinal Richelieu had kept his promise. Sister Laetitia would return the favour.

The nun stripped off the heavy habit and stood in shirt and trousers. Then the male clothing was discarded, exposing a shapely, female figure.

Then the shapely, female figure was discarded. The layers of psychoform skin were peeled off, and the illusion of femininity disappeared as the body-morphing skin was stripped away. A stocky male physique emerged. A final tug at the head mask . . .

And a bald-headed Aleister Crowley stood by the fourth window, mouth spread in a wide grin.

He donned the shirt and trousers, listened to the polyglot in his ear, and murmured a low, 'Yes, I'll set him up now. Remember, leave plenty of space between me and the window, and no armed guards, or I'll denounce *you*.'

Crowley crept into the Chamber Sumptuous, making sure that the seated Agostini had his back to him.

When a slide-panel opened in the wall, he stepped speedily to Agostini's side, looped an arm around the chair's backrest, and leaned forward with a friendly smile.

'Wha—' gaped Agostini.

Cardinal Richelieu, Torquemada and Altzinger entered through the secret panel, accompanied by two unarmed guards. Crowley feigned surprise, backing away.

Richelieu jabbed an accusatory finger at Agostini and his satanic companion. 'There is your proof, gentlemen. Agostini has been consorting with the Beast, Aleister Crowley.'

'Devil-worshipper!' screeched Torquemada, glaring pure hatred at Agostini.

Crowley took his cue. He ran for a connecting door, shouting. 'You swore no one would find out, Agostini! The deal's off!'

He raced through two chambers to the fourth window, pressed the release catch, and leapt through the gap as the window slid upward.

The cloaked Angelus, as he'd earlier perceived, was pressed tight to the wall of the Apostolic Palace. Right under his feet.

He dropped. And kept on dropping.

The Angelus wasn't right under his feet. All that was below him was a clear hundred metres' fall.

Crowley's heart dropped faster than his descent. Slippery Richelieu had pulled a fast one on him. Left an Angelus to reassure him, then removed it after the reassurance. Suicide, that would be the verdict.

So much for the cardinal's promise to pave Crowley's way to the title of Official Antichrist. Must have done a side-deal with Faust from the start.

Crowley stared down at the hard, hard ground that rushed up to meet him, and searched for a word of farewell to the world.

'Bugger.'

Domain Purgatorial boiled with Switzia Guardians. Scores of them, with scores more rushing in from all angles. The seven trespassers were outnumbered to an extravagant degree.

Sarah quailed at the forest of barbed halberds as the foremost guards closed in. Watching a swashbuckler movie was one thing, being inside one was another. Those steel barbs would make an unromantic mess of her anatomy, and that prospect was mere seconds away.

Miles Dashing's sword danced in the torchlight, skewering the first of the Switzia Guardians. 'For God and Saint George! Come on, Crocker — show the flag.' He darted a swift look around. 'Where's Crocker got to?'

'Up here, sir.' Crocker was clinging to a gargoyle a full three metres from the floor, where only the rawest of raw panic could have powered his jump.

'Come down this minute!' ordered Miles, despatching a second guard while Mary Shelley took another in the chest with the point of her épée.

'I'd only get in the way, sir,' Crocker called down to Miles. 'Cramp your style. Anyway, I can act as a lookout up here.'

Giving up on his servant with a disgusted snort, Miles laid into the soldiers, blade flashing to the manner born.

Byron slashed two men with a single stroke of the sabre.

Casanova's rapier took an attacker clean in the throat.

Faust struggled to hold his own with an unsteady sword.

Sarah was ducking and dodging for all she was worth, and pondering whether she might manage a leap to the nearest gargoyle.

'Stay behind Miles, Sarah!' Mary shouted out as she ducked a swing from a halberd. 'He's the finest swordsman in all of —' Two charging guards demanded her complete attention.

Sarah took the advice, diving behind Miles's tall figure. He had cleared a space before him, his adversaries temporarily daunted by the Britannian's dazzling dexterity. 'That's it, milady,' he said over his shoulder to Sarah. 'Staying behind me with your back to the wall will preserve your life for perhaps as much as a full minute.'

He drew a long-barrelled pistol. 'See how you like a taste of Hellfire, base-born Vatican acolytes!' He fired the weapon into the liveried ranks with a thunderclap report and a lightning flash. When the smoke cleared she perceived that the pistol had made mush of dozens of guards.

'I'm out of Hellfire ammunition,' he called to the others. 'Does anyone else possess secret weapons?'

In response, Casanova whipped out a length of slender rope, and lassoed a gargoyle. 'I'll show you what an expert can do with autoknot rope,' the Venetian declared, hurtling into the air.

'You're not the only expert, Giacomo!' Byron laughed mirthlessly, drawing out a similar length of rope and lashing the end around a stony face four metres above his head. 'Let's go to the Devil with a dash of panache!' He soared above the soldiers' heads, his sabre parting several of the heads from their shoulders.

The extraordinary ropes, like two horizontal pendulums, swung the men to and fro above the fray, the rapier and sabre wreaking havoc. Then Byron swung too low, and a well-aimed halberd severed the rope. The poet went down under a press of soldiers to a cry of dismay from Mary.

Miles, meanwhile, had disposed of an astounding number of opponents. At least a score of Switzia Guardians were heaped around him, and his darting épée was adding to the score by the second.

But one guard managed to slip past him, halberd hoisted to cleave Sarah in half. The soldier swung the weapon. And the swing went astray as Crocker landed feet-first on the helmeted head. The servant scuttled on all fours to Sarah's side.

Miles caught the action out the corner of his eye. 'Well done, Crocker —' During the fleeting distraction, a halberd, flat side on, slammed Miles on the temples. The lord reeled, his sword dangling. Then Miles and the sword dropped as one.

Casanova swooped to Sarah's rescue, flooring several guards with double-kicks in his flight. He landed in front of her, rapier stabbing the attackers in a streak of light.

For the best part of ten seconds, he put up an amazing performance against absurd odds. But sheer weight of numbers threw him off-balance. And steel barbs tore into his stomach. He spun round, and another halberd stabbed into his back. Swaying, Casanova saluted Sarah with his sword. 'My regrets, madam, on leaving you undefended against these graceless oafs.' Then he thudded to the floor, lips moving in a final whisper to a someone only he could see: 'Ah, Milady La Charpillon – how you broke my heart.' Then Casanova breathed his last.

Sarah and Crocker shrank back against the wall from the advancing halberds.

Sarah shut her eyes and readied herself for a fatal jab in the stomach or throat. She hadn't a hope in Hell.

Twenty-Nine

Agostini, recovering from shock and assessing the situation with a speed derived from a lifetime's practice of diplomacy and intrigue, was hot on Crowley's heels and making for the Passage Furtive's slide-panel.

Wily Richelieu had outwitted him. He should have killed that old fox first. But too late now for regrets.

His eyebrow raised a fraction when Crowley jumped out the window, but his pace didn't falter. He was in the passage and had slammed the panel shut before the guards entered the room.

Keeping up a brisk pace down the secret corridors, he turned several options over in his mind. Means of escape – the Angeli. Not feasible; the Angeli were closely guarded.

Hiding-places – numerous, but a refuge could easily become a trap.

He required a fast vehicle, preferably one capable of outdistancing an Angelus, but where would he find a Draco?

A vehicle. There was one, far outstripping any Europan craft. His spies in Dimensions Extraordinary Office had informed him of what little they'd learned of the Doctor's transdimensional blue police box, and Maroc had let slip a few hints.

The box, up in the Crypt of the Seven Sleepers, might possibly contain a mini-universe. What better place of refuge? And, according to the experts, it was some form of space-time vehicle. With luck, he might work out how to operate it.

A dash through several tunnels took him to a door leading to an Ascension Tower. He would steal the Doctor's transport, and no one was going to stop him.

Altzinger gave a reluctant nod to Cardinal Richelieu. 'The pope's absence from his apartments suggests that your account is correct, eminence. I'm inclined to believe the true pope was killed on Eighth Night, and the pope who returned was an imposter. As for Agostini – his guilt is evident.'

'The situation is grave, Altzinger,' said Torquemada. 'The Devil is loose in the Vatican. We need a leader at the helm now, this moment. We are all that's left of the Enclave. A new pope must be voted in on the spot.'

'Amen,' agreed Torquemada.

Altzinger shifted from foot to foot. 'Well – if the title's simply that of Pope Designate – agreed, I suppose.'

Richelieu subjected the Germanian to a stern stare. 'Do we have your solemn word on that? You agree that we must elect a pope here and now?'

Altzinger threw up his hands. 'Very well, you have my solemn word, if that's what you want. Now, my name as pope will be –'

'Not you, eminence,' Richelieu said firmly. 'Torquemada or myself – we're the candidates.'

'But – but you're Reprises! The Nicodemus principle . . .'

'Will be revoked once one of us is nominated. The issue is simple. Torquemada wishes to become pope. So do I. Neither of us will vote for you. Which of us do you support?'

'I – What can I say?'

Richelieu folded his arms. 'You say, in front of these guards as witnesses, either "Torquemada" or "Richelieu". I would have thought the choice was obvious.'

A bemused Altzinger looked from Torquemada to Richelieu, from Richelieu to Torquemada. Then he knelt and kissed Richelieu's ring.

Torquemada bit his lip so deep the blood trickled to his chin.

'Release the Dominoes!'

The command resounded through the mouths of the Gargoyles Parlant in the Domain Purgatorial.

Sarah, pressed tight against the wall, opened her eyes at the booming voice.

The Switzia Guardians hesitated a moment at the sound of Richelieu's voice, then drew back from the embattled Dominoes.

'I am Pope Designate,' boomed Richelieu. 'Cardinal Altzinger and Inquisitor General Torquemada will confirm the appointment. They will also confirm that Cardinal Agostini has committed heinous crimes and is to be apprehended.'

As both the appointment and Agostini's guilt was confirmed via the Gargoyles Parlant, Faust breathed a loud sigh of relief. Sarah breathed a louder and longer one.

'Talk about Divine intervention,' she gasped.

'God and the cardinal are not yet identical,' Mary said, her eyes straying to where Byron lay in red ruin.

Miles, blood streaming from a head-wound, was struggling to his feet. 'I see the guards are retreating. Some fortunate happenstance has clearly worked in our favour.'

Crocker wore a wide smile. 'I knew everything would turn out all right.'

Sarah's gaze descended to the butchered Casanova, and her elation evaporated. He had given his life to save hers. And Lord Byron — another casualty.

She shook her head. Everything turned out all right? No way. Two good men were dead. And Persona was about to transform everyone into poor players on his Europan stage. If Mary Shelley's calculations were right, they were too late to play their part in averting the disaster.

'Miles . . .' called out a familiar voice. Byron was rising painfully from the floor, blood escaping from several stab-wounds. 'Bring some of that healing ointment of yours, will you? Mary used hers up on the Doctor.' He gave a wink at Mary. 'You didn't think you'd be rid of me so easily, did you?'

She flashed him a smile, then glanced at Sarah, a question in her gaze. Sarah was all too aware of that questioning glance. The Doctor – Persona – a failed mission.

Rubbing his head, Miles made his way to Byron as Mary walked to Sarah's side. The two women exchanged stares. Mary held up the trionic key to the Doctor's vehicle.

'The TARDIS,' they chorused.

The Crypt of Seven Sleepers was empty.

'Thank God,' wheezed Agostini, hearing the thump of guards' boots at his back.

He rushed to the open door of the blue box. And recoiled, as if obstructed by a transparent membrane. He tightened his lips, refusing defeat.

I'll think my way in, he told himself. I'm walking in – there's no barrier. An open door. I'm walking through an open door.

He was still thinking of walking through an open door when he realized he was already inside the white-walled interior.

'Safe,' he sighed. Then his face clouded. Any member of the Dimensions Extraordinary Office could penetrate the vehicle. Even a guard could follow his example.

He put a shoulder to the door and heaved. The door refused to budge. Well, if the door wouldn't shut . . .

Move the blue box somewhere safe. Somewhere *nobody* dared go. He sprinted out the door as the guards charged into the crypt, pressed a lever on the Altar Ipsissimus, and raced back to his refuge.

He leaped through the door just in time. The drop-slab

he'd activated fell through the crypt floor, taking the police box with it.

Breathing heavily, he edged away from the open door as the dark smear of a transit tunnel sped past the doorway. He was on his way down to the safest, and most dangerous region in Vatican City, the Pit of Perdition.

He turned and ran to an inner door leading to a corridor. Before the vehicle plunged into the Pit, where none dare approach, he wanted to put as much distance as possible between himself and that open door. Who could tell how far the Pit's lethal plenum-vacuum would reach into the mini-universe?

In time, he'd learn how to pilot the craft out of the Pit, but first, he had to gain time.

He ran for all he was worth.

Richelieu, Pope Designate of the Catholic Church Apostolic, sped across the Domain Purgatorial in a small hover-flier.

Faust raced to meet him. 'You did it! You really had me worried back there. Talk about a close call!'

The flier halted and Richelieu dismounted, his expression indecipherable. Sarah and the Dominoes approached the tall prelate, a partially recovered Byron leaning on Miles for support.

Faust glanced over his shoulder at his former comrades. 'You can have them killed now. I'm safe.'

Sarah darted a glance at Mary, but the young woman pressed a silencing finger to her lips.

Richelieu shook his head and sighed. 'Faust, Faust – so naive. You have betrayed the Dominoes, and thus deserve the severest of punishments.'

'But you hate the Dominoes!' Faust spluttered. 'They're your enemies – you never stopped saying so.'

'That's what I thought,' Miles said, frowning.

'Perhaps, like that Shakespearean lady, I protested too much,' said Richelieu. 'My only enemies are those of Francia. What better way to serve Francia than as pope, and fly the Exalted Vatican to hover over Avignon? As for the Dominoes, my prime concern is defending Francia's borders against other Dominions. The Dominoes have a destabilizing effect on Dominions. However, I have Mary Shelley's word that they will stay clear of my realm. Mutual convenience. At this stage of the game, our interests converge. At a later stage – Well, later is later.'

Faust boiled with rage. 'You swine! I transmitted everything to you, passed on every word in the Villa Diodati.'

'Yes,' growled Byron, pushing aside Miles's supporting arm. 'I know that – *now*, thanks to a message passed from Richelieu to Mary. You were sitting beside Albé – I thought the signal came from him. No wonder the Doctor looked at Albé's severed head and said, "Wrong man". He knew you were the culprit. I killed the wrong man.'

'Fortunately,' said the cardinal, 'all messages came to me. Now, please, let's waste no more time.' He signalled to Byron. 'I suggest you give Faust an appropriate finale to his career.' His gaze swerved to the Pit.

'But you'll drive the Anti-Church underground!' Faust yelled. 'I thought you wanted it kept official, where you can keep an eye on it.'

'Paracelsus will keep it official,' said Richelieu. 'Once he's instated as Official Antichrist.'

'Oh no! Not bloody Paracelsus!'

Byron grabbed Faust by the scruff of the collar and dragged him to the immense black hole. 'No!' Faust screamed, arms flailing, legs kicking.

'You can't let him die like that!' Sarah protested.

Miles squared his shoulders. 'So die all traitors.' His gaze moved to Casanova's corpse. 'Let his death pay for Giacomo's.'

Crocker made a wry face. 'Could have emptied Faust's purse of money first.'

Byron had pulled his captive to the rim of the abyss. He lifted a boot and slammed it into Faust's back. It propelled him straight over the edge.

He plunged into the blackness, a thin scream fading into the distance: 'Mephistopheles!'

Richelieu met an interrogative stare from Miles. 'Mephistopheles won't honour his pact with Faust. I've made certain – arrangements.' He stepped into his hover-vehicle. 'Did you know, one authority has it that the last words of the original Faust were "I'll return my library books", but I suspect the story is apocryphal.' With that, the Pope Designate glided away.

From below, the pitch of Faust's scream rose an octave as he faced his worst nightmare.

Sarah turned away, sickened. 'I wouldn't have expected you to let that happen,' she said to Mary.

Mary gave a shrug. 'You don't live in my world –' She broke off, jabbing a finger at the ceiling. 'Is that what I think it is?'

Sarah looked up, and saw the familiar shape of the TARDIS plummet from the shadows of a lofty dome. It streaked down, a blur of speed.

And plunged straight into the Pit.

'Oh *no*,' Mary groaned, seeing their sole hope vanish. 'That finishes everything.'

'No it doesn't,' Sarah said, swiping the trionic key from Mary's hand. 'There's a hope in Hell.' She sprinted hell-for-leather to the Pit. She raced across the flagstones, not daring to think what she was doing. Not daring to think.

'Sarah!' Mary yelled.

'*Dum spiro, spero,*' Sarah shouted back.

She ran to the rim of the Pit.

And jumped straight in.

Thirty

What Sperano pulled out of the box was the head of everyone in the audience.

Each of the thousands in the Theatre of Sighs saw his or her own head in the Dramaturge's hand, held by one ear.

'The first item from Pandora's box,' he announced. 'Your own face. Look on the face of the small fear.'

No one was heckling now, no one was laughing. He had their head by the ear. If he should drop it, or push a thumb in its eye . . .

He put the head back in the box. 'And now, ladies and gentlemen – the large fear. But first, I must prepare you. This is a special night, the grand opening of the Europan shock show. Europa is my stage, my drama, my amusement, and all of you here are privileged to have front seats at the first-night performance, introducing a new era in earth's history.'

He strode to the front of the stage and, with an exaggerated gesture, pulled off his Doctor Sperano face.

'I,' he declared, 'am Persona.'

Each of thousands of faces stared at the blank non-face, a pink, smooth shell. They looked, and couldn't look away.

'I am Persona,' he repeated in a paradoxical whisper that shook the auditorium. 'Persona, all things to all men.'

He allowed a long, dramatic pause.

'But this absence-face you see is only another mask. Shall I lift it off and show you what lies beneath? Do you dare confront the Gorgon?'

They trembled in their seats, struggled to avert their eyes, but Persona had captured the sight of one and all.

'Ah, but of course, you have no choice. It's written in my script, and what I write, happens. If I should massacre a Nederlandian town in a play, that same massacre will take place in the outside world. With a stroke of my quill, I can set army against army, bring the Eiger crashing down in thunderous ruin. On a less grandiose level, with a spoken word, I can squeeze your heart. At last, the pen is truly mightier than the sword. But first, let me teach you the fear that the elect among the mad know so well. The soul of nightmare. For this is Thirteenth Night, the extra night, like the thirteenth month, the extra month. A night out of time. My night. An endless night.'

He slid fingernails under the Persona mask and started to peel it loose. 'Once you have seen my face, I will show you your own from the box. It will never be quite the same again.'

The mask was partially lifted when a prodigy manifested behind the Dramatist.

To the accompaniment of groaning timber and sundering masonry, the Globe Theatre pushed itself on to the stage from nowhere, cramming its wooden O into the proscenium arch and splitting it asunder.

The Globe was just too much for the stage of the Theatre of Sighs. It cracked wide open. The psionic backlash flung the audience to the floor.

Swinging wildly in the maelstrom, the chandeliers flickered and died.

In steady pulses, light blinked from the theatre-crammed stage. Ghost illumination. In the intermittent glare, a dark figure swung wide the gates of the Globe and rushed into the wings.

Persona, his unmasking curtailed, crawled along the footlights, almost as stunned by the Globe's appearance as the onlookers.

Incarnadine assisted the Dramatist to his feet. 'Milord, what wonder is this?'

'Not what,' he snarled. 'Who?'

The sound of clopping hooves and rumbling carriage wheels echoed from the wings. Persona raised a fist in rage as he witnessed the entrance of his own Rite of Passage carriage on stage.

The driver was the Doctor. He grinned, and lifted his hat. 'Room for one more inside, sir.'

Then he shook the reins and the mechanical horses veered into the Globe's open gates.

Roaring with fury, Persona raced in pursuit. The gates slammed shut behind him.

Then, in a flare of spectral light, the Globe Theatre emitted a vast groan from the mother of all timbers and departed the Theatre of Sighs in a neither-here-nor-there direction.

The Globe Theatre spun through the exuberant sense and nonsense of the Passing Strange, tossed by rivers of rumour, currents of thought, streams of ideas, an extravaganza of possibilities and impossibilities.

The Doctor jumped out of the carriage and leapt on to the Globe's stage, ready to confront Persona.

It had been an arduous trip from Londia to Venice, initiated by a frustrated kick against a wooden upright. Funny that, just how often you got a machine started by a good kick.

The Globe had kicked back, as it launched itself into the Passing Strange, a borderland between space-time and the vortex. The theatre lacked the shielding to protect the passenger from the turmoil of the Passing Strange. And the fabric of the primitive TARDIS, soaked in Managra's essence, was inimical to the Time Lord. It was a fight to stay alive in transit to Venice as the theatre travelled to its focus, the being known as Persona.

He kept an eye on the chaos sky above. Its muddle and discord was wreaking havoc on the Globe, unravelling its fabric in a process that would result in one, long ontological string. Trouble was, the same process was at work in his own psyche-soma.

'Doctor!'

He summoned up a grin at the Dramaturge's stealthy approach. You're only as brave as people think you are. He spun on his feet and circled the stage, arms lifted, head tilted, and spoke in a strong but wistful tone:

> 'All the world's a stage,
> And all the men and women merely players:
> They have their exits and their entrances;
> And one man in his time plays many parts . . .'

He flashed another smile. '*As You Like It*. Or – as you don't like it?'

'Don't quote perfidious Will's play at me!' stormed Persona. 'He stole all my ideas, all my lines. The Thief of Stratford!'

The Doctor paced to the front of the stage. 'Come now, Pearson. There *is* a trace of Francis Pearson left in you, isn't there? You know perfectly well you stole and mangled every idea and line from Will Shakespeare, and he didn't raise a single protest. Sweet Will, they used to call him. Good-natured, a loyal friend, generous to a fault. Admit it, you envied his genius. Lacking originality of your own, you aped his works, and, quite frankly, you aped them with a lack of skill and wit that verges on the breathtaking.'

Persona sprang on the stage, lunging in wrath. 'I'll turn you inside out, Doctor!'

The Doctor evaded the lunge, whipping off his scarf and looping it round the man's legs. Persona went sprawling and the Doctor took to his heels, aiming for the more efficient TARDIS of the Rite of Passage carriage.

He jumped inside and pulled the door shut, then scanned the spacious Jacobean interior, with its dark, polished wood and hefty furniture. He glanced at his scarf; it was starting to unravel from the chaos effect of the Passing Strange. Time to play for time, on the off-chance that Mary had located his TARDIS and managed to punch the correct code into the console. He had given her the code, along with the trionic key, back in Londia. It was up to her now. If she didn't arrive in a few minutes, he'd be unravelling a lot faster than his scarf.

He peered through the window, a mullioned, diamond-latticed affair from this side of the glass, and saw Persona's eggshell face looming close.

The Doctor shook his head. 'Sans teeth, sans eyes, sans taste, sans everything.'

Darting across the main living room for the stairs, he glimpsed a portrait on the wall, the original of that crimson-clad girl in the Theatre of Sighs. Elizabeth Bathory. The Blood Countess.

'I'm sorry,' he muttered, recalling a girl's face from the Castle Bathory. 'I should have tried harder to save you.'

Then: 'Sarah . . .'

He took the stairs three steps at a time, hearing Persona's boots thumping the ground floor. He scanned the upper floors, and a frown creased his brow. The upper storey held room after room, ranging to apparent infinity. Downstairs, the rooms, including the kitchen, amounted to four, at most. The house was top-heavy to the point of insanity. An unstable structure for a TARDIS.

The house was mad to the soul of its timber.

He prowled through room after room, then came across what might have been a man, spreadeagled on the floorboards. Throwing light on the subject with a holo-candle, he inspected the sprawled shape.

The figure was dressed in the Doctor's own clothes, from brown fedora to multi-coloured scarf. But the body had been transmogrified. Reassembled. A thick mane of curly hair sprouted from the gaping mouth. There was a blue eye in the throat. A mouth in the forehead, teeth bared. Each feature had been transposed. A jumbled face. An anagram of a face. The victim had looked on the visage of the Gorgon.

He pressed the chest, and felt the contour of a hand

bulging from the sternum. A faint pulse, but no beat of hearts. A quick examination disclosed that one heart beat in the brain, another in a foot.

The eye in the throat swivelled up and looked at him. The mouth in the forehead opened its slack lips.

'The countess fooled us with her masks, didn't she?' said the mouth. 'Killed so many of those poor young women. Quite a spot of bother. She taught Persona a great deal, but she kept so much back. So much. *We* know how much, don't we?'

The Doctor reeled away, trying to retrace his steps to the stairway. The stairs were nowhere to be found.

'LOST, DOCTOR?' Persona's voice was the loudest whisper in the world, echoing from below. 'OF COURSE YOU'RE LOST. YOU'RE IN MY WORLD. THIS IS THE HOUSE THAT PERSONA BUILT.'

He ignored the booming whisper, pushing open a door. Inside the door was a small room. On the far wall was a large mirror. It reflected him in uncanny detail. He stepped back to leave.

But his image stayed frozen on the mirror.

'WANT TO SEE A GOOD TRICK, DOCTOR? IT'S A TRICK I'VE PULLED BEFORE.'

The mirror crazed into a thousand pieces in its wooden frame, each piece a hologram of a man in a hat and long scarf.

Then the mirror exploded across the room, hurling a blizzard of sharp-edged shards straight at the Doctor.

'CAT LICK YOUR HEART!' Persona's voice exulted.

Thirty-One

A gale raged down the limitless corridors inside the small blue box.

Agostini tumbled down the corridors, hands frantically scrabbling for purchase on a lever, a handle, a doorknob.

The suction of the void outside the vehicle was too strong.

Now he was being dragged down the passages into the blackness of the Pit, the dreadful plenum-vacuum, seat of soul's fear. Whether it was the vacuum that was drawing him or the Doctor's vehicle that was rejecting him, he couldn't tell, and it wouldn't have made any difference.

A whimper escaped him as he was flung across the control chamber. The whimper rose to a scream when he was sucked through the doorway.

There was a fleeting sensation of speed. Then stillness. Silence. Utter dark. He looked where he thought was up, and saw the dark. Looked from side to side, and saw the dark. Looked down, the dark.

He waited, in fear, for fear to come.

It came from above.

A ceiling formed above his head, its wide expanse covered in a fresco. For a moment, Agostini thought he was in his bed, woken from a nightmare. It was the frescoed ceiling of his bedchamber. In a tangle of tormented limbs, howling heads, and demons rampant, the Sufferings of the Damned were depicted in all their inglory. Skewered on a roasting spit, Pope Lucian glared down at the cardinal from his heights of anguish.

'Done to a turn,' grunted a demon with the body of a

reptile and the head of a fish, tilting the spit so that the pontiff slid off. The creature's gaze shifted down to Agostini. 'Now your turn.'

Pope Lucian protruded from the ceiling, hands extended into hooked claws, scorched eyes fixed in the cardinal. 'Your turn, Agostini.'

'No!' He fought to escape the descending pope, but his legs thrashed impotently in the void. He felt a burning embrace as Pope Lucian's arms enfolded him. Then he was hoisted up to Hell and shrieked as he was skewered on the spit.

The pope lifted a hand in farewell. 'I'm for Purgatory, and you – you're where you belong.' He departed like mist, leaving Agostini in the company of the damned.

'Welcome to Hell, Cardinal Agostini,' said the fish-headed demon. 'My name's Hieronymus. We're all on first-name terms here. First I'll toast you over the fire a while, next you'll be introduced to the excretion tubes . . .'

Agostini howled at the flames that ravaged him to the very soul. He was in the supreme nightmare, religion's *tour de force* of horror. Hell itself.

But he was also in the Domain Purgatorial's Pit, enduring his worst fear. The fear that kills. At least that was cold comfort in so hot a place. The terror would usher in the blessed oblivion of death.

'Death will save me,' he croaked from blistering lips.

Hieronymus peered at Agostini through his fishy eyes. 'There's no death in Hell.'

Sarah soon lost all sensation of falling. She hovered in the black void, weightless, directionless.

Wherever she looked, black night.

She focused her thoughts on the TARDIS. There was a degree of affinity between the Doctor and his vehicle. And there was a bond between herself and the Doctor.

The Doctor was the link.

'Doctor,' she whispered. 'Doctor.'

If she could only call the TARDIS to her. She had the key, tight in her fist, but the door would probably still be open, if she was any judge of the old craft's sly little ways.

'Doctor . . .'

A light flashed in the dark.

A rectangular outline spun in her direction. The flashing beacon soon illuminated the advancing object.

It was a blue police box, the door wide open. She reached out, and found she could move, by an act of thought alone.

The TARDIS is enclosing me in its field, she realized, breaking into a smile. It's saving me. Thanks, thanks, thanks. Oh, God, thank you.

She caught the doorframe and stepped inside.

The inside was slightly smaller than the outside. It was an ordinary police box, except for the missing telephone. There were sweet wrappers on the floor. And a pool of stale urine.

The door slammed shut. She whirled round, frantic fingers probing the surface. There was no door handle, just a smooth expanse. Smaller on the inside than the outside.

Smaller inside. And getting smaller.

Her heart set up an erratic drum-beat.

The phone box was contracting. She could hear her panicked breathing as the ceiling came down to touch her head. Within a few harsh breaths, the walls pressed against her shoulders.

She wrestled with the door, struggling to force it open. *Come on. Oh God, come on.* The door stayed obdurately closed. It might as well have been welded shut.

'Let me out!'

The enclosing walls forced her into a crouch, then compressed her to an embryonic posture.

The terror broke in full flood, and she released it in a stream of tears, thumping on the tiny door and bawling. 'Let me out! Let me out!'

She'd soon be a small, crushed shape, tinier than a little girl. A tiny tot, crying for her Dad.

The lights went out.

Now she knew where she was — back in that old fridge on the rubbish-tip, on the way home from school. Bob and Tommy had shoved her in and shut the door, and there was no handle on the inside.

'Daddy!' she screamed, giving the door another thump. 'Help! Daddy!'

Her lungs laboured to breathe. 'Daddy!'

The door opened and in a flood of daylight she saw her Dad's face. Saw his wonderful, big arms pull her out of the fridge. Yes, that's what happened — he'd been out looking for her, and heard the thump of her fist on the door. She was free.

She was free.

And the dark was back. And her Dad was gone. She glanced around in the blackness of the Pit of Perdition, free of that hideous box. The memory of her Dad had saved her. She felt her face; wet with tears.

She flinched at the sight of a blue police box approaching through the blackness, its roof-beacon flashing, the door wide open in invitation. She couldn't see inside.

Another trick. It must be. And this time, it would crush her to death, she was sure of it. She'd sooner hover forever in the void than step into the box and risk being crunched to a pulp.

It was a trick. An open door to her worst terror.

She reached out, pulse pounding, and pulled herself through the door and into the box.

Miles and Mary stood near the edge of the Pit. An exhausted Byron and solemn Crocker sat nearby.

For a long time, no one spoke.

Finally, Mary lowered her head. 'She'll be dead of fear by now.'

Miles gave a sad nod. 'Better for her if she is, Mary. Better it's all over.'

Byron darted a glance at the abyss. 'I'd give anything to

see that brave young lady once more, if only to praise her heroism.'

Gaze still downcast, Mary wheeled round slowly. 'We'd better go.'

A blue police box ascended from the black of the Pit and glided to the rim, settling gently.

A familiar face popped out the door. 'Hello, folks,' Sarah smiled. 'Room for lots more inside.'

The Doctor flung himself at the door when the mirror detonated, and had swerved round the door-frame as the lethal shards poured through. He suffered no more than a cut on the back of his hand.

'Enough, Persona,' he said softly. 'No more games.' He took a sliver of glass, dipped it in the blood welling from his hand, and scribbled a sentence on the wall. 'Mimesis is a game two can play,' he muttered to himself, eyeing the red scrawl.

He let drop the shard and marched through the rooms. A door led into a series of passages, and at the end of one passage he saw a mullioned window, identical to the one downstairs. Peering through the glass, he saw the floor of the Globe a mere couple of feet below.

It was the *same* window as the one on the ground floor, or rather, both were aspects of the same window. He pushed open one of the panels and jumped on to the floor of the theatre. The as-above, so-below structure of the carriage interior had saved him the trouble of sneaking back down the stairs. Persona had been lured inside the house; now the Doctor had to ensure he stayed there.

He glanced at the Globe's wooden O. Long ago, Pearson had burned down the real Globe, home to the greatest dramas in history. This recreation had witnessed mockeries of those plays. With a huge bound, he landed on the stage and spun round, arms outspread:

'Heat not a furnace for your foe so hot
That it do singe yourself. We may outrun

By violent swiftness that which we run at,
And lose by over-running.'

Summoned by drama, the ghosts of the past came back to haunt. The ghosts, and the fire. A red flicker at the edge of the pit heralded the conflagration. Persona's Globe was about to go up in a ghostly inferno, and in the Passing Strange, ghost fire was as real fire.

Glancing up at the mounting turbulence of the nonsense sky, the Doctor sped to the carriage door, and slammed it tight shut behind him. Standing in the downstairs room, he studied the door's mullioned window interior. The apparent glass was part of the carriage's plasmic shell, unbreakable.

He gave a grim nod. 'Good.' A hand dived into a pocket, and pulled out a flute. Putting flute to lips, he warbled an intricate melody, and watched with satisfaction as the wood of the door melded with the frame into a seamless whole. The door, in all its aspects, upstairs, downstairs, and in my lady's chamber, was sealed tight. The sonic bonding would last a good ten minutes, and that was more than enough time.

Outside the latticed window, Jacobean phantoms were fleeing a greedy blaze. Persona's Globe was going up in smoke.

'DOCTOR – WHAT GAME ARE YOU PLAYING?' boomed Persona from the upper floors.

'You're the player of games, Persona!' the Doctor shouted. 'Couldn't resist adding that cryptic signature to *The Last Judgement* in the Sistine Chapel, could you? The ever-changing mask on the back of St Benedict's hand. What were you trying to say, that you are the author of the Last Judgement, of all our woes?'

A silence greeted his words. He strode across the room and was pulled to a stop by a sensual, feminine voice from Countess Bathory's portrait: 'A cat will lick your heart . . .'

He kept his gaze averted from the painting. 'You're a nightmare that's over,' he said.

'Am I?'

'For now, at least,' he murmured, then made for the stairs and sprinted up the steps.

'NOW I'LL SHOW YOU THE WAY TO MY PRIVATE LITTLE PLACE, DOCTOR, IF YOU HAVE EYES TO SEE . . .'

'I thought you might,' he said, arriving on the landing. His mouth tightened as he saw a human heart plumped by the far wall, and a black cat licking its pulsing valves.

Beyond the heart, he spotted a flight of angled stairs, almost hidden in shadow. 'Ah, I think I spy your sanctum, Persona. Is that where you keep your masks?'

'CONGRATULATIONS, DOCTOR, YOU'VE FOUND THE VISAGE ATTIC. DO COME UP.'

The Doctor ran up the stairs and thrust open the attic door. Persona stood on the far side of the loft, framed by a latticed window, and surrounded by open chests brimming with masks.

'Welcome to my little treasure trove,' laughed the blank face. 'Care to try on a new look?'

The Doctor shook his head. 'You're a fool, Persona. You've kept your attention on me, instead of our course. I've rigged the Globe to fly out of the Passing Strange, and into the vortex. These makeshift craft of yours may withstand the fringes of the vortex that you call the Passing Strange, but they'll start to tear asunder once they enter the true wilderness of space-time. However, the Rite of Passage will implode before that. Its plasmic shell is too weak, its structure too unstable.'

'Nonsense!' snorted Persona.

'Look out of the window. See for yourself.'

Persona whirled round and looked through the window. 'You've set fire to my theatre! Torched my palace of masques!'

'The least of your troubles. Let me enlighten you. Do you know what's likely to occur if you place one TARDIS inside another, particularly two crude examples like the Globe and the Rite of Passage? I'll tell you. Implosion. The house that you built will come crashing down.'

Persona gazed up at the sky. 'You maniac! We're already in the vortex. If I don't drive the carriage out of here we'll be destroyed.' He reached for the window, and pulled at the catch several times before noticing the fused wood of window and frame. 'We're sealed in. You've condemned us both to death!'

The Doctor's tone was quiet. 'Yes, it won't be long before the house folds in on us. You gave me no alternative. I can't let you loose on the world. I don't want any more deaths on my conscience.'

Persona spoke in a sibilant whisper. 'Like that girl in Castle Bathory? You still have nightmares about that castle, I know you do.'

'As do you. I saw an example on the landing. You've imposed your bad memories on this world. The image of a cat licking a heart, part of the ritual the Countess forced you to endure.'

'I was glad to endure it! I bared my heart with my own hands, and never cried out once at the harsh tongue of the cat.'

The Doctor lowered his gaze. 'We all have our nightmares.'

'Then let me give you a new one now!' Persona jabbed a quill into his wrist and wrote red words on the air: *The Doctor was no longer able to resist Persona, and Persona controlled him thereafter*.

'Now kneel,' Persona commanded. 'The torture begins.'

The Doctor remained upright. 'I've already written my own words of mimesis, in my own blood on a wall. The words say "Persona lost all his arts of mimesis and never regained them." '

Persona flung his quill aside in fury.

'I got there before you, Persona,' the Doctor continued. 'All you are is a mimic. The entity you merged with copied Gallifreyan arts, but I *am* a Gallifreyan. An original. Did you seriously believe you could defeat me with mimesis, a deadly skill developed on my own planet?'

'You are still in my own form of TARDIS, Doctor.'

'Yes, but this vehicle of yours is breaking down. Can't you hear the wood creaking – cracking?'

Persona listened, and flinched at the noise. There was a fracturing sound. He glanced up at the rafters. The beams strained as they bent with the ceiling.

The Doctor nodded. 'Yes, I'm afraid so. You have a sizeable house at a transdimensional angle to a carriage. But the house is moving into the carriage's dimension. The carriage is a plasmic shell, so the house won't break through the carriage –'

'Everything in the house is being squashed into the dimensions of a carriage,' Persona breathed hoarsely. 'Timber, furniture, flesh and bone.'

The walls bulged in. 'Stuck in a box,' Persona croaked. Then he drew himself up to full height. 'But you're stuck in here with me. Stuck in the box. Let me – rearrange you before the box makes an end of us. You'll meet your fate with a jumbled anatomy. Look on the face of the Gorgon.' Slowly, he peeled off the Persona mask.

His voice was a whisper, large as night: 'WE ARE THE DEVIL.'

The Doctor looked into Persona's secret face, and saw his own countenance, jumbled as an anagram, the features constantly transposing. A mad facial pavane. Faces within faces.

The Doctor looked upon Managra. And, according to mimetic art, when you saw Managra, you became what you saw.

Unless you had inured yourself to the Gallifreyan art of mimesis.

The Doctor studied the jumbled and jumbling parody of his own face, and shrugged his shoulders. 'Most unattractive. I should have that seen to if I were you.'

Persona sprang at the Doctor with a roar.

The walls rushed in with an almighty thunder.

And the Doctor heard grating gears and a noise akin

to an asthmatic engine, the unmistakable sound of his TARDIS materializing.

He spun round as the blue police box phased into the attic, and sprang through the opening door. 'I thought you'd never come,' he said, as the door shut behind him and the TARDIS phased out of the Rite of Passage.

'I know the face of your nightmare, Doctor!' Persona shrieked above the thunder of the imploding interior. 'And *she* knows! She knows!'

Beams shattered and transfixed his quivering form.

The dramatist lifted his arms and declaimed as the house closed in with a boom. 'I brought the house down!'

Then timber and plaster stormed in and compressed Persona to a pulp, part of the house he had built, packed up neat in a carriage.

The Rite of Passage, inside the blazing Globe Theatre, spun into the vortex on a voyage to nowhere.

In an alleyway off the Grand Canal in Venice, the Doctor leaned at an acute angle against a wall, beside a blue police box.

'So that's what became of Persona,' he said. 'If Sarah and Mary hadn't activated my vehicle's homing mechanism, I wouldn't be here to tell the tale. I'm sorry about what happened to him. I wish it hadn't been necessary.'

'The same fate almost befell you, Doctor,' Miles Dashing pointed out, downing a glass of red wine and replacing the glass on the alfresco table. 'If it were not for this brave lady here –' He nodded at Sarah, sitting between Byron and Mary Shelley. '– your strange vehicle would not have arrived and you would be confined in a nutshell, isn't that how the Bard put it? My heartfelt congratulations on your successful endeavour. You are a true aristocrat. Crocker – more wine.'

Crocker glanced up from his investigation of the money-bag, a guilty look in his eyes. 'Er – yes, sir.'

Byron chuckled, then winced at the pain of his wounds. 'I'd prefer to acclaim you as a real man, Doctor.'

'As a matter of fact, I'm not. But I appreciate the sentiment.'

Mary Shelley lifted her glass in salute to an empty chair. 'And let's not forget absent friends.'

'Casanova,' they chorused, Sarah more fervently than most.

Sarah lowered her eyes. 'If he hadn't chosen to save my life, he wouldn't have lost his own.'

'Have a cheer, milady,' Miles said. 'He would have wished it no other way.'

She nodded, half-smiled, then rose from the table. 'The Doctor's giving me one of his looks. It's time to go.'

The Doctor had already opened the police-box door. 'Ah, it's good to have the old girl back safe again.' He glanced at Sarah. 'I think you need a break after your recent ordeals. This time I really will land us on that Shalonarian beach.'

'That's what you said last –' She smiled wryly. 'Never mind. Perhaps we ought to get back to UNIT; we're *supposed* to be on our way to it, after all.' She pulled off her tangerine gown and cast it aside, revealing the skimpy black cloth of a bikini. Miles politely averted his gaze.

'On second thoughts,' she said, 'I vote for the beach.' She gave a wave to her companions. 'See you. And keep an eye on Richelieu.'

Mary smiled. 'Don't worry, we will.'

Miles straightened his back. 'Even now, I suspect, he moves against the Dominoes, now his goal is attained. I must away ere sunset to join forces once more with the Four Musketeers.'

'Michael York,' Sarah sighed wistfully, then gave a shrug and a final wave as she stepped into the police box.

'Goodbye – hope it doesn't take too long to rebuild the Theatre of Sighs,' the Doctor said cheerily, but was halted from entering the door by Mary Shelley's low tones.

'If you're ever in Europa again, drop in and see me.'

He flashed a grin. 'You never know.' Then, with a swish of the scarf, he was gone.

The police box shimmered, emitted a teeth-grinding din, and faded from the alley.

Mary Shelley swirled the wine round in her glass. 'Did you notice his eyes?'

Miles pursed his lips. 'Not really. I suppose they were fairly jolly – he seemed a cheerful sort of fellow.'

Mary gave a slight shake of the head. 'I think, sometimes, he has bad dreams.'

Available in the *Doctor Who – New Adventures* series:

TIMEWYRM: GENESYS by John Peel
TIMEWYRM: EXODUS by Terrance Dicks
TIMEWYRM: APOCALYPSE by Nigel Robinson
TIMEWYRM: REVELATION by Paul Cornell
CAT'S CRADLE: TIME'S CRUCIBLE by Marc Platt
CAT'S CRADLE: WARHEAD by Andrew Cartmel
CAT'S CRADLE: WITCH MARK by Andrew Hunt
NIGHTSHADE by Mark Gatiss
LOVE AND WAR by Paul Cornell
TRANSIT by Ben Aaronovitch
THE HIGHEST SCIENCE by Gareth Roberts
THE PIT by Neil Penswick
DECEIT by Peter Darvill-Evans
LUCIFER RISING by Jim Mortimore and Andy Lane
WHITE DARKNESS by David A. McIntee
SHADOWMIND by Christopher Bulis
BIRTHRIGHT by Nigel Robinson
ICEBERG by David Banks
BLOOD HEAT by Jim Mortimore
THE DIMENSION RIDERS by Daniel Blythe
THE LEFT-HANDED HUMMINGBIRD by Kate Orman
CONUNDRUM by Steve Lyons
NO FUTURE by Paul Cornell
TRAGEDY DAY by Gareth Roberts
LEGACY by Gary Russell
THEATRE OF WAR by Justin Richards
ALL-CONSUMING FIRE by Andy Lane
BLOOD HARVEST by Terrance Dicks
STRANGE ENGLAND by Simon Messingham
FIRST FRONTIER by David A. McIntee
ST ANTHONY'S FIRE by Mark Gatiss
FALLS THE SHADOW by Daniel O'Mahony
PARASITE by Jim Mortimore
WARLOCK by Andrew Cartmel
SET PIECE by Kate Orman
INFINITE REQUIEM by Daniel Blythe
SANCTUARY by David A. McIntee
HUMAN NATURE by Paul Cornell
ORIGINAL SIN by Andy Lane
SKY PIRATES! by Dave Stone
ZAMPER by Gareth Roberts
TOY SOLDIERS by Paul Leonard

The next Missing Adventure is *Millennial Rites* by Craig Hinton, featuring the sixth Doctor and Mel.